About Jude Hayland

Jude Hayland is a writer and tutor. For many years she wrote commercial short fiction for magazines and was published widely in the UK and internationally. After graduating with an M.A. in Creative and Critical Writing, she began to write full-length fiction and has published three previous novels. A Londoner by birth and upbringing, she now lives in Winchester, but also has a home in a village in north-west Crete.

Follow her blog and latest writing news on:
www.judehayland.co.uk
Facebook: Jude Hayland Writer
Instagram: judehaylandwriting
Twitter: @judehayland

Also by Jude Hayland

Miller Street SW22

Beautifully written – an uplifting story about a group of disparate people coming together for a celebration, and how their lives change through that.

A terrifically good novel – an absorbing read.

So realistic – painfully true – the stuff of ordinary lives in 21st century.

The Legacy of Mr Jarvis

The writing is simply extraordinary.

The author handles all the tender aspects of the story with great sensitivity and draws such compassion for the characters.

I would recommend this book to anyone who is looking for a literate and compassionate look at the lives we lead.

Counting the Ways

It made me think, it made me feel. It has everything that a good book should have.

A rare treat to read a book that manages to portray all the foibles and failings of its characters while allowing their ordinary human kindness to shine through the story with remarkable subtlety and grace.

The author manages the near impossible task of writing about the quietly heroic love of women without sentimentality or cynicism.

To Deborah

THE ODYSSEY OF LILY PAGE

*Love,
Jude x*

JUDE HAYLAND

Copyright © 2023 Jude Hayland

The moral right of the author has been asserted.

Apart from any fair dealing for the purposes of research or private study, or criticism or review, as permitted under the Copyright, Designs and Patents Act 1988, this publication may only be reproduced, stored or transmitted, in any form or by any means, with the prior permission in writing of the publishers, or in the case of reprographic reproduction in accordance with the terms of licences issued by the Copyright Licensing Agency. Enquiries concerning reproduction outside those terms should be sent to the publishers.

This is a work of fiction. Names, characters, businesses, places, events and incidents are either the products of the author's imagination or used in a fictitious manner. Any resemblance to actual persons, living or dead, or actual events is purely coincidental.

Troubador Publishing Ltd
Unit E2 Airfield Business Park,
Harrison Road, Market Harborough,
Leicestershire LE16 7UL
Tel: 0116 279 2299
Email: books@troubador.co.uk
Web: www.troubador.co.uk/matador

ISBN 978 1 80514 170 9

British Library Cataloguing in Publication Data.
A catalogue record for this book is available from the British Library.

Printed and bound in Great Britain by 4edge Limited
Typeset in 11pt Aldine by Troubador Publishing Ltd, Leicester, UK

Matador is an imprint of Troubador Publishing Ltd

*To George
As always*

Acknowledgements

With grateful thanks to close friends for their unwavering support: Carol Randall, Elizabeth Stacy, Marie Armstrong, Deborah Sampson, Lynn Scott and Sue Harris-Kokotsaki. To my sister, Jane Gaudie, always a source of strength and, of course, to the rest of my beloved family for always being there. Come what may.

Why look you now how unworthy a thing you make of me. You would play upon me, you would seem to know my stops, you would pluck out the heart of my mystery ... 'Sblood, do you think I am easier to be played on than a pipe?
Hamlet Act 3 Scene 2 – William Shakespeare

★★★

Happiness depends upon ourselves.
Aristotle

1983
London

1

The first time she saw Stella Fox seemed insignificant. The last was an incident hitched to memory. But the first.

Clerkenwell Road on a Wednesday afternoon early in the New Year of 1983, the light beginning to fade after a day of cold brittle sun. She was leaning languidly against the bus stop as if appropriating it to serve only her needs, assuming the object for her purpose.

Lily Page should have known then.

Later, she was to remember the servility of that bus stop. And the knives of ice in the cruel January air that threatened snow.

But at the time she saw only the girl. The young woman clad defiantly in an enormous amount of fur – sable or perhaps squirrel – staring indifferently down the road, detached, remote. Lily envied her. Admired her air of self-possession, noted the perfection of her pale, flawless face. And was reminded of her late mother's fur coat, the smell of cedar and dust and stale perfume when she opened the door of that large wardrobe on the top landing of the house.

And then the bus arrived.

And Lily, who usually walked, got on alone somewhat guiltily, found an empty seat, swiftly shifting her mind away from the girl, the young woman, onto the prospect of her evening. A fire lit in the upstairs living room to offset the chill of the day. Some supper, that soup left over from Sunday lunch with her aunt Dorothy. The bit of Stilton still lurking from Christmas. And a glass of wine, perhaps two, considering the ordeal of the day. She would leave her father's papers for one night. Disregard the need to sift through more of his books, the endless, stacked shelves occupying floors as well as walls. Ignore the letters of condolence requiring acknowledgement which persisted in arriving months after his death. After all, the day had already seen her spend several uncomfortable hours devoted to his memory. That awkward, strained lunch she should have resisted. The subsequent Service of Thanksgiving attended by too few to merit the event at all. Her fingers were numb inside her gloves, her thin-soled shoes chosen for the formality of the occasion inadequate to the task of warming frozen toes. Perhaps there would be snow by morning, a light frosting on the roofs of houses, sufficient coating on the roads to deaden traffic noise for an hour or so, the city's plane trees dense with the stuff like winter blossom. Lily liked snow. She admired its way of disrupting routine and entrenched habit with a simple natural offering. At least in London. She assumed the countryside was a different matter. Concerted efforts with snow ploughs opposing the stuff, an urgency to get milk through to its destination. Chains on car tyres. She preferred the city's haphazard, helpless response.

The bus shifted itself wearily up Rosebery Avenue, sat in clogged traffic then at red lights so that she began to regret the impulse to catch it. Even in such shoes she could have been close to home by now. Or at least in Upper Street and within comfortable reach of it. She had been stubborn, refusing a lift from that man who had read one of the lessons, badly, hesitantly, as if sceptical of the sentiments. She had forgotten his name, but had noted that he had not even bothered to hide his boredom, his sense of exasperation over the whole affair. Privately, she had sympathised, but could not bring herself to accept his offer, still compelled by her late father's expectations. Consequently, she had lied, told him she was meeting a friend and that yes, of course she would check for any first editions among her father's books, inform the university of any such discovery before despatching most to the second-hand shop in Highbury.

No doubt they all thought of her as ill-informed about such matters.

Now that her father was gone, they probably pitied her, saw her as sadly solitary and out of her depth. And if she was honest, she knew she gave them little reason to think otherwise.

After all, Lily Page knew how ordinary she was.

A woman who reaches middle age with little to show for her five decades beyond compliance and respectability is marginal, a side note at best. And thus, they would view her, those remote acquaintances of her father who had obliged with their appearance at the service. And they would be right on the whole. About Lily Page. A woman of routine, she conformed to a prescribed, contained life, the only one, after all, she had ever known. And one adapts, one accepts. And anyway, it was not as if an alternative had presented itself.

For the most part, at least.

At the Angel, she got off the bus, walked rapidly the short distance to Alfred Street, up the few steps to her front door, slipping out of her court shoes as she fumbled keys, gloves. A hole had appeared in her stockinged left foot, two toes coldly protruding. They required cutting, she noted, her toe nails. And the toe joint was threatening a bunion.

Only when she was inside the house, welcomed back by the familiar smells and warmth of the place, the cat, Hector, demanding food, affection, did she think briefly again of the girl at the bus stop.

The young woman.

Of her certain air of contrariness and the wisdom of that defiant fur coat.

Of the contempt, she would no doubt have, for people like Lily Page.

2

Toby Jenner had been absent. He had written, excusing himself from the *well-merited university memorial service for your father*, the requisite condolences noting *Professor Walter Page's long and admirable life spent encouraging and supporting the academic careers of so many*. Easy, glib sentences that gilded more than they revealed. But there was nothing inappropriate about that. What Lily had sought in his conventional letter was some semblance of connection, at least a familiarity in his tone. After all, what would have been the harm after so many years? Close on a quarter of a century now. Toby Jenner, however, had always been adept at reinvention, capable of excising past events as if they were mere figments of someone's fevered imagination. A man skilful in shedding exoskeletons to allow him to move on, blithely untethered. And he had moved on, personally, professionally, not so much steadily climbing career ladders as discarding inconvenient steps along the way in cavalier style.

No.

People like Toby Jenner did not hold onto sentimental, potent memories unless they were of use to him. And thus any intense if brief entanglement with Lily Page could swiftly be discarded to oblivion.

She rang Dorothy early on Thursday evening. Her father's only surviving sibling, younger by six years, she had refused to make the journey from Harrow to Bloomsbury for the service and spent most of the phone call reiterating her reasons.

"So unnecessary, so morbid. My brother is gone. Dead. That ghastly crematorium business last August with that appalling vicar with the speech impediment was bad enough."

"It wasn't an impediment. He was from Sunderland, I believe."

"Couldn't understand a word he said, anyway. No-one knows how to project these days, that's the trouble. But why go through the whole business again? Were there hymns?"

"Just two. And a lunch first for a selected few. You might have enjoyed the lunch."

Lily had loathed it. A stilted affair with institutional food in a small room off a cavernous dining hall. It had been cold, the air frigid, and attempts at strained conversation with two current members of the department over tepid beef and flaccid sprouts had failed to warm the mood. Only one of her father's former colleagues had been there, most already inconveniently dead, and he had at least provided mild relief with his accounts of similar services which seemed to be the mainstay of his diary. Walter Page's memorial, he had declared expansively to Lily over his second helping of Eve's pudding and copious amounts of custard, was the first in what he expected to be a demanding year for him.

"And a lot of waffle, no doubt, trying to fill up the allocated hour or so. Speeches?" Dorothy went on.

"An address. By the current faculty head. He spoke well. If a little – ponderously, shall we say?"

"A bore, in other words."

"He was highly complementary. Referred to several of father's important publications."

"I should think so too," Dorothy said. "Although as you know I could never quite grasp my brother's obsession with the ancient world when there were so many more relevant matters he could have pursued."

"He thought it was all relevant, remember. Understanding ancient civilisations was the key to grasping our own precarious handling of the 20th century."

"Lily, there's no need to remind me of one of Walter's favourite obsessions. But just tell me, why?"

"Why ancient Greece?"

"No! Foolish girl, you're being perverse." Dorothy always spoke to her as if she was a wayward child instead of a placid woman of fifty. "Why have a memorial service at all? Your father retired close on fifteen years ago and even that was testing the patience of his department, I seem to remember, delaying departure until they nearly had to kick him out."

"He wanted one. A service. You know that. He expected it and spent the last few months of his life talking about it in considerable detail. It seemed to give him a lot of pleasure. Rather like most people gain from planning a party when you think about it. And he left full instructions so it was easy for me simply to ensure they were carried out. In conjunction with the university, of course."

It had, in fact, been far from simple. When Lily had eventually raised the matter with her father's erstwhile department, she had been passed from one bewildered voice to another, clearly at a loss with how to handle her request. Walter Page had, it seemed, assumed rather than agreed such an arrangement. She had persisted. The classicists had eventually capitulated. The whole affair had been fraught with embarrassment.

Just like his ashes.

The one subject that her father had failed to instruct upon had been the location for the scattering of his ashes. Adamant about a desire for cremation, he had left Lily with the dilemma of what to do with the residue. Consequently, a large container still resided on a shelf in his study, the best place Lily could think of to avoid confronting the problem on a daily basis.

Dorothy had moved on.

"You can give me chapter and verse when we next meet, Lily. If you insist, that is. But your phone bill for the past six months is no doubt excessive. In ten days, then? I will expect you at midday as usual. Or thereabouts. The North Circular on Sundays gets more exasperating every week."

And she was gone before Lily had time to confirm their arrangement, back to her substantial second floor mansion flat, her dwindling circle of stalwart friends from civil service days, her prescribed habits. *The Times'* crossword before breakfast, a sizeable Scotch on the stroke of six. A game of bridge alternate Fridays. Whist once a month.

A defined life.

Like most of us lead, Lily thought, one way or the other. Anything less prescribed seemingly too precipitous to consider. Hector clawed at the carpet. She bent down, picked up the cat and carried him to the kitchen to assuage his demands.

For as long as she could remember, the three of them had met weekly for Sunday lunch in Alfred Street. Her father's death in August had only modified the arrangement for Dorothy appeared to have decided that the loss of her brother clearly heralded her own decline. Thus she announced that she would no longer be using the Metropolitan Line to travel to Baker Street, where Lily was in the habit of picking her up, but would require transporting by car for the entire journey. Her concession to these increased demands was to change their weekly meeting to a fortnightly arrangement. Her aunt always implied, with some justification, that her niece was permanently in debt to her for providing the maternal care that her birth mother had failed to supply. Since Helen

Page had died from puerperal fever three days after giving birth to Lily, the fault could hardly be considered hers yet Dorothy spoke as if the gesture had been somewhat wilful and inconsiderate. Dorothy had occupied the role not with warmth, but with undeniable practical efficiency, treating the young child a little like an anomaly she might find in her department at the London City Council. In consequence, Lily had experienced rather a rushed, truncated childhood with the inference that it would really be better for all concerned if she simply skipped that passage and fast forwarded to the convenience of self-reliance. Her widowed father, bereft, helpless, bewildered by the abrupt turn in circumstances, had loved his only child inordinately, but had been relieved to follow his sister's instructions to chivvy Lily through the tedium of her early years to occupy a more companionable, resourceful role at his side. Dorothy, who had always implied that her brother's marriage to an attractive, vibrant woman fifteen years his junior had been somewhat imprudent, had viewed their venture of goading Lily to premature, responsible adulthood as an unqualified success. *And remember*, she would often add to anyone she could convince to listen, *we had a war on*. As if hostilities had been solely, spitefully declared to hamper their attempts to raise motherless Lily.

★★★

There had been no snow overnight and the next few days saw the temperature rise so that by the time Lily drove to the AGM of the Play Reading Society the following week a stream of mild dank air had set in that seemed inappropriate for January. She was the first to arrive in the cavernous back room at the former working men's college, a late Victorian building in a narrow street near King's Cross where the society held its monthly meetings. She arranged chairs for what she expected to be a small attendance – after all, no members were likely to challenge current practice sufficiently to turn out for the dull, obligatory annual meeting on a winter's night – set out agendas and had time to go down to the refectory in the basement, which, in spite of efforts with rubber plants and framed posters of impressionist paintings, never quite lost shadows of the gymnasium that had once occupied the space. The coffee served, however, was surprisingly good and the place usually felt convivial. But this evening it was close to deserted with only a couple of solitary figures occupying a long trestle table, another hovering by the notice board, since most of the evening classes and clubs that occupied the college in term time had not yet resumed after the Christmas break. She was disappointed. Used to finding the atmosphere of the whole building positive, a shared common purpose of learning providing a hook between relative strangers, her attention was now drawn to the dispiriting cream and green painted walls, the stale smell of cigarettes from the smokers' area of the room. Perhaps she had overestimated its charms.

But coffee.

Carrying a substantial cup over to a table in the corner she sat down and scanned through the brief agenda, pencilling in a couple of points she wanted to raise in Any Other Business.

"Excuse me, would you mind?" She looked up, startled. A man was at her side, taking the chair opposite before she had a chance to speak. "You see, I'm worried I've come to the wrong place entirely and you look like the sort of person who could put me right." Lily said nothing. The remark seemed intrusive and without foundation. The man smiled, clearly unaware of any impropriety. "I was expecting to sign up to a class, you see, or whatever the process is to get the ball rolling for one of these courses. Sign my life away to a term of tuition on

Tuesday nights. But I have obviously been ill-informed. The place is as near as empty. The woman on the phone was a little vague now I think about it. Would you be able to help, direct me to where I should be headed?"

"I think you've come on the wrong day. And no, unless you are planning on joining the Play Reading Society, I'm afraid I'm of no use to you at all."

She was indifferent to sounding rude. His manner was too direct and she wanted to stall conversation. She glanced at the clock and concentrated on drinking her coffee, waiting for him to apologise, move away. But he continued to sit as if unconvinced by her words.

"I was looking for Italian. Beginners' class. I picked up something in the library about this place – the college – and thought, why not? Get the ageing brain into gear before it's too late!" He continued to smile, assuming engagement. Lily swallowed the remains of her cup too swiftly, burnt her tongue. She stood up. Gathered her coat, her bag.

"Strictly speaking," she said, "the Play Reading Society is not even part of the college. We simply rent the room so I have no idea about the formalities of enrolment. But I'm sure the languages department has its procedures and you would certainly need to pay the fee before your first class." She started to walk towards the door dismissively, but he caught up with her.

"Well, that's put me firmly in my place, then!" he said. "I knew you would be the person to ask, a fount of information."

"Anyone would tell you the same," she said, irritated by his persistence. "The adult education term starts next week, I believe. I'm merely here for a meeting."

And swiftly she left the room and headed for the stairs.

As anticipated, there were only seven in attendance, with only one non-committee member, and matters were sorted within an hour, the agenda covered with little hesitation. No-one opposed the re-election of chairman or treasurer and Lily's long-standing position as secretary was unsurprisingly confirmed. Most people belonged to the Play Reading Society to do little more than that and had no wish to involve themselves in any administration. On the final Tuesday of each month, the society met to read whichever play had been chosen, taking roles allocated to them either out of choice or necessity. Lily's role as secretary confirmed casting in sufficient time for some preparation. On the whole, the system worked well, with members sensitively aware of the extent of their talents and rarely was she required to negotiate conflicts. Tonight, no-one seemed to want to linger, deterred by the emptiness of the college, the sense of trespass in the quiet corridors. The chairman and treasurer were the first to go, the two men clearly despatching themselves to the local pub, a somewhat dubious place in the nether region of King's Cross station. As usual, Lily offered a lift home to Agnes Wills, an elderly, faithful member of the society who rarely missed a meeting, but resisted always taking a vocal part. A retired hospital almoner, she lived alone and appeared to have little family. Whilst she always insisted on making her own way to the college, she was clearly gratified by the assumed arrangement of a lift back at the end of an evening.

"How have you been, Lily?" she said as they drove down Copenhagen Street towards Agnes's flat on the edge of Barnsbury. "It must have been difficult, the first Christmas without your father. A lot of adjustment for you, I can imagine."

"It was hard, of course, and not easy for my aunt either," she said. "I know she misses him terribly, although she would find it awkward to admit it. But my father was an old man, Agnes, and wouldn't have wanted to linger once his health was so poor."

"The intelligent ones never do," Agnes said, "and of course your father was such an esteemed academic."

"In his day."

"That must be a comfort to you, knowing he lived such an admirable life. And you were always a part of it, of course. What with your skills and ability to support him in so many crucial ways."

"My father never learnt to use a typewriter efficiently, that's true," Lily said, negotiating her way around a wavering cyclist with inadequate lights. "In fact, he was really very stubborn about the matter and insisted that writing by hand was his only way of doing things. And it worked out well for me, of course. Gave me a role. It was always the plan."

"Secretarial training in preparation, I suppose?" Agnes asked somewhat bleakly.

"Yes. It was the obvious choice. And I always felt that I was lucky in having a watered-down further education without ever having a formal one. You can't imagine how much I learnt about the classical world simply by being my father's typist. Or at least about Athenian civilisation between the third and seventh centuries. That was his particular area of interest. Somewhat narrow, I suppose."

"Would you have liked to have gone?" Agnes asked. "To university, I mean?"

Lily turned into Wheelwright Street and slowed down as they drew close to Agnes's flat.

"Me?" she said, "There was never any question about that as I simply wasn't clever enough. And when you think about it, so few women went in those days. And I've been lucky with the substitute I've had through helping my father. Plus the travel, of course. We went to Greece every summer for years. I was very fortunate."

Agnes found her keys in the pocket of the dark heavy coat

she wore most of the year, peered out at the unrelievedly bleak façade of the building where she lived. Graffiti scotched a tall brick wall. Sheets of discarded newspaper freewheeled along the pavement. She sat for some moments as if resisting the need to leave Lily's company, the comfort of the warm car against the dank night.

"Until *A Woman of No Importance* in a couple of weeks, then," she said suddenly with resolve, "I shall look forward to it. I always enjoy Wilde. It's the elegance of the language as much as the wit. Such a joy to hear. Thank you for the lift as always, Lily. You are so very thoughtful."

It was on the way back to Islington and Alfred Street that Lily saw her again.

Or thought she saw her.

The girl, the young woman enveloped voluptuously in the fur coat.

Afterwards, she told herself she could so easily have been mistaken.

It was by a bus stop again, this time in Liverpool Road, but the figure Lily briefly glimpsed was not passive or languid on this occasion, but pacing back and forth on the pavement as if barely containing impatience. Spontaneously, Lily slowed down then realised the foolishness of the gesture, heeded to the horn of the car behind and picked up speed. She was unsure why the young woman had lingered at the back of her mind to resurface so effortlessly. No doubt it was the bold defiance of that coat, the tangible hook to her late mother.

Particularly at a time of recent loss, of inevitable mourning.

★★★

Dorothy said, "Will you stay? In this house, I mean. Obviously, it's always been the family home, in the Page line for generations, but it's solely yours now, you lucky girl. You should do with it what you like." She took another potato from the dish in the middle of the table. Lily could never understand how her aunt always remained rake thin considering her voracious appetite.

"Everyone keeps asking me that. About the house. Or hinting at least. I've never thought of leaving."

"Well, hold onto it as long as it suits you," Dorothy said. "Think of it as your pension."

"I am already in a pension scheme of sorts," Lily said. "I don't need to turn my home into a source of income."

Dorothy looked across at her, raising her eyebrows scathingly.

"My dear girl, do you have any idea what this place is worth? You sound as naïve as my late brother."

Lily poured water from the jug into her glass. Filled her aunt's.

"People say," she said cautiously, "that prices in Islington have risen considerably. That it's suddenly become terribly fashionable to live here. What has that got to do with me? It's simply home. It always has been."

"Apart from that year or two in Buckinghamshire."

"During the war. Yes. Nineteen months, actually. And it was very dull, I seem to remember. A lot of fields and cows. I didn't feel I belonged."

"You were far too young to make such a judgement or have a view about it, Lily. It was for the best, after all."

"I know. Of course."

"There was hardly a child left on the streets of London during those early days. We would have been very remiss not to send you off."

Dorothy dug a serving spoon into the cauliflower, hefted a wedge onto her plate to nestle next to the remaining meat.

"Now, this business about your job at the school. You've never quite explained this demotion of yours."

Lily felt herself flush. She looked down at her plate, quartered a carrot unnecessarily.

"It's a change, not a demotion. A restructuring of administrative staff, that's all."

"You used to be secretary to the headmistress. Now you're not."

"I was secretary to the old head. When she retired last summer, it was thought to be the right moment for a new regime. That position is now covered by someone called a P.A. A terribly smart young woman, actually. Wears what look like very expensive suits. High heels."

"And you stepped aside willingly?" Her aunt's conversation so often sounded adversarial.

"I was offered a job in the school's general office instead so there's a wider range of responsibilities for me now. I'm kept just as busy." Lily hoped Dorothy would not ask more. It would take little for her to confess her initial sense of humiliation at losing her own office for the bustle of the admin room where the photocopier was constantly in use and phones perpetually ringing. Or it had been at first. Now she had adjusted, accommodated her disappointment and had settled quietly into the routine pattern of her working days which were undemanding. Fortunately, Dorothy's interest seemed peripheral.

"As long as you are content, my dear, that's all that matters to me. And I know Walter's finances were in order so you should be able to manage even if there's been a drop in salary for you."

"Of course," Lily said, "I can more than manage. I'm very lucky."

"You are indeed. There's nothing worse than an impoverished single woman and no excuse for it either in this day and age."

"I'm not sure that's entirely fair. Or true, come to think of it," Lily said. She thought of Agnes Wills, living on inadequate state and frugal occupational pensions in a small, rented flat at the edge of a sprawling disadvantaged estate. She pushed her knife and fork together. These large Sunday lunches that Dorothy liked in the middle of the day challenged her and she struggled for sufficient appetite.

"One has choices," Dorothy said firmly, continuing to eat. "Take me. I decided not to marry so I could keep my job. And even after the civil service decided graciously to retain married women, attitudes hadn't shifted particularly. Wives were considered a nuisance. Spinsters were accommodated far more willingly. Therefore I took advantage of that situation. And let me tell you, Lily, I had my chances."

"Chances?"

"With men. Or lovers, as they'd be called these days. But as you know well, these things are not always straight forward or appropriate. One has to make sacrifices." She paused, fork loaded, looked across the table. "Is he still alive? Not that it's of any interest to me. Or to you, for that matter."

"Oh yes," Lily said, "Toby Jessop… he's certainly still alive." Her aunt's allusion was clear.

"I suppose he would be, come to think of it. Decades younger than Walter. Although older than you, of course."

"Ten years older," Lily said.

"Should have known better then, shouldn't he?" She tidied up the remnants on her plate, soused all in gravy, added a dollop of mustard and swiftly finished it. "Now, do we have a pie? Or a steamed pudding with custard would be nice. You haven't made one of those in a long time, Lily. And it's always wise to stoke up the calories in these winter months."

3

Lily had been named after her ill-fated mother.

Or at least an attempt had been made.

Returning home from her funeral service on an unseasonably wet day in August 1932, Walter Page had looked at his small daughter asleep in the enormous pram cluttering the narrow hall in Alfred Street, and decided that, in some attempt at perpetuity, the child should not, after all, be called Lily, but Helen. A week later the baby had been duly registered and a birth certificate produced in the name of *Helen Lily Page*.

But her original name had already stuck.

At least with Dorothy.

And since her voice was the only one to be heard clearly in the confused months and early years after the young mother's death, it was the one that carried. Lily remained Lily.

She had always been relieved. To bear a name given to the infamously beautiful and arguably most significant woman in Greek mythology seemed a burden best despatched. And as Dorothy had said countless times over the years, *my brother might be a professor of classics, but there's no need to bring that sort of thing home and label your children accordingly*. Lily in response would remind her aunt that the sole idea had been to honour her late mother rather than suggest anything trojan, but covertly she had agreed. After all, her appearance had never been considered startling. Only very occasionally in her childhood, never in adolescence, had people called her pretty. Rather, they tended to talk of her even, neat features as if floundering for a compliment. But Lily had been unconcerned. Her face, she had concluded equably enough, was suitably commonplace for a woman who had no desire to be infamous. The name Lily sat well with her disposition, her occupation of the life that appeared to have been allotted to her and she had been happy to relinquish all claims on anything more illustrious.

Somewhere around Act 3 of *A Woman of No Importance* at the first meeting of the New Year, Lily's attention was caught by a man, vaguely familiar, slipping through the double doors of the hall to occupy a chair at the back and spend the rest of the reading leaning forward with apparent concentration. It was only at the end that Lily remembered who he was. As the meeting closed, members broke into small groups to talk or swiftly scattered, some remembering to stack chairs on their way out. The man stood up and walked directly towards Lily, who was gathering the usual collection of abandoned cups since it appeared to have become one of her unspecified responsibilities as secretary to ensure their safe return to the refectory.

"I jettisoned the idea of beginners' Italian," he said, "as you can see." He smiled, assuming recognition. And she obliged. The same dark jacket and head of brown hair noticeably silvering around the temples. The same familiar, direct manner and distinctive voice that were hard to ignore.

"What a pity," Lily said as she balanced three cups in her left hand and two more in her right. He stepped forward, relieved her of a couple.

"Ah, but you are to blame! You had whetted my appetite, you see. Suddenly, the idea of spending one evening a week attempting to acquire another language seemed too much like hard work. Whereas joining a play reading society seemed much more my kind of thing." He followed Lily as she headed down the stairs to return the crockery, still talking. "And of course, as you told me when we first met, the society is not actually run by the college so no hope of registering with them. I assume you can help me with that. With the relevant forms and any paperwork business?"

"It doesn't work quite like that," she said crisply. "The normal pattern is for people to be recommended or introduced by a current member." Even as she spoke, however, she knew this system had been largely abandoned since the society suffered from a serious lack of men. It was getting increasingly difficult to cast plays unless several of the female members were willing to play substantial male roles and too many, like Agnes Wills, simply attended in order to listen. Going to the theatre in London was expensive. For some, this was their substitute. But Lily was wary of this man's assumption. He was not tall, only two or three inches taller than her, but his manner suggested dominance, as if he believed implicitly that he was of interest to others. No doubt to women in particular.

"Of course," he said. "You probably have an audition process. Rather like joining a choir, I imagine. I would be quite happy to do a trial reading."

This disarmed her, and turning away from him she busied herself with lining up cups on the counter to delay the need to respond. He waited. Eventually, she said,

"If you like to give me your name and address, I could get in contact before the next meeting. I am, in fact, the secretary of the society so I could send you details about how things are run, membership forms and subscriptions, for example. It's going to be *Twelfth Night* in February so perhaps you would like to read a small part? That would give you a chance to get a feel for how we work. After that, you could decide whether you would like to join us. Whether we suit each other, as it were." She felt pleased with her compromise and waited for this mildly imperious man to turn her down. Instead, however, he held out his hand and took hers in a firm handshake.

"Hugh Murray," he said. "Appalling of me not to have introduced myself before. And I think you'll find I could be quite useful to you. I'm an actor, you see. Although to be frank it's all a bit past tense these days. Still do the odd bit here and there and the Equity card's lurking somewhere at the back of a drawer. And even in the good old times it was provincial stuff mainly, weekly and fortnightly rep. That sort of thing."

"Lily Page," she said. And wondered whether Hugh Murray expected an acknowledgement of the society's good fortune in attracting his membership. It was not, in fact, unusual for out-of-work or hopeful jobbing professionals to join them for a year or so, the chance to play major roles if only for one evening in the back hall of the former working men's college. Several, Lily suspected, claimed their performances for dog-eared and inadequate resumes with vague reference to the King's Cross location as if it were some theatrical pub or club venue rather than an amateur society. Hugh Murray's reasons for joining them could be similarly motivated. On the other hand, there had been that business about the Italian classes and the muddle over enrolment week. And this man was considerably older than the usual juvenile suspects, her own age at least and appearing to seek friendship. There was something marginally lonely about the way he had attached himself to her on this second occasion as if acceptance was important to him. By the time they were back upstairs, everyone had left. Only Agnes Wills remained, sitting somewhat self-consciously next to Lily's bag and coat. Lily ferreted for her notebook, a pen, turned to Hugh Murray. "Your address?" she said, "I can get everything in the post to you within the next few days."

Hugh Murray silently took the biro and notebook from her, turned to a clean page and began to write.

"Do excuse my handwriting," he said. "I broke my index finger when I was six. I've always blamed the hospital's bad setting for my subsequent scrawl." He returned them to her and she glanced down to check what was, in fact, perfectly legible large script. "Am I allowed in?"

"Sorry?" Lily said, confused.

"All the way from Balham. Although, strictly speaking, it's more Clapham South. And actually, it's my sister's address. I'm living with her for a short time while I have some work done on my place in Fulham."

"I see," Lily said, somewhat overwhelmed by the unnecessary detail. She glanced at Agnes, saw her excuse to leave. But Hugh Murray was already retreating towards the door. As he reached it he turned, smiled warmly as if at an established friend.

"It's been so good to see you again, Lily. I look forward to hearing from you and joining the ranks, so to speak."

Agnes stood up, buttoned her coat.

"Whoever was that?" she said as the double doors banged behind him.

"Actually," Lily said, "I'm not entirely sure. But I have a feeling that we'll find out."

★★★

The basement of 8 Alfred Street was hard to negotiate. On Saturday morning Lily stood in the first of the three small rooms determined to sort some order out of the chaos. It had been a task she had delayed for months and was determined to start the New Year with resolution. But looking around at the boxes, wooden and tin chests, ugly filing cabinets, old leather suitcases, even a school satchel, she wondered fleetingly whether it would be easier simply to call in a clearance company to dispose of the contents. The idea appealed yet equally appalled her. Over the years she had so often suggested to her father that they should make some attempt to sift through the possessions that had been delegated to the bottom of the house to linger for decades. But he had been a man given to hoarding, disinclined to think that anything once owned should be easily discarded.

She began with the back room and the filing cabinets. Dense with dust – but not, she was relieved to see, with mouse droppings – they revealed endless pages of her father's handwritten lecture notes, essays, manuscripts, their ink faint, faded beyond clarity. In the first of several wooden chests, she uncovered files of typewritten articles and recognised her own work in the copy, even differentiating between her early error strewn attempts that later became flawless. Academic journals, dating back decades, filled three packing cases and she wondered whether any would be of interest to the university. She imagined the department's library was already substantial with such material, but could not easily resign them to Islington's refuse collection before checking. Her father's habit, Lily thought ruefully, stuck. The largest room at the front of the basement with access to the stairwell and steps up to the street was the repository for old furniture. Or rather pieces of furniture: wooden chair legs, legless stools, drawers, the carcass of a chest, a Lloyd Loom nursing chair without a seat. There were even parts from a Singer steel and cast-iron treadle sewing machine that Lily assumed must have belonged to her mother or possibly to an earlier generation. Her aunt might remember although Dorothy's unsentimental regard for the past made that doubtful.

By midday, Lily felt she had made minor progress, although it hardly showed. Some floor space had been created by lining the narrow hallway at the bottom of the stairs with boxes of papers intended for the dustbin. She had then used them as a surface to pile up mounds of black-out curtains left from the war, blankets, abused by generations of moth, and carrier bags from obsolete department stores – Gamages and Marshall and Snelgrove and Daniel Neal – full of old woollen socks, scarves and single shoes. Already, some light filtered in from the windows and in the back room the small patch of city garden could be glimpsed through the locked French doors. The key, Lily thought vaguely, must be somewhere. Possibly. She tried to remember when the doors had last been opened, when there had been any functional use of the basement at all, but failed. It had always been a space referred to by her father as "down there" when telling her to look for something he had mislaid or to take a damaged lampshade, a cracked vase or unstable chair. She turned away, went upstairs to prepare for the rest of her day, washing thoroughly to remove the inevitable grime that had collected, and changed her clothes. Then she saw her hair. Wisps of cobweb giving an ethereal effect, Miss Havisham without her veil, shrouded her head and she stared at her reflection for a moment, startled, as if it bore some sort of portent or an alarming foreshadow of the future. She picked up a brush, attacked her hair vigorously, watched white flakes fall onto the dark carpet of her bedroom. There was no time to wash it now. Besides, no-one would even notice or bother to remark on the sight of a middle-aged woman with a dubious dousing of something indeterminate on her dull-coloured hair. Her invisibility was secure.

 The day was bitterly cold, but dry and Lily walked to the Barbican, relieved to be in the crisp winter air after her laborious morning. She found Eileen in the café as arranged and they sat for an hour or so over coffee before the start of the matinee. Lily had known Eileen Shaw for years, initially as a colleague at the school and since Eileen's early retirement five years before as a close friend. They had met frequently, usually for theatre visits, the occasional exhibition, until the previous year when Walter Page's health had become too precarious, his dependence on Lily absolute for her to feel she could make plans of her own. Now Eileen looked across the table at her and asked,

"All sorted now? All that ghastly business after someone passes on?"

Lily smiled. "My father always hated that euphemism. He was very particular about language, you know. But yes, I'm getting there. Of course, it's been very simple since he'd put the house into my name years ago. And I'm the only beneficiary. Apart from the odd grant or bursary to the university. My aunt made it clear to him that she didn't want a thing as she considered it would complicate her estate and add to the taxman's profits when she died. A very practical woman is Dorothy."

"I was wondering," Eileen said hesitantly, "how you were feeling. Coping, shall we say? It's a big change for you."

"The house did seem very empty at first. As if it was all temporary. I quite expected my father to walk in any moment. Even though he was always rather a silent man, there still seemed to be a vacuum. I suppose I felt rather redundant, really. Still do in a way."

"A notable academic, Walter Page. You must be very proud."

"Of course," she said automatically and wondered whether she had been too rash in her plans to discard the cardboard boxes dense with old lecture notes. Perhaps she should sift through them more thoroughly with due reverence.

"And you have your work," Eileen said. "How is the place? I heard that there's a new head in charge. And some changes as a consequence of that. Your job, for example, Lily."

Eileen leant across the narrow table in an inquisitorial manner. Lily glanced down at the programme for *A Winter's Tale* sitting between them, traced the lettering with a forefinger and saw that she had badly snagged a nail during her morning of sorting.

"Yes, inevitable really. I had to take time off during the summer term to look after my father, which was obviously inconvenient for the school especially at a time of change in the leadership and by the time I came back in September a new arrangement was in place and my job didn't really exist anymore. Or at least not in the same form at all. And it was considered that I was no longer the most suitable person for it. I lacked, apparently, some of the new essential skills. As simple as that," Lily said, aware that her defence sounded rehearsed.

Eileen was dismissive. "How foolish. Still, a sign of the times, I suppose. And no doubt you're making the best of it, Lily. You always do."

Lily stood up. "Shall we find our seats? It's my first visit, you know. I've walked around the Barbican estate itself, but I haven't been to the theatre since it opened. And it's one of my favourite plays."

"Really?" Eileen said, "I always find it a bit fey, statues coming to life and all that business with the oracle and Apollo. And there was me thinking of you as a pragmatist, Lily. You must be more of a romantic than I took you for."

They had planned to have dinner after the performance, but Eileen had a bad cold and was loath to delay her journey home to Potters Bar. They crossed the high walkways of the Barbican, stopping every now and again to look at the residential towers, the terraces of houses and flats, lit up against the early evening winter sky, pools of light reflecting in the lake. At Moorgate, Lily left Eileen to catch her Tube train and intentionally took a long and circuitous route through the city streets. She always found their weekend desertion appealing, a place in stasis, suspended from activity. Even local residents seemed absent or in self-imposed hibernation. By the time she reached City Road and Upper Street, however, Saturday had reinstated itself, pubs loud with post-football fans and wine bars already busy. But Lily was still engrossed by the play, detached from her immediate surroundings as she thought more of the temple of Apollo and the king's consultation with the oracle than of the familiar streets. She and her father had been to Delphi several times over the years, driving up to the marginally cooler temperatures of Mount Parnassus after two or three weeks in the sultriness of an Athenian summer. Walter appeared to endure the heat with an air of martyrdom as if it was a requisite of his profession whilst Lily relished it. Even after his late retirement their travels had continued since he was always hatching ideas for a paper, contributing chapters for scholarly publications. It was only his increasing frailty in the past couple of years that had brought the trips to an end and Lily in consequence had also relinquished holidays since it had seemed insensitive, let alone impractical, to leave him when he was railing against his own restrictions. But now, perhaps, she could begin to think again. And the thought of going back to such familiar places that held a repository of memories was heartening.. Even alone, she would not feel solitary.

She had turned off the main road into Camden Passage, absorbed so much by her thoughts that she almost tripped up, stumbled over someone's feet, and had to steady herself against the frontage of an antique shop to right herself.

It was the girl again.

The young woman from the bus stop.

And this time, Lily was certain it was her. The same fur coat was hanging from her shoulders, arms lost in its folds as she leant heavily against the wall, crying.

At least Lily assumed she was crying although there was little sound, her head down, strands of dark hair covering her face, rubbing her eyes as if to staunch tears. A shoulder bag lay at her feet, the contents – a hair brush, lipsticks, pens, tissues, a mirror – scattered on the ground. Later, Lily questioned what had made her stop. Why she had not simply sidestepped the woman, the way she normally would, coming across the common sight of an abject troubled stranger on a London street. Why instead she had been direct, unusually bold and suspected that it was the fact of seeing her yet again as if there was a purpose in such coincidence.

"Excuse me," she said, placing a hand on the furred shoulder, speaking close to the young woman's face, "but you seem to be in some sort of trouble. Can I help you?"

There seemed no surprise or confusion about the girl as she looked up at Lily, stared straight at her for some moments with clear, unclouded dark eyes as if she was checking Lily's veracity. Eventually, she spoke in an even, precise voice, her tone measured and calm.

"Yes, you could. Thank you. That would be kind. I could certainly do with some help right now."

4

Lily stared out of the back window of the dining room, at the meagre clutches of snowdrops in her neglected patch of walled garden and thought of Toby Jenner.

They had driven out of London in early February in that ridiculous car of his that was prone to breaking down or refusing to start without cranking the engine. Surrey or possibly Sussex. Some distance, anyway, from his home in Dulwich, a snatched opportunity while his wife was away for the weekend visiting her mother. He had spotted the endless beds of snowdrops in the hedgerows, had pulled up abruptly, taken a spade from the boot and swiftly dug up a wedge, deposited it by Lily's feet, the fragile flowers firmly embedded in dark sodden soil. A worm had wriggled out, disturbed from its cold, natural habitat. Lily had looked at him, shocked. Enthralled.

"Do you always carry a spade for such purposes?" she had asked.

"Always," he had said, encouraging the car to start again.

"Isn't it against the law? Digging up things in the countryside like that?"

"Whose law?" he had said. "The countryside belongs to everyone." Adding, "We'll come back next month for daffodils."

But they had not gone back.

A few weeks later she had sat with her father and with Dorothy in the first-floor sitting room in Alfred Street and agreed not to see Toby Jenner again. Walter Page, awkward, inadequate with such conversations, had turned to his sister who had been forthright. *Lily, this is not the behaviour expected of you. You know what you have to do, don't you?* And Lily, already bereft at the prospect of not seeing him again yet also bewildered by this sudden intrusion of intense passion into her prosaic life, an awakening she had not anticipated, had concurred. After all, as Toby Jenner himself said, he could not leave his wife. As Roman Catholics, neither of them would counter the idea of divorce however unhappy their mutual situation. *This is simply inappropriate for you*, Dorothy had added conclusively and her father had nodded, muttering something about the possibility of meeting someone else in the future if Lily really felt herself amenable to the idea of marriage. In early May of that year, in her aunt's mansion flat in Harrow, Alfred Street yet to boast a television set, they had watched together the wedding of Princess Margaret to Anthony Armstrong-Jones. *Of course*, Dorothy had said after they had both commented on the bride's beauty, the exquisite dress and endless train, *it should be Peter Townsend at her side. He was the real love of her life, not this convenient substitute of a husband who will never be able to make her truly happy.* Dorothy, an unobservant woman when it came to others' sensibilities, had not noticed Lily's stricken face, the tears that had flowed uncontrollably down her cheeks and onto the Peter Pan collar of her dress. At the end of the transmission, her aunt had stood up, switched off the television, closed the doors firmly on the unwieldy piece of furniture that housed the set and had gone to make a pot of tea. Sparingly buttered some dry scones.

The following year, Toby Jenner had left his wife, an annulment was arranged and he was married again within six months.

Lily had not been particularly surprised to hear the

news. And she had not allowed herself to be devastated by it, accepting it instead with a sense of inevitability. She was well aware that she was not the kind of woman anyone would consider a suitable subject to trouble Rome, too insignificant for papal debate and dispensation. And as for attempting to fall in love again, to seek out that precipitate state of turbulence and unrest, she felt unequal to the challenge. Besides, look at Princess Margaret. Her compromise had clearly been unwise.

She turned away from the clutches of frail snowdrops and went back to the kitchen, sat down at the table to resume work on the final casting of *Twelfth Night* for the Play Reading Society. Ken Adamson, a pedantic accountant by day, had requested Malvolio, but so had Trevor Martin, a more obvious choice, although neither were ideal, and one of them would have to be appeased with Sir Andrew Aguecheek. Firmly, she wrote down Trevor's name next to Malvolio, allocated Andrew to Ken. There was a knock at the front door and Lily was glad of the distraction.

The girl in the fur coat stood on the top step.

The young woman from Camden Passage.

"It's Lily, isn't it?" she said, in her clear precise voice. "I'm glad I remembered your address. Didn't write it down, you see."

Lily was relieved to see her again. To see Stella Fox, her name easily coming to mind. She had slept badly the previous Saturday night, contrarily concerned that her response to Stella had been both gullible yet also overly restrained. Stella had needed money. There had been a row, she had explained to Lily, with a friend of hers and he had disappeared with her wallet in his pocket. Unintentionally, she had added, as if anxious not to suggest she was a victim of crime and in need of police assistance. But Stella had no means of getting back home, or rather, she had added, where she was currently staying. Not at her usual flat share in Dalston, but somewhere near Shepherd's Bush where she was spending a few days. Lily had gently enquired whether she could go to the Dalston flat instead, given the situation, its proximity, but Stella had seemed upset by the idea, had shaken her head and said that, unfortunately, that was simply not possible. Lily had liberally handed her a £5 note. She had wanted to offer more in practical terms. She had been tempted to go home and collect her car, offer to drive Stella to the Shepherd's Bush address, thought fleetingly of inviting her back for something to eat although the idea of asking a stranger into the house was patently absurd. But Stella Fox did not seem like a stranger. Lily already felt she knew something of the young woman from the times she had seen her in the Clerkenwell Road, caught that possible glimpse in Liverpool Road.

And then there was the coat.

That sentimental link to her late mother's fur, hanging mostly undisturbed for over fifty years in the wardrobe on the top landing. So when Stella Fox had firmly folded her hand over the £5 note, thanking her, insisting she would pay her back, Lily had automatically given her name and address, without thinking of any negative consequences. After all, she appeared entirely respectable, presented no suggestion of potential threat or intimidation. No evident signs of drug or drink addiction. And she was, as her aunt Dorothy would have noted with class-conscious approval, well-spoken, articulate, as if the unfortunate situation she had found herself in was entirely unfamiliar. There was surely no reason to be suspicious of everyone in need of help on a London street. Even so, Lily had not expected to see her money returned. Now here she was, Stella Fox, having taken the trouble to find her, going out of her way to repay her debt by hand. Lily felt vindicated.

"There really was no need," she said. "It's good of you to bother. Most people wouldn't, you know."

Stella stared as if the idea had not occurred to her, put her hand in her pocket and took out five clean and crisp £1 notes. Handed them to Lily.

"Thank you," she said. "I don't know what I would have done without you. People are not kind, you know. Not in general."

"I think perhaps they are just suspicious. Naturally wary and alarmed by strangers."

"But you weren't, were you?" Stella said and smiled, displaying exemplary even and very white teeth as if carved with extraordinary precision out of precious ivory. She turned, starting to leave, to take the three steps down from the front door onto Alfred Street.

Lily said, "Your coat."

"My coat?" Stella sounded defensive. "What about it?"

"It's beautiful. It's real fur, isn't it?"

Stella shrugged. "Everyone disapproves. Nearly everyone, anyway. These days."

"I know. But it suits you so well. You're brave to wear it."

"Brave?" That shrug again. Although whether in concern or indifference was hard to tell.

"Was it inherited? A grandmother's, perhaps. They used to be so fashionable, of course."

"No," Stella said. The denial lay vacantly between them and Lily felt embarrassed by her intrusion. To cover her awkwardness, she said impulsively, "I can't let you go without offering you a cup of tea. Or coffee, of course. Now you've taken the trouble to come all the way here. From Dalston, possibly? Or even Shepherd's Bush? Do come inside for just a few moments. The kettle's just boiled." Lily held the front door open wide to encourage her inside. Stella took a step back, looked up at the house, then peered beyond Lily into the narrow hallway.

"Do you live alone?" she said. The cat sneaked between her legs, neatly camouflaged by the long coat. Lily picked him up and tucked him under one arm.

"Yes," she said, "apart from Hector here." Stella's caution was reassuring. "Please don't worry, it's just the two of us. Unless, that is, you're allergic to cats."

"Cats," Stella said and stepped firmly forward past Lily and Hector into the narrow hall, casting her eyes momentarily at some pictures on the wall, "Oh, I'm quite used to cats."

She was extraordinarily beautiful.

Lily wondered if Stella was aware of it.

Or if, in fact, women with such remarkable beauty were too used to their appearance to consider it anything out of the ordinary. To fail to see it as a burden, something untoward to tilt the equilibrium of their lives. She sat in Lily's kitchen, drinking tea, eating cake. Her slim fingers broke the slice of cherry madeira into four small squares and she ate each piece slowly, carefully, while looking around at the room. Lily, refilling their cups, noted the way her eyes, almond-shaped, the colour of navy ink, seemed to take in detail as if methodically attaching it to memory. Her fur coat had fallen to the floor, but she had resisted Lily's attempts to pick it up, hook it over the back of the chair as if she was nervous of her coming too close. Lily respected her wariness and dismissed any mild qualm she might harbour about the wisdom of her impromptu invitation.

"It's like being in a time warp here, isn't it?" Stella said. She pushed her fringe away from her face with one hand and a couple of light cake crumbs deposited themselves on her hair, like snowflakes. "This kitchen, I mean."

Lily looked around, blankly. At the heavy dresser with

its assortment of willow-pattern plates, large soup tureen, earthenware milk jugs and jelly mould. At the gas cooker with the temperamental pilot light and erratic grill. The larder cupboard in the corner with the replacement handles once intended as a temporary solution. That glass cake stand. Objects too familiar to be noted as anything other than unremarkable.

"I'm not sure what you mean," Lily said hesitantly. "Everything still works. Well, in its way. So there's never been a reason to replace anything, I suppose. Or buy more. There are probably enough plates and cutlery in this house to serve the whole of Alfred Street, in fact!"

She attempted to make her tone light. For some reason she felt a need to please Stella, to provide an answer she approved.

"Is the whole place like this?" Stella asked. She pushed her cup away, the tea half-drunk, and leant back in her chair, folding her arms. She was dressed entirely in black, a polo-neck sweater and long skirt over heavy boots.

"I suppose so. I've never really thought about it. Not looked at the house with fresh eyes, I mean. It's always been home and you grow accustomed to what is around you, don't you?" Then added, almost apologetically, "But of course it's different for you. You're young and are bound to see things from a modern perspective. This whole place must seem very old fashioned."

Stella shifted her position, rested her elbows on the table, her chin on her clasped hands.

"Of course not. Nothing like that at all. I am just observing, that's all. I find it interesting. The way people choose to live." She stood up and started to wander around the room, her fingers lightly grazing surfaces. When she reached the front window she looked down into the basement stairwell. "Is it all yours? The whole house?"

"It was my father's home. He died last summer," Lily said. "So yes. It's mine now." Then added, as if in propitiation, "but it's not big. I mean it's not a big house by the standard of a lot of the others in the area. And of course, it's been in the family for generations. My father inherited it from his father, you see."

"Your mother?" Stella leant against the wall by the window. The paintwork, Lily saw now, was scruffy, the wainscotting scuffed. Hector had sneaked through the open kitchen door and headed for Stella, rubbing his head against her boots. She leant down, scooped him into her arms and stood stroking him.

"I never knew my mother. Or only through a few photos and what other people have told me. She died was I was three days old." She waited for the predictable murmur of sympathy. But Stella said nothing. Simply went on stroking Hector, who purred contentedly. "And you live in Dalston?"

"How do you know that?" Stella said, a brief flicker of uncertainty across her very pale face.

"You mentioned it. Last Saturday. When – when you had lost your wallet."

"Oh that," Stella said, "at the moment, yes. But not for long. I've been a lodger in the flat of friends of mine. Well, not so much friends as brief acquaintances. People I met through other people. But all that's coming to an end. Soon enough, anyway."

"I see," Lily said. And waited for more. She was loath to seem too inquisitive like an irritating maiden aunt and had no wish to alarm Stella by prying. But she was curious and the girl's company on this bleak winter afternoon was a diversion from mundane tasks, obligatory phone calls. She said lightly, "Hector's taken to you. He's a fastidious cat so you should feel flattered."

Stella looked down at the circle of purring fur in her arms as if she had forgotten what she was holding and said, "Hector?"

"My father named him. He was a professor, you see. Of classics. The ancient Greek world in particular."

"Oh. Homer. And Euripides. Aeschylus. All that lot." She peeled herself away from the wall and sat down at the table again, carrying the cat with her. "I did all that stuff at school, I think. Classics. In the sixth form. Ages ago now, of course, but some of it must have stuck." Lily tried not to feel reassured by such a claim. Knowledge was no guarantee of morality, after all, and it was pure intellectual snobbery to think so. Yet somehow it connected Stella to the house, to her father's house, and legitimised her place at the kitchen table.

"And what are you doing now?" she asked tentatively, half expecting an evasive answer.

But Stella said, "Nothing."

"Nothing?"

"Not right now. I was in France, you see. Near Paris. Until a while ago. Working as an au pair."

"That must have been good for your French."

"Oh, I'm fluent," Stella said dismissively and put Hector down, suddenly disturbing him from her lap so that he tottered for a moment in surprise. "My grandmother is French. Was French. She's dead now."

"I see," Lily said. "What a gift. To be bilingual, I mean. Such an advantage in all sorts of jobs."

Stella looked puzzled for a moment as if the idea had never occurred to her. Then she shrugged her shoulders, pulled the high neck of her sweater over her chin so that it rested just beneath her mouth.

"Jobs," she said eventually, pulling out the monosyllabic word as if testing it for appeal. "That's the next thing, I suppose. Decide what I want to do. And get one."

"I would have thought," Lily said, feeling increasingly confident to broach matters, "your priority must be to sort out where you are going to live. If, as you say, your situation in Dalston is changing."

"Yes," Stella said. "That too." And she sighed, putting her head down onto folded arms on the table as if hiding from the dilemma. Then as abruptly she sat up again and said, "But something will turn up, I'm sure. It always does. I just have to ask around."

"Have you been there long? At the flat in Dalston?"

"Not really. Just a while. And now they're moving on. The people I lodge with. The way people do, I suppose."

Her mood seemed to have shifted and she looked troubled as if the impact of a kind of abandonment had suddenly been realised. The phone went in the hall. Lily wanted to ignore it, but Stella waved her away and began to gather her coat from the floor.

"You don't have to leave. I don't suppose it's anything important. It never is," Lily said. But Stella continued to shrug on the coat, lifting her hair to arrange it on the large collar.

"Actually, I do have to go. I'm meeting someone a bit later, you see. And I've kept you too long already. Thank you for the tea, Lily. And the cake. I really like your cake."

"If you're passing any time again soon," Lily found herself saying, moving ahead of Stella into the hall. "I mean, if you find yourself in Islington by chance, do pop in. You would always be welcome." She surprised herself by the openness of the invitation. She was not by nature a particularly gregarious woman.

Stella reached the front door, her hand on the latch. She turned, stared at the ringing phone, the black Bakelite sitting on the hall table.

"I didn't know anyone still kept their phones in their halls.

Like people used to, years ago. And a phone like that! How… unique." Then she looked at Lily and smiled warmly. "Thank you so much. For everything. You're a kind woman. Not many of your type around these days, I can tell you that. I might just take you up on the offer and visit again. As it seems to be all right with you." Lily, feeling inordinately flattered, reached for the receiver. "And by the way, I do like your cat," Stella added, opening the door onto the darkening evening, "and I don't always. Like other people's cats, I mean. But I've quite taken to Hector. And him to me, I'd say. He really seems to be fond of me already."

5

Neither Ken nor Trevor, as it happened, was available for Malvolio. The evening before the society's reading of *Twelfth Night*, Trevor had rung to report, hoarsely, a bout of laryngitis and Ken had suddenly become adamant that he wanted to read Sir Andrew, claiming considerable preparation for the role. Lily began to regret the committee's choice of a play with a substantial male cast in February. It was never an easy month for the society. People caught coughs and colds and variations on flu. Some of the more affluent members went skiing. Others simply peered out and decided that the weather was too unpleasant, the darkness too challenging to venture from home. Lily, searching for a parking space in the streets around King's Cross hovered behind a car that seemed about to pull out from an ideal spot, trying to ignore the competition from another driver. It was foolish to drive at all from Alfred Street when she could so easily walk or take the bus in far less time. But Agnes would be relying on her for a lift home and she did not want to disappoint. Her moment's distraction about the absence of a Malvolio from the evening's casting caused her rival in the larger, far more assertive car to slip into the vacated space. Lily, ignoring the look of triumph on the man's face, moved on, eventually managing to park in a distant side road so that she arrived with only a couple of minutes to spare before the reading was due to start.

Already, people had formed the usual semi-circles, principals in pole positions, servants and stray lords and ladies appropriately arranged to complement. And then the "audience", the members like Agnes with no wish to read at all who placed themselves to avoid any possibility of selection for even the lowliest of walk-on roles.

Hugh Murray was in conversation with the evening's Maria.

As soon as Lily walked in, aware of the large clock in the room looming towards seven, he looked up and immediately broke off, coming towards her and proffering one of two mugs of coffee.

"I had to guess," he said, "or try to remember. Milk and no sugar, I believe. You don't look like the kind of woman who would take sugar, anyway!" He spoke to her with a familiarity that Lily expected to find alarming, but instead felt gratitude for his thoughtfulness. He went on. "As a first timer, I wasn't sure where to sit. I didn't want to step on anyone's toes, as it were. And as I'm reading – Valentine, is it? And Fabian, I believe? That's what you indicated on the bumph you sent me all about how things here work. Thank you for that." He looked down at his copy of the play, turned to pages where he had clearly marked and pencil underlined the text as if in conscientious preparation. "The also-rans, as it were. Which is only to be expected given this is something of a probationary period for me with the society." He smiled, a certain self-deprecation in his manner that, however studied, still managed to appease.

"Actually," Lily said, moving swiftly towards the front of the room and a couple of empty seats, "I wonder if you would mind doing me a huge favour. I quite understand if you would rather not, but you see we have no Malvolio. It's easy enough to cover Valentine and Fabian, but such a principal role really needs – well, someone with the confidence and expertise to take it on at the last minute."

Remaining stragglers were taking their seats, chairs scraping the floor, an excess of coughing and then voices stilled in anticipation of Act 1. Orsino, an endearingly intense young man, leant forward in his seat, script poised, ready to speak the first line. Hugh Murray took the seat next to Lily, craning close to her as they sat so that she was aware of the scent of his skin – sandalwood soap, possibly, or citrus shaving cream – and said, "Now that's two favours you owe me, Miss Lily Page. Of course I will be your Malvolio for the evening as you ask so nicely. And for the record, I drink my coffee black."

★★★

Agnes was enthusiastic on the drive home.

"I have to say the new man certainly brought out the pathos of poor Malvolio. He can so easily be played for laughs so that the darkness of his situation is lost. I do so hope he will stay with us, become a permanent member. We need people to play the strong senior male leads with conviction. What did you say his name was?"

"I didn't," Lily said. "But I believe it's Hugh. Hugh Murray. An actor, he said. Or at least he used to be one in the past."

A pedestrian ran out suddenly in front of her car, causing Lily to pull up sharply. He glared at her as if the near collision had been her fault, continued to dance his way precariously across the road.

"Ah, well, that explains it. You can always tell, you know." Agnes lapsed into silence, fumbling instead in her deep bag for front door keys and the small torch she always liked to use in spite of the well-lit city streets. *A hangover from wartime and the blackout – a habit I've never quite managed to shift after all these years, I'm afraid*, she frequently apologised. Hugh Murray had certainly read well considering he had no time to prepare and he had received particularly effusive comments from the woman, Bridget James, who had played Olivia. But he had swiftly left Bridget and joined Lily as she had stacked chairs, picked up forgotten scarves and stray gloves that she would present as Lost Property at a subsequent meeting. The room had already emptied as people scurried out into the night to clear ice from windscreens or negotiate their way on hazardous pavements to bus stops and stations.

"You made, may I say," he said, with the suggestion of a mock bow, "an admirable lady in waiting and monosyllabic courtier, but I do hope you don't always give yourself such insignificant roles."

Lily had felt herself flush. The compliment was needless and she tried to diffuse it.

"I know my limitations as a performer. I'm really far happier listening to others read, but there are always walk-on characters, servants and housemaids and the like, that need filling and since I'm on the committee – well, I suppose I feel a certain obligation to help the evening along."

"Nonsense, Lily, you have a good voice with a very pleasant tone. Such clarity is rare, you know. You really should be bolder in your casting and give yourself some major roles."

She shook her head. "That's very kind, but unnecessary. Besides, we have a lot of women in the society and already too few strong parts for them so I'm surplus to requirements in that respect."

Hugh had picked up a cup lurking near one of the large cast-iron radiators in the hall. Held it out to Lily.

"You should insist that people return their own crockery to the refectory or whatever it calls itself. Perhaps an announcement when the reading comes to an end before people scatter? Hardly fair to land you with the job each time."

"I know," Lily said. "I did try it once, but it seemed to break the mood. As if I was some hectoring caretaker. It felt intrusive."

"That's very commendable of you, but people can be so inconsiderate," Hugh said and placed his hand lightly on her shoulder, letting it hover there. Lily, feeling embarrassed by his gesture, chose to bend down to retrieve a woollen hat from the floor so that his hand inevitably slipped away. "And what play have you got lined up for us next month?" he went on. "I was expecting some sort of formal announcement at the end, but then I assume it's only newcomers like me who don't already have the season's full programme."

"Are you definitely going to join us as a member?" she said. "After all, I realise tonight was something of a try-out for you. To see if we came up to your expectations." She realised with surprise that his answer seemed to be important to her.

"Of course," Hugh said emphatically. "You sent me all that information and those forms, remember? Fulfilling your role as society secretary with what I am sure is your natural efficiency. And I have them here, all completed and the cheque duly signed for my annual fee." He took a thick brown envelope from the inside pocket of his jacket and held it out. "All addressed to you already, you see. I've been meaning to find a stamp to get it into the post all week, but it suddenly seemed foolish to entrust something to the Royal Mail when I could deliver it personally."

"Thank you," she said, staring at her name and address in bold black ink as if the details were unfamiliar to her. "I'll be in touch, then, about next month's casting. It's Chekhov in March. *The Cherry Orchard*. Of course, you're perfectly welcome to state preferences. For what you would like to read, that is. It's how things work."

Hugh had cupped his chin with one hand as if considering the matter. He wore a signet ring on his small finger and for some reason it brought to Lily's mind the wedding ring that her father had worn all his life despite his early widowhood.

"I'll have to give that some thought for a day or two. The casting, that is. All right if I ring you about it? Or if you prefer, I could drop you a line."

Lily, somehow anticipating that the failure of a call or a note from this man would disappoint and therefore even the chance of it was best avoided, had said, "It's not essential, of course, I can just as easily cast as I think best."

Hugh had smiled and his hand rested, more firmly this time, on her shoulder again.

"I'll certainly be in touch, Lily. You can be absolutely sure of that!"

And he had left the hall as if in a hurry, passing Agnes who was patiently waiting at the back, as if the need to be somewhere else had all of a sudden occurred to him. The smell of sandalwood or possibly citrus soap had lingered in the space he had left.

Lily pulled up outside Agnes's building. A couple of figures hovered on the pavement, hands deep in pockets, heads lost to hoods and scarves, mildly sinister in their mutual absorption.

"Be careful, Agnes, on the way to your front door," Lily said, "there's ice on the roads already and the pavements are uneven."

Agnes gathered her bag, gloves. Her torch. Then sat for some moments staring through the windscreen as if trying to remember a train of thought.

"So what does he do now?" she said eventually, turning to Lily in the darkness of the car's cold interior. Lily stared at her blankly. Impatiently. The heater of her ten-year-old Morris was inadequate.

"Who? What are you talking about?"

"Our new man, of course," Agnes said. "Hugh, did you say? Only you mentioned that he used to be an actor, but that's now all in the past. And I saw you talking to him at the end."

"About membership, yes," Lily said firmly, as if correcting some implication in Agnes's words. "I have absolutely no idea what he does now, Agnes. How he learns his living, that is. But he certainly came to our rescue this evening and yes, he'd be an asset to the society for sure. We'll have to see if he comes back next month. Who knows? People can be so unpredictable." She was aware that she was speaking out of self-preservation. Hugh Murray's cheque was currently in her possession, but it could be bounced or stopped. Or perhaps he was a careless man who took out memberships, but failed to comply with attendance. Hope, Lily knew, was best quashed before it attached itself too firmly to expectation. And for some irritating, inexplicable reason, she had begun to wish to see Hugh Murray again. Agnes's hand rested on the door handle.

"Well, time will tell," she said. "But some new life blood into the society is always to be welcomed so do encourage him if you can, Lily."

"Encourage him?" Lily said, alarmed that her thoughts might be transparent. "Whatever do you mean?"

Agnes opened the door, appearing to sniff the temperature of the night air in Watkins Road. She turned to Lily in surprise.

"As the society's secretary. Surely it's your responsibility to follow up on people who have shown interest in us? You must make sure to keep in contact with him, don't let him slip away without a struggle."

"Of course," Lily said. "I'll make sure I do that. You're absolutely right. Goodnight, Agnes."

The house was cold. Hector was curled up under the small radiator in the upstairs sitting room, but there was no heat in it. Lily pulled the cat onto her lap where he circled three times and obligingly settled down in a heap, providing her with a fur comforter. It had taken years to persuade her father into installing any form of central heating and even once the battle had been won, he had agreed to only a partial system. Bedrooms, he claimed, should be cold. And they were. Very. His study, on the top floor of the house, rarely caught the sun and seemed to occupy a micro climate that chilled the flesh, but he claimed it as conducive to thought. Even in the last year or so of his life when he had struggled with the stairs and had been mainly sedentary he had resisted Lily's encouragement to make use of two electric heaters she had bought to supplement the scant radiators, rejecting them as superfluous to his needs. Perhaps it was habit. Walter Page had spent his entire life in the house and it never seemed to have occurred to him that the privations of early 20th-century domestic living had become redundant in the post war years. Lily occasionally wondered if her father's pre-occupation with ancient Greek civilisation had removed him from the advances of his own. Now she looked at the empty fireplace, the cold embers and ashes from the night before and was tempted to create a small blaze to warm the place before she went to bed.

But no.

Hardly a necessity, an indulgence, in fact, given the late hour. And the shadow of her father's habits was not entirely erased. Hector, responding with pleasure to the attention from Lily, purred rhythmically.

Hugh Murray has been excessive in his praise of her speaking voice. It was typical, Lily supposed, of someone in the acting profession to offer such exaggerated acclaim, no doubt assuming similar in return. And yet she was touched by his words, resistant to dismissing them as superficial. There had been a time, after all, in her remote past when she had not shied away from seeking main roles. Schoolgirl productions, the enthusiastic efforts of fourteen and fifteen-year-olds at her secondary school in Highgate in those years just after the end of the war had been enjoyable. Convivial. *She Stoops to Conquer* and *The Importance of Being Earnest* with all-female casts, necessitating binding burgeoning breasts with bands from the P.E. department and borrowing hats and cravats and corsets and waistcoats from obliging relations.

But it had all stopped abruptly. At least as far as Lily's involvement was concerned.

And her memory of the particular circumstance of her retreat from performing had been left unconsidered for years. Decades. But tonight, Hugh Murray's casual, no doubt inflated, comments had dredged it up like a piece of telling evidence from a long-forgotten crime. And now, sitting with the contented cat on her lap, digging numbed fingers into the depths of Hector's deep coat, she confronted it.

Auditions for the 1948 production of *The Tempest* at the girls' grammar had not been open to people like Lily Page.

For Lily was to leave school at the end of that summer, regardless of the number of credits she gained in her School Certificate Exam, to begin her secretarial course at the college in Holborn in the autumn. It had been decided. Arranged. Settled. No chance of the likes of Lily staying on to take her Higher Schools along with those considered potential university material and the school, in their blinkered, elitist wisdom, had decreed the play as material suitable only for such students with, apparently, the intellectual heft to handle Shakespeare. Lily had duly taken her place in the audience for the performances of *The Tempest*, had warmly applauded and had made a mental note of her position, her place in the scheme of such things.

She had never seen a reason to revise it since.

★★★

Three days later, coming home late from work on Friday after too many hours spent in the company of the photocopier preparing test papers for school exams, Lily found a picture postcard on the mat. A pre-Raphaelite woman with cascading auburn hair stared up at her from among the muddle of pedestrian buff envelopes. She carried it into the kitchen, turned it over and read:

Leonid Gayev? The Cherry Orchard? But as a newcomer happy to oblige wherever. Perhaps better discussed over a cup of coffee? I am hopeful! Hugh.

And his phone number. Underlined. Mechanically, Lily filled the kettle to make tea then, as the water began to boil, remembered that she had already drunk endless cups at work, noticed the time and turned to the fridge. She stared too long at the shelves, at the single piece of chicken, two small cutlets. The remains of the meat pie. Then closed the door and went upstairs to change her clothes, wash her hands to remove the taint of chemical printing ink that clung to them. In the sitting room, she drew the curtains, lit the fire and encouraged it with kindling until it produced a reasonable heat. The weekend was going to be busy. She had promised the librarian from school the chance to look through her father's books on Saturday morning to see if any were of use before despatching more to the second-hand sellers. Then in the early evening there was an invitation to the house warming party next door. *All very informal*, Anna and Simon Dickenson had stressed when they had invited Lily, *but you really must come as you are something of a curiosity!* Evidently, as the third generation of her family to have lived at 8 Alfred Street, Lily had a certain interest, a cachet of sorts. It made her feel as if her longevity in the place was the only criteria for her inclusion. And then Sunday was

Dorothy's day, her aunt's fortnightly visit for a substantial lunch. Tea with homemade cake. The fire well established, she went downstairs and chopped some vegetables, turned the sluggish oven to a temperature setting higher than the heat it would produce, slid peelings and discarded circulars still sent to her father in the bin. The gaze of the Pre-Raphaelite beauty reached her from the kitchen table. Lily picked up the post card, considered its use as a convenient bookmark, then changed her mind and swiftly despatched it along with onion skins, apple peel and the outer leaves of a savoy cabbage.

6

Anne Turner, school librarian, gave a cursory glance through the books Lily had placed on the desk in her father's study. At some stage, she would have to stop thinking of the room as his and find some alternative purpose for it. Until then, his shadow hovered. No doubt the casket of his ashes, sitting discreetly on the top shelf out of sight, did little to relieve the feeling.

"As I suspected, Lily," Anne said hesitantly, "a wonderful collection without doubt. For the scholar. But for our girls... well, all a bit specialised and academic, I'm afraid."

"Of course," Lily said, "I didn't think of that."

"Not to decry their value, naturally. In the right hands, these books would be treasured, I'm sure."

"I was thinking," Lily said, "of the pupils who take classics. And isn't there an ancient Greek A level class?"

"There is indeed," Anne said, "with one student. A special request from her parents. And evidently, she is struggling. As you know, we are not the most academically rigorous of the London day schools. More a haven for the daughters of the sufficiently affluent who would flounder under more intellectually demanding regimes. And they do like a lighter touch, our pupils."

"A lighter touch?" Lily's hand hovered protectively over one of the slenderer volumes: *Towards an Understanding of Athenian Democracy* by Walter Page.

"Lots of illustrations. Bright, bold presentation. Some humour, if possible."

"Humour?" Lily thought of mentioning Aristophanes. The significance of ancient Greek comedy. But she felt Anne Turner probably meant something else.

"Irony, if you like. A certain style to make the girls feel they are not studying anything terribly serious."

"I see."

"Did your father teach you ancient Greek?" Anne turned away from the desk and quickly scanned the shelves that had been thinned in recent months, books now stacked singly rather than in double-decker fashion.

"Oh no," Lily said, "he never attempted to. It really wasn't necessary. Not for the work I did to help him."

"And you fulfilled such a useful role, I'm sure."

"I suppose so." Lily said, looking away from Anne's insistent gaze, her mildly patronising air, and out to the garden. She noticed the windows badly needed cleaning. One of the curtains was partly unhooked from the runner. The partial view of her immediate neighbours' back garden showed care and loving attention as if they treated the space as an extension of their home. Anna and Simon had already planted dwarf shrubs and evergreens and the boundary walls appeared to have been repointed. Lily turned back to Anne. "But I've often thought of learning modern Greek," she said. "Or at least it was something I intended to do when my father was alive and we went there every summer."

"And no point now, naturally."

"No point?"

"Without your father. All that part of your life is over now, after all." Anne turned back to the shelves. "Perhaps the art department could use something on Greek vases. Anything along those lines?"

She refused coffee and left with a guide to the Parthenon and a book about Greek theatre that she said could be of some interest to the fledgling drama department. In the kitchen Lily put away the tray of cups, coffee pot and plate of shortbread she had prepared for the two of them, turned her mind to the rest of the weekend. A roast, possibly, for Dorothy's lunch the next day. Although it seemed foolish to buy a joint for just the two of them, she knew her aunt's expectations and her occasional resort to casseroles had been tersely received. And a cake for tea, most of which would be transported to Harrow along with the remains of the meat. In spite of living in relative material comfort on her civil service and state pensions as well as prudent savings, Dorothy had never lost the habits instilled by years of war rationing. Always she arrived with offerings – a packet of biscuits, a pint of milk, some apples – and expected to return home with some similar token. Walter had tried to reason his sister out of the unnecessary gesture, but had only managed to curb it for a few weeks. Lily did not even attempt to try. Fleetingly, she wondered what to wear to the party that evening, what would be deemed suitable for *a small informal housewarming*. No doubt there were a set of implicit rules attached to such a gathering that eluded Lily.

But her concern proved pointless.

Just before she left to go shopping in the Holloway Road, the phone went. The housewarming party was, regrettably, cancelled. Or rather, postponed.

"We think it's chicken pox, you see," Anna said, "the baby, that is. When I was changing him this morning, I noticed it all over his back. Sort of red rashes. And I looked it up in the childcare book and Simon's down at the chemist now. For the calamine lotion. Isn't that what you need? I don't suppose our GP will want to know. He's fine in himself, actually – Thomas, the baby, that is, not Simon – but clearly we might all be contagious. Probably are. And even if you've had it and most of us no doubt have, evidently it can come back as shingles. In adults. That's what you hear, anyway. So we don't want to risk that."

"Very sensible," Lily said. "I quite understand."

"These things happen, of course, once there are children in the house, I suppose. Although not measles, obviously. Or mumps now, come to think of it. Thank God for 20th-century advances in vaccination!"

"Yes, indeed," Lily said. "Well, if there's anything I can do to help. Although, as you say, your husband can pop out and do any shopping you might need."

"Actually," Anna said, "it's the opposite. We're rather overstocked with food ordered for the party tonight. We'll be eating canapes and sides of salmon and fancy cheeses for weeks!"

"Of course," Lily said. "I didn't think of that." The *small, informal housewarming* appeared to have grown in size and status. Or perhaps it was simply how people now entertained. People of a certain affluence and aspiration in Islington, anyway. Lily was sure she possessed no clothes that would have been appropriate.

"But there is something, Lily," Anna went on, "if you're genuinely offering and are at a loose end today."

The single woman of an indeterminate age is always considered to need occupation to fill her vacuous life, Lily noted wryly, as Anna enlisted her help in letting all the other guests know of the cancellation.

"Best thing is for me to pop the list through your door, actually. Don't even want to risk breathing over you. It's mostly neighbours and a few from further afield, but Simon is terribly organised with these things so all the info is here. Names, phone numbers and everything. I've got my hands full with the little ones and no doubt Simon will take ages getting back from the chemist or obviously we'd do it and I'd like them all to know straight away so they can make other plans. You know, being Saturday night and all that." Lily promised to make it her priority for the morning. "I knew you were the ideal neighbour as soon as we moved in!" Anna continued. "Not like the nightmare family next to us in Camden. Neighbourly spirit? You have to be joking! And as soon as this little mite is free of all unsociable lurgies, Lily, you must come round and tell us all about the history of the place. Alfred Street, that is. We can't wait to hear about our predecessors as it were!"

And within moments, a substantial list of names was thrust through her letter box. Lily could see by its length that the task would encroach well into the afternoon.

Still. She had offered.

And Anna and Simon had a sick baby demanding their attention as well as a toddler to occupy. The only minor inconvenience to her was delaying her shopping for a few hours and in all likelihood missing the Saturday street markets. But there was, after all, always the supermarket.

She bought the last joint of beef just before the butcher closed. The bakers had run out of wholemeal. The supermarket supplied, naturally, but Lily always felt some unease in the aisles of the large, garishly lit store with its bewildering range and choice. Her father had disapproved of such places. Saw them as counter to the spirit and tradition of the urban high street with its bevy of earnest shopkeepers pursuing their livelihoods. Back home, Lily tried again to contact the more elusive on Anna's list, a couple from Clapham who appeared either to be away or to refuse to answer their phone, a man listed only as Blake whose line seemed disconnected. Swiftly, she found a postcard, wrote a note to alert her neighbours that these unwanted guests might still appear on their doorstep and pushed it through their front door. She made a pot of tea, weighed out ingredients for Dorothy's cake and thought of *The Cherry Orchard*. With an evening unexpectedly free ahead of her, she could now spend it sorting out the casting for the next meeting. On the whole her Saturday nights were occupied by a film or a play, usually alone, sometimes with a friend, but staying at home for once was hardly a misfortune.

Only the young could possibly view such an occurrence as calamitous.

Stella Fox, for example.

Lily could not imagine young women like Stella Fox ever being content with a solitary Saturday night at home with only a fastidious cat for company.

Dorothy did not ring until nearly eight. Lily had already made a chocolate cake and iced it liberally to suit her aunt's rich tastes and had moved onto the play, allocating most of the principal parts in line with stated preferences with only one or two roles left to fill. Her aunt sounded strained.

"I'm not coming tomorrow," she said as soon as Lily picked up the phone. "It wouldn't be wise, considering the state I am in."

"I didn't know there was anything wrong," Lily said, alarmed. "What is it? You should have rung me earlier."

"It's this cold of mine. It hasn't disappeared. In fact, it's been getting progressively worse and no doubt pneumonia will set in now and you know what that's called?"

"Pneumonia? It's a respiratory problem, surely. Caused by a bacterial infection?"

"The old person's friend, Lily, that's the somewhat euphemistic description. The way most of us are carried off. And naturally I'm next in line. After Walter, that is."

"Don't say that. It's just a cold at the moment." Lily felt a draught around her stockinged feet, noticed how flat and thin the hall carpet had become. "How do you feel in yourself?"

"Ghastly. At least 104 and of course I'm not far off that. It's quite the worst cold I've ever had, Lily. And now a cough has set in." She broke away from the receiver for a moment as if to demonstrate.

"I'll drive over to you," Lily said swiftly. "I could come now if you like. Or first thing in the morning might be better. I can just as easily cook lunch at your flat."

"Nonsense, Lily. I just want to be left alone. Besides, the idea of eating is really not appealing and even the smell of food would probably make me nauseous in my present condition."

"I could make you soup. You should be eating something, you know. Keeping your strength up."

Dorothy was adamant.

"Don't fuss over me, Lily. That's the last thing I need. I will ring you tomorrow evening if it makes you feel better. Best not for you to ring me as you're bound to choose a time when I'm resting."

"If you are sure," Lily said. She twisted the cord of the phone around her finger, felt her response was inadequate. "But if you change your mind in the morning just ring me then. In fact, ring me whenever you like. There might be things you need, after all. Aspirin and perhaps barley water? Lemons and honey? I'm sure I could be of use."

Hector padded up the stairs from the basement, intertwined himself between her legs, then stretched out prostrate at her feet, making plaintive sounds in demand of dinner.

"I have everything I need, thank you, Lily," Dorothy said. "The only thing remaining is to be left quietly alone to nurse myself back to health. If, of course, that's possible given Anno Domini."

In the kitchen Lily filled Hector's plate with food, watched him eat sparingly as if he too was feeling frail. She had not eaten herself and went to the fridge where the absurdly large joint of beef immediately confronted her as if to underline some folly of hers. She was not hungry enough to bother cooking a meal and instead hacked off a lump of Cheddar from the slab in the larder. Buttered a piece of the new loaf and stood eating in the middle of the room. The foundations of her weekend had suddenly imploded. Earlier, she had blithely accepted the prospect of a solitary Saturday evening, but now the emptiness of the landscape until Monday morning disturbed her. It was not acceptable to find oneself so alone, so exposed to the threat of loneliness. And the future could only offer her more of the same sense of isolation. Naturally, her aunt's death would follow that of her father, hardly a revelation yet she had never considered the implication of this for her own sense of worth. For her own definition. Dorothy, in spite of her unshakeable intransigence, was no more immune to mortality than any other elderly person. And once she was gone, Lily's purpose, any significance she might harbour would seem obsolete.

Even the business of the books that morning had affected her.

Anne Turner's dismissal of them had felt foolishly personal. As if Lily herself was implicated in their uselessness, their irrelevance for a current generation. That memorial service should have been sufficient warning to her. She should have grasped more willingly the transitory nature of her father's scholarly reputation, that such a thing is mutable rather than an edifice cast in limestone.

She went upstairs to the sitting room, tried to settle again to the casting of *The Cherry Orchard*, hovering with her pen over the character of Leonid Gayev. Then, remembering the note on his postcard, firmly wrote Hugh Murray next to it. She moved to the window where she had not yet drawn the heavy curtains. It was her habit to hang on to as much daylight as she could, to wait until the sky was dense until giving in and now the winter was beginning to show slight signs of shifting into marginally longer days, she welcomed the extra hours of light like one emerging from hibernation. Outside in the road, several loaded skips occupying precious parking spaces marked Alfred Street's rapid transition. Houses subdivided into basic bedsits for decades were being reclaimed as large family homes by new owners who saw the location as not only convenient, but aspirational. Fashionable. Islington was no longer a destination purely for the working classes of London, Lily's neighbours far more likely to be city bankers, lawyers, even politicians than the shopkeepers and commercial travellers of her grandfather's day.

She could imagine his astonishment.

Back in the kitchen, she convinced herself to eat something and placed two slices of bread under the grill, forgetting to watch them with the eagle eye required resulting in inedible charred remains. Turning to the dregs of a bottle of white wine, she swiftly drank a glass, vinegary, warm. Lily had always thought of herself as naturally sanguine, little affected by a change in circumstance that altered the expected course of a day. A weekend. Yet now she moved restlessly from room to room as if in search of a satisfactory diversion to ward off the shadow of a fear she was not willing to define. She stared at the kitchen rubbish bin, noticed that the lid no longer fitted adequately, refilled her glass with the last of the unpleasant wine.

The Pre-Raphaelite beauty on the postcard was called *La Ghirlandata* and apple peel had attached itself to her harp, a tea bag to a golden tress.

But Hugh Murray's message was unscathed.

Lily placed the postcard next to the phone in the hall and went back to the kitchen, finished the wine. Ran the tip of a finger through the icing of the rich chocolate cake. Then returned to the hall and swiftly dialled before she could change her mind.

No doubt he would be out.

She listened to the repeated ringing tone with some relief and was on the point of giving up when he answered.

"Could I speak to Hugh Murray?" Lily knew his voice, but it seemed inappropriate to assume. It was his sister's house, after all.

"Speaking," he said.

"I see. Good." Lily realised that she had absolutely no idea what to say next. She had concentrated purely in summoning the courage to ring and was without a further plan.

"And to whom am I speaking?" he said with the suggestion of mock provocation. Somehow it encouraged her.

"I am so sorry, it's Lily Page. From the Play Reading Society. And I appreciate that it's a very foolish time to ring you, on a Saturday evening."

"Not at all, Lily," he said. His voice was warm, reassuring. "It's very good to hear from you. I have been worrying that you might have been thinking me too presumptuous."

"Presumptuous?"

"With that postcard of mine."

"Oh no, of course not." Lily picked up *La Ghirlandata* with her free hand. "I have put you down to read the part of Gayev. That will work well, you see, as we already have one of our younger members desperate for Lopakhin. In fact, the suggestion that we read the play came from him in the first place so naturally he was first choice. And the other male leads seem to be covered too." Lily was aware that she was speaking too rapidly. As if she had information to impart and was wanting to extricate herself from the call as soon as possible. Which, in a way, she was. "So that's the reason for my call, to confirm things. Gayev, that is. To save me dropping you a line. You know how unreliable the post can be."

There was a pause. Lily began to wonder if the line had gone dead. Then Hugh said, "I was hoping you were ringing to follow up on my other suggestion."

"Your other suggestion?"

"Or shall we call it an idea? For the two of us to get together over a coffee. A drink. Lunch, even. Before the next society reading. After all, just meeting once a month is really rather unsatisfactory, don't you think?"

"I suppose so." Lily had no idea what she meant by her answer. Or what Hugh was implying by his question.

"Excellent! So we are agreed on that," he went on. "And since next week is already looking hectic for me – numerous work obligations and unavoidable social gatherings, you know the sort of thing – how are you fixed this weekend? Tomorrow, in fact?"

Lily thought of the possibility of a sudden decline in Dorothy's condition. Her duty to keep Sunday free in case an impromptu trip to Harrow was required. She found herself, in fact, craving such an excuse to avoid Hugh's proposal. Yet at the same time she was aware of an unusual sense of pleasure, of anticipation at the prospect of seeing him.

"Tomorrow?" she repeated. "By chance, I am going to be free. Unexpectedly."

"Then that's settled," Hugh said definitively. "Shall we say eleven o'clock? No, far too early for a Sunday morning. Noon. Will that suit?" He did not wait for an answer. "The question is where, of course. I can't possibly ask you to venture south of the river to my neck of the woods so how about I come to you? Or at least we could meet somewhere near you. I am sure Islington can provide us with a suitable spot for a rendezvous of sorts. A café or a salubrious pub that you might know?"

Lily was unfamiliar with pubs to suggest. Women went to pubs with partners. Husbands. At least the sort of women she knew. Her father used to go to a pub in Upper Street before he became too frail. On Saturday lunch times it was his habit to leave the house around twelve and return an hour or so later for the soup and sandwich snack she usually prepared for them. Occasionally on a warm summer's evening, the two of them would go to one of the pubs close to the Regent's Canal. Beer or Cider for Walter, a glass of Cinzano or Vermouth for her then home to a light salad supper. And of course, there had been those few visits to country pubs a long time ago. Discreet, out-of-the-way places down winding Kentish lanes, oast houses on the horizon. Inconspicuous inns in home county hamlets. Toby Jenner's knowledge of such places had been comprehensive.

But no. Lily was at a loss to make any feasible suggestion to Hugh Murray right now.

"Angel station," she said, floundering. "Why don't we meet there?"

"Excellent suggestion!" he said. "Then we can make up our minds together. See what looks to be the most inviting. Tomorrow, then, Lily. At noon. I'm looking forward to it. And thank you so much for ringing. You've brought a little brightness into my weekend!"

In her bedroom, Hector had curled up on the black jacket she had left on the chair, pounding the cloth thoroughly with his paws. She shifted him to the floor and sat down on the bed, trying to remember why she had come up to the room in the first place. Hector stalked out of the room, displaying disdain at his ignominious removal.

Hugh Murray was simply being sociable.

No more than polite. There was really nothing personal in his gesture. No doubt, as an actor, his manner of speech was somewhat flamboyant. Inflated. She placed her hands against her cheeks, wondered why she felt flushed, warmed by a sentiment that she could not name. She was used to receiving commonplace gratitude, of course. Those appropriate, obligatory gestures of appreciation from people like Agnes, her new neighbours, staff at school when it was the task itself that was the focus of their thanks.

But this was different.

Hugh Murray had said *you've brought a little brightness into my weekend* as if Lily herself was the cause of his optimism. She was offering, after all, simply her company and it appeared to be sufficient, the sole reason for his anticipation. On the other hand, Lily swiftly reminded herself, the man was seemingly in possession of an empty Sunday in late winter that required filling. Anything and anyone, was, no doubt, preferable to allay that situation for Hugh Murray while temporarily lodging with his sister.

Her availability was a convenience to him. No more than that.

7

The walk from Alfred Street to Angel was less than five minutes. Lily allowed fifteen. Getting the event underway seemed to be the best method of despatching its significance, already having spent far too long trying to decide what to wear. Informal house warming parties suddenly seemed far less of a sartorial challenge than coffee with a man who was virtually a stranger and she had grown exasperated by her own indecision. Clothes had never been a preoccupation for Lily. She liked to look appropriate, neat, unobtrusive. She owned navy and grey woollen skirts for work which were exchanged for their linen cousins in cream and pale blue for summer. There were a couple of good suits, one in burgundy, the other in black, that she had worn in the past when she had been the headmistress's secretary, now consigned to the back of the wardrobe. And she possessed some simple dresses she wore for what she viewed as occasions – the theatre, a concert, dinner at a friend's house. But nothing, she thought, staring hopelessly at what she now saw as an inadequate selection, at all suitable for a casually sociable Sunday in London. Trousers were probably needed. But although she owned three pairs, they were all functional, disagreeable in colour or shape and decidedly unbecoming. It was a very long time, Lily realised, since she had looked at herself in the mirror with the scrutiny that others applied on a daily basis and the result was no doubt balefully evident.

He was ten minutes late. She saw him first and worried for a moment that he had failed to recognise her as he stood and scanned the handful of people hovering by the entrance. Then suddenly, he waved and came towards her, talking rapidly.

"So sorry, Lily. What must you think of me, keeping you waiting like this? Blame the Northern Line as always. Some delay at London Bridge for an unexplained reason. Still. I'm here now and I'm so grateful you didn't give up on me and decide to do something else with your Sunday."

"I've only just arrived myself," Lily said fraudulently. "It's fine, really. The Tube at weekends is never reliable."

"And while I'm stuck down in Balham – did I mention it's not my usual home?"

"I think you did say something about it. And of course, it was the address you gave me."

"Address?" he seemed surprised.

"For sending the society membership forms," she reminded him.

"Of course. Exactly. Just a temporary measure. There's long, drawn-out work on my own house in Fulham, you see. Such a nuisance. But you know how these things always overrun. Should have been back there by now, but no, evidently according to the builders – well, let's not bring the tone of the day down by burdening you with my domestic problems. Now, Lily, this is your stomping ground, so where do you suggest we go? Recommendations from a local please!"

He was wearing the same dark jacket she had seen him in before, but this time with a red polo neck sweater, a grey checked scarf that seemed to strike the carefully offhand style that people nowadays adopted at weekends. Affluent people like her neighbours in Alfred Street, at least. And jeans. Lily had not realised that men of his age still wore jeans. Perhaps it was the thespian in him. She hoped her eventual choice of camel skirt and jacket looked vaguely appropriate. While she hesitated, he took the lead, striding them along Upper Street as if he was more familiar with the area than he claimed.

"I seem to remember quite a decent café along here somewhere," he said, "that actually manages to stay open on a Sunday. Do you know it? Of course, there's always the King's Head, if all else fails on the café front. But perhaps we can go on there later."

The café was open, but crowded. Lily had not been to Esme's for years and had barely been aware of the transformation it had undergone since the days when it had been somewhere she had liked to meet friends. Then, large pots of strong tea, solid scones and cakes with a sawdust texture had been served by mildly belligerent waitresses to an entirely female clientele. It had been a place favoured by spinsterish types who would sit discreetly alone at small tables over a high tea of poached eggs in the late afternoon until closing time. Lily remembered looking at these solitary, single women with pity, even with fear. But Esme's was no longer the refuge of the lonely. Gone were the stained, seersucker table cloths, replaced by bare stripped pine surfaces and families with small children talking in loud voices or couples with broadsheet newspapers spread out between them, reading with apparent absorption. Hugh led them to the only free table, wedged between two others so that they had to negotiate chairs, legs and coats before they could claim it. Already, a small queue had formed behind them at the door.

"Hungry?" he said. "Or just coffee? I have to say breakfast seems very remote if I even remembered to have any."

Lily had eaten a single slice of toast around seven. But now she resisted his attempts to persuade her into anything more than coffee, feeling that the very act of conversation was sufficiently challenging without complicating it with food.

The thought that she had initiated this meeting through that rash phone call was already haunting her. How much easier to be spending the day companionably alone, sifting through more of her father's books, making further inroads into the clutter of the basement rooms than negotiating some sort of friendship with Hugh Murray.

"Do you know the play well?" she said abruptly after he had ordered. "*The Cherry Orchard*, I mean. It's a long time since the society has read any Chekhov so you've joined at a good moment. That is, if you particularly like Chekhov."

It was a question she had prepared as a sort of insurance. If there was swift evidence of regret from Hugh at setting up the meeting at all, she could pretend that its sole purpose was to confirm casting rather than anything more ambiguous. Hugh smiled.

"Played Lophakin in my youth. Or relative youth. Dreadful under-rehearsed production that took place somewhere north of Derby, if I remember correctly."

"Of course," Lily said, grateful for the clutch, "you must tell me about all that, your professional roles in the past, I mean."

"Oh that," Hugh said, dismissive, as if the subject bored him. "All so long ago, Lily."

"But you must miss it."

"Well, yes, to a point." He unwound the grey scarf from his neck, hung it around the back of his chair where it promptly fell to the floor. "There were certainly some good times. Not that rep theatre wasn't challenging, of course. Standing in the wings on a Monday night still learning Act 3 moments before going on. But audiences were very kind and forgiving in those days, I suspect. Grateful for any entertainment."

"And now?"

"Now?" Hugh looked at her somewhat expectantly. His

apple Danish pastry arrived. He ignored it. "Now, Lily? What do you mean?"

"I mean," she said, looking away from his stare, which for some reason she found disconcerting. "If you're not acting any more, what do you do? For a living, that is."

"Oh, work!" he said as if the notion was a disturbance to polite conversation. "The rat-race, the day-to-day humdrum business of our lives. Yes, set against that, the theatre was a marvellous existence, it has to be said. But I'm not entirely lost to the profession, you know. Although in a somewhat diminished capacity, it has to be said."

She wondered if she had offended him by implying he was no longer an actor. Coffee arrived. Hugh turned to his pastry, ate it swiftly.

"I can imagine," Lily conceded, "it must be such a precarious profession with little stability. At least, that's what people always say."

"And people are right, of course. Acting's no game for the faint-hearted. And these days – well, we live in an era where the soaps rule. And commercials, of course. That's where the money is. All a bit of a travesty, really, but one has to move with the times, I suppose. Or try to."

Lily said something non-committal, concentrated on her large cup of coffee. Hugh pushed together careless flakes from the pastry that had gathered between them on the small table. She noticed the signet ring again, a faded scar on a forefinger. His red polo neck sweater had a small hole on his left wrist. Details that felt curiously intimate to note. He drank his coffee swiftly, somewhat restlessly. Placed cup and saucer to one side.

"But Lily, all this talk about me really won't do. It's your turn now."

"My turn?"

He smiled. Folded his arms on the table and leant forward towards her.

"It's time I heard all about you. So that we are no longer strangers to each other."

"Well, I'm not sure that there is that much to say." She felt inadequate. And aware suddenly that it had been years since she had met anyone who had shown any particular curiosity about her. Even her new neighbours only seemed to want to befriend her from self-interest to gain knowledge about the history of their home. She had worked at the same school for over twenty years and was now no more than an inconspicuous cog in the wheel of the place, deflecting rather than attracting attention. But here was Hugh Murray, looking across the narrow table at her in the crowded, noisy café, waiting for her to talk. Valuing, even, his time spent with her. She tried to gather her thoughts.

"Start with birth and work up to the present day!" he encouraged her.

"That sounds very dull," she said, and wondered whether her prosaic life was really worthy of examination. But Hugh was an attentive listener as she swiftly ran through the facts and details of it, an account that managed to deal with fifty years with alarming brevity. When she came to an abrupt halt, he said nothing for a moment and she wondered whether he was disappointed, had expected something less pedestrian of her. Then he reached across the table and lightly placed a hand on hers.

"The loss of your mother at birth must have cast such sadness over your childhood, Lily. I am so sorry."

"Not really. Not then. I mean, I never knew her," Lily said. "It was later that I began to wonder how different things might have been if she had lived. When I got to the age she was when she died. Really, it was my father who never entirely recovered from her death. He was forty when I was born and my mother only twenty-six. I was named after her, of course."

"Your mother's name was Lily?"

"Helen Lily. But somehow the first bit got lost, I'm pleased to say."

"But why?" Hugh looked appalled. He leant back in his chair as if puzzling over the fact. "Helen is such a gift of a name that I would have thought any woman deserving of it would be proud to claim it. And you say your father was a classicist so what could be more appropriate?"

"I've never thought of it like that." Lily fiddled with her cup, wished there were coffee remaining in it so that she could occupy the awkward moment. His compliment was excessive and she suspected sarcasm. Hugh went on.

"Naturally, it might have been difficult for your father, the poor man in mourning, to hear the name of his late wife constantly called. Perhaps that was the reason for the substitute, as it were. And I suppose you just grew up with it, dear Lily, and didn't give the matter a second thought."

"Perhaps," she said, "you are probably right." Dear Lily. The endearment struck her. No doubt just a manner of speech. Even so.

Hugh suddenly smiled broadly. "I shall call you Helen, I insist on it! In private, anyway. I can imagine it would be a little confusing for everyone at the Play Reading Society if I started referring to you in that way, but when we're alone I shall make every effort to reinstate your birthright, as it were!"

Lily looked around the café, desperate to seize upon something as a distraction. This meeting had clearly been an error on her part. She had been so foolish in acting upon that postcard of his, should have left it dwelling along with the cabbage leaves and carrot scraps for it was clear now that she was to be the target of some subtle humiliation. A man like

Hugh Murray, someone others would judge as still attractive, striking even, with his gregarious manner and easy confidence, was not the sort of man to talk of being alone with a woman like Lily Page.

But *In private*, he had said. *In private*.

In the queue by the door, a woman with a small child at her side seemed to be glaring pointedly at the empty cups in front of them.

"We should go," she said in relief. "Our table's needed," turning to shrug her arms into her coat. Hugh placed a hand on her shoulder.

"How considerate you are. But I'm sure we can justify just five more minutes. Or perhaps you would prefer us to move on somewhere else? It's not particularly warm, but maybe a brisk walk could be on the cards? I'm sure that's how people in salubrious areas of north London occupy Sundays, isn't it?"

Mechanically, Lily headed them towards Highbury Fields. Hugh talked rapidly as they walked briskly northwards, past closed shops, St Mary's Church, the town hall, the noise of traffic relieving her of the necessity of saying anything much in return. His sister, he told her, was still kindly accommodating him at her maisonette in Balham while the protracted work on his own house went on at snails' pace. Underpinning, Lily thought she caught, subsidence issues and something about dry rot. She nodded. Sympathised. Not an ideal situation, he said, but needs must. Another reason for his delight in finding the Play Reading Society was to get out from under her feet for the occasional evening although he wished the meetings were more frequent and hadn't the society ever thought of a more regular arrangement? They had reached Highbury Corner and Lily's reply was swallowed as they negotiated the hectic A1 and crossed into the Fields. Here, Hugh paused. Looked across at the expanse of green and turned to Lily.

"Now, if this was summer or even a warm day in late spring, we could spread ourselves out on the grass and have a splendid picnic lunch. Do you ever do that with friends, Lily? On fine Sundays, I mean."

"Not really," Lily said blankly. "Or at least not for a very long time. When I was much younger, perhaps, although even then – Sundays have always been for my father and my aunt, you see. Or they were. Now of course there's just Dorothy and we meet every other week. It's habit, I suppose."

"Well," Hugh said, "habits can always be broken, wouldn't you say, Lily?" He smiled at her conspiratorially. "And new ones formed. Or are you too much a traditionalist to join me in my subversive ways?"

"Of course not," Lily said swiftly. Yet immediately felt fraudulent. Her obligation to Dorothy was too entrenched to shift and she had a moment of concern again for her aunt's health. She had, perhaps, been too eager to accept Hugh's invitation and should instead have insisted on driving over to see her.

They began to walk past the substantial houses overlooking the green, progressing slowly, peering down into basement level rooms and up numerous floors to attic windows.

"The desirable residences of the rich," Hugh said. "Quite something, aren't they? But then, as an Islington inhabitant yourself, homes like this are no doubt quite commonplace."

She shook her head. "Of course not. And probably most of them are subdivided into bedsits, anyway." Adding, "or at least some of them, I imagine," as a front door opened and a couple stepped out with two young children, offering a brief view into a graceful hallway.

"Nevertheless, Lily, you rub neighbourly shoulders with the affluent and successful with an address like yours."

"It's simply where I live," she said with some confusion.

"And the strange thing is that when I was at school people used to feel sorry for me, living in Islington. There was nothing smart about it at all back then. Quite the opposite, in fact."

"I think you said earlier that your grandfather bought the house?"

"The family were just tenants for years, I believe, although I'm a little vague on the details."

"But then it was purchased?"

Lily nodded. "Sometime in the 1920s. My grandfather appears to have been rather resourceful financially. He was a shopkeeper, but had all sorts of other interests, evidently. Owned various freeholds on properties or had inherited them. Something along those lines."

"And your father inherited the house?"

"As the only surviving son, yes. His two brothers were killed in the First World War, you see. In fact, you could say that my father never left home."

"Like you, Lily. Or rather Helen. I must remember to call you that."

"Please don't. I'm not sure I could accustom myself to a change of name at my age and time of life."

Hugh shook his head as if in amused exasperation. For a moment, Lily thought he was going to take her arm as they crossed back onto the Fields and she moved imperceptibly apart from him then felt foolish as he stooped to tie a shoelace instead.

"I'll have to do a good job at persuading you into the idea," he said, resuming his step, "make it a mission of sorts. And as for age – Lily, you are clearly a decade or so younger than me so we'll have no more talk of that."

"I was fifty last August."

"And I hope you celebrated your half century in appropriate

style!" He fielded a football heading in their direction from a game between two young boys, firmly kicked it back to them.

"No," she said. "It was the day after my father died, you see. So understandably, it was entirely forgotten."

Hugh turned to her and said, "Poor Lily. But did you know that belated birthday celebrations are permissible? In fact, it's said that they are the best kind!"

Lily tried to smile, to share his lightness of tone, but was abruptly overwhelmed by her memory of that day when she had felt bereft not only by the loss of her father, but by the failure of anyone to acknowledge its added significance for her. She was appalled now to sense tears in her eyes, looked up at the sky, tipping her head back to discourage them falling.

"I think it might rain," she said. "The forecast predicted showers."

"In that case," Hugh said and this time made a deliberate move to take her arm which she did not resist, "I suggest we find ourselves a quiet pub before closing time. I think we've earned ourselves a glass of something. Any recommendations, Lily?"

He was fifty-four, he confided as they sat in a discreet corner of the saloon bar of the Nag's Head. He had lived in London for years, although had been born in Devon, in Barnstaple, where his parents had run a guest house. He had been married, but his wife had died some six years before and now his sister was his only living relative apart from some remote cousins with whom he had lost touch. There had been no children. He still had a theatrical agent, but the man appeared to have lost interest in him at least a decade before and since then he had mainly fended for himself in pursuit of work.

"How?" Lily said. She imagined Hugh haunting stage doors and persistently pounding Shaftesbury Avenue. The image was faintly glamorous to her. She drank steadily from her glass of red wine.

"Oh, *The Stage* is a good friend for the jobbing actor," Hugh said. "And you get to hear of things by word of mouth. Someone knows someone who's looking to hire for a stand at an exhibition, promotions in need of silver-haired middle-aged men, that sort of thing. Last week I spent two days pretending to be a difficult client in a training session for executives at an insurance company. And there's always film extra work if you're really desperate and can handle the tedium of long days spent doing very little. I jog along all right. On the whole, at least." He drank steadily from his pint, glanced at her glass. "Is it unpalatable? As sharp as a knife, no doubt. You know, Lily, next time we must go to a wine bar. They're the places to drink decent wine these days and there are enough of them about. Have you noticed how they seem to be springing up virtually overnight everywhere you look?"

Next time, Lily thought. *Next time*. And was confused whether his assumption terrified or consoled her.

By the time they left the pub, Hugh glancing at his watch and saying something about a promise to his sister to devote some of his Sunday to sorting a blocked drain, Lily felt disorientated. As if the day had taken on a quality that was unfamiliar to her, precipitous. She would not have been surprised to look around and find herself not in Upper Street near her home, but in some foreign place where she was ignorant of the language. The rules of engagement. At Angel Tube, Hugh leant towards her, kissed her briefly on each cheek, his woollen scarf brushing her chin. The smell of smoke from the pub had sunk into their clothes. Seeped into the pores of their skin.

"Let's be in touch," he said, "preferably before *The Cherry Orchard* reading in ten days or so. Although things are very hectic for me for the next week or so. As I'm sure they are for you, Lily."

"Yes," she said. "Of course. Very busy."

"And Lily – forgive me, I mean Helen – it really has been delightful."

He turned away, heading for the escalator before stopping suddenly and turning back towards her.

"And I hope you're going to give yourself a decent role this time. For the reading, I mean. Not just a serf or monosyllabic servant. What do you think?"

There was no need for her to answer as someone at that moment stepped in front of Hugh and by the time she had a clear view again he was gone.

She tried to resist walking straight home, aware that the silence of the house would give her too much opportunity to review the day, recast their conversation in her mind. But there seemed something dispiriting about walking alone on the quiet Sunday streets as if her few hours with Hugh had given her an appetite for conviviality. Back in Alfred Street she rang Dorothy and was relieved to find her no worse. In fact, her aunt seemed to have recovered remarkably swiftly and dismissed Lily's concern as excessive. Pneumonia and other dire complications seemed to have been forgotten and Lily was reprimanded for unnecessarily inflating such a trivial matter as a common head cold.

She busied herself with menial jobs about the house, tidying, cleaning, distractions from thoughts of Hugh Murray. Theirs had simply been a pleasant meeting of two acquaintances, as inconsequential and insignificant as that. After all, a friendly kiss on each cheek when parting appeared obligatory these days. At least in London. At ten o'clock she went upstairs to bed, worn out and anxious only for sleep before facing the prospect of Monday morning and the bland tedium of the school admin office. But coming out of the bathroom, she stopped, assaulted suddenly by the sense of Hugh's face close to hers. The smell of his skin that had seemed both alien yet strangely familiar as if touching a remote memory. With deliberation, she went to the oak wardrobe that had stood solidly on the narrow top landing for as long as she could remember. After some reluctance, the key turned and she opened the doors onto scents of dried, musty lavender, cedar and dust. Heavy overcoats hung, her father's old-fashioned suits, discarded mackintoshes, two panama hats she recognised from their Greek travels.

And the coat.

Her late mother's fox fur coat.

Lily stood, stroking the soft pile, the warp and weft of the fur, buried her face in its folds. Then suddenly, swiftly, there on the landing, she took off all her clothes, skirt, sweater, tights, underwear, dropping them with measured carelessness onto the floor. She shivered for a moment, standing naked in the chill of the unheated space, then lifted the heavy weight of the coat from its wooden hangar and slipped it on. In the long mirror behind the door, she stared at herself in the ostentatious fur as if at a figure she knew only remotely. She closed her eyes, focusing solely on the sensation of the silky lining against her skin, trapping folds of fur between her bare legs, her thighs.

Lily had entirely forgotten, she realised, or at least long suppressed, an appetite for sensual pleasure. For physical desire.

And the fundamental animal-like need to burrow with abandonment into another's embrace.

8

Dorothy ate the breast and a leg. Poured more gravy over the peas.

"Strange how cheap chicken is these days. Used to be a treat in the past. And of course, in the war people would pass rabbit off as chicken. And now rabbit seems to have all but disappeared. Possibly the fault of myxomatosis."

Lily glanced at the table then stood up.

"I forgot the parsnips. They must still be in the oven or perhaps I just left them in the kitchen."

Dorothy waited for her return and let Lily place several parsnips on her plate. Tried one.

"As I thought. They're cold now, Lily. Although I suppose if you were to heat up the gravy I could stomach a few. Wouldn't want to waste a roast parsnip."

"No," Lily said, sitting down again and pushing her remaining food to one side of her plate. She refilled their glasses with water. Drank. Dorothy waited. Then, with a sense of resignation, doused the cooled parsnips and ate them rapidly.

The phone rang.

"Lily, leave it," Dorothy said. "Anyone who rings over Sunday lunchtime deserves to be ignored."

"But it seems so rude," Lily said, already hurrying to the hall. "After someone has bothered to ring."

It was Agnes Wills.

And immediately she felt herself flush with foolishness at her expectation. In her turn, Agnes was apologetic for interrupting Dorothy's visit, had forgotten Lily's Sunday obligation to her aunt and the call was brief. Lily was back at the table within a moment or two.

"Sorry," she said, "just my friend Agnes who comes to the Play Reading Society. She's going to be away next week, a last-minute invitation to an old friend. Or was it a niece? Someone in Bognor, anyway."

"Not ideal," Dorothy said, rejecting the final parsnip in favour of the last roast potato, pronging it firmly with her fork as if staking a claim. "Bognor in late winter. Actually, I'm not sure Bognor is ever ideal. But then I've never been fond of the south coast."

"No."

"Nor any English seaside resort, come to that. Even Brighton is not what it was."

"Probably not."

Dorothy placed her knife and fork together and looked inquisitorially across the table.

"Lily, whatever is the matter with you today?"

"I don't know what you mean."

"You seem so jumpy. As if you can't relax and fix your mind on anything. Even on our conversation."

Lily tried to dissemble.

"I'm fine. It's nothing, just rather busy at work at the moment so I might seem a bit distracted. The admin office is under siege with end of term photocopying and meeting deadlines."

Dorothy pushed her empty plate towards Lily.

"End of term already? Surely not. It seems to me we've only just recovered from Christmas. Is Easter really upon us so soon? The church has a lot to answer for, you know, insisting we keep up all these outmoded religious festivities." A devout atheist, Dorothy always liked to gibe at what she saw as Lily's sentimental attachment to religion. For her own part, Lily was uncertain whether she harboured a particularly strong faith or belief in a deity, but she lacked Dorothy's conviction to deny it entirely. The idea of a higher power, some sort of sagacious upper chamber devoid of the frailties and perversities of the human race seemed a consolation of sorts. She brought in the treacle tart, cut a generous slice for her aunt, offered cream.

He had not rung, of course.

Hugh Murray had failed to follow up their Sunday outing with a call to suggest another ahead of the society's next meeting. But he had not promised, Lily reminded herself. It had been only a vague remark, simply the way people ended conversations, out of politeness rather than with intention. And what possible reason would cause a man like Hugh Murray to seek out her company? She knew her limitations as a woman. She was no longer young. And whilst the same could be said of Hugh Murray, she was aware of the inconsistencies between the sexes. Single women past middle age were faintly embarrassing, objects of mild suspicion and more of an encumbrance than an asset unless in possession of startling, original intelligence, great wealth or age-defying beauty.

Whereas men.

Even the most ordinary appeared to be useful, viable currency. And Hugh Murray, with what Lily supposed could be called raffish, gracefully ageing good looks, that somewhat theatrical air about him, was far from dully ordinary.

No.

Any more contact from Hugh would have been out of obligation, a need to reward her for steering him towards the society where clearly, he would make his mark.

Even so.

She had found herself hovering by the phone in the hall when she came in from work, lifting up the receiver to check the line was not out of order. She had caught herself turning down the radio in the kitchen in case she failed to hear it ring. She had looked through her wardrobe of lighter clothes now that the days were longer, milder, in case there was a sudden, last-minute invitation to meet. Pointless, self-defeating gestures that fed rather than assuaged her sense of futility.

Dorothy said, "No treacle tart, Lily? It's quite good, I must say. Your pastry was always reliable. My brother was lucky, I'll give him that."

"Lucky?" Lily cut herself a small slice to satisfy her aunt.

"Having a daughter who could cook. Or at least provide sensible meals every day. Of course, I always encouraged you in that direction."

"Did you?"

"It never mattered for me until my retirement as there was always a solid, sustainable lunch available at the office. Three courses, too, except during the war, naturally, although even then with rationing we were pretty well provided for. But Walter needed someone who could provide for him. Especially after he retired."

"I suppose so." Lily had never liked treacle tart, she remembered now. The cloying sweetness of the syrup seemed unpalatable. She put down her spoon, wondered if she could persuade her aunt into a walk. There were at least three hours before she could suggest driving her home and she felt unequal to the task of occupying the time with conversation.

There was a knock at the door. However irrational, Lily thought of Hugh. And swiftly squandered the idea as she went to open it amidst Dorothy's complaints about more interruptions on a Sunday.

It was Stella Fox.

The fur coat was gone. Instead, she wore a long, quilted garment, heavily beaded, vibrant, the sort of thing that Lily had seen for sale on her very occasional visits to Camden Lock market. Her hair had been cut shorter, barely grazing her shoulders.

"Hello, Lily, I hope you don't mind me calling," she said hesitantly. "Of course, if it's very inconvenient I can come back later. Or tomorrow. But I do need to ask you something. Need some help, actually, some advice. And I thought you would be the perfect person. In fact, it was you, Lily, who immediately popped into my head."

She looked anxious, biting her bottom lip with her row of even, very white teeth, fiddling with the strap of her large tapestry bag. Hector, who generally absented himself during Dorothy's visits, sensing her antipathy towards pets and cats in particular, leapt down from the low wall between the houses and wound himself around Stella's ankles.

"Me? You thought of me?"

"Yes, you. You've lived here forever so must know everyone."

"Hardly. People come and go so much these days."

"Even so. You're established. Here." Stella indicated the street with a sweep of one hand.

"Well, yes," Lily said, a little bewildered. Dorothy had left the dining room and was at her side.

"Do we have a visitor, Lily? Whyever are you keeping her talking on the doorstep? Do invite the poor child in instead of conducting your conversation for the whole street to hear."

"Oh, but you have someone here!" Stella said, "I'm so sorry, really thoughtless of me. I forget that other people do things like have lunch. With guests. Proper Sunday lunch, that is." She sounded nostalgic as if for a bygone event.

"Nonsense," Dorothy said. "We've just finished, haven't

we, Lily? Anyway, I am Lily's aunt so family rather than a guest. A friend of my niece's is always welcome company." Lily felt redundant as Dorothy stood back and encouraged Stella into the hall. "In fact, we were just on the point of having some coffee so perhaps you'd like to join us for some in the sitting room?"

Her aunt never drank coffee after lunch, always insisted it was something to have only before midday. But Dorothy, proprietorial, was already leading the way upstairs and Stella, who had casually discarded her boots in the narrow hallway as if out of habit, followed. Lily went into the kitchen, made coffee, carried it upstairs. The two of them appeared already to be well acquainted.

"Of course, all these stairs wouldn't suit me anymore," her aunt was saying as she pushed open the door. "Still, that's London town houses for you. Vastly overrated, in my opinion. And certainly overpriced. Give me my sensible mansion flat any day. Do you know Harrow, Stella? Suburban, naturally, but very civilised. No doubt you take your coffee black? All young people do, don't they? Or perhaps I am woefully out of touch these days."

Stella took a cup, added some milk, retreated to the window seat and curled her legs underneath her, looking out at the street.

"I love this room of yours, Lily. It's got the best view of all, almost down to Regent's Canal." She turned to Dorothy who had waved the tray of coffee away. "We usually sit in the kitchen when I come round, don't we Lily?"

"I suppose so," Lily said and wondered for a moment if she had forgotten visits from Stella, conflating several into the single one she remembered. The pot of tea and those slices of cake. Her fur coat among the crumbs on the kitchen floor. Stella's familiarity with the house was confusing.

"How do you two know each other?" Dorothy asked with a hint of surprise in her voice. "I don't think I've heard Lily mention your name before."

"Oh, we've not known each other very long, actually. I mean we don't go far back or anything like that. We kind of fell over each other, you could say. Sort of more or less close neighbours, but not quite. Wouldn't you say that describes us best, Lily?"

"Yes," Lily said. "Something like that." She was grateful for Stella's evasive reply. She could not imagine her aunt being amused by the truth of how they had met yet at the same time there seemed a certain duplicity in claiming an established friendship that could hardly be said to exist. Stella suddenly swung her legs down from the window seat to the floor and looked from one to the other with intent.

"Actually, that's almost exactly why I'm here. Today, that is, barging in without the usual invitation. It's Lily's local knowledge I'm after."

"No-one has lived here longer, that's for sure," Dorothy said, "she'll have told you that this house in Alfred Street has been in the family for generations. Therefore, it was my childhood home as well."

"Quite," Stella said, with the mildest hint of irritation at the interruption. Swiftly, she went on. "I'm homeless. Or as near as. I mean obviously not actually living on the streets or anything like that, not quite in cardboard city yet, but close to it."

"The homeless situation in London is appalling," Dorothy said. "I was only reading about it in *The Telegraph* yesterday. Who would have imagined it, in the affluent 1980s? Here we are, coasting our way to the next millennium and people still without a decent roof over their heads."

Stella turned directly to Lily, her face once more anxious as it had appeared at the front door. She chewed for a moment at a fingernail, then said, "I'm about to be thrown out, you see. I think I said it was on the cards the last time we met, but now it's actually happening. Told to pack my bags, you could say. Nothing personal, of course, it's just that they – the couple I'm lodging with – are getting out. Of London. Going somewhere really rural. Norfolk, I think. People seem to be taking themselves off to East Anglia these days. Anyway, I immediately thought of you, Lily."

"Me? Why would you think of me?"

"Well, what with you being such a long-term resident I thought you must know someone who lets rooms. Attics. Basements. That kind of thing. People live in these enormous houses around here and lots of them probably like to have lodgers. For security for a start. Even company. Maybe some of them are even a bit short of money and could do with some rent. Not that I can afford much. Which is why I'm thinking just a room and not a whole flat."

"Of course she'll be able to help you. Won't you, Lily?" Dorothy said firmly. "What with all your contacts at school. Let alone your neighbours. And anyone would be delighted to let to a friend of yours, someone with a personal recommendation, as it were. I've heard it's very common these days, letting a spare room."

"There are agencies for this kind of thing," Stella said, "but they charge the earth in commission fees and want references, which all takes forever and anyway, who wants to be filling the pockets of greedy, iniquitous landlords?" She drained her cup, replaced it on the tray and sat down on the floor, cross-legged, her fingers fiddling with thin strands of her hair, twisting them into a skimpy plait. The effect made her look younger, vulnerable, like a child at school assembly.

"Absolutely," Dorothy said. "One reads such dreadful things about what goes on."

"There's always the classifieds, of course. Perhaps I should go that route. You know, in the *Evening Standard* and *The Times*. The trouble is anything decent gets snapped up before the newsprint is even dry. And one never knows, naturally, what one could be getting into, moving in with an entire stranger."

Dorothy was adamant. "There is no need for you to be put in that situation, Stella. Trailing around dubious streets on a wild goose chase. Not with Lily here to help. You'll be only too glad to do what you can for your friend, won't you, Lily?"

Lily hesitated. She felt an overwhelming need to satisfy the assumptions of her aunt. She was inordinately flattered by Stella's belief in her ability to help and the prospect of their gratitude was warming. Yet she also shrank from the thought of approaching people, of drawing attention to herself in such a way. And more significantly, she knew so little of Stella. It was surely fraudulent to claim an established friendship with the young woman when in fact she was a near stranger. But it was too late to retract. She had allowed Dorothy to believe they knew each other well, had failed to counter Stella's claim and would simply have to adjust, to go along with this version of events.

"I certainly could ask," she said tentatively, "sometimes people advertise on the staff room board at school. Rooms to let, that sort of thing."

"And then there's that society of yours," Dorothy said. She seemed animated by the subject of Stella's search as if her day had been brightened by her arrival in their midst. "There must be so many members involved in that and you can surely badger them to help out poor Stella. Make some sort of announcement at the start of a meeting."

"Exactly, I just knew you were the person who could help, Lily. And I'm quite flexible about where I'm willing to live, but obviously I need to be close to Tubes and buses for work. Good connections and all that. Somewhere central, in other words."

"So we'll leave all that in your hands, shall we, Lily?" Dorothy said. "To sort out your friend's housing problem?"

The two of them looked at her, Stella's elfin-shaped face now composed, its anxiety and pallor lifted. Dorothy drummed one hand lightly on the arm of her chair.

Lily said, "Yes, all right. Of course."

Already, she sensed something slipping away from her, her entire grasp of a situation moving just beyond her reach. Like floundering in waves that threatened to overwhelm. But she dismissed the feeling. Compliance, after all, was all that was being asked of her and there was no logical reason to refuse.

It was past five o'clock when Stella looked at her watch and seemed surprised by the time.

"I so envy you your family Sunday," she said wistfully as she pulled on her boots, took her bag from where she had hung it on the banister in the hall. "How nice to know there's still that tradition going on, the roast and all that. With people you love. Not something I've known in a very long time." Then, as Lily was about to reply, she glanced at her watch again and skipped down the three steps to the path. "Do your best for me, won't you, Lily? Just so kind. It's wonderful to know I can rely on you."

On the journey back to Harrow, Dorothy said, "Well, I must say, Lily, she doesn't seem your usual sort of friend."

They passed Park Royal and Hangar Lane in dense traffic, the weekend drawing to a close and pulling people home.

"What do you mean?"

"I'm surprised, that's all," her aunt went on. "A young woman like Stella Fox. The few friends of yours I've met all seem to be – well, lame ducks, one could say. Friends in need."

"You hardly know any of my friends," Lily said defensively. "Not these days."

Dorothy said nothing for a moment. She stared hard through the windscreen as if intent on recall.

"There was that sad child who seemed to attach herself to you when you were at school. What was her name?"

"That was a very long time ago," Lily said. "Hardly relevant now." Yet immediately she remembered the girl. How she had assumed a dependence and apparent need for Lily's friendship that had felt novel since as a rule it was the prerogative of others in the class to be so selected. Jean Cook. That was the girl. Or Joan. Those others, of course, the prettier, more assertive and confident of their year had spurned girls such as Jean or Joan with her shabby third-hand uniform and hair prone to grease. Those bitten fingernails. Lily, however, had been amenable.

"I believe you felt sorry for her," Dorothy went on, "brought her back to tea and even on visits to my flat. I remember thinking she needed feeding up. A thin little thing and not awfully bright. Appalling spots. Or perhaps it was eczema? One forgets."

Lily said, abruptly changing lanes and picking up speed after clearing a bottle neck of traffic, "There's nothing so very lame duck about my friends at work. Or from the Play Reading Society, come to that. And you haven't met any of them." Then, emboldened, went on. "Hugh Murray, for example. An actor. You might well have even seen him in something. A play or in a television series. Or even heard him on the radio. Afternoon plays, possibly." She tried to think of something that her aunt would not watch since she had no idea whether her claim was accurate. Hugh had been clear that his appearances belonged to the past and that current work was far more prosaic. But Dorothy was still focused on Stella.

"She is an extraordinarily beautiful girl, of course. The

type to wreak havoc with men, no doubt. And clearly highly intelligent. What does she do? For a job, I mean. I didn't seem able to pin her down."

Dorothy and Stella had talked animatedly about the London housing situation, about rents and inflated prices and Stella had seemed intrigued by Dorothy's long account of her civil service days and had asked pertinent questions. Lily had sat back, offered more coffee, later retreating down to the kitchen to bring up tea and cherry madeira cake.

"I believe she's temping at the moment," Lily said vaguely, "until the right thing comes along."

"She did mention," Dorothy said, "that she was thinking of going back to studying. Drama school, isn't it?"

Lily said, "Something like that," and concentrated on the car accelerating past her in the inside lane.

"Hardly a steady, reliable profession, although I suppose the young never think of that. They are convinced of their own talent and think only of their name up in lights and all that sort of glamour. Well, you never know, of course, somebody has to succeed. Perhaps it will be Stella. You will do your best for her, won't you, Lily? Find her suitable accommodation. A sign on your staff room board should sort that within a day or two, surely. And a reliable and pleasant young lodger like Stella in the house would be ideal for anyone looking to fill a spare room."

Lily watched her aunt walk to the communal entrance of her block of mansion flats after refusing as always help to her front door. Her string bag in one hand held the remainder of the treacle tart and cherry madeira along with two of her brother's books that she had swiftly selected from the shelves in his study. Lily knew that Dorothy had never read anything that he had written and had blatantly claimed to lack any curiosity about his work when he had been alive. But equally, she liked to conjure a kind of vicarious intellectual status by displaying some of his books around her flat for her few visitors to see. They were dwindling in number now, that band of rather terrifying, opinionated women that circled around Dorothy and claimed her friendship. Some were, like her, single and from her civil service days. Others appeared to have shed husbands, through death or divorce, and now gravitated towards Dorothy, to her coffee mornings or her soup lunches or sandwich teas laid out in the living room of her substantial flat where they would talk of the past, bemoan the present and refuse to counter the future. Lily had been invited, from time to time, and had endured the oppressive atmosphere amongst these formidable women, had felt insignificant in their company. She could see that her own few friends, whilst in no way lame ducks as Dorothy described them, were indeed undefined, shadowy in comparison.

But not Stella Fox, of course. There was nothing undefined or shadowy about her.

Except that, in truth, there was.

Or at least to Lily. She knew, after all, so very little about her.

The next day she arrived at work early, scanned the staff room board, sifted through pleas to offload kittens and outgrown children's bikes, but found no spare room or attic space to let. Casually, over their sandwich and salad lunches in the admin office, she mentioned to her colleagues that a young friend of hers was looking for somewhere to live, but drew nothing. She drove home, partly relieved of the burden of effectively standing guarantor for Stella yet at the same time feeling inadequate at her failure to provide, to fulfil the belief placed in her. She made some tea and sat down at the kitchen table with the day's post, thinking of the silent house around her, the emptiness of her father's rooms. It was now well over six months since his death yet she had done little to his study, even less to his bedroom. The clothes from the wardrobe were gone, the chest of drawers had been emptied, his pills and reading glasses and the bowl of boiled sweets he liked to keep by his bed had been taken away. Slippers removed.

Only the photograph remained, clutching at the room as if to hold on to its long-term occupant.

Lily went upstairs to the first floor and opened the door. It felt chill yet airless, a certain staleness lingering as if still harbouring shades of the sick room, her ageing, failing father. She crossed to the bedside table and picked up the photograph, the frame, she now saw, cracked and fragile.

There were few photographs of her mother.

And those few inevitably small, indiscernible representations of a young woman, displayed in frayed old albums.

But this.

A full-length studio portrait of Helen Page at the age of twenty-four or twenty-five taken in the months after her marriage. Of course, Lily had seen it before. Endless times she had stared at it as a child, out of curiosity as well as implied filial duty. And inevitably she had mythologised her, felt a reverence that had seemed appropriate in view of her obvious beauty and the poignancy of her premature death. The loss to Lily's father had been inexpressible, a shadow that had qualified the rest of his long life. Walter had rarely spoken directly to Lily about her mother. But on her twenty-first birthday he had given her the string of seed pearls that she recognised from the photograph. On her thirtieth, he had passed on a ring, a single garnet in a chip diamond setting, that he had eventually admitted had marked their engagement. There had been an awkwardness in these gestures, a reluctance at parting with them as if compelled only by a sense of duty. Lily had rarely worn either item and never in his company. She thought of them now, the seed pearl necklace, the garnet ring, nestled in a box deep in her dressing table drawer, items that had taken on a significance far in excess of their material worth.

A layer of dust had collected itself on the back of an upright chair. Similarly, on the mantelpiece. Lily moved to the window, pushed up the sash and let the room fill with fresh evening air. It was not quite dark and within a week or so the clocks would move forward with their gift of an extra hour of daylight. Outside in the street, she saw her neighbour, Anna, talking to someone who had recently moved into one of the houses opposite. Lily had watched the removal van unloading endless packing cases, the new occupants directing their actions somewhat imperiously. Now Lily saw that the woman was heavily pregnant, her pale blue dress billowing, her arms possessively cradling her shape. She moved away from the window, caught her foot on the ragged end of the rug that lay on the oak floorboards and steadied herself with difficulty on the bedhead. More dust imprinted itself on her hands. It was time, Lily told herself, firmly closing the door of her father's bedroom, leaving the windows open for another half hour of airing, for some serious spring cleaning. For considering even, whether a young lodger in the house might be a positive step. She carried the photograph of her mother into the sitting room, placed it on the long sideboard. A concerted attempt was needed to remove the grime and obvious neglect of the house during the long winter months.

The season had, after all, shifted.

9

He was late. Lily was on the point of asking someone else to read the part of Gayev when Hugh arrived hurriedly through the swing doors of the hall on Tuesday evening. She felt conscious of overwhelming relief, tried to suppress it as he caught her eye across the room, mimed an apology and sat down in a spare chair just in time for his first line. Acts 1 and 2 were run together before they took a break and people dispersed to the refectory, opened thermos flasks, or went outside to smoke. Immediately, Hugh was at her side.

"Appalling timekeeping on my part," he said, "although the Northern Line is partly to blame as always."

"It doesn't matter," Lily said, "you didn't miss your entrance."

"Never guilty of that in my long career and I must say you've got a good cast tonight, Lily. Particularly strong. Your Lophakin is most impressive and no age at all. Quite a presence there, I'd say." He looked across the hall where the young man was still sitting scanning his script, as if loath to break his focus on the play.

"Luke Andrews. Yes, he's not the most reliable of our members, but he's certainly good and very useful as a male lead. When he remembers to turn up, that is."

"And that very pretty girl playing the maid with such a spark about her. Perfect casting I'd say. But you're still resisting casting yourself prominently, I see. Shame on you!"

"It's useful to have an understudy," Lily said swiftly. "In case we're let down at the last minute."

"Of course, very resourceful of you."

"Do you want to get some coffee? Only the refectory has a habit of abruptly shutting and we can only take a short break with two more acts to go. People don't like staying too late, you see."

He ignored her suggestion. Instead he took a step closer to her and said in a low voice, "I do hope you forgive me, Lily. I've been very remiss this past couple of weeks. And I wouldn't want you to get the wrong idea."

"The wrong idea?" She looked at him blankly. One of the members of the committee, the treasurer, Colin, was hovering behind Hugh clearly trying to catch her attention. She ignored him. "I don't quite understand. The wrong idea about what?"

"I had every intention of following up that delightful Sunday we shared with another invitation. At least I was going to risk asking you. A gentleman should never assume, I've learnt over the years."

"Assume?"

"But it's been one of those hectic times," Hugh went on, "you know how it is. Fraternal duties, a couple of leads to pursue for potential work, a day or two actually in front of camera in a lowly capacity – and suddenly I realised that tonight loomed and I was going to have to face you and explain. I don't like breaking promises, you see."

"I don't think you promised anything." She felt marginally out of step with the pace of their friendship as if she had missed a key conversation, misunderstood a message. And perhaps she had, she told herself. She was, after all, so unfamiliar with the way of such things, an ingénue even, since her only knowledge was hitched to an era faintly archaic.

"Oh good!" Hugh said with evident relief and grabbed

one of her hands. "Dinner then, you'll have dinner with me? This coming weekend, ideally. How are you fixed for Saturday night?"

"This Saturday?" She stalled, unprepared by what felt like an abrupt acceleration of events. She had anticipated at most another civil Sunday outing, innocuous, bland. She could see Colin, an overbearing, pedantic man, growing impatient behind Hugh, glancing at his watch, at people starting to return to seats searching for Act 3 in their play copies. Lily continued to ignore him. Even enjoyed the look of exasperation on his face. "Saturday evening," she said, "I think I'm free. Yes, in fact I know I am. Dinner would be lovely."

"Splendid!" Hugh said. "That's a date, then. Pick you up around seven. Or more like eight? Thereabouts, anyway."

Lily nodded.

She heard little of Act 3. Lophakin triumphantly bought the land, Lubov Ranevskaya wept copiously while her daughter tried in vain to comfort her. They moved into the final act as lives shifted, changed forever and the family left the old house and the estate, keys turning in the locks and carriages driving away. Leaving only Fiers, frail and thoughtlessly abandoned, to sit and listen to the sound of the axe striking down the first of the trees in the cherry orchard. There was a moment or two of silence before the first chair scraped, then a flurry of coughing and gathering of coats and bags and the hall swiftly began to empty. Lily saw Hugh hastily break away to catch Luke Andrews, saw Elaine West who had played Lubov, join them, all talking animatedly for some minutes. She stacked chairs, rubbed a spillage of coffee into the floor with her foot hoping it would be easily camouflaged by other stains.

"He's thinking of going into the profession," Hugh said, eventually joining her as Luke and Elaine left. "Was just offering him a word or two of advice."

"That's kind of you. What did you tell him?" Lily said.

"Don't! Avoid it like the plague. Unless you want a life of frustration and penury. Become a taxman. A bookkeeper. A funeral director. They're the jobs that are needed for life."

"I'm sure you don't really mean that," Lily said, flinching as she pinched her finger in a sandwich between two chairs. "People need dreams, after all. And surely you consider your career to have been reasonably successful. It's sustained you, at least."

"You're very kind and complimentary, Lily. Just what I would expect of you!"

His familiarity, however inappropriate, warmed her. Already Hugh spoke in the terms of an established friend. Perhaps more. But words were easy, no more than conventional tropes to sustain conversation, she reminded herself. They stacked the last of the chairs.

"I enjoyed your reading of Gayev," she said, groping for safer ground. "You gave the character depth. A sincerity so that one felt an empathy for him." Hugh inclined his head, smiled. He found his jacket, his scarf, hung them around his shoulders.

"He can be played as a bit of a buffoon, head in the clouds, vacuous, that sort of thing. And in a way I suppose he is. But Chekhov layers all his characters, wouldn't you say?" Lily nodded, was about to say more, but the caretaker appeared at the door, a large bunch of keys signalling the end of the evening. "Our heavy hint to go, wouldn't you say, Lily? We'll have to leave further discussions until Saturday evening."

Outside, Hugh straightaway headed down towards King's Cross while Lily hesitated for a moment, watched him, wondering whether he would turn round to say goodnight. Confirm their arrangement for dinner. After all, it had sounded somewhat loose. Resignedly, she crossed the street where for once she had managed to park close by. Then he was beside her again.

"Appallingly remiss of me. I didn't even ask. Any preferences for dinner? I really should book something as it's a Saturday night."

"Preferences?"

"Italian? French? Greek? People can be quite particular, I find, and I want to get it right for you."

"Anything," Lily said. "Really, whatever you like."

He smiled, hand on her shoulder for a moment.

"Excellent! Leave it to me, then. Until Saturday," and he rapidly retraced his steps, turning up the collar of his jacket against the night air.

Lily sat for several minutes in the car before starting the engine and heading home. The experience of being regarded by another, the focus of their concern, was remote from her, and she wanted to hold on to such singling out, simply marvel at it.

★★★

Of course, the idea had been fleeting. Impulsive.

On Friday evening, she went back to her father's room, returned the photograph of Helen Page to its place by his bedside, pulled the coverlet tight over the mattress and left the room. Already she could not imagine why she had even briefly considered the thought of relinquishing his place to someone else. It was far too soon to think of such a thing, not while his ashes remained in that large container on the high shelf in his study, their final resting place unresolved.

Still. The thought had occurred.

It had seemed logical in many ways. Stella Fox was in need and had turned to her for help. To Lily. And her desultory efforts to find her other suitable accommodation had produced nothing.

Of course, she could always suggest the idea as temporary.

While Stella was taking time to find something suitable for the long term, she could offer her lodging as a respite. For a few days, a week or even two at a pinch. That way, Lily would feel she had not disappointed Stella's expectation of her.

But not her father's room.

There was that other space next to it, hardly a room at all and probably once intended as no more than a dressing room, but it narrowly fitted a single bed, a chair. Inappropriate for anything more than a very brief stay, but Stella might be grateful for it. For a few nights at least.

She went down to the kitchen, started to push the ingredients for some supper together, urged the reluctant gas burner into some sort of action and wondered what it would feel like to have someone in the house again.

Since her father's death, Lily had not felt lonely.

She had anticipated it. Had waited for a sense of dread in returning each day to the empty rooms, the silence of the place, rather like waiting for the full onslaught of flu after initial shivering and sense of encroaching fever. Undeniably, the first few weeks had been difficult. She had been reluctant to shift his chair from its favoured position by the standard lamp in the living room. Had resisted fluffing the back cushion since it would cause the imprint of his shape to be lost. The book he had been reading had sat for too long on the dresser in the kitchen. A favourite mug had remained draining by the sink. Yet once she had dealt with such tokens of her father, she realised that her grief was complex, signalling not only loss, but also release. Walter Page had loved her, of course. Lily had never doubted his paternal affection for her. At the same time, she had sometimes allowed herself to wonder whether he had ever chosen really to know her. To see her as anything more than a biddable and obliging child who had grown unexceptionally into an acquiescent, amenable woman suited to fulfilling a certain kind of life. She had never been quite sure whether she had consciously shaped herself to fit his expectation or if she was conciliatory, diffident, even, by nature. After all, a brief and ill-judged passion for a married man hardly merited evidence of a suppressed subversive side. She was the sort of person who served rather than led. Hadn't she overheard someone saying just that about her once? Her aunt, Dorothy, of course. Left to her own devices, no doubt she would have chosen always to fit rather than break out of any mould.

Even so.

There had been a moment soon after his death when she had allowed herself to think that his absence offered her a freedom and the possibility of change, not just in circumstance, but in herself. She was no longer hitched to her father, an accoutrement and accessory to his well-being. Now she could surely forge a life self-determined rather than living one fashioned according to the needs of another. And had wondered as the weeks had stacked up into months what shape this brave new life of hers would take. With good fortune, inheriting the genes of her father, her aunt, she could live a long life now devoid of obligation, of conformity. She could negotiate her way through the remaining years of the century and tip into the new millennium in a way she had fashioned and honed to her own satisfaction. She knew how fortunate she was materially, how privileged, and had felt a qualified excitement at the prospect of what lay ahead. It was not until the year had turned and she had attended the memorial service in early January, suffered the awkwardness of that stilted lunch, those thinly voiced hymns, that she had accepted that nothing would essentially alter.

That was the truth of it.

She had been dependent on satisfying the needs of others for too long to shrug off the habit and without such a crutch she was nebulous.

But so be it.

After all, it was simply the way for so many women of her generation, of average talent and attraction who, with increasing years, inevitably became somewhat marginalised, peripheral, lacking the habit and initiative to steer their own course.

It was entirely different now.

At least for women like Stella Fox.

Which brought her back to the room.

By now, Stella had no doubt found herself somewhere to live, a bijou studio in Kentish Town, a house share in one of the substantial terraces in Highgate. Even a berth on a house boat on the Regent's Canal. She would hardly be awaiting a phone call from Lily for reassurance. Besides, Stella had not even left a number or an address where she could be contacted. Clearly, she had sorted matters out for herself and would be troubling Lily no longer for help. The thought, as she sliced an onion, grated a carrot, grilled a fillet of fish for supper, felt like a reprieve of sorts.

★★★

Hugh arrived just after eight o'clock.

At seven-thirty Lily decided he had changed his mind. By ten to eight she had slipped off her shoes, hung her coat back over the end of the banister, convinced that he was not coming. And was relieved. After all, the evening was bound to be a disappointment from his point of view, an invitation he would regret and certainly not repeat. It was better, therefore, for her to quell expectation, accept defeat at an early hurdle.

And then the doorbell rang.

"So sorry, am I late? Couldn't remember what time I'd said." Hugh stepped into the narrow hall, closed the door behind him.

"No, you're very punctual," she said. Then looked down at her stockinged feet. "As a matter of fact, I haven't even got my shoes on yet. And my coat..." She swiftly retrieved shoes and coat. Her handbag from the hall table. But Hugh had already stepped through the open door of the kitchen and stood looking at the room as if appraising it. For a moment, Lily worried that there had been a confusion, that he was expecting to spend the evening with her in Alfred Street. Dinner, perhaps, was what she was supposed to be providing. Then he turned to her and she caught the faint smell of alcohol on his breath.

"Ready, then, Lily? I have our table booked for eight-thirty so there's no rush. Of course, I'm a little unfamiliar with the area so had to rely on a friend's recommendation for a suitable place. I do hope it will be all right. I know I could have rung you to ask for advice on the dining front, but it seemed a little – well, shall we say ungallant? For a first proper date, at any rate."

The word startled her. Since Hugh's invitation on Tuesday night she had tried to tell herself that there was no significance in having dinner with a fellow member of the Play Reading Society. It was what friends did, after all. Even she and Agnes had occasionally been to the trattoria in Camden Passage for plates of pasta and a half carafe of Chianti. But Hugh had now inflated the occasion. Consequence, one way or the other, was inevitable. And as if to confirm it, he took her arm lightly as they began to walk along the road in the direction of Upper Street.

"I don't mind telling you I've been very nervous about this evening," he said, lowering his head towards her conspiratorially. "I got here a bit early and had some Dutch courage at the King's Head. You see, it's years since I've done anything like this. Taken a woman out for dinner on a Saturday night. I really am out of practice."

"Me too," Lily said clumsily. Yet felt better for the confession.

"Well, I suppose neither of us is of the age to make it a habit. A regular occurrence, shall we say? And the last six or seven years for me have been somewhat difficult. After losing my wife, I rather withdrew into my shell. Didn't feel up to much, socially."

"That's only natural," Lily said. "It must have been a very distressing time for you." She wanted to ask more, but felt it would be tactless.

"But one has to go on, make a new start. Wouldn't you say, Lily? Or does that sound too heartless?"

"Not at all."

"Good. My sister is all for it, may I add? Tired of having me hanging around the house like a wet blanket. She certainly thinks it's time to get myself a life again. Get out from under her feet. Not that the arrangement will be forever, of course. Once the builders actually let me repossess my own house again, that is."

"Of course. It must be such a nuisance." Lily felt too warm in her coat. The evening was mild and hardly warranted its weight yet her only alternative was a thin jacket that always creased and the colour had seemed wrong over her dress. Did such things matter, though? Hugh had abandoned his usual dark jacket for camel coloured suede that appeared entirely appropriate for the season. He began to talk about loose roof tiles and brick work that needed repointing and something about the foundations in danger of sinking.

"Houses are such a drain, are they not, Lily? Although I must say your place looks in good shape. They certainly knew how to build in the 19th century. Such attractive terraces. Early, is it?"

"Early?"

"Regency is my guess," he went on. "Domestic Regency architecture is so pleasing to the eye!"

"Oh yes," Lily said. "We think the street was built around 1820. Or rather that's what my father used to say. I've never really looked into it."

"Shame on you!" Hugh said. "Social history is fascinating. Streets tell stories, don't you think?"

"I suppose so. Certainly the demographic of the residents of Alfred Street has changed radically in recent years. What about your house?"

"Mine?"

"Your house in Fulham, I mean."

"Edwardian," Hugh said. "A typical Edwardian terrace. Nice enough, if it hadn't decided to start being temperamental and showing its age and running up bills for me with careless abandon. But then my attachment to it is nothing compared with yours. Your hook to your family home. Were you evacuated during the war? Surely Islington wasn't the best place to spend one's childhood during the Blitz."

"We left for a while," Lily said. Hugh's pace had slowed as if thoughtfully trying to match hers. "Although my father disliked being away from the house for long. He used to say he'd rather take his chances with the bombing. Which, when you think about it, was somewhat foolhardy of him. Very rash, in fact. We went to Buckinghamshire for a few months, stayed with some remote cousin of his in the Chilterns and I was sent to the local village primary school. Although I can't remember a great deal about it other than a sense of not belonging. Which, of course, I didn't. So it was hard to make friends. And then my father came back to London and left me there, which made things even worse. After that, I spent some time living with my aunt Dorothy in her flat in Harrow. Although, quite frankly, I think she found giving house room to someone so young even more troublesome than the air raids."

"Poor motherless Lily. How difficult for you."

"We were far luckier than many people. The house survived whereas others lost so much."

"And your father?"

"My father? Oh he was too old to fight so he joined the local Home Guards."

Hugh had headed them northwards on reaching Upper Street and as they passed by a shop, she caught a glimpse of their reflection in the window lit up by the street light, and was warmed by it, by the normality of being part of a companionable couple out on a Saturday night.

"Of course, all this ages us terribly, all these reminiscences about the war. Do you realise that, Lily?"

"That's true, but my father rarely spoke about it. At least not to me. My aunt once told me that he became very distressed about the number of young men he knew from the university who had lost their lives. The appalling waste of it. Especially after he had lost his own two brothers in the previous war."

Their reserved table was at the far end of the dimly lit restaurant.

"I've just realised that I'm being negligent," Hugh said as he sat down opposite her. "I had every intention of calling you by your rightful name of Helen and here I am already slipping into old habits."

"Please don't, I would find it very confusing suddenly to be called Helen."

"Why?" Hugh said, leaning across the table towards her. "It's your rightful birth name, one specifically chosen for you. You must own it."

Lily picked up the menu lying in front of her as a distraction from his gaze.

"I've never felt it suited me," she said simply. "I prefer Lily."

"In that case," Hugh said, "I shall see it as my mission to convince you otherwise. Alter your perception of what suits you. Now what would you like to drink? By the way, is this place all right? When one has lost the habit of regularly dining out it can be difficult to make the right choice. No doubt it's boringly local to you. We will have to be more adventurous another time, venture further afield from N1."

"It's certainly very popular," Lily said, looking around her, "not an empty table in the place. That's a good sign, surely."

Hugh smiled. "You're such a comfort. Always saying something consoling. Or maybe you're just a master of tact. And I have to be honest with you from the start in saying how much I enjoy your company, Lily. Or rather, Helen. Hugely enjoy it. I do hope you might feel something of the same by the end of the evening."

Lily looked down at the menu again, seeking some semblance of composure as she studied it. *Poulet Bonne Femme, Boeuf Bourguignon, Cassoulet, Coq au vin, Confit de Canard*. Then she felt a light touch on one hand. "I am so sorry, Helen, I am being far too forward. Forgive me," Hugh said. "As I say, I'm so out of practice with this sort of thing. Don't know the rules any more. Let's order some drinks. Gin? Vermouth? Or perhaps we'll go straight onto some wine."

"Wine, yes, thank you, that would be nice," Lily said and, looking up and seeing an uncertainty in his eyes that matched her own, felt reassured by his apology. Allowed herself to begin to enjoy the evening, even dispensing with her inclination to predict its failure.

She barely noticed what she ordered, whether she ate, but

presumably both steps were accomplished since a couple of hours went by, food was produced, wine drunk and plates removed. Hugh was easy company, affable, entertaining, yet equally curious to know about her, insisting on hearing how she had supported her father's career, suggesting tentatively that it might have been at the expense of her own. Lily had been adamant.

"Not at all. I had few ambitions of my own worth pursuing so I was very fortunate to have my father's profession to embrace, you could say. To be at the side lines of it, anyway. He never really stopped working, writing, researching, you see."

"Not many women are as self-effacing as you. Or dare I say as sacrificial?"

"Oh no, that's not how it was at all," Lily insisted. "I've always had my own job, after all."

"Ah yes, the girls' school. Tell me about that."

And she did. Although there seemed little to say of particular interest and very soon the conversation returned to Hugh and his career. Amusing stories about the days of weekly rep, touring and the trials of inhospitable boarding houses and intractable landladies.

"You must stop me being a bore about the old days," he said after a complicated tale about understudying for two actors who both fell ill on the same night. "I have such a store of stories and tend to forget that not everyone finds them as amusing as me."

"I think they're fascinating," Lily said. "It's a world I know so little about. Was your late wife an actress?"

"No. Not at all." His answer was abrupt.

"Sorry," she said, "perhaps I shouldn't have asked."

"But why not?" Hugh said. "A perfectly reasonable question. But no, she was – Louise, that is – she worked in a bank. And no, there were no children, as I believe I mentioned before. I'm afraid it simply didn't happen for us. A family, that is. But every life has its regrets, doesn't it?"

Lily said nothing. She sensed a sadness in Hugh and was resistant to responding blandly.

"And you?" he went on. "No long history of spurned lovers, adulterous husbands or possessive brothers, I presume."

"Nothing like that at all," Lily said. "I've never been married." She was loath to mention the matter of Toby Jennings. Swiftly she went on, "And I'm an only child."

"Sensible," Hugh said somewhat ambiguously and drank the glass of cognac he had ordered. The restaurant was emptying, their table one of the few still occupied. Hugh turned, signalled to a waiter to bring their bill.

"Are you going to be available for casting next month for the society?" Lily said.

"Naturally, I have every intention of being there. I wouldn't by choice miss any of the meetings as they've become quite the highlight of my scant social calendar. Apart from occasions such as this, of course, Helen, that goes without saying." He smiled, leant across the table so that his face was close to hers. Then suddenly drew back. "Although I have to say my schedule is somewhat uncertain for next month. It's work, you see. And one can't afford to turn any of it down, however uninspiring the engagement."

Instinctively, Lily felt disappointed. "It's *The Deep Blue Sea*," she said. "A strong play, although I know some people think of Rattigan as dated these days. We always need a play with a small cast at the meeting close to Easter as people tend to be away. School holidays, that sort of thing. But obviously, your work must always come first, your career. I quite understand that." Lily wondered if she was mildly drunk and consequently rambling. Or not so much drunk as liberated from her usual reserve by the mood of the evening. By Hugh's attention.

"Well, needs must and all that." Hugh reached for his wallet, Lily produced her purse. He placed a restraining hand over hers. "Let me take care of the bill tonight. I know we live in an age of aspiring equality – or so I hear my sister say in one of her rants – but you have been so good as to accept my invitation with such grace." She started to protest, but he insisted, summoned the waiter and dealt speedily with the bill.

"Then it will be my turn next time," Lily said, surprised by the boldness of her assumption.

It had started to rain, not heavily, but with an appealing mistiness when caught in the beam of the street lights. Hugh took her arm, apologised for the lack of an umbrella to shield her. At the corner of St Peter's Street, he stopped as if intending to divert from his direct route to the Tube station.

"There's no need to go out of your way," Lily said.

"My mother brought me up with appropriate manners," Hugh said, "towards women, that is. I should see you safely home to your front door." His light suede jacket was marked with rain spots. Lily wondered whether it would stain.

"Please don't," she said. "It's quite unnecessary."

He nodded. Took one of her hands and squeezed it tenderly.

"I wouldn't want to overstep the mark, get things wrong at this early stage. I'll be in touch, then. If that's all right with you. I don't want to presume."

"Of course," she said, adding, "please presume. And thank you for a lovely evening."

He leant forward, kissed her on both cheeks, lingering as if he wished the social gesture to imply more.

"Until next time, then, Lily. I mean Helen. Dear Helen. I'll have to practise that. We'll talk soon."

10

Lily was unsure what she expected. She examined his words, anatomised them forensically. Foolishly. Like an adolescent with an inappropriate crush.

And reminded herself constantly that it was 1983. Hardly an era when a woman was obliged to wait patiently for gentlemen callers to make the first move. There was no reason why she should not pick up the phone and ring him.

Even so.

Hugh had implied that he would contact her. So she waited.

Anyway, it was Easter.

End of term at school meant a week or so of leave to take and she drove home planning to ring Dorothy, to check what she wanted to do about holiday arrangements. For a woman who dismissed any significance in religious festivals, her aunt could be intransigent about how she marked associated events. They should be family occasions, she had often said perversely, times to gather together, to observe certain rituals. Lily knew she was thinking more of hot cross buns and roast lamb with extensive trimmings than three-hour church services surveying the wondrous cross, but always obliged. She parked conveniently close, for once, to number 8 and wondered if some of her neighbours had already headed to Cotswold or Cornish cottages for the holiday.

And then she saw Stella.

Stella Fox stood on the pavement talking to her neighbour, Anna, who was dismantling a pushchair with one hand, clasping her youngest child with the other. Stella, as if in acknowledgement of the season, was wearing a long vibrant daffodil-yellow dress. The fur coat lay on the ground at her feet looking like an animal's shed skin. A scuffle of carrier bags was deposited next to it.

"Lily!" she called. "I was so worried I'd got things wrong. Dates, that is. And that you'd gone away or something. But Anna didn't seem to think so."

Stella Fox was the sort of person immediately on first name terms with strangers.

"I was just about to invite Stella in for a cuppa while she waited for you," Anna said. "I knew you wouldn't have forgotten an arrangement with a friend and were just delayed at work."

An arrangement. Lily groped in her mind for any possible confusion between the two of them. A letter lost in the post. A message through her door that had somehow disappeared. But at the same time found herself relieved to see Stella. Dorothy was bound to ask if her housing dilemma had been sorted.

"I'm so sorry, last day of term and numerous jobs to sort out in the school office then nightmare traffic," Lily found herself apologising.

"I'm leaving you in capable hands then, Stella," Anna said. "And I'm sure Lily will have the solution for you. Good to meet you. And the best of luck!"

Stella followed Lily up the steps, deposited her coat, heavy boots – surely inappropriate for the mild spring day – and the carrier bags in the hall, went straight to the kitchen and sat down at the table. Lily followed her in.

"Tea? Coffee? I'm afraid I don't have any cake, but perhaps a sandwich?"

"God yes, the lot," Stella said and put her head down on the pillow of her arms as if overwhelmed by exhaustion. "I've had such a time of it, I just can't tell you, Lily, quite how bad it's been. Well, actually, I can. As you know, you were the first person I thought of when it all started. Because I knew you'd understand and want to help. It's in your nature, isn't it?"

"Is it?" Lily said, putting on the kettle. She found bread, the butter dish. Cheese, a jar of chutney.

"You're one of those helpful sorts, salt of the earth, isn't that the expression? Someone who can be relied upon, anyway. I don't seem to have come across many of those in my life. People like that. Like you, in fact."

"Is it still your accommodation problem, Stella?" Lily said. "I'm afraid I've not had much luck in finding anything suitable. Anything that you might be willing to accept, that is."

"I'd accept anything right now," Stella said and scooped up Hector, who had begun to rub his face against her legs, fussed him until he curled up on her lap. "Lily, things are at crisis point. I am officially homeless. I mean, it was bad when I saw you before, but now it's critical. In fact, most of my possessions are in those bags in the hall. I've left some stuff at work in the staff room – I've been temping at Liberty's for a couple of weeks, sales assistant stuff in the scarves, but I'm about to leave – and what with Easter coming up and even the agencies will be shut over the bank holiday, well, I've reached a dead end. Even a space on someone's hearth rug would do."

Lily made a pot of tea. Poured two cups. Took time to make a substantial sandwich and put it in front of Stella.

"What about family?" she said tentatively, sitting down opposite her at the table. "Just as a temporary stop gap, I mean. Your parents, perhaps, could help you out?"

Stella shrugged. Looked down at the curled fur ball of Hector, purring volubly.

"You'd think that," she said in a quiet voice. "I mean, that's what parents are supposed to do, isn't it? Be there in times of need. That's what everyone assumes. But mine? Well, for a start, they're not even living in the country. They're in the middle of France somewhere. Not even sure exactly where it is as they haven't bothered to keep in contact. Just took themselves off some years ago and left me to my own devices more or less. The moment I reached eighteen, they seemed to despatch all responsibilities. Saw me packed off to university and even when that all went wrong, they weren't there to pick up the pieces, help me sort things out. So effectively, I'm on my own." She shrugged again as if resigned rather than resentful of her situation and began to eat the sandwich with evident hunger. Lily was shocked. It was not that she was ignorant of the prevalence of irresponsible parents and the consequence of their neglect, but she had never imagined that people like Stella could be a victim of such desertion. Her world view had been too narrow, no doubt.

"I'm so sorry, Stella," she said, "and London is a very challenging place for someone like – well, someone young and in need of some support. To help get you on your feet, as it were. I'm aware of how spoilt I have been in that regard. Always having a home and never having to worry about rent. Another sandwich? I'm sorry it's only cheese."

Stella shook her head, drank the tea. She looked worn out, as if even the effort of talking was now eluding her. Her hair hung lankly, looked unwashed.

"Of course," she said eventually, picking up stray shivers of cheese with her finger, "there's always a squat. There are lots of those around at the moment in empty houses. I could find a place in one of those, I suppose. Someone mentioned one down the Liverpool Road. A bit rough, of course, and there tends to be a problem with rats and inevitably there'd be drugs, but at least it would be a roof over my head."

"Isn't that illegal?" Lily said. "Squatting?"

"Not really. The law's a bit vague. And squatters' rights mean the police can't get you out easily so it's quite a valid option for me."

Lily was resolved.

"I had been thinking that perhaps I could help you out," she said cautiously. "Just for a while. It's not ideal or what you need in the long term, but for the time being, it might suit. And certainly save you from squatting."

Stella looked up. Stared at Lily keenly.

"Anything you can suggest. Just anything. I am truly desperate." She looked close to tears.

"You could stay here," Lily said. "There's a small room on the first floor at the back of the house, nothing special and not even a proper spare room, really. But it would be something. For a week or two, anyway."

Stella said nothing. Lily sipped her tea and began to feel awkward. The idea was clearly preposterous to Stella and she was no doubt unsure how to decline without offending. Then suddenly her face changed, broke into a wide smile. Abruptly, as if disturbed by her excitement, Hector jumped off her lap and stole out of the room.

"Lily, I can't tell you what this means to me. I am simply so grateful. It's just so… so generous and thoughtful. Do you really mean it?"

"Perhaps you should see the room first," Lily said, touched by Stella's gratitude. By the prospect of bringing so easily some relief into this young woman's life.

Upstairs on the first floor, Stella eagerly began to open the door into her father's room.

"Actually, it's not that one," Lily said swiftly, pulling the door closed and opening its neighbour. "It is rather small, as you can see."

The room, as they stood on its threshold, appeared monastic. The single bed, upright chair and small table too utilitarian for comfort. But Stella seemed unconcerned.

"It is small, but perfect for me for the time being. Very cosy, in fact. And it's not as if I have been used to luxury these past few years, I can tell you, sleeping on sofas in overcrowded flats. If you are really sure, Lily. And of course, we will have to come to some arrangement about rent. That's only fair. I must pay my way."

Lily had not thought about rent. She was simply offering the room to satisfy Stella's needs. Stella had turned to her and she wanted to provide. Besides, there was the matter of their fledgling friendship that her aunt, her neighbour Anna and, apparently, Stella herself seemed to assume. This was a gesture of friendship.

"There's no need for that," Lily said. "Any payment, I mean. After all, I'm sure you will soon find something better suited to you, a proper flat share with friends of your own age. So think of this as just a convenience."

Stella moved towards the bed and sat down. Her hair fell over her face as she examined the heavy paisley eiderdown, stroked the fabric, tracing the intricate floral patterns with the fingers of one hand. She looked up, flicked back her hair, smiled warmly at Lily.

"Thank you. Thank you so much. This is just perfect. And I suppose you could say we are helping each other out. After all, you must be so lonely after your father's death and living here on your own not easy for you, I'm sure. It will be good for you to have someone else in the house. I can see that now. So that's settled then. Fixed, we could say?" Stella pulled her legs up under her, the daffodil yellow fabric of her dress billowing out across the paisley pattern like an indelible stain of paint.

Lily shivered, suddenly cold.

Yet the window was closed and the room was in the habit of catching shafts of afternoon sunlight from the west facing courtyard garden. She pulled her cardigan tightly around her against the chill. Rubbed her arms.

The phone rang.

"I'm sorry," she said, "I ought to get that. In case – well, it might be my aunt. Asking about Easter."

Or Hugh Murray. There was always a chance, after all. Stella waved her away.

"I'll just sit here tuning into the room if that's all right. And the bathroom? Don't worry, I'll investigate while you're gone, Lily. Take your time."

It was not Hugh, of course. Nor Dorothy. Eileen Fisher apologised for not being in touch since they had met at the Barbican in January.

"I had every intention of asking you over for a meal, Lily. So remiss of me. But what with one thing and the other – well, anyway, here we are with summer just around the corner and I thought we ought to make some plans."

"Plans?"

Hugh had, of course, said he was going to be busy. Lily knew that. She was being unreasonable expecting him to ring. And after all, it was barely ten days since they had met for dinner. She was not, she reminded herself, a priority in his life.

"Stratford-upon-Avon," Eileen went on. "We talked about the idea of going to the summer season there in June or July. Do you remember?"

"Of course," Lily said blankly.

"It's just that tickets sell so fast, especially the cheaper ones. And we did think of even staying over in a B and B and making a weekend of it, didn't we? Now you've absolutely no ties at all at home."

Eileen made such freedom sound like an aberration rather than a gift.

Lily said, "It's a lovely idea, of course. But it's a long way off, isn't it? The summer, I mean, and hard to make plans so far in advance."

There was a silence from Eileen. Lily heard sounds from upstairs, doors opening and closing.

"Of course, if you'd rather not commit yourself," Eileen eventually said, "I can always ask someone else. Naturally, I just thought of you first, Lily. After what you said when we met in January. You seemed so keen."

Lily felt contrite. Yet still resistant to committing herself to outings hitched to a time ahead as if it had become necessary to suspend forward planning and abandon herself instead to the laws of chance. To the laws of Stella Fox and Hugh Murray as if she suddenly had a significance in their lives that she needed to nurture and cherish. Whatever Eileen Fisher thought, she was not entirely free and without ties.

"And I am still keen," she compromised, "at least in theory. It's just that I've not looked that far ahead yet. To the summer, I mean. Not checked my diary." She heard her cliché. Flinched. Went on. "Let me get back to you in a week or so. Would that be all right?"

"Fine," Eileen said, pacified. "Just don't leave it too long, Lily. Advanced booking has already started. Any plans for the Easter weekend? I suppose you'll be seeing your aunt, as usual."

"Probably," Lily said. "On Easter Sunday, at least. And you?"

"Oh, family. You know how it is. Our daughters and various partners and hangers-on. A full house for a couple of days at least."

"Of course," Lily said. And then impulsively added, "Actually, I'm expecting a friend over the holiday and she's going to be staying with me for a while. Stella Fox. In fact," she added, "she's moving in any time now so I'm really very busy getting everything ready for her."

"Moving in?" There was a note of surprise in Eileen's voice.

"Yes," Lily said firmly. "Just for a short stay to help her out a bit. So if you'll excuse me there's a lot to see to right now. But I'll be in touch as soon as I have a moment, Eileen. A very happy Easter to you all."

Stella stood at the bottom of the stairs. In her bare feet, the hem of her long yellow dress partly torn, there was something faintly childlike about her, vulnerable. Lily put the receiver down.

"Was that the aunt? The lady I met the other week?" she asked.

"No, just a friend. But nothing important. I'll have to ring Dorothy later. Make some plans for Sunday."

Stella hopped down the final step.

"A traditional Easter celebration!" she said. "Do let me cook, Lily. I'd adore that. Unless of course…" She knelt down on the floor next to Hector curled on her coat, buried her face in the two of them so that her voice became muffled. "Unless I'd be intruding. I mean, if you want to keep it to just family, I'd quite understand."

"That's quite unnecessary," Lily said. Stella looked up, beamed.

"Good, that's settled, then. You really are my saviour, Lily, you know that? Not only have you rescued me from homelessness, but now you're sharing your family with me."

"It's only Dorothy," Lily said. "I'm afraid I don't have anyone more alluring to offer. My father was the most interesting member of the family. Always with an opinion on every subject and with such a fine mind. I'm sorry you won't meet him."

"You must have lots of friends, though, Lily. Interesting friends. Especially having lived in the same place for so long. I've always envied people that, a sense of stability and connection."

Lily said nothing. She looked at the pile of Stella's carrier bags still sitting in the hall. They appeared to contain clothes, scarves. Some books. A toothbrush had toppled out onto the floor. Stella followed her gaze.

"So would it be convenient for me to move in straight away?" she said. "Get myself established, as it were. Unless that's awfully awkward for you."

"Now?" Lily said. "Yes, of course, why not?" In spite of her bravado to Eileen, she had to hide a sense of panic at the prospect of such a swift change of circumstances. Her circumstances. Events had acquired a pace that was unfamiliar so that there was no time for her to adjust to relinquishing her quiet, solitary evenings for the foreseeable future. Then there was the need to find suitable bed linen, supplying, she supposed, supper for the two of them. Perhaps she really had been too rash, too precipitate about the whole matter.

"Good," Stella said, "I'll just settle in, shall I? Get myself unpacked. And would it be all right if I had a bath? It's just that this morning I only managed to splash my face in the staff cloakroom at Liberty's as I was already persona non grata in Dalston."

"You must make yourself at home, Stella," Lily said. And wondered fleetingly if the somewhat inadequate tank would provide sufficient hot water for the two of them. Her father's needs had been scant. Someone like Stella would no doubt expect a more luxuriant supply. And she made a mental note to turn on the immersion heater regularly.

She made a pie to eke out scant chicken and laid the small table by the kitchen window. Stella ate with enthusiasm.

"Rather last minute, I'm afraid," Lily said. "I need to shop tomorrow so you must tell me if there is anything you don't eat. And any particular preferences."

Stella shook her head. "I eat everything," she said and neatly lined up her knife and fork as if following careful etiquette. "I'm not at all fussy, you'll find, so you needn't worry about that. And no doubt I'll be out for meals most of the time. Although I have to say this is so nice, Lily. I mean sitting in your cosy kitchen having a proper home cooked meal. It's so... comforting." She drew one hand through her hair, which was still damp from washing. It had regained its lustre and now hung sleek and straight as if under order to resist random wave. "And you must let me cook. For both of us, I mean. You'll find I'm pretty resourceful in the kitchen if I have free rein. Quite inventive with the right ingredients." She looked around the room as if inspecting its potential. Her eyes focused on the gas stove. Smiled with evident pleasure. "And that will be my first challenge! A bit like your bathroom, Lily. I don't think I've ever seen anything quite so... quaint. Yes, that's the word. Absolutely quaint. And charming too, of course. Like the whole house."

"I'm just pleased to be able to provide you with a stopgap," Lily said. "Until you find somewhere more permanent to live."

"Oh that," Stella said and stretched her arms above her head, yawned extravagantly. "It's an impossible business, I can tell you. Sometimes, I feel as if my whole life is on hold, Lily, do you know what I mean? And has been for ages. And it's unsettling. An unsettling, disturbing feeling."

"It must be," Lily sympathised. "But you are still so young, Stella."

"But you were never in this situation, were you, Lily?

Everything seems always to have been mapped out for you. Preordained as it were. Whereas me – well, I suppose you could say I've always lacked roots. My parents being my parents. And a compass. I'm definitely without a compass."

"But there's time," Lily said consolingly, "for you to achieve anything you want. Whatever that may be."

She really did know so little about her. Nothing of any substance at all. But then the young woman was merely occupying a small room in the house for a week. A fortnight at most. And it was common, surely, for people to have lodgers in their home who were near strangers.

"You're so encouraging, Lily," Stella said. "And now I think I'll take myself off to bed if that's all right with you. I've got work tomorrow, after all. One last ghastly day selling scarves to tourists and appalling men buying last-minute birthday presents for their wives. Or for their lovers, come to that. I'll be very happy to walk through that staff entrance for the very last time, I can tell you that."

"I suppose Liberty's takes on a lot of temporary staff," Lily said, beginning to clear the table and pile their plates on the draining board. "For busy holiday times like Easter."

Stella looked at her in surprise.

"Oh, it isn't temporary. The job. Didn't I say? At least, it's not supposed to be. I just can't stand it anymore. So I'm not going back. Not after I've collected my first week's wages tomorrow and stuff from my staff locker." She went into the hall, gently lifted Hector from where he was still curled up on her coat. "Good night, Lily. And thank you. You're just one of the best."

"Really, it's nothing, I'm happy to be in a position to help you."

"Just one more thing," Stella said, hovering in the doorway. "Keys."

"Keys?"

She held out her hand.

"Yes, for the front door to the house. And back door if there is one. To let myself in. After all, I don't want to be bothering you all the time, Lily. Best if I have my own set."

11

Dorothy was most complimentary.

"I have to say, that was a splendid Easter lunch, Lily. Or perhaps it's Stella I should be thanking. I could certainly detect a certain flair there. Have you been formally trained, dear?"

Her aunt rarely used endearments. Lily was unsure whether she had ever been on the receiving end of one. Stella shrugged, nibbled at a piece of glazed apple from the slice of tart on her plate.

"I did one of those courses ages ago. You know, a week learning to do posh dinner party food. Cordon bleu and all that. Think I got a certificate or a diploma or something. But it's all a complete waste of time when you're living in a bedsit or worse."

"A valuable skill, nevertheless," Dorothy said. "We all need to eat, after all. Have you ever thought of making a profession of it?"

"What, cooking?" Stella sounded mildly offended.

"Well, I believe smart catering is quite the thing these days. People's standards have inflated, their expectations. No doubt all this foreign travel they do now is to blame. Sophisticated palates and ideas don't come from a week in a guest house in Clacton or Scarborough, that's for sure. Still, it could be something to consider, Stella. A viable career for you to pursue?"

"I don't think so," Stella said. "I don't like my clothes smelling of cooking all day long."

"Ah, there is that," Dorothy said, conceding. "And clearly, you are a highly intelligent young woman and need a profession to satisfy that lively mind of yours. I was much the same as you when I was your age. You need to be stretched. Intellectually."

Dorothy had never spoken to Lily in such terms when she had been young. A job was what she had been encouraged to find, something convenient and satisfactory to complement what had already been defined for her. She began to clear the table.

"Of course, I'm still thinking of acting," Stella said somewhat wearily, leaning back in her chair. "Drama school. Perhaps. I mean I did start a degree, of course. Did university for a while back, but it wasn't really for me."

"Was it the exams that worried you? Understandably, they can cause a lot of anxiety," Dorothy said.

"Oh no." Stella looked surprised by the suggestion. "The exams were all fine. Easy, really. It was just all a bit dull."

"Perhaps it was your choice of subject. Not the right one for you. What were you reading?"

"Philosophy," Stella said with the suggestion of a sneer. "With a subsidiary in psychology." There was a slight pause. Lily's tray was loaded, but neither offered to help her.

"Well, of course it's important to find the right path," Dorothy said eventually. "And you were brave to abandon something that clearly didn't suit you. That takes courage. Someone like you, Stella, needs to be doing something that enthuses you. And, of course, you are still so young."

Stella smiled, looked warmly at Lily.

"That's what Lily always says, no need to rush these things. She's made me feel so much better about myself, I can't tell you."

"Well," Dorothy said, "what are good friends for? And my

niece has always been such a supportive and caring person."

Lily could only remember one brief conversation with Stella about her career plans and her own contribution had been scant. Still, compliments were too rare to question their validity. She lifted the loaded tray with difficulty, carried it to the kitchen while the other two headed to the sitting room. She heard their voices drifting down the stairs as she soaked and washed the numerous pans and bowls that Stella had piled up on every surface in the kitchen. It was a relief to have someone else to make conversation with her aunt, to retreat for a while safe in the knowledge that Dorothy could not complain of being ignored. Stella seemed at ease with her, content to talk inconsequentially, to listen with apparent curiosity to her stories about her past. The young were rarely so gifted in the art of social exchange, their concerns generally too self-obsessed, which made Lily wonder whether Stella had strong bonds with her grandparents in spite of a detachment from her parents.

She had seen little of her since she had moved in the week before. Stella had headed out most mornings, talking about avenues to explore, people to consult, and was rarely back before six. They had eaten companionably on a couple of evenings, but she usually then left the house to meet friends and Lily was always in bed and mildly startled by the unfamiliar sound of a key in the front door, steps on the stairs, when she came home much later. On Good Friday, Lily had gone to church, slipping into a back pew at St Mary's for just an hour or so of the three-hour vigil service and had seen nothing of Stella all day. On Saturday morning, however, she had been sitting at the kitchen table drinking tea when Lily had come downstairs around eight and hesitantly, as if expecting objection, had asked whether she could take responsibility for preparing Easter Sunday lunch. She had then proceeded to dictate a precise and detailed shopping list that had impressed Lily, even reassured her, in spite of an awareness that knowledge of such elaborate ingredients, an ability to cook sophisticated food, hardly guaranteed moral standing. Snobbery was a despicable trait, she knew, but one no doubt ingrained and she felt a need to believe that her father would have approved of the temporary resident at 8 Alfred Street. Later, when Stella had left the house around ten, explaining that she was unlikely to be back until evening and entrusting the shopping to Lily, she had gone up to the bathroom and hung several wet towels along the banister to dry, attempted a quick wash herself since there was inadequate hot water for more. It might be more sensible simply to leave the immersion heater on all day. That way, neither she nor Stella would be inconvenienced. And after all, she could afford the inevitably higher bills. There was absolutely no need to be mercenary when it came to expenditure and it might even help the marginal guilt she sometimes felt at the ease of her financial situation.

They ate hot cross buns around six. Dorothy took two followed by a substantial slice of simnel cake. Then Stella produced Easter gifts for each of them, small chocolate eggs from a specialist shop in the King's Road that, she patiently explained, made all products on the premises.

"It's what people want these days," she said, "in London, anyway. Something different and not mass-produced."

"If they can afford it," Dorothy said curtly. "Not everyone is riding high with the times, you know." But she examined the elaborate ribbon and wrapping around the minuscule eggs with interest. "Well, thank you, Stella. Quite unnecessary, of course, for you to give us anything at all, but I have to say you are bringing the two of us quite up to date. Making us aware of what is fashionable. In Chelsea, at least. Wouldn't you agree, Lily?"

"Thank you, Stella, it's very kind of you." She resented her aunt's implication that she shared the same outmoded outlook. Yet no doubt she would seem as remote from the habits and values of Stella's life as octogenarian Dorothy.

On the drive back to Harrow, she seemed to be in a mood of rare gratitude.

"A lovely day, Lily, I must say. Especially considering it's the first Easter without my brother. These occasions inevitably bring back such memories. Walter always welcomed spring and the year waking up, as he put it said it was the time his full enthusiasm was revived."

"Yes, he did," Lily agreed. "He liked to start planning the long summer trip to Greece around Easter. Even after he retired, there was always more he wanted to see or revisit. And he used to say that the longer evenings offered him more energy especially as he grew older."

"Did you mind?"

"Mind?"

Dorothy fiddled with the cameo brooch on her blouse, as if checking it was still fastened.

"It never occurred to me at the time to wonder, but I suppose it wasn't the most exciting way for a young woman to spend her summers. I don't think either of us ever considered that, your father and I, if I am honest. But then people didn't travel abroad in those early days, certainly not young people, so you were fortunate to have the opportunities given to you."

Lily turned on the windscreen wipers against the light shower. The day had been humid and rain had threatened since lunch time.

"The last few trips were difficult," she said. "Father was obstinate, still insisted on packed itineraries in the height of the summer when clearly it was all getting too much for him. Ancient sites tend to involve a lot of walking and climbing on uneven surfaces." And for a moment Lily was at Epidaurus, pulling up in their hire car, trying to convince her father that the intense heat of the July day was unsuitable for climbing the steps of the ancient theatre to test its extraordinary acoustics. After all, he had done it so many times before that it was surely unnecessary for him to do it again. And just as she thought he had capitulated and she was on the point of driving them back to Nafplio and the quiet cool rooms of their small hotel, he had turned to her, face resolute, declaring that, on the contrary, a visit to the sanctuary of Asclepios was surely most timely for an eighty-eight-year-old man intent on reaching another decade.

Perhaps he had been right. He had at least nudged his way a year or two past his 90th birthday.

"Yes, you were certainly very fortunate, Lily," Dorothy went on forcefully as if anxious to override her moment of brief concern. "Few have had your advantages. Life was so terribly dull for women in those years after the war if they had made the mistake of getting married. Housewives! What a destiny to reap after emerging unscathed from the threat of Hitler. You were sensible there, Lily, to avoid that trap. To choose to remain single."

Mechanically, Lily turned off the main road and down the suburban streets of 1930s houses leading to her aunt's block of flats. The journey was as ingrained as her own to Alfred Street requiring little conscious navigation and, inevitably, she thought of Toby Jenner. It had not felt like an act of choice in parting from Toby. More a bleak sense of submission, of helplessness in her misery as she had endured the days and months after their separation. And after that, after Toby, she had been unaware of any profusion of choices falling in her path the way her aunt implied. Choice, in fact, seemed a word remote, on the whole, from her experience of life.

The beds and borders in the gardens of Regent Court were neatly resplendent with spring flowers.

Lily admired them.

"I should think so too," Dorothy said, "residents pay enough for the upkeep of the grounds. Can't imagine what they pay the so-called gardeners. Anyone can stick in a few bulbs, after all." Lily opened the car door and she eased herself out, clutching the carrier bag with the remains of the simnel cake, Stella's gift. "Don't come up, not necessary in the light and I'm not geriatric yet. You get yourself off home before traffic builds up." A neighbour of Dorothy's waited by the entrance to the flats and waved to Lily. Reassured, she quickly kissed her aunt on the cheek and turned back to the car.

"By the way, Lily," Dorothy said, "please thank your young friend again for that delicious meal today. Quite a treat, I must say."

"I will."

She put a hand on Lily's arm for a moment.

"And remember, won't you? Don't allow any dependency to grow."

"Dependency? Oh, but Stella is just staying for a few days and no doubt I'll be delighted to have the house to myself again once she moves on somewhere permanent. Don't worry about that."

"I wasn't thinking of you, Lily," Dorothy said, "I was thinking of Stella." She turned away, calling over her shoulder, "See you in two weeks as usual. Goodness, we'll be half way through the month by then and well on our way to summer."

★★★

At first, she thought Stella must be out. The kitchen and sitting room were empty and there was no sound from her room.

Lily thought of ringing Agnes to see if she would like to go for a walk the following day. Across Hampstead Heath, possibly. Primrose Hill or Clissold Park. Bank holiday Mondays were no doubt dispiriting days for the retired already awash with leisure time. And Agnes, without family or close friends living nearby, had probably spent the entire Easter weekend alone in her flat. But just as she was about to ring her, she heard a noise from the basement as if something was being moved, shifted across the bare floorboards.

Stella stood in the middle room of the three, packing cases pushed back against the walls.

"Lily!" she said, "I had no idea this existed! A whole section of the house that's just revealed itself to me. You know, just like Narnia!"

"Well, it's just a storage area, really," Lily said, noticing that dust had already coated the hem of Stella's long pale skirt and her bare feet were grey as if she had been treading ashes. "I have done some sorting in recent months, thrown a lot away, but it's an uphill task. Decades of unwanted things have simply been deposited here. My father was not good at discarding. I think it was a consequence of the war. Two wars, in his case. Make do and mend. Except that we never did. Mend, that is. Things simply festered here and we just forgot about them."

Stella did not seem to be listening. She knocked against the walls dividing one small room from another, went to the front room and tried the door that let on to the narrow stairwell beneath street level.

"Do you have a key?" she asked.

"Somewhere around," Lily said vaguely. "But I have no idea where. I don't think we've bothered to unlock that door for years. Although I have some memories of using it when I was a child. Or perhaps it was simply left unlocked. Quite possibly in those days."

"But you are missing such an opportunity here, Lily!" Stella seemed enthused. "Haven't you seen what a lot of your neighbours have done with their basements? Half of London seems to be doing it, in fact."

"Not really," Lily said. "What would that be? The rooms are small, after all."

"Knock them through!" She moved to the back room with Lily in tow. "That's what people are doing. Knocking the walls to make one big open space."

"Why?" Lily said, imagining the jumble of discarded objects and boxes becoming even more unnegotiable without walls to divide.

"To create a wonderful kitchen, of course. These internal walls aren't load-bearing, I'm sure." She tapped at them again, this time more forcefully.

"But the house already has a kitchen," Lily said reasonably. "Why would I want another?"

Stella looked at Lily the way an adult might look at a child incapable of grasping a simple concept. Sympathetically yet with the compulsion to instruct.

"It would so improve the house," she said, "put value on it, obviously. As it is, the basement is just…" her voice trailed off as she looked around her, sniffed the air as if suspicious of undiscovered contents. "A sad waste of inhabitable space. In fact, Lily, you have a potential gem here, a phoenix waiting to rise. Aren't you fortunate?"

"I've never thought of it like that," Lily said. "When you live in a place so long it just becomes comfortable and what you are used to."

"Exactly!" Stella said. "It takes a fresh pair of eyes to spot these things. There is just so much potential here currently going to waste."

"I see," Lily said doubtfully and moved back into the front

room, looked out at the stairwell and steps up to street level that were encrusted with moss and mud. And thought of the numerous skips frequently sitting in surrounding streets, in roads close to the school where tall houses, unremarkable, serviceable for decades, suddenly seemed to have become subjects for transformation.

"Naturally," Stella's voice reached her from the back room, "you should just tell me to mind my own business, Lily. It's your home, after all. And such a lovely one at that. The basement clearly works for you as it is. A large storage space."

"But you're right," Lily said. "Of course you are, Stella. I really should give the whole matter of home improvements some thought, I suppose. While my father was alive, you see, it would have been inappropriate. To consider changing a thing. Although, to be frank, I find the prospect all a little alarming. I mean I wouldn't want the house to lose its character, to change it entirely and betray its history."

Stella came and stood next to her. On the pavement above them a young boy ran a stick against the railings, backwards and forwards several times until his father caught up with him and they walked on past.

"Absolutely not," Stella agreed firmly. "I'm all for sympathetic renovation. But when you think about it, Lily, the basement probably housed the kitchen and the scullery when the house was first built. When there were servants for such things. So you could look at it as taking the house back to its original state."

"I suppose so. I know there's an old stone sink somewhere in the back room, the one overlooking the garden."

"There you are, then!" Stella said triumphantly. "Restoration rather than change, Lily, that's what you would be doing. Anyway, it's all up to you. Please don't think I'm interfering. I really shouldn't have said a thing, should I?"

She looked concerned that she had offended. Her face,

chameleon-like, changed expression in a moment. Lily reassured her.

"I'm very grateful, Stella, of course I am. And I value your opinion. You've certainly given me a lot to think about. It's just that – well, I can understand people like my neighbours, Anna and Simon, wanting to make changes with a growing family to accommodate. But there's only me living here. So a large kitchen is hardly essential."

Stella said, "Dear Lily! You're a very modest person, aren't you? And I really admire that about you. But everyone is entitled to some creature comforts these days. Unless, of course, it's a question of money."

"Money?"

Stella put a hand to her face, fiddled with a loop earring, looking contrite.

"Finances, Lily. I do hope I haven't put my foot in it. Perhaps there are simply insufficient resources for such work. After all, I know how poorly admin jobs pay. And as a single woman living on one income – I do hope I haven't embarrassed you."

"No, of course not, Stella. I'm very fortunate, more fortunate than most women in my situation. My father was a frugal man on the whole. His only expenditure tended to be on books and trips to ancient sites. And even then we always stayed in very modest rooms. And I suppose as a result I have benefitted."

Stella said nothing. She removed the earring, rubbed her earlobe then replaced it. Lily wondered whether she had said too much. For some reason that eluded her she knew that people were reticent where money was concerned, that such matters were rarely aired. Stella moved out into the narrow strip of hallway and stood at the bottom of the stairs, her fingers caressing the oak newel post.

"Well, I'll leave you in peace now, Lily. Just forget all my chatter, won't you? Do you mind if I make a couple of phone calls? Only swift ones to friends locally. We're planning a picnic tomorrow, you see, Battersea Park, probably. Or somewhere like that. But you know what people are like, promising one day, forgetting all about it the next. I would use the public phone box in Upper Street, but last time I looked it had been vandalised again."

"There's no need for that, Stella," Lily said. "Help yourself to the phone whenever you want it. You know where it is."

"Can hardly miss it! I thought it was only in old films that people made phone calls in their hall. Have you ever thought of an extension? Another line somewhere? Just imagine if there was an emergency in the middle of the night or something, a suspected burglar downstairs, for example, you wouldn't want to come down to ring the police, would you? I mean one has to think of these things when you live in a city. And a woman on her own, especially."

"You're right, of course, Stella. I often used to think it would have been convenient for my father to have a phone in his study or his bedroom. But somehow it seemed – well, excessive. Unnecessary."

"There you go again!" Stella laughed. "A woman content with very little. That's such a refreshing thing to find these days, believe me. And you are such a calming presence, a positive influence on me, Lily. Do you know that?"

"I really don't think I'm any different to most people," Lily said. Yet she could not help feeling inordinately flattered.

She stayed in the basement for some time while Stella made several phone calls, her low, measured voice faintly discernible from the hall upstairs. Then she heard the front door bang and the house grew silent again. Although Lily had made some inroads into the tea chests earlier in the year, her reluctance to be sufficiently ruthless was evident. Resolutely, she started to unearth their contents. An old leather briefcase, a holdall with a broken strap, remnants of a large umbrella, folds of black fabric hanging like bats' wings, objects utterly worthless once detached from the sentimentality of memory. In another chest, a substantial number of envelopes bearing attractive foreign stamps had been banded together, presumably with the intention of starting a stamp collection or preserving them for future potential value. Rapidly, Lily tore the envelopes in half.

On the floor of the tea chest was a dense pile of newspapers.

Faded, torn and fragile in some cases, their dates drifted back forty or fifty years and more. This was entirely different. Surely this would prove a worthwhile discovery amongst the rubbish and Lily turned on the harsh bare light bulb to look at them, expectant of poignant content. No doubt these newspapers would bear witness to some of the events of atrocity that had been all too commonplace in the 20th century and she prepared herself for startling headlines, salutary reporting on places that trailed their own appalling mythologies. Guernica, Dunkirk, Dresden, Dachau. Nagasaki, Saigon, Phnom Penh. With images, no doubt, underpinning the inhuman level of the suffering.

But no.

Nothing of such significance.

Not even close.

Instead, in the dog-eared copies of *The Times*, the *News Chronicle*, *The Guardian*, several editions of the *Islington Gazette*, Lily found marked paragraphs, highlighted references of interest and relevance solely and only to her father.

To Walter Page, Professor and Reader of the Ancient Classical World.

Academic matters mostly. University concerns, wartime bomb damage to a lecture theatre, appointments of chairs and fellows, retirements and obituaries of his predecessors and contemporaries. One or two laudable reviews of books he had written. Even a photograph in the local paper, a very blurred image with the heading, *the longest-living resident of the borough opens library extension*. And then endless correspondence in the Letters section, his objection, apparently sustained over many months, to the *pitiful, pathetic eyesore plans of deluded and demented redevelopment of our area* and other hyperbolic phrases. He seemed to have been in a particularly contentious and long-drawn-out dispute with a councillor named Reginald Higgins.

Her father, always a colossus of erudition and wisdom. A man of substance and superiority.

As parochial and self-obsessed, apparently, as the ordinary of mankind.

Lily switched off the light and went upstairs. Tomorrow, she would ask Stella to help her cart the entire contents of the tea chests to the dustbins for the collection the following day.

She went into the kitchen to make a drink and as she waited for the kettle to boil noticed with surprise how very small and narrow the room suddenly seemed.

And, considering the amount of space lying dormant in the basement below, woefully inadequate.

12

There were few members at the society's April meeting and consequently, the choice of *The Deep Blue Sea*, with only a handful of characters, had been well-judged. Even so, Lily felt deflated by the evening. Perhaps it had been unwise to attempt something so dependent on two convincing leads when their strongest members had already indicated they would be away. She liked the play and had found it hard to listen to an inadequate reading. There was also, of course, the fact that Hugh Murray had been absent. She had not expected him so feeling disillusioned by his failure to appear was simply foolish. Yet she was aware of an anticipation, a possibility, that brought with it a faintly nauseous sense of unease throughout the evening. Like a kind of seasickness that robbed her of her usual composure and self-possession. It was a sensation that had been remote from her for over twenty years and she was unsure whether she resented or welcomed its return. She dropped Agnes back at her flat, remembered that they were short of milk and drove a long route home via a late-night corner shop in Camden.

Stella was in the hall, pulling on a bright sequinned jacket that Lily had not noticed before.

"Oh, milk!" she said. "Good timing, Lily. I've just used the last of it in a bowl of cereal and I was worried about breakfast." Stella's tastes appeared to veer from gastronomic sophistication to childish habits and, consequently, large boxes of cereal now nestled in the larder next to bottles of various oils and vinegars, several sorts of rice, dried pulses and beans. Her father's tastes had been simple. Traditional. Lily saw Stella as providing her with a culinary education. She peered out of the open front door at the light drizzle that had started. "Actually, perhaps I won't go out after all. And now you're home with the milk, how about we make some tea or coffee or something and have a catch-up at last? I never seem to get to see you now you're back at work." She was already shedding her jacket and heading back to the kitchen to put on the kettle, placing mugs on the table. Lily followed, inevitably gratified by such desire for her company.

"Any luck with the job-hunting?" she said, pushing Hector from a chair to sit down. "You said something a few days ago about a new employment agency that sounded promising."

Stella rolled her eyes. "Like I said, that's because you're too busy with work these days so I never have a chance to tell you stuff."

In truth, Stella was rarely in when Lily arrived home from school and never awake when she left in the morning. She was unsure whether Stella's constant absence meant a determined search for a job and permanent accommodation or solely a demanding social life.

"Advertising," Lily said, "You said you were keen to get into that industry. And it certainly seems to be a burgeoning one right now."

Stella pulled a face, slopped milk into the mugs.

"Oh, advertising agencies! Dreadful places, Lily. So superficial and cut-throat, you just wouldn't believe. The trouble is I think I've been born out of my time."

"Really? I would have thought this was an ideal moment for young women to take advantage of all the opportunities now open to them."

"But that's just the point, Lily. I'm not like the others. Not like you're supposed to be. Like you have to be to survive in these places. Ambitious, driven, ruthless. It's all her fault, of course."

Lily was confused. "Her?"

Stella said, "Our prime minister. First woman to have the job and it has to be someone like her. Thatcher."

"But surely, it's progress. Isn't it?" Lily felt her convictions slowly thaw as Stella looked at her with intensity across the kitchen table as if ready to rebut her claim. "I mean we've always voted Liberal, my family. My father and I, at least. I believe my aunt is somewhat more right-wing."

"Good old Dorothy!" Stella said. "In fact, now I think of it, she's probably a paid-up member of the Thatcher fan club. She's just the type. You have to admire that." Stella's allegiances were confusing. Lily drank her tea, waiting to hear more of the news Stella apparently had to share. But after draining her cup, she suddenly stood up, picked the sequinned jacket from the floor where she had dropped it and slipped it on. "Actually, I think I might go out after all. There's someone I did sort of promise to see for a drink and there's just time before last orders. It might lead to something. Work, that is. If you don't mind."

"Of course," Lily said.

"Oh, and I nearly forgot. There was a message for you. When you were out earlier this evening."

"A message?" It will be Eileen, Lily told herself. About that Stratford business. She really should have got back to her. Or possibly the plumber she rang about the inadequate supply of hot water.

"In fact, it was a bit odd. This man was asking for Helen. He said it several times, insistent kind of thing, even when I said that there was no-one called Helen living here. Then he sort of laughed and said that this person was also known as Lily. So I guess he did mean you. It's there by the phone, anyway. A number and name and that."

"What did he want?" Lily said unnecessarily.

"Want?" Stella said. "Well, presumably you to ring him. Yes, that's what he said. Why he left his number. You won't forget, will you, Lily? He sounded really keen for me to pass on the message."

Lily stood by the phone. She glanced at her watch. Of course, she could not ring Hugh Murray at this time of night. It was nearly a quarter to eleven and such a gesture would say too much. Yet delaying might suggest indifference. She walked back to the kitchen, collected their mugs and put them in the sink. He had asked for Helen. She had told him to ignore the name and his persistence should irritate. Yet instead she was touched by his use of it. By the fact that it had lingered in his mind and he had hitched it to the woman he had met. To very ordinary, prosaic Lily Page. It was, perhaps, a sign of his growing affection for her.

But not tonight. There must be no phone call tonight.

After all, anticipation was potent.

★★★

"I have to say I am so relieved to hear from you. I was beginning to wonder if I had offended you, dear Helen." It had taken her several attempts to reach him. She had begun to expect the sound of the phone endlessly ringing in his sister's Balham maisonette. "I have been very remiss. Work, of course, that's my only excuse. I really have been unexpectedly busy."

"Good," Lily said. "I mean that must be satisfying."

"One can't claim that it's been inspiring work. In fact, I hesitate to divulge any details. Still, when one is a jobbing actor and a mature one at that – but I've bored you with all this before." There was a silence on the line. Hector rubbed against her legs, his fur wet from a recent downpour. "So, providing you are willing to forgive me for such neglect," he eventually went on, "we really must get together again."

"Well, there's always next month's play reading meeting, of course," Lily said.

"I was thinking of an outing somewhere," Hugh went on. "What do you think? Could you bear my company for an entire day? Or an afternoon, at least."

"An outing?" Lily saw snowdrops and clods of dark earth in Toby Jenner's hands. That unreliable and ridiculous car of his. "Did you have somewhere in mind?"

"Actually, the British Museum was an idea of mine, if that doesn't sound too terribly tedious for you. I can't remember the last time I went. In fact, I suppose I must have gone once upon a time, but the truth is… well, Helen, I thought you could educate me."

"Educate you?"

"Don't tell me that the daughter of a renowned classicist doesn't have insight and knowledge into the ancient treasures of the place! You were the professor's right-hand woman, after all, from what you've told me. Perhaps you could be my guide. Although, of course, if you'd rather not, we could always just meet for coffee."

"Yes," Lily said. Hector began pounding the door mat aggressively, glaring at her for attention. "I mean, of course, the museum is a lovely idea."

"Excellent!" Hugh said, "I'm so glad you approve – that's settled then. What about this Sunday? Or Saturday, even? But no doubt you already have plans for the weekend."

No, Lily told him, no particular plans for either day. A Sunday free of her aunt, as it happened. And swiftly arrangements were made for Saturday afternoon, although

not before she had protested the superficiality of her own knowledge to dispel any expectations. He had laughed, said she was no doubt being characteristically modest. Just before he rang off, Hugh said,
"Is your niece staying with you for long?"
"My niece?"
"The young lady I spoke to on the phone. I just assumed."
"I am an only child," Lily said, "so no nieces or nephews."
"Of course! I was forgetting. So that was…?"
"Stella. Stella Fox. A friend. She's staying here just for a few weeks while she finds somewhere more permanent. It's not easy, finding accommodation in London, it seems."
"Absolutely. What a kind gesture, Helen. So until Saturday? Great Russell Street at two o'clock. Now don't let me down, will you? Stand me up or anything? I can't tell you how much I'm looking forward to it."

Lily stood in the hall for some moments. A shaft of sunlight filtered through the narrow window above the front door. She felt too warm, inappropriately dressed for the mild April day. The previous year she had hardly noticed the shift in seasons, failed to acknowledge the arrival of summer, too preoccupied with what she knew would be her father's final months. She remembered looking in her wardrobe the morning of his funeral for something suitable to wear and finding she had forgotten to unearth her summer clothes, pack away winter woollens. This year, however, was different. Even Hector was preparing, already shedding fur on the furniture, on Stella's discarded clothes.

This year, Lily was determined to inherit a summer.

★★★

She saw Hugh from a distance, waiting for her under the

colonnaded portico, and quickened her step. He leant forward, kissed her on both cheeks.

"At last!"

"I'm not late, surely." Immediately, she doubted her watch. He laughed.

"Absolutely not, Helen. As punctual as ever. What I meant was that it's been far too long since our delightful dinner. And I've had such good intentions of being in touch."

"You were under no obligation," Lily said.

He looked surprised. Chastened. "But I wanted to be in touch. To see you again. Very sincerely, in fact. Is that better? Now come on, I'm expecting a tour. I'm placing myself in the hands of the expert.

"I was merely the secretary rather than the academic, remember. And actually, I'm ashamed to say it's ages since I've been here myself. Was there anything in particular you wanted to see today? It can be rather an overwhelming place."

Hugh took her arm, headed them towards the doors.

"I'm with you. That's what matters. Let's just wander, shall we? See what catches our attention."

"Yes, if you like," Lily said as they sidestepped around a group of young tourists hogging the entrance for photographs, taking turns behind the camera lens. "Or we could simply concentrate on the ancient Greek world. I feel more at home there."

As a young child, her father had brought her to the museum frequently. Indeed, he rarely took her anywhere else and it had come as a considerable surprise when friends' parents offered to take her to see dinosaurs in South Kensington. The zoo in Regent's Park. Lily had rather assumed that the enormous edifice in Bloomsbury had been the extent of the capital's attractions. The closure of the museum during the war had ended such outings, but, once it was open again, visits seemed to have been stepped up as if Walter had been anxious to make up for those lost years. Curiously, Lily remembered not so much her father's enthusiasm in explaining artefacts and objects to her as simply a desire to alert her to their existence in a compulsive manner. She had vague memories of trailing behind him, peering into glass cases, attempting to read citations and copy his silent absorption. In his long retirement he had been invited to deliver occasional lectures at the museum, had given several series of talks, but he had never asked her to any of these events; on the contrary, he had insisted that she would find the content too obscure, of specialist interest only and she had concurred. Later, too late, she wished she had ignored his stipulation and sneaked into the back row to hear him speak.

They progressed through Minoan civilisation, moved onto the Mycenaeans and Bronze Age Greece.

"I suppose all this was your father's back yard, so to speak," Hugh said as they stopped by a statue of Achilles. "A clever man, indeed, knowing all there is to know about the ancient world."

"Not quite," Lily said. "He wasn't terribly interested in anything too early. Or too late, for that matter." Hugh laughed. Then turned towards her and adjusted her silk scarf that had begun to slip from her neck. The casual intimacy of the gesture startled her. "His particular interest was in the politics of Athens. And in the philosophers and histories. The drama too, of course."

"Ah yes," Hugh said, "those desperately long tragedies with endless speeches and declamations and desperately unfunny comedies. I can't say I've ever had the chance or the desire to appear in any of them."

"My father would disagree with your view heartily, of course," Lily said, "and no doubt do his best to persuade you otherwise."

"Did he persuade you to become enamoured with them? Drag you along to numerous performances?"

"Oh no," Lily said, "he wouldn't have thought they were my kind of thing at all. But I do remember typing up numerous lecture notes and reading some of them in translation. The tragedies, mostly, Sophocles, Euripides. And Aeschylus, of course."

"Of course!" Hugh said. "You undersell yourself, Helen. Do you know that? You possess such an extraordinary wealth of knowledge that I am entirely in awe of you!"

They moved on to another gallery and Hugh drew apart to study in more detail the marble relief from the Temple of Athena. Lily stood watching couples, family groups, small tour parties making their way through the rooms, content to be with Hugh, attached to this personable man, the focus of his afternoon. It had never occurred to Lily to consider herself an anomaly. While her father had been alive, she had been tethered by given responsibilities, an accessory to his work, to his life, which had provided her with definition. Status, even.

But now?

She knew she had done little since his death for people to adjust their view of her as now rudderless, insignificant. Chance opportunities were, after all, the prerogative of women like Stella Fox with youth and exceptional beauty to boast and allure. But if a man such as Hugh Murray chose to single her out, even to admire her qualities, there was perhaps hope of redemption.

He glanced towards her, smiled. Came back to her side.

"Shall we move on? There's only so much I can absorb at any one time. The mind is getting increasingly cloudy, I find. Age, no doubt."

"Do you want to go to the Egyptian section? That's what most people seem to want to see when they come here."

He pulled a face, took her arm and steered her away.

"Would you think me very defeatist if I asked to leave them to another time? After all, we'll be back, won't we? Now you've begun my classical education, Helen, I'm not letting you off the hook with only one visit!"

"Of course," she agreed. "Then perhaps a cup of tea or coffee?"

"An excellent idea," he said. "But perhaps we can stop off in the shop if there is such a thing? These places usually have gift shops, I believe. I'd like to buy a postcard or two to remind me of what I've seen. Even a book, maybe? So I can read up before our next visit."

"There's no need to buy a book," Lily said swiftly. "I have so many of my father's. I've got rid of a lot, but that still leaves far too many cluttering the house."

"How kind, Helen. And if you're really sure we'll find something accessible to my limited brain power among the collection... that's settled then. If you don't think it too forward of me, I'll invite myself over to your house one day and pick out something instructive to fill my blank evenings."

"You'd be doing me a favour."

He squeezed her hand, took her arm as they left the gallery.

"Ah Helen, it warms me to hear you say that! After all, one just does not know how to play things these days. I'm not sure what the 1980s guidebook is to matters like – well, the word courtship is certainly not applicable, but one does not wish to lose sight of all proprieties, after all."

Outside, a rain shower and sun were competing.

"There'll be a rainbow at this rate," Hugh said and hurried them down the steps and out into Great Russell Street. They passed one or two impossibly crowded cafes, then found themselves in the myriad of streets between Bloomsbury and Clerkenwell, offering nothing.

"We could," Lily said suddenly before the idea appeared too charged and significant to her, "go back to Alfred Street for tea. Then you could find this book you're after while the idea is still in your mind."

Hugh appeared to hesitate. Her sudden need for his company, for some sort of affirmation of what lay between them was no doubt too evident in the invitation. She fastened then unfastened the top button on her navy jacket. Her raincoat would have been the wiser choice.

"What a splendid suggestion!" Hugh said, grabbing her arm again. "And shall we walk there? The clouds don't look too ominous, do they? Lead the way, Helen, I'm entirely in your hands!"

He was deferential with her father's books. Lily insisted he was welcome to borrow them, to keep any, in fact, since what remained was the residue after the university and the second-hand book shops had taken what was of interest to them. The room, she said to Hugh, feeling suddenly resolute, could not reside forever as Walter Page's erstwhile study and it was time she cleared it entirely, thought of a new use for it. Stella, for example, her temporary lodger, would be more comfortable in the bigger space rather than crammed into an apology of a room on the floor below. And after Stella had moved on – well, she was sure she would find other uses for it. Lily was aware of speaking too fast as if her thoughts needed sharing in order to convince her of their merit.

"Yes," Hugh said, "life does go on, doesn't it? And one has to accept change and live accordingly. That's why I am so frustrated with my present situation."

"Your house, you mean?"

"Exactly. The progress on it is minimal. Where had I got to in telling you my woes over it?"

"Something about the builders being unreliable?"

"Worse than unreliable. It's a disaster. The company I was using has gone bust. In liquidation or whatever the term is. So now it's back to square one, find a new one, get more estimates and it's all so much harder this time around. Taking over a job half started doesn't seem to be popular among the building trade."

"At least you have your sister."

"My sister? Oh yes, the back bedroom in her Balham flat," he said bleakly. "Not a very dignified way to be living, I can tell you. But you're right, Lily, she's been very – accommodating, shall we say?"

He picked up a copy of Homer's *Odyssey*. "I suppose I should read this. Will I find your namesake in it? Not worth reading it otherwise!"

Lily said, "Helen does appear, actually. Although the focus is more on Penelope, naturally."

"Naturally!" Hugh smiled, patting Lily on the shoulder, "You see, you are quite the classical scholar, your humility misplaced."

"I certainly could not begin to read this version," Lily said. "And nor could you. It's in Homeric Greek."

"Ah!" Hugh said, "yes, something of a stumbling block for both of us!"

From downstairs, there was the sound of the front door opening, keys tossed onto the hall table where they regularly fell to the floor.

"That will be Stella," Lily said.

"Stella?"

"Stella Fox. I believe you spoke to her on the phone the other day."

"Indeed. How nice, a chance to meet one of your friends, Helen. Important, I think, when getting to know someone in the way we are. Don't you think?" Briefly, his hand returned to her shoulder, lingered.

Lily, her eye suddenly caught by the casket containing her father's ashes still residing on a top shelf, swiftly led the way out of the room and down the stairs.

13

Hugh stayed for the evening.

By seven o'clock it was clear he was in no hurry to leave and when Lily tentatively offered dinner, he beamed.

"I should refuse; please don't feel obliged. Are you sure I won't be outstaying my welcome?"

Stella said, "Fine with me. We enjoy having impromptu guests at the weekend, don't we, Lily?"

It was the first Saturday evening that Lily could recall Stella not going out. Neither had they ever entertained any guests, impromptu or planned apart from Dorothy on Easter Sunday. And her aunt was a fixture and therefore did not count. The point, however, was irrelevant. Hugh clearly wanted to stay. Lily was quietly elated.

"I would, of course, have brought a bottle of wine as some sort of contribution to the meal if I'd known there'd be such an invitation."

"You can bring two bottles next time," Stella said, "but we've got something stashed away that we can drink tonight, haven't we, Lily?"

"I could pop down to the nearest off-licence, of course." Hugh padded his top pocket as if to check for his wallet.

"Really, there's no need for that." Lily was alarmed by the idea that Hugh might leave the house and not return. It seemed imperative to keep him there in case he should change his mind about the course of his evening.

"We do have some basic stocks, don't we?" Stella said with a knowledge that surprised Lily. "We can run to bottles of *vin ordinaire*, both red and white. And I believe we have both gin and vermouth." There was half a bottle of Campari on the floor of the larder, another of Martini and some dry sherry. And the scant remains of her father's final purchase of a bottle of Teachers' whisky. Stella swiftly retrieved them, apologised for the lack of Gin as if the oversight had been hers and placed them all on the table. Lily found glasses, explained that the freezer compartment of the old fridge was stubborn when it came to producing ice. "Don't you think, Hugh, that Lily's kitchen is so – well, extraordinary? Like we're privileged to see something so original. Utterly authentic."

"The whole house," Hugh said, "is so perfectly preserved. From what I've seen so far, that is. Quite delightful."

"Although Lily is about to make some changes. Has she told you about that? She's got all sorts of ideas brewing."

Lily was taken aback. Their conversation over the basement had been brief, inconsequential and they had not spoken of it since.

"I wouldn't say I have any definite plans," she said hesitantly, "but of course, it's important to maintain houses. And these days everyone seems so – well, ambitious where property is concerned."

"You are absolutely right. Or at least certain sectors of the population are. I'm sure most of the country is simply grateful for a roof over their heads. But thus was ever the divide. And Helen, I'm sure any ideas you might have for this house would be most sensitive and appropriate. Shall I help myself?" He unscrewed the bottle of whisky. Poured himself a small dram. "And yes, if we can afford it, we all have to live with the times, move on and embrace fashion. Otherwise – well – where does that leave us? Sad relics of the past, clinging to outmoded ways. You and I were only saying something like that earlier, weren't we, Helen?"

"Helen?" Stella said. "Of course, you're the man from the phone call. I thought I recognised your voice."

"Hugh likes to use my birth name," Lily said. The explanation implied affection, intimacy even.

Hugh smiled. "And she's kind enough to indulge me!"

Stella insisted on cooking. She laid the small table in the kitchen window for the three of them.

"It's where Lily and I always eat and I think it's so much cosier than the dining room which, if I'm honest, is a bit too formal for my tastes, don't you think?" she said. "Fine for lunches with Aunt Dorothy, of course, but not quite right for a relaxed Saturday night supper. Have you met the redoubtable Dorothy?" Hugh shook his head. "Oh, she's quite something, isn't she, Lily?"

Briefly, she disappeared upstairs and changed into a long pale pink dress and then found some stubs of candles from the back of a cupboard, remnants from power cuts one winter, and arranged them on the table so that it took on a sense of occasion. Hugh was complimentary about the meal she conjured from the contents of the larder and fridge.

"So you're chief chef of the household, are you, Stella?" He opened a bottle of wine and filled their glasses.

"Oh, we take it in turns. Whatever works, really. But I have so much more time, don't I, Lily? I'm between things at the moment, you could say, Hugh. Whereas Lily has her job and then there's her reading society thing. And her aunt, of course, that's a big responsibility for her. Let alone keeping this big house going. She's a very busy woman, I can tell you. But no doubt you know that already, being a close friend."

Since her father's death, Lily had not thought of herself as particularly busy. If anything, some guilt hovered about the expansiveness of her time, the unencumbered nature of many of her days. Stella's impression, however, was a preferable face to present to Hugh.

"Stella is thinking of applying to drama school," she said. "Hugh is an actor so he could no doubt offer you some advice."

"An actor! Lily, I had no idea that you had famous friends!" Stella leant forward across the table so that her face was close to Hugh's. Her long earrings hung perilously near to the candle flame. "Should I know you? Come to think of it, there's something about your profile that's familiar. Stage or screen?"

Hugh laughed expansively. He picked up his glass and drained it before returning Stella's intense stare and said, "My dear, I take whatever is going. Years ago, it was the stage, naturally. And that is still closest to my heart. Nothing like it."

"That's fascinating," Stella said, resting her chin on her cupped hands. "So tell me, what were some of your favourite roles?"

"Oh it's all so long ago," Hugh said, "one forgets. But I think I can safely say I had a stab at most things. While in rep, that is. It was the way things worked in those bygone days."

"Hamlet?"

"Of course – the Danish prince himself – when I was little more than an adolescent myself."

"Iago?"

"I believe so. In fact, I have to say I rather preferred playing the villains. So much more interesting. But as I say, Stella, it's all past history now. I could probably look out the old programmes if I had a mind to – I'm sure they're all in the attic somewhere in some battered suitcases."

"I'd love to see them sometime," Stella said, picking up the bottle of wine and filling Hugh's empty glass. "Lily, shall we open another? We seem to have got through this one rather swiftly."

There was only one other bottle in the cupboard, a prize from an end of term staff room raffle still bearing its ticket that Lily swiftly removed.

"I'm afraid it's white and not chilled," she said apologetically. "I should have thought ahead and put it in the fridge."

"I think it's a case of us needing to get more organised, isn't it, Lily? Now we are clearly going to be entertaining the company of famous actors on a regular basis."

Hugh grabbed the bottle and rapidly removed the cork.

"Your young friend, Helen, is an expert in flattery!" He filled Stella's glass, splashing a little onto her fingers. "Introduce me to more of them if they are all of this nature!"

"Certainly not," Stella said, "you've already got two of us holding on to your every theatrical word and memory. If we provide you with a coterie of fans, Lily and I would be lost in the crowd of adorers!"

Lily felt herself blush. No doubt it was the wine in addition to the glass of pungent Campari she had drunk. But neither Stella nor Hugh seemed to have noticed. Their conversation had moved on to drama schools and auditions and agents and Lily had little to contribute. At one point she suggested some cheese, fruit, and unobtrusively placed small plates and knives on the table. Stella was vivacious, vibrant, Hugh constructively helpful and practical in his advice. Were her parents happy with her choice of career? Did they not think it unwise to chance her luck in such a precarious and cut-throat business? After all, even the most talented often fell by the wayside. Stella shrugged, briefly seemed deflated.

"Lily knows the situation with my parents. Basically, I'm on my own and they show little interest in me. In fact, if I'm honest, I think I was always a bit of an encumbrance to them.

They are very wrapped up in their own lives, you see. Always have been."

Hugh sympathised, but said that such freedom and the lack of a cautionary voice could be seen as advantages for the aspiring actor.

"And, after all, remember, Stella" – he warmed to the subject – "any negative experience of childhood is potent material for performance. Tapping into lived emotions is vital for acting." Stella nodded her head vigorously, said how true that was and that she was certainly unfettered by fear of failure.

"After all, someone has to succeed. Why shouldn't it be me?"

Hugh laughed, broke off a small bunch of grapes and said how much he admired the optimism of youth.

They talked on animatedly while Lily sat back, her thoughts in freefall. Suppose, she indulged herself, she had met Hugh instead of Toby Jenner. Suppose, rather than squandering time with a married man whose protestations of devotion were clearly, ultimately, baseless, she had stumbled across Hugh Murray as he was leaving a stage door, and the two of them had met, talked, befriended, and ultimately fallen in love. Marriage would have followed with Hugh moving into the family home in Alfred Street and thus tonight Hugh and Lily could be sitting here on an ordinary Saturday evening in the company of their only child, their daughter, now on the cusp of adulthood.

And why not?

Why should Lily Page not be allowed what vast swathes of women seemed to consider commonplace and perfectly normal? She was not, surely, unlovable. Her appearance, whilst not exceptional, was not unpleasing in a neat, satisfactory sort of way. And whilst she had never considered her life to be unfulfilled, frustrated in any way, now she could see that to many it could be considered just that.

It was past ten when Hugh looked at his watch.

"I really must be making my way home, I had no idea it was so late."

"What a pity," Stella said, "do you have far to go?"

Hugh mentioned Balham. The Northern Line and its unpleasantness on a Saturday night.

"Hugh has a house in Fulham," Lily explained, "but he's staying with his sister while building works are going on."

"Fulham!" Stella said. "I have friends somewhere around there, in fact I lived on their sofa for a few months last year. Which road?"

"Which road? Oh, just off Munster Road. Thereabouts, anyway."

"What about a last drink before you go, Hugh? Lily, what do we have in the way of liqueurs – cognac, that sort of thing?"

"I don't think we have any. There used to be some brandy, but I believe I gave the bottle to my aunt some time ago."

"Tell you what," Hugh said, "if you really insist, Stella, I am happy to take another small measure of that whisky I had earlier. Just one for the road, or rather the Tube journey in this case."

Stella stood up, went and fetched the bottle.

"There's so little left," she said, "you might as well finish it up. Is that all right with you, Lily?"

"Of course," Lily said. And watched as Stella poured the remains of her father's last bottle of whisky into a tumbler and passed it to Hugh. For a moment she felt a slight betrayal and something in her throat thickened, constricted her from speech. The room was now almost dark. Lily had resisted putting on the kitchen's unsympathetic strip lighting and the stubby candles were nearly burnt down. The street lamps, however, offered such light to render Hugh and Stella silhouette-like, insubstantial figures, devoid of detail.

"And you will come again soon, Hugh? Lily, you must arrange something as soon as possible, you can see how essential he is to me with his advice. In fact, Hugh, if I really begged you, would you consider coaching me for my auditions? It would give me so much confidence, I'm sure."

Hugh smiled. Swallowed the remains in his glass.

"I would be delighted. And as for another invitation, that's rather in Helen's hands, isn't it? We are dependent on her gracious hospitality."

The two of them turned towards her. Lily knew she would oblige.

★★★

Of course, the credit for the success of the evening was not really hers. It had been Stella, after all, who had insisted that he stay for dinner, Stella who had prolonged the evening through lively conversation and plenty of alcohol. In truth, Lily herself had been more of an observer at their table, the provider as always.

Still.

Hugh Murray's manner had been avuncular towards Stella. But it had been Lily's hand he had caught, warmly, briefly, as they had sat down at the table, Lily who had been the recipient of a kiss, not lingering, but nevertheless more than a mere gesture, as he had left the house.

The next afternoon, she tried to concentrate on the casting for the society's next reading which was proving difficult, too many members proffering excuses with the longer May evenings inevitably pulling people away from the dubious attractions of the Young Men's Working College. Hugh had been unenthusiastic about the prospect of the Wesker play.

"Lily?" Stella came up to the sitting room, with mugs of

tea for the two of them. "I thought I might find you outside in the garden. Isn't that what people do on Sundays at this time of year, get their gardens ready for the summer?"

Stella's tea was always too strong, but Lily was grateful for the gesture.

"It's only a courtyard and it's been rather a disgrace for years. In fact, I can't really ever remember a time when it was paid any attention."

"Shame on you!" Stella said. "A bit of your own private outdoor space in the middle of London, however small, should be treasured. You're really very lucky to have it."

"I know. And you're absolutely right. It's just that I know nothing about gardens, however small. My father was the same. In fact, I think he hardly noticed his immediate surroundings at all. Not in any objectively critical way, that is."

"Steal," Stella said.

"Steal?"

"Steal ideas from other people, I mean. Have you been into Anna and Simon's garden next door? They've done wonders with the space."

Lily was unaware that Stella had been into her neighbours' house. But then no doubt Anna had invited her in one day. After all, she had little clear idea how Stella spent the hours when she was at work.

"They seem to have done a great deal to the whole house since they've moved in, I must say," she agreed.

"Your trailblazers, so to speak – like so many of your neighbours," Stella said, moving to the window and gesturing down the street. "But don't worry, you'll catch them all up, Lily, once we get your plans in motion."

"Yes, I suppose so." She sipped cautiously at her strong tea. "Although nothing is actually decided yet, Stella. About changes to the house, I mean. Costs and estimates would be needed for a start. It will quite a long process. If I do decide to go ahead."

"Of course, you are so right," Stella nodded in agreement. "Absolutely no need to rush anything especially about such a major project. You have to be certain you really want the considerable expense and upheaval of it all." She perched on the arm of the large chair, flicked her fringe out of her eyes. "Although, of course, the summer is nearly here and that's an ideal time for these big jobs."

"Is it?"

"Think of it. Open windows and doors to let the dust out, long hours of daylight for the builders to work. Actually when I think about it, you've hit on just the right point of the year for such a project, clever you! If you do decide to go ahead."

Lily knew that procrastination was natural to her. It was a trait she suspected she had inherited and found difficult to shift. Now, however, she reminded herself that the house was entirely hers, her father's views an irrelevance. And Hugh, too, had been positive about the idea of renovation.

"It certainly wouldn't do to neglect the house, I can see that," she said tentatively.

"It's your greatest asset," Stella said.

"Asset?" Stella sounded like her aunt. It was clear she needed to adjust her attitude to property if this was how everyone now thought. Stella said nothing for a moment, then turned to face Lily.

"I can't tell you what this means to me, Lily. A sense of belonging after so many rootless months – years, in fact. Sundays in particular can be so dreadfully lonely if you don't have a place to call home. I know it's only temporary, me staying here, and as soon as you tire of me, I'll be off, of course. But I want you to know how I value it. Your kindness. Of making me feel like part of a family." She looked close to tears, rubbed a hand over her face, smudging mascara on her cheek. "And ignore my nagging you about bringing the house up to date. Making useful changes. It's just my way of trying to contribute, to give back, as it were, and to repay what I think of as my enormous debt to you."

"There's no need to feel like that, Stella. Absolutely none at all." Lily was touched by her sentiment. And thought of the ease of the three of them round the kitchen table the night before, the incidental meeting with Hugh at a moment when Stella, too, had stepped into her path as if the configuration was intended. A vacuum filled. "And you can stay as long as you like," she added impetuously. "Of course you can. You really must think of this as your home, Stella. For just as long as you need it."

★★★

It had been Stella who suggested that she should take over the shopping. She pointed out that it simply made sense, that Lily's hours at school meant most shops were closed by the time she left and that it would be her way of repaying her hospitality.

"I've so much more time than you, after all," Stella pointed out. "I mean I can't spend all day haunting the employment agencies, it's just so depressing. And if in the meantime, I can take over some of the household load from you, it will serve us both. I just want to be the best house guest that I can, you see."

Lily could see no reason to object.

Stella seemed immediately cheered by the responsibility as if her days now had a direction they had lacked. She began to go out less, was in most evenings to cook and Lily became used to finding her in the house when she came back from work. Initially, she found this disconcerting. Even when her father had been alive, his habits had meant that the house was always quiet, but she reminded herself that there was consolation in such perpetual company, that a preference for solitariness and silence was unnatural.

"Think of me as your housekeeper and cook all rolled into one!" Stella said as she added up the first week's outgoings with the new arrangement and presented Lily with the total. "At least I am doing something for my keep at last. As you won't let me pay rent, that is. Although, of course, if you change your mind on that do let me know. Not that I have any income just at the moment, but I could possibly borrow some money if necessary. And there's always the dole, of course."

"Nonsense," Lily said. "Naturally there's no need for you to pay any rent. The room is there, after all, and it's very small."

Stella smiled. "Yes," she said, "it is a little. Do you know if Hugh eats fish? I was thinking of sole for when he comes to dinner next Friday night. Lemon or possibly even Dover if I can get it."

"I'm sure he does," Lily said. "Eat fish, I mean. At least – well, most people do, don't they?" Her father had been fond of cod. Smoked haddock with a poached egg on a Saturday evening. Never sole. Stella went back to the stove, adjusted the wavering flame under the simmering spaghetti.

"How long have you two known each other?" she said, glancing over her shoulder at Lily. "I mean, I take it you are actually a couple rather than just friends." Lily took out her purse and occupied herself with counting notes and change to cover her awkwardness. "Because it's clear he adores you. I've seen the way he looks at you when you're unaware of it."

She had insufficient cash to meet Stella's bill. Clearly, she needed to get into the way of withdrawing more each week from the bank, to adjust and shake off a lifetime of cautious spending.

"Sole," she said firmly to Stella, "sounds lovely. Of whatever type you think best."

Later, she lay awake, trying to dismiss Stella's words as fanciful, wildly exaggerated. Lily was entirely unaware of Hugh looking at her in a way that could be considered anything other than companionable. Affable.

And yet.

Hugh's visits to Alfred Street had swiftly ingrained themselves since that initial spontaneous evening. He had called on the off chance four days later after some location work as an extra in Canonbury, cheekily cadging, as he phrased it, a cup of tea. Somehow an invite to dinner the subsequent Saturday was in place before he had left. Since then, it had begun to feel more like the rule than the exception to expect him at the house, to anticipate his voice in the hall, his jacket on the back of the chair. But the ease with which he had slipped into such familiar habits could be seen simply as a platonic friendship rather than moves in a mating game.

Lily did not believe that she had fallen in love with Hugh Murray.

Or at least not love in her understanding of the term. The precipitate state she had known when Toby Jenner had been the focus of her affections had been something other, a sense of heightened elation, perilous in its intensity.

This felt entirely different.

But then she was no longer a young woman. And here he was, an agreeable man seeking out her company at a time when she feared for the vacuity of her future. There was the matter, of course, of his current living arrangements, his provisional lack of a suitable location to woo her, to escalate matters from mere friendship into a relationship.

Lily could, if she so chose, take the lead. She could provide.

14

Dorothy said, "Are you planning a holiday this summer, Lily? I know how you used to love your Greek trips with Walter, although I could never understand that. Traipsing around ruins in that appalling heat."

They had finished lunch. Stella was out and Lily felt weary at the prospect of conversation for the next few hours before she could reasonably drive her home to Harrow. In the winter months, Dorothy was usually anxious to return as soon as it was dark, but the long, light days of early summer offered no such respite. Hugh had stayed very late the night before and she was tired. Wanted only to sit with a book, the Sunday papers, allow her thoughts to drift freely. Dorothy picked up one of the petits fours that Stella had made, ate it swiftly and took another.

"Anyway," Dorothy went on, "clearly you will be at a loose end this summer so I was thinking that you could run me down to Wales for a few days."

"Wales?"

"Yes, Wales, Lily. West Wales, I believe."

"West Wales?"

"I have an old friend who lives there. You probably remember me speaking of her. Norah? A former colleague from service days who went and got herself married late in life after retirement and ended up marooned out in – well, Wales. He had pretensions of being an artist, I think. Or a potter or something of the sort."

"Who?"

"Who? The husband, of course. Or rather late husband by now. So foolish to bother marrying at that stage in life when no doubt caring duties followed by swift widowhood is going to be one's fate." Lily was barely following. She was thinking of Hugh's seeming reluctance to leave the previous evening, his joke about the dubious attractions of the night bus. She had felt inadequate, gauche even, as they had stood in the hallway, his arm sliding lightly around her shoulder to pull her close. "She's asked me to go and stay." Dorothy's voice intruded. "More than once, actually, but I've always excused myself because of Walter. Not wanting to be too far from him in his last year or so just in case and I couldn't ask you to take me then when you were clearly needed by his side. So this summer seems ideal. Would late July suit? I've pencilled in the 24th to travel with a return on the 30th. How does that sound to you, Lily?"

"Did you say Wales?"

"Yes, Lily, have you not been listening? Pembrokeshire, if I remember rightly. No doubt miles off the beaten track, in some God-forsaken hamlet. Norah always was impractical, come to think of it."

"Perhaps," she said tentatively, "you could go by train. I could take you to Paddington. You could even travel first class."

Dorothy stared at Lily as if her suggestion was subversive.

"I don't do trains any more, you know that, Lily. No. That's out of the question. You can drive me there and have a little holiday yourself into the bargain. I'm sure Norah has space for the two of us. In fact, come to think of it, she's mentioned enough times about the enormous house they bought for a shoe string once she'd sold her flat in Chiswick so there won't be a problem there."

She said nothing. Her aunt's suggestion was rational. Of course it was. She could hardly offer merely to ferry Dorothy back and forth to West Wales without staying herself. Yet Lily was annoyed by her assumption and equally by the knowledge she would comply.

"I'll have to check summer holiday dates at work," she said.

Dorothy looked surprised.

"Surely that's unnecessary. You're always well clear of school by late July, aren't you? And especially you're now just in the admin department rather than fussing around the headmistress's needs. That's clearly one advantage of this demotion of yours. So that's settled. I'll ring Norah tonight and confirm which will please her."

"I haven't really thought about the summer yet," Lily tried to protest.

Dorothy looked across the table as if glaring at a truculent child.

"I'm sure you'll manage to squeeze me into your summer, Lily. I'm only asking for six days of your time."

On the way home from Harrow, she stopped at a small convenience store near the Edgware Road that managed to rebel against permitted hours of weekend trading and bought random items that she did not particularly need out of a desire for mild defiance. Stella was still not home and, restless after a day inside with her aunt, she left her shopping in the kitchen and walked briskly up to Highbury Fields, the light of the May evening encouraging others so that there was a sense of conviviality, of shared celebration at the promise of summer. Although there was a sharp breeze and rain was forecast for overnight, people appeared to have shed layers of clothing as if a little self-willed belief would help herald the new season. Returning to Alfred Street, a neighbour from the house opposite waved at her before disappearing down the steps to the basement. Anna and Simon, the baby clasped to her chest in a shawl-like arrangement, the toddler on Simon's shoulders, turned the corner into the street and similarly greeted her.

Stella was back.

Her large patchwork bag was lying at the bottom of the stairs as if discarded in a hurry, spilling out most of the contents. Hector was occupying a small corner of it.

"Is that you, Lily? I'll be down in a minute, just looking at something while the idea is in my head," she called. Lily went into the kitchen to put on the kettle, but Stella had taken out glasses and opened a bottle of wine, arranged the table with the items from Lily's impulsive shop in the Edgware Road. She poured herself a half glass, waited for Stella. After a few moments she came downstairs and joined Lily at the table.

"Sorry to miss seeing Dorothy," she said, "only I've been busy making contacts. Getting in touch with people who could be helpful."

"There's no obligation for you to see my aunt," Lily said. "She's hardly ideal company for someone of your age."

"But I find her fascinating, Lily. Such a character."

"Yes," Lily said, cutting a piece of the Camembert she had bought. Her knife slipped easily through the runny, ripe cheese. "She is certainly that."

Stella filled her own glass. Drank. She seemed buoyant. "So don't you want to hear about my new idea?"

"Of course," Lily said. Smiled and sat back. Stella's enthusiasms were uplifting. Even if only brief and fleeting, she found them a respite from the ordinary round of a day. Particularly a day spent with Dorothy. She waited for her to outline a new thought for a career, a course, a job opportunity that within days would lose its attraction.

"Well, it's the sitting room upstairs," she said.

"The sitting room?"

Stella picked up the bottle and filled Lily's half glass to the brim so that splashes of the pale straw-colour wine pooled onto the table.

"Yes. Had you thought what you would do with the space once the basement is renovated? I presume you have plans to use this current kitchen as your main sitting room. So the one up on the first floor will become redundant, won't it? Maybe you're considering another bedroom?"

The smell of the Camembert seemed to fill the room. Lily wondered whether such overripe cheese was unwise. No doubt it had been festering in that shop, unrefrigerated, for months.

"No," she said. "I hadn't really given the matter much thought."

Stella's face had been animated. Now it changed as if slapped. She sat back in her chair. Chastened.

"I'm so sorry, Lily. I've completely misunderstood and been utterly insensitive. It's the money, isn't it? The budget for the renovations. You just haven't got it."

"No, it's not that at all," Lily said.

"You see, I wouldn't have gone ahead and devoted so much time to the project on your behalf if I didn't think you could manage it. Financially, that is. I feel really awful if I've embarrassed you."

"You haven't. Please don't think that."

"Are you sure?" Stella looked keenly at Lily as if for reassurance.

"It's simply that it's all a little overwhelming. The idea of such changes to the house. I can't help, but wonder what my father would have thought."

Stella said nothing for a moment. Then abruptly she stood up, tucked her chair into the table and looked up at the kitchen clock.

"I've just remembered I said I'd meet a friend for a drink. Alistair? I think I've mentioned him before. Didn't realise the time. See you later, perhaps."

She was out of the front door before Lily had time to say anything. To remind her that she had left her bag behind at the bottom of the hall stairs. To suggest she might be cold only in her thin slip of a dress.

She cleared the table, threw away the Camembert cheese then found her diary, turned to late July and marked in the dates of her aunt's proposed trip to West Wales. She finished her glass of wine, refilled it and sat down again at the table, staring out at the street. At the time of her father's death, Lily had barely glanced at the sums she automatically inherited. There had been a brief meeting with the solicitor handling the probate when he had advised her to consider shares and investments, but she had paid little attention. As far as Lily was concerned her father's savings could remain just that. The only difference would be a shift into her name at the top of the bank statements which duly arrived every quarter showing interest accrued. She occasionally glanced at them, comforted in an abstract way by the evident cushion of the increasing sum, but content to leave the money as if she was its custodian. Which, in a way, she supposed she was. Just as the house was now her sole responsibility.

So there was really absolutely no reason at all not to agree to Stella's plans.

In fact, her fortune was in meeting Stella.

Alone, she would lack the vision to make such radical changes. After all, the house was satisfactory for her own needs. But that was before she met Stella.

Before Hugh.

Lily thought again of his reluctance to leave the night before. If she had a spare bedroom, an invitation to stay could be seen simply as a practical solution rather than a gesture loaded with implication. In fact, she could even extend her hospitality, suggest he might like to spend every weekend in Alfred Street until his current domestic situation was resolved, his own home reclaimed.

After all, it would only be a short-term arrangement.

Stella was back just after midnight. She was wearing a man's red sweater that swamped her small frame, long sleeves dangling. She smelt of smoke as she leant against the doorframe of the sitting room.

"You're still up, Lily? Thought you'd be in bed hours ago. Monday morning tomorrow and all that." Her face, half-lit by the first-floor landing light, looked drained. Sullen. Her vivacity of hours earlier had entirely disappeared.

"I wanted to see you, Stella. To apologise. I'm so sorry if I seemed ungrateful," she said. "Naturally, I'm happy with the ideas for the house. In fact, I'm thrilled. We really must talk through all the plans and come to some decisions as soon as possible."

Stella did not move from the doorway, but her expression softened.

"No need to apologise, Lily. I quite understand how hard such changes are for you. I mean, you've had a lifetime in this house. But now I'm here and I can help." She wrapped her arms, elongated by the woollen sleeves, around her like an embrace. "That is, if you want me to."

"Of course I do. I know so little about these things. I'd welcome all your suggestions."

"Oh I can do more than make suggestions," Stella said firmly, "in fact, if you like, you can just leave things entirely to me. The arrangements, that is."

"I suppose the first step is to get some estimates, decide a budget," Lily said to show her commitment. "And then, presumably, we need plans drawn up."

Stella shrugged, yawned. "That's certainly one way of approaching things. Methodical, but painfully slow. Actually, I think we can short-cut a lot of that. I do, after all, have some reliable contacts. And good people too. Not mere fly-by-nights who will take your money and disappear with the job half-finished. One has to be so careful these days."

"Of course," Lily said. She thought of Hugh and the problems he was experiencing with his house in Fulham. Stella was right. "Recommendations are key, I can see that."

"Exactly." Stella waved her hand in the direction of the stairs. "But it's late now, let's talk it all through tomorrow. God, you have work in the morning, Lily, have you seen the time? You'll be a wreck when your alarm goes. Not a great way for you to start your week."

Lily smiled. Said goodnight.

No-one, she thought, as she went downstairs to lock the front door, put out the lights, had shown such spontaneous concern for her since she was a young child.

And possibly not even then.

★★★

Agnes Wills said, "Well, I enjoyed that. Such an interesting play, *Roots*, and a good reading, Lily. A pity there weren't more members here."

"At least we had a full cast, although it was a bit of a scramble to reach even that."

They tidied the few remaining chairs, headed out into the mild evening.

"People have better things to do in summer, don't they?" Agnes said, adding wistfully, "at least some people do. A pity Hugh Murray wasn't here, though. A shame to lose him as we're a little thin on strong older actors."

"We haven't lost him," Lily said swiftly, finding keys and trying to remember in which of the myriad side streets she had parked the car. "He was busy tonight, but he's promised to be here next month for *Our Town*."

"I do hope he's not going to be one of those people who only turns up when there's a prime role for them to read," Agnes said censoriously.

"Well, you can't blame him," Lily said. "No doubt he couldn't exactly see himself in Wesker."

"My point entirely. It's not an audition process. It's a play reading society and loyalty is required."

"But you can't expect people to read just out of obligation." Agnes looked at her, said nothing. She had always been in the habit of sharing Agnes's views on dutiful membership and the two of them frequently spent the short drive back to her flat complaining about irregular attendance. They reached the car. Lily unlocked the doors. "Anyway," she went on, "I've already cast him for *Our Town* and he's very enthusiastic about that. Says he played the part years ago in summer rep somewhere and has always loved the play. We are so lucky, aren't we, to have some professional actors among our membership?"

"Has he had many parts lately? I imagine that's all rather behind him if he is willing to join us."

"Perhaps," Lily said evasively. She had not shared with Agnes the extent of her friendship with Hugh, uncertain herself of its parameters. "And a difficult profession, of course."

"Overcrowded, certainly," Agnes agreed.

Her car had been hemmed in, bumper to bumper.

Lily stared at the ingenuity with which two other drivers had managed to sandwich her with their larger, weightier vehicles so that there was barely a hand separating them. She started the engine, attempted to edge forwards then shifted into reverse. There was little progress. Agnes sighed. Lily felt exasperated. If it was not for her established habit of giving Agnes a lift home after the meetings, she would not be in this situation. She could easily walk to King's Cross and back again from Islington. She tried once again, this time coming into contact with the car behind, rocking it marginally in an effort to extricate hers. At that moment, she caught sight of a man in her rear mirror, coming down the road, increasing his pace as he saw the slight movement of his car. Lily flinched, waited for the onslaught of abuse she expected. Instead, the man walked slowly around his car inspecting it, scrutinising both bumpers, every inch of paintwork then took out a pen from his pocket, stared exaggeratedly at her registration plate and made a note of it on the back of his hand. There seemed to be something more menacing in his calculated actions than in a swift torrent of expletives. Eventually, he got into his car and after further delay, a protracted business with combing his hair, lighting a cigarette, flicking ash out of the window, he drove off.

"Did you see that?" Agnes said. "Driving without wearing his seat belt. And it's become law now, you know. Mandatory."

"I know," Lily said weakly, pulling out from the parking space at last.

"Not that I ever go in any cars except for yours, Lily. And I've never driven, of course. Well, no need, living in London, and of course women of my generation simply didn't. Learn, that is. Then there's the expense of maintaining a car. All beyond me, I'm afraid."

Lily wondered why Agnes Wills was irritating her. She had always thought of her with affection and respect, but her implied humility, her self-effacement, were suddenly exasperating. Yet equally, she felt fickle, as if the company of Stella and Hugh had rendered Agnes redundant.

She had spent the previous evening finally stripping her father's bedroom. Now the space was freed from any remaining tokens that hooked it to Walter Page and could serve another purpose. The photograph of her mother was removed to her own room where she placed it on the chest next to one of her father in a light jacket, squinting in the strong Athenian sunlight as he stood on the slopes of the Acropolis. Stella's belongings had spilt out from her inadequate room over the weeks and now clogged much of the landing, making it difficult to negotiate a path to the sitting room. But once she moved into the main bedroom, that problem would be sorted. It needed attention, of course, the room requiring an update after years of relative neglect. The wall paper was dated and stained, skirting boards and paint work shabby, but a couple of days of decorating would uplift the room.

And then the curtains.

Swiftly, Lily had unhooked the dark, heavy velour drapes and carried them downstairs and into the back garden where she deposited them in a heap, her clothes now covered with dust mites. After a couple of hours of cleaning, she felt the room sufficiently purged of the past and ready to present to Stella when she came in.

"Thank you, Lily," she had said complacently, "I can certainly do something with this space. I do understand how hard this must have been for you with such warm memories of your father. But life goes on, doesn't it? We all have to travel onwards."

Lily had thought of the photograph of her mother. Of Helen Page now in touching distance of her father in his summer jacket, that stick of his that he carried in later years. And said,

"Yes, if we are fortunate enough to be given that chance. You are absolutely right, Stella."

★★★

There were plans spread over the kitchen table when she came in from work a few days later. Lily found it hard to make sense of them since they seemed to bear so little resemblance to the present house. There were no walls where walls currently existed. Doors appeared to have changed places. A second bathroom had sprung up on the first floor. The current kitchen, stripped of sink and stove, was an open space with little to suggest its new purpose. And the basement that the plans labelled as *lower ground floor/garden level* had taken on a character entirely unrelated to the depository she had always known. Lily had never liked the idea of fast fairground rides. But once, at Battersea Funfair, in the company of Toby Jessop, who had sat at her side, holding her hand, she had endured minutes of spinning round and round on a garishly painted machine at such speed that her sense of equilibrium, even of self, had entirely left her. She remembered that sensation now, unable to separate feelings of exhilaration from alarming loss of control.

The phone rang.

It was Hugh.

"Helen – not ringing at an awkward time, I hope? I never know what's acceptable to people."

"It's fine," Lily said, "in fact, I was just looking over the plans for the changes to the house."

"Excellent," he said. "What an inspired idea on your part, to have such vision for it. One has to keep up with the times."

"Yes, I suppose one must."

"Not that I would expect anything less of you, Helen. And I'll look forward to seeing what you have in mind."

"Stella is really the driving force behind it."

"You are too modest as always. But I can see that the two of you together are an ideal partnership. You are doing absolutely the right thing, investing in bricks and mortar. Especially in

Islington." His approval consoled, any harbouring hesitancy on her part dissolved. "But onto other things, Helen. I was thinking about this weekend. I feel we should be a little more adventurous. I am guilty, I fear, of taking your hospitality for granted rather than behaving as I should."

Hector padded down the stairs and came to settle by her feet expecting attention.

"You are always very welcome here."

"What I mean, dear Helen, is that I should be inviting you out on dates. Because that's what people do. What new couples do. They see films, go to pubs, plays, that sort of thing. I have been very remiss in my behaviour. But it's been so long since I have been fortunate enough to have someone with whom I wanted to share such things. Forgive me, Helen."

"It's quite unnecessary."

"So I'm springing a surprise on you this Saturday, to make up in some very small way for my neglect. How does the Royal Festival Hall sound to you?"

"A concert?"

"Something of the kind," Hugh said. "I presume you're free Saturday evening. Of course you are, you were expecting me to slope along for dinner as per usual in my lazy way. Well, that's all settled then, wouldn't you say? It's a seven-thirty start so let's meet for a drink first. I expect there's a decent bar there. In fact, I know there is. Shall we say a good thirty to forty minutes beforehand?"

Effortlessly, arrangements appeared to have been made and he moved on to talk of his week, ask about hers. He broke off at one point, shutting a door against loud voices, apologising on his return. "By the way," he added, "I do hope the concert will be your sort of thing. I just had to guess at your tastes and you must be sure and tell me if I've got things wildly wrong."

"I'm sure it will be lovely," she said and whilst Hugh

continued to talk she thought of the substantial stack of LPs somewhere in the house, overlooked for years so no doubt now warped through neglect. The usual light classics, acquired over the years, but in addition her own purchases of Judy Garland, Ella Fitzgerald, Sarah Vaughan. A weakness for sentimental music, Toby Jenner had once chided her, inappropriate according to him for someone who could access Elvis Presley, Bobby Darin, Adam Faith. Toby had prided himself on tastes that Lily had considered suitable only for teenagers pushing coins into juke boxes in dubious coffee bars in Soho and had suspected that in truth he rarely listened to anything later than Mozart. He had been a shape shifter, adapting to the moment, eyes sharply attuned in every direction for the next chance. Whereas Lily had been steadfast, faithful in her adherence. After Toby, however, she had set aside such music, avoided the potency of those exquisite songs of love and loss.

"But I mustn't keep you any longer, Helen." Hugh suddenly truncated a tale Lily had barely followed about a cancelled casting. "I'll be looking forward to Saturday tremendously, I can assure you. Something to lighten the dreariness of the week."

Hector stretched, turned round in a circle and settled again at her feet. Stella's key was turning in the front door. She came in, bringing cool evening air into the narrow hallway. She smiled broadly at Lily, handing her a large box of tea bags and two packets of biscuits.

"For the workmen," she said. "Essential supplies. They start tomorrow."

15

Two days later, the partition walls in the basement were gone.

Lily came home from school to find a skip in the road already full of masonry, the door in the basement stairwell, stubbornly shut for years, wide open. For a fleeting moment she thought of homes bombed during the war, the carcass of buildings precariously exposed. Stella, in denim dungarees, her hair hiding under a headscarf, was sitting at the kitchen table with a ginger-haired young man wearing only shorts and a sleeveless T-shirt. They broke off abruptly from a conversation that seemed intense.

"Lily!" Stella said, "I had no idea it was so late. We were just recovering after a day's hard slog."

"Some of us," the young man said without looking up to acknowledge Lily.

"Ok, that's true, Crispin's done the heavy stuff. Not without help, of course. But we sent the others home hours ago."

"The others?" It was somewhat startling to think of an invasion of strangers while she had been at work.

"Yes, Crispin's got a good team, you know. Not that those walls needed much encouragement to fall. Paper thin, actually. A quick wielding of the sledgehammer was all it took."

Crispin rolled his eyes at Stella, but remained silent.

"So what's the next step?" Lily said, summoning enthusiasm. "Now that the walls are gone?"

"Slow down, Lily!" Stella said. "There's a long way to go before you'll be sitting down in your state-of-the-art new kitchen, you know. You've looked at the plans, haven't you?"

"Of course," Lily said firmly although her glance had been scant. "I was just wondering whether we had any idea of a time scale."

Crispin looked across the room at Lily, staring at her as if he had only just noticed that she was there.

"These things, you know," he said slowly, drawing out the words as if he found some effort in articulating them, "take as long as they take. After all, you can find problems."

"Problems?"

"With old buildings. Damp. Wiring. Plumbing not fit for purpose."

"I see," Lily said. She felt like a patient receiving negative news. "But these are well-built houses, surely. They've stood the test of time, after all." She tried to locate a space at the table, but was aware that it would mean sitting uncomfortably close to Crispin. A faint cloying smell of sweat filled the room.

"Take no notice of him, Lily," Stella said. "He's just being cautious. Of course, it is true that one has to be ready for the unexpected when embarking on major projects like this. Costs can rise, naturally."

"I suppose so," Lily said.

"Talking of budgets," Stella said, "we need to keep the lads happy. It's only fair so would it be all right if you made the first payment to everyone tomorrow? It's along the lines of what we discussed and agreed so no nasty surprises there."

"Of course," Lily said automatically and tried to remember what had been agreed. She knew Stella had briefly presented her with a list of break-down costs, but had insisted that it was just a preliminary figure. *After all*, Lily had vaguely recalled her saying, *there is always going to be a need for contingencies*. "I can write cheques this evening if you give me the names they should be made out to."

Crispin rocked back in his chair. The old lino squeaked as if in protest.

"Cash, Lily," Stella said firmly. "Unless that's going to be a problem?"

"No problem at all. It's just that – I'm not sure if I will have time to get to the bank tomorrow to draw the money out. What with school and Fridays are always extra busy."

"Your lunch hour?" Crispin said. "Surely they let you out at lunch time."

"Crispin, that's unfair, don't put pressure on poor Lily," Stella said. "If she is going to find getting cash out tomorrow just too difficult, I suppose we can tell the lads not to come in at all for a few days. Leave this job for a while."

Lily had heard stories of workmen who abandoned jobs half way through and disappeared, never to be seen again. The house already felt in a precarious state and she was anxious to return it to stability.

"There's no problem with the cash," she said swiftly. "Of course I can get to the bank at lunch time. Silly of me not to think of that."

"Good!" Stella beamed. "That's all sorted then." She stood up as if finding it hard to contain her excitement. "Now for it! A little tour of your new lower ground floor – you won't believe the light that has flooded into the space. It's going to make the most wonderful room. You are going to be thrilled, Lily, I know you are!"

★★★

Hugh was standing close to the crowded bar, trying to gain attention, a note held out in one hand. Lily had arrived too early out of her habitual fear of being late, had sat in her car for half an hour then wasted time walking along the river terrace hoping that her dress was not a mistake. She wished she had asked Stella, but her response might have been diplomatic rather than truthful. The season was partly to blame. According to shop windows, it was a time for pastel florals and diaphanous fabrics as if Londoners spent their summers solely attending elaborate weddings or garden parties, yet her own wardrobe was woefully inadequate. She had seen the dress in the window of a small boutique in Upper Street that morning, a shop that she had always assumed as inappropriate for her needs. Inside, the smell of joss sticks had nearly driven her straight out, but she had persisted, asked the assistant if it came in her size. There was only one size, Lily was told with indifference. She had bought it without trying it on, anxious to retreat from the place, cowed by its unfamiliarity, an irrational sense of trespass.

Hugh turned and saw her. Smiled warmly.

"Wine?" he said over the gaggle of heads. She nodded. Said something about red, but he had turned back and after a couple of minutes appeared at her side with two glasses of white.

"Hope that's what you said. What a crush in this place! Let's find somewhere quieter. Is it too chilly for you outside?" He led the way without waiting for an answer and she followed, losing him for a moment as he slipped between people queuing for programmes. "No hope of getting a table, I'm afraid, but at least we can breathe out here." He was wearing a pale blue shirt, no tie, a jacket she had not seen before. Linen, no doubt, because it was creased in a way that made it seem authentic. "And you're looking lovely, Helen. Should have said that straight away. I certainly thought it. You'll have to excuse my lack of gallantry as always."

"There's no need," Lily said, "to apologise, I mean." Yet his compliment was reassuring. Fleetingly, she looked around at the other couples on the terrace and was comforted by a sense of belonging. Like the solitary child who eventually gains friendship, she felt she was acquiring the habits that permitted inclusion. And the dress was undoubtedly a success. Just before the performance started, sitting in their seats in the rear stalls, Hugh bent his face very close to hers, placed one of his hands momentarily on her knee.

"Those muted, subtle colours suit you so well, Helen. I don't think I've seen you in that dress before. You see, I do notice these things!"

She was barely aware of the entrance of the conductor, the obligatory bow and audience applause. The opening chords of Mendelssohn's Overture to *A Midsummer Night's Dream*, then the scurrying business of the violins was lost to her and she closed her eyes, acutely aware of Hugh's presence next to her, of the alarming level of physical desire it provoked. When the interval came, she resented it for the suspension of mood and the awkwardness of an audience shuffling out of seats, clogging aisles, shouldering towards exits.

"You look thoroughly absorbed," Hugh said, turning to her. "Obviously the consummate concert goer, unlike me. But come on, let's try and grab ourselves another drink before the second half."

Lily followed. Again, she lost him for a moment as he darted swiftly in the direction of the bar, skilfully weaving his way around the ice cream queue and signalling for a barman's attention so that by the time she caught up he had two glasses in his hand. She had intended asking for orange juice. Suggesting coffee instead. She had eaten little all day, too preoccupied by the prospect of the evening to warrant much attention to food.

"I do hope it's all right," he said as they headed towards a quieter part of the foyer. "My choice of concert, I mean. I have to confess to being rather a philistine when it comes to classical music. Whereas you, Helen, are the sort of woman I would expect conversant with opera and no doubt highbrow chamber music and such like."

"Not at all," Lily said. "I wonder why you have that idea of me."

"I think it's because you are the daughter of a professor of classics. It suggests a certain gravitas. As if you are someone only concerned with the more serious aspects of life."

"Surely you don't think that," Lily said. "It makes me sound so dull."

Hugh laughed.

"Nonsense, Helen, you are far from dull, I assure you. It's more a case of me being aware of my inadequacies. Intellectually, shall we say? I fear I am no match for you."

"I am not my father," Lily said firmly. "Really, I am very ill-educated in so many ways. The ways that seem to count in the real world, that is."

Hugh slipped his arm around her shoulder, pulled her away from the group of young people standing close to them and talking animatedly about the music.

"Do you know how lucky I feel to have met you, Helen? I simply didn't think that such women like you existed any more. Humility is a quality in short supply these days, I can tell you that."

Lily drank, grateful for the sense of liberation afforded by the second glass of wine.

"Perhaps I am more like my mother," she said, raising her voice to speak over the foyer noise. "Rather than my clever, serious father. But I have little way of knowing. My father never really spoke about her in any depth."

"And you were never curious enough to ask? That seems extraordinary, if I may say so."

"He was a very private man," Lily said. "And it would have seemed intrusive. You sense, don't you, when people find things too painful to talk about?"

"I suppose so," Hugh said. "You are probably right."

"And when you think about it, they knew each other for such a short time before her death. Just three years or something like that. Hardly a lifetime in which to get to know one another."

A warning bell for the end of the interval sounded.

Hugh swallowed the rest of the wine, took her empty glass.

"Do you realise that we've barely said a word about the programme – the music? Shame on us! We're growing too mutually absorbed, Helen, that's our trouble. But hopefully the second half will be equally light weight with no insistence on a bit of discordant contemporary stuff to disturb me!"

"You chose the concert," Lily reminded him.

"True," Hugh said swiftly, "but I'm hopeless at reading detail."

"It's Tchaikovsky's overture to *Romeo and Juliet* and his *Serenade for Strings*. So yes, we're on very safe ground."

He insisted on paying for the tickets. When Lily tried to object after the concert had finished, he swept away her protestations.

"When I think of the number of meals I have had in Alfred Street, I am badly in your debt, Helen."

"There's no need to think of it like that. Besides, Stella so often does the cooking, so really, things have never been easier."

"The ideal house guest, then!" The audience slowly dispersed and they made their way out of the hall onto the South Bank. Lily pulled her light shawl around her. "Not too cold for you? I thought we might stand here for a few moments admiring the river view rather than jostling along with the crowds. As usual, I'm putting off the prospect of the Northern Line for as long as I can."

"Let me drive you home instead," Lily said. "It won't take long at this time of night. I'm parked in Upper Ground."

"So kind of you, as always. But I couldn't possibly expect you to do that." He took one of her hands, held it firmly in both of his. "No need to tarnish your evening by a trip to dubious areas south of the river. I have to say that although tonight has been absolutely delightful, I am feeling a little deprived of my weekend visit to Islington. Perhaps it's a sign of sedate middle age, a need for a reliable routine!"

"There's still tomorrow," Lily said.

"Tomorrow?"

"Come to lunch," she went on before she had time to check herself. "It's one of my aunt's Sundays, so as long as you don't mind the company of an octogenarian. And Dorothy can be quite entertaining in small doses. You'll be able to inspect the progress on the house renovations too. Actually, I'd be grateful for some moral support in case Dorothy is critical of the changes. I'm rather dreading her reaction, if I'm honest."

Hugh's acceptance suddenly seemed crucial to her in a way that was faintly disturbing. He hesitated for a moment then drew her close to him.

"Sunday lunch with the infamous, indomitable aged aunt sounds delightful, Helen. I can't think of a better invitation. About noon? Or is that too early? I'm a little unversed in the hospitality habits of salubrious north London neighbourhoods, you see."

"That should be fine," Lily said. "I'm usually back from picking my aunt up by then, but if we're delayed by traffic, Stella can let you in. She's planning to be home tomorrow so you can be assured of a good lunch."

It was how normal people behaved, Lily thought, as they continued to stare out across the river. Lights of small tugs and larger pleasure boats illuminated the dark waters. In particular, it was how couples behaved. Friends for long Sunday lunches, the burden of obligatory relations shared, lightened by younger company. She felt a sense of appropriateness, as if at last she understood the rules of engagement with a life that should be hers. Even the layers of dust from the basement renovation, the skip outside the house, the considerable cash flow of payments to the labourers were confirmation of her newly acquired status. Hugh kissed her on one cheek then took a step away, made a mock bow.

"Until tomorrow, then, Helen. How good that sounds, I must say. Tomorrow around noon. Drive carefully, won't you? Lock your doors and avoid the Saturday night drunks and loiterers. Shall I accompany you to your car? Yes, that's the least I can do."

Lily noticed the man before Hugh.

He was standing in the shadow of the Festival Hall watching them and as they turned to walk in the direction of her car he approached.

"Hugh Murray! I thought it must be you. Fiona said I must be mistaken, but no, I was right all along."

A woman about Lily's age stood back as if uninterested in the encounter. Hugh looked confused for a moment and Lily wondered whether there was some mistake. Then he said somewhat brusquely,

"Ralph. What a surprise. I thought you'd moved out of London."

"Oh, we have. We're country bumpkins these days wallowing in the depths of Dorset, aren't we, Fi? But we come up fairly regularly and stay with our daughter in Greenwich."

"Were you at the concert?" Hugh said.

"Concert? Not at all. Just had dinner in some exorbitantly priced restaurant and thought we'd take a stroll along the river before heading back."

"To Dorset?" Hugh spoke without warmth.

"To Greenwich, of course. Not back to the country until Tuesday." The man, Ralph, turned to look at Lily with blatant curiosity. "Aren't you going to introduce us, Hugh? I don't think we've met, have we?"

Lily felt uncomfortable under the man's gaze. Hugh said blankly,

"This is Helen. She's a friend. Now if you'll excuse us, Ralph, it's been a long evening and the two of us have to get to our respective homes."

"No time for a drink then, the four of us?" He glanced behind him to Fiona who smiled, but showed little enthusiasm for the idea.

"No," Hugh said firmly. "Sorry, Ralph."

"Another time, then," he said. "I'd like to catch up and hear how it's all going for you. Last time we met things were... complicated, shall we say?" He laughed as if his evasive comment was amusing. "Of course, that must be a while back now."

"It was," Hugh said, "exactly. A long time ago." He started to walk away from the couple so that Lily had to hurry to catch him up.

"Good bye then, Hugh and... Helen, was it?" he called after them. "Good to see you. I'll get in touch next time we're up from the country, shall I? So we can arrange to get together – the four of us, perhaps?"

Hugh muttered something into the night air that Lily did not catch. They were in Upper Ground by her car within moments.

"Sorry about that," Hugh said, "objectionable man."

Lily found her keys. Hugh seemed restless, looking around him as if concerned they had been followed.

"Really? He seemed pleasant enough. How do you know him? Ralph and – Fiona, was it?"

He waved a vague hand.

"I don't really. That's my point. He is – ingratiating."

"I see." The mood seemed broken. Swiftly she opened the car door and said, "Thank you again for a lovely evening, Hugh. Until tomorrow, then."

He said nothing for a moment, staring down the road as if expecting Ralph and Fiona to hove suddenly into sight. Then he snapped round and surprised Lily with a close embrace.

"Apologies. That was uncalled for. A streak of moroseness as a result of someone spoiling the end of our evening."

"Nothing was spoilt," she said and wanted to remain in his arms, the comfort and consolation of another's flesh so close to hers. He pulled away, held her at some distance as if looking at each feature of her face then embraced her again.

"Enough!" he said and took a step away, this time more firmly. "Parting is such sweet sorrow and all that business. Alfred Street at noon. Until then, Helen."

16

Dorothy was silent for most of the journey. Only when they drew close to Islington did she allow her curiosity to show.

"A man is having lunch with us you say? A friend of yours?"

"Yes," Lily said. "Hugh Murray. I think I might have mentioned him before."

"Possibly. You do seem to be branching out, Lily. First there's young Stella and now you're harbouring male guests in your father's house."

"My house now," Lily said. "And you make it sound immoral, subversive somehow."

"And is it?"

"What?"

"These sudden friendships of yours?"

"I have no idea what you mean," Lily said. "I've invited Hugh to have lunch with us, that's all."

Dorothy relapsed into silence for the rest of the journey until they pulled up in Alfred Street. Then she placed a hand briefly on Lily's arm.

"I'm an old woman. I dislike change. And since my brother is no longer around to keep an eye on things, on you in particular, it's fallen to me to take over the mantle, as it were."

"I am fifty years of age," Lily said firmly. "I don't need anyone to keep an eye on me."

"Everyone," Dorothy said, gathering her large handbag from the floor, "needs someone to perform that task for them. Believe you me, Lily."

Dorothy was still reserved when they sat down to lunch, sufficiently cordial over a glass of dry sherry with Hugh, but unusually quiet. She listened patiently to Stella's animated account of progress with the house changes, but showed no interest in seeing the evidence.

"Lily has been wonderful," she enthused as she served Dorothy with second helpings of roast pork. "Just given me and the builders carte blanche, really. Isn't that right, Lily?"

"Well, we do have proper plans drawn up," Lily said, anticipating her aunt's concern. "I approved those first, of course. And it does seem to be what everyone else in the road is doing. With their basements, I mean."

"I have such admiration for Helen, embarking on a project like this," Hugh said expansively. "It's so easy just to be complaisant about one's home and I know to my cost that I've been guilty of that."

Dorothy looked up sharply at Hugh.

"Helen? Who is Helen?"

Lily was flooded with embarrassment, but Hugh put down his fork and calmly explained his habit of using her birth name. Dorothy took time to answer, spooning more apple sauce onto her plate and taking a Jersey potato from the bowl, examining it before nestling it beside a roasted cousin.

"Well," she said calmly, "I've always thought that the name did not particularly suit my niece. And once her mother was dead – very unexpectedly and inconveniently, as you no doubt know if you have any knowledge at all of our family – it seemed a little morbid to perpetuate her memory by continuing to call the child after her."

Hugh turned to Lily and smiled warmly.

"I don't think you have any objection, do you Helen? At least you've not said so. But as long as I am not treading too heavily on any family traditions and causing upset, of course. I do realise how sensitive such matters can be."

"Goodness, not at all," Dorothy said firmly. "There's only me and Lily left now and I've never been one for sentiment, I can assure you."

Hugh switched his attention entirely to Dorothy. Skilfully, with restrained charm, he made her the focus of conversation and soon she appeared no longer wary of his company, but affable and relaxed. Lily felt pleasingly redundant, marvelling at the way both Hugh and Stella managed to entertain and divert her for on Dorothy's own admission she was a generally intractable and stubborn woman. She left the three of them and went to find the usual impact of Stella's cooking in the chaotic state of the kitchen. By the time she had finished they had moved upstairs to the living room and were talking about the general election the following week. Dorothy's staunch support for Margaret Thatcher was countered only mildly by Stella, who shrugged and said where politics were concerned one side was, on the whole, as bad as the other. Lily noted that she seemed to have lost the fervour she had expressed only the week before when she had said she was thinking of canvassing on behalf of the local Labour candidate.

"What about you, Hugh?" Dorothy asked. "Where do your sympathies lie? Not for that appalling Mr Foot, surely. The man doesn't even appear to own a decent suit."

Hugh smiled. "I believe in the discretion of the secret ballot box," he said. "But of course, one can't deny that Thatcher has the success of the Falklands War to boost her ratings."

"How awful," Lily said without thinking. The three of them turned towards her and immediately she wished she had not spoken. "I mean," she hedged, "any war is a tragedy and to think that there is political advantage to be made, exploitation, if you like, seems so very wrong."

There was a silence. Then Dorothy sighed too loudly for the others to ignore. Hugh looked across at Lily and said warmly, "That's exactly the response I would expect from you, Helen. Compassionate and sincere."

Her aunt, however, clearly considered her answer naïve.

"Oh, my brother was like that, Hugh, too liberal for his own good," Dorothy said. "Actually, I suspect he was a bit of a conscientious objector on the quiet if I'm honest. Definitely a man to sit on the fence, anyway."

Lily was about to say something in support of her father when Stella jumped up from where she was sitting cross-legged on the window seat.

"This is all getting terribly serious when there's cake to be eaten. I've made an angel cake for tea which takes the most ridiculous amount of egg whites so, Lily, it's going to be yolk omelettes for us the whole of next week unless you can think of another use for ten of them. Hugh, how about I show you the basement, the phoenix rising from the ashes and all that, while we wait for the kettle to boil?"

On the journey home, Dorothy again said very little. Hugh had been solicitous towards both of them as they had left, saying he wished he could offer to drive himself to save Lily the trouble, but that he had long dispensed with car ownership. He hoped, he said, taking Dorothy's hand, finding her scarf that had slipped to the floor, to see her again very soon if he could contrive another Sunday invitation to Alfred Street. Lily was so relieved at what she saw as the success of the day, her aunt's apparent capitulation to Hugh's easy company, that her silence did not bother her. She was no doubt tired, the day more demanding than when it was just the two of them. Once they had pulled up outside the block of mansion flats and the engine turned off, however, Dorothy became more animated.

"Well, Lily, you are full of surprises these days, I must say. What's come over you?"

"I don't know what you mean," she said evasively. There seemed a cyclical pattern to the conversation of the morning that she had hoped to avoid.

"Not content with one addition to the household, you now appear to be entertaining another who seems well-dug-in, if I may say so. And an actor, at that. I can't imagine what your father would think."

But her tone was light-hearted.

"He wouldn't have wanted me to be lonely, that's for sure," she said.

"Of course, Lily, but there is no reason why any female in this day and age should resort to loneliness. Only a fool allows herself to be that when there are so many opportunities and diversions out there to avoid it. In my youth, it was different for a woman, naturally."

"Did you like Hugh?" Lily felt in need of affirmation. "You certainly seemed to get on well with him."

Her aunt was equivocal.

"He seems pleasant enough although one can hardly tell on a first meeting." Then she turned to Lily, studying her face. "Does it matter to you whether I like him?" Lily said nothing. She was too unsure of her answer. Dorothy went on. "Of course, a single man at his stage of life can trail an appalling history. One knows that all too well. A widower, however, cannot help but gain one's sympathy. Particularly given the circumstances of his late wife's death."

"The circumstances?"

They were both distracted for a moment by two dogs, straining at their respective leashes, coming face to face on the pavement and barking ferociously at each other. Their owners pulled them smartly apart.

"The road accident," Dorothy went on. "A collision with a drunken driver, Hugh said. What an appalling way to lose one's life. So unnecessary. Really, the penalties for drink driving should be so much more severe."

Lily was confused. Surely Hugh's wife, Louise, had died after suffering from a long, debilitating illness. But perhaps she had simply assumed, failed to gain the full facts out of her usual reticence to pry. Dorothy, in her forthright fashion, had clearly delved more deeply while she had been out of the room. She gathered her belongings. The remains of Stella's angel cake, some slices of pork. A portion of gooseberry fool and accompanying shortbread.

"I meant to ask you," Lily said, "if this visit to Wales has been arranged. If you still want me to take you there and stay for a few days. Or perhaps—"

"Of course," Dorothy said. "July 24th. And I've decided we should make it a full week. After all, one doesn't want to waste petrol going all that way for such a short time."

"You didn't say anything about a whole week," Lily said, irritated. "You should have checked with me in case I had other plans."

"Don't be tiresome, Lily. What's a couple of extra days to you? You have the time, after all. See you as usual in two weeks, then."

The car door closed firmly and, watching her progress to the entrance of the flats, Lily wondered why her aunt always managed to render any protest futile. It was true that a couple of extra days in Wales was no particular hardship for her and if matters were different she would no doubt be welcoming the prospect of a summer that was structured and defined in some small way. But not now. Now she had other obligations, other people whose needs were paramount.

And there was the work on the house to consider. To use as justification for refusing invitations, avoiding commitments. And she had done just that. To Eileen with her plan for that trip to Stratford, to Barbara, a long-standing colleague at work who had suggested some days away at the Edinburgh festival. Lily resented the way these women now no doubt viewed her: single and without dependents and therefore a prop and a convenience to their own lives. She had enjoyed talking airily to both of them about workmen to supervise, plasterers and plumbers to direct, suppressing the truth of the matter that Stella was the driving force of such employment and that she was merely the financial provider. She slipped the car into another lane to avoid a break-down ahead and thought again of Louise. Of Hugh's late wife and wondered whether there were still photographs of her displayed in his house in Fulham. Whether she had been dark or fair, attractive or faintly plain. Now that she thought about it, the tragedy of her death in a road accident had no doubt caused Hugh to sell his car and abandon the idea of driving. Suddenly, that made entire sense.

He was still there.

She heard his voice from upstairs, Stella's laugh, as she came into the hall and went up to join them.

They were standing in the middle of her father's bedroom.

Or rather, as Lily swiftly reminded herself, the room that had previously belonged to Walter Page and now had a new incarnation. Her face betrayed her surprise. She had not realised that Stella had already started work on the room, painting the walls, discarding some furniture, adding a vibrant rug.

"I was going to wait to show you until I'd finished it," Stella said. "But you did say that the room was all mine now. I haven't got that wrong, have I? Or have you changed your mind?" She looked concerned.

"No, of course not, Stella, it's quite all right," Lily said quickly. She wanted to sit down to accommodate herself to the room's shift, but there were dustsheets over the bed and the single chair seemed to have disappeared.

"She's making a very splendid job of it, I'd say," Hugh said. "Bang up to date, this rag-rolling effect."

"I do hope you like the colour, Lily. I did think of checking with you, but then knew you would simply say it was my choice as I was the one having to sleep here and that I needed to do whatever would make me feel at home. Those would be your very words."

The walls were pale peach with a sponge effect that managed to look, Lily thought, both extraordinarily complicated and crassly error strewn at the same time. An infant's early experiments or a priceless abstract painting.

"It's lovely," she said. "Very original."

Stella pulled a face.

"Not really. I was a bit afraid I was going for the obvious, what everyone is doing on walls these days. It's very early 80s, actually. But you can't help getting caught up in the vogue of things, can you?"

"It seems to me you have a real eye for these things, Stella," Hugh said. "I'd forget all this idea of drama school and theatrical ambitions and think about interior design as a career if I were you."

Stella inspected a small area of wall near the window, scratched at it with a fingernail.

"Oh, I have," she said. "Given up on drama school and acting, that is. Not enough money in it."

"You're spot on there, Stella."

"So possibly interior design," she said slowly. "That's quite an idea, Hugh. But really, the renovation project here is so much more about the personal involvement. I mean I'm just doing this for Lily, really, helping her out to repay her kindness for all she's done for me."

"The house is certainly taking on a new lease of life." Hugh looked at Lily with a certain mutual pride. "That basement of yours is going to be quite phenomenal."

"Ah yes, Lily. We need to start talking kitchens this week," Stella said. She lifted a corner of the dust sheet and propped herself on the bed. "I'm wondering what you have in mind for the units and fixtures and fittings. And the colour scheme, naturally, of course."

Lily had imagined if she had thought about it in any detail at all that the arrangements in the current kitchen would serve the new. That the cupboards and shelves, the fridge and washing machine would simply be transplanted downstairs to the new space. It was, she had conceded, possibly time for a new cooker. Now she saw that her assumption had been woefully wrong. She tried to cover her sense of inadequacy.

"I'd be interested to hear any thoughts you might have, Stella. Obviously, I have some ideas of my own, but you clearly have a good eye for these things."

Hugh slipped his arm around Lily's shoulder.

"If you can bear to put up with me just a bit longer, Helen, I think all this calls for a celebratory drink, don't you? How about the three of us pop along to that pub by the canal and toast the resurgence of 8 Alfred Street? We can even debate kitchen appliances over a glass or two if you insist, Stella!"

The evening was warm and the terrace of the pub crowded, but eventually they found a table, cleared it of overflowing ashtrays and discarded crisp packets and managed to acquire drinks. Lily was aware of a feeling of blithe happiness as Hugh and Stella began to discuss the relative merits of tiles and work surfaces, every now and again expressing a preference, randomly chosen since she had no particular opinion on what seemed to her periphery concerns. It was the moment that mattered, the contentment to be found in such companionship and not only in the immediacy of the event, but in the promise of a future entirely unimagined.

"So, you two," Stella said, "any holiday plans? Summer's just around the corner, after all. Are you jetting off somewhere exotic for August? Or is it a summer season at the end of the pier in Brighton or Bognor Regis for you, Hugh?"

He laughed.

"No such luck these days," he said. "Long gone, I'm afraid. Although one still has distant memories, of course, of those years in the late 50s and 60s. And as it happens, my last summer stint was in 1976."

"The heatwave summer. A good year to spend months by the sea, I would have thought."

"Yes. Except that the first fortnight was in Hull in some ghastly digs, followed by a month in Crewe. Or somewhere like it. I forget now. I believe we were granted a week or two in Sidmouth followed by Truro at the end of the run. Reward for good behaviour the company used to joke. Do you know Devon and Cornwall at all, Lily?"

She shook her head. Theatrical summer seasons sounded enviable whatever the privations.

"Lily's spent every summer of her life gadding around Greece, not prosaic English seaside resorts," Stella said. "Lucky Lily."

"Not every summer," she corrected, "but it's true I'm quite ignorant about most English coastal towns. I'm sure I've missed a lot."

Hugh drained his glass.

"We had a particularly good time in Sidmouth, now I come to think of it. Lovely town. And a small theatre at the end of the pier. Always receptive audiences at those shows as everyone was in a relaxed holiday mood and determined to enjoy themselves. It was all very light stuff – farces, broad comedy, that sort of thing and I can't pretend to have had leading roles, if I'm honest. I seem to remember autograph hunters hovering at the stage door after every performance even though none of us were particularly well known. At least, not in the grander scheme of things," he qualified.

"I can just imagine you, Hugh," Stella said, leaning her elbows on the table and gazing at him as if aping a star-struck fan. "Gorgeously glamorous in those days, in your youth, no doubt. The classic matinee idol! Don't you think so, Lily? You would have been an avid fan, one of those hungering for him at the stage door, no doubt!"

"You are embarrassing her!"

"Not at all," Lily said, but she found Stella's remark, however playful, awkward to answer. It was easier to shift the subject. "Anyway, I suppose the renovation will dominate my summer. I have to say I wish I could see everything through your eyes, Stella, as I'm finding it hard to visualise what everything will look like once it's finished."

"Which is why," Stella said, stressing each word as if for emphasis, "I've suggested to Anna and Simon that we both pop next door to see what they've done with their place. Or we could knock on Meg and Charlie's door as the paint is still virtually wet after their enormous renovation. You know, the ones at number 18 just a bit down from you?"

Lily tried to recall the couple at number 18. She remembered taking some post there one day that had been delivered in error and coming face to face with a very tall man and a thin auburn-haired woman who were just leaving the house. They had been briskly grateful, but barely exchanged a word. She could not imagine how Stella had gained first name acquaintance so swiftly, let alone acquire knowledge of their home. At times, Lily wondered if living with her father, a man who dwelt so ineluctably in the ancient past, had caused her to atrophy, to become detached from the present so that it was easy for others to eliminate, to overlook her significance. No such fate could ever befall Stella Fox. Or, come to think of it, Hugh Murray. They would always be noticed. Observed.

"I suppose that might be a good idea," she said hesitantly. "If they don't mind."

"Or," Hugh said, taking one of her hands and entwining his fingers firmly through hers, "you could just leave things entirely to Stella. She's got such style, after all. I'd employ her any day to add some allure to my woefully neglected Edwardian semi. Once I'm sure it's not sinking into the ground, that is."

"I'll let you know my charges!" Stella said playfully. "But seriously, Hugh. You need to get the place structurally secure before you worry about the interiors."

Hugh raised his eyebrows.

"Don't I know it. Try telling that to the bunch of cowboys I seem skilled at employing."

"You should send Stella over to Fulham," Lily said. "She seems very adept at directing matters in Alfred Street."

"I might just consider that," Hugh said. "Now, anyone for another drink?"

Stella shook her head. "Actually, I'm off. Got some friends to meet about stuff over in Kentish Town so I'll leave the two of you in peace. I'll probably be late, Lily, really late, I mean, so catch up with you tomorrow."

They watched her go, slipping rapidly between tables, turning a few heads as she went.

"Oh to be so young!" Hugh said.

"And beautiful," Lily murmured. Youth alone did not bring unalloyed happiness, she knew. Hugh turned to her.

"As far as I am concerned, I am sitting opposite the woman

I find most attractive in north London today. There, will that do? But sadly, I suppose I really must be heading off soon myself, Helen, I've occupied far too much of your weekend already."

His compliment, even if excessive, warmed and encouraged her.

"I have been thinking about the small spare room that Stella used to have," she said, brushing away a wasp that was hovering over a sticky patch of spilt beer on the table. "Obviously, it's empty now she's moved into my father's old room. And while you have these problems with your house, well, it could be helpful for you to have the use of it. I mean it would save all the tedious business of getting back to Balham late at the end of an evening and disturbing your sister into the bargain. It's only a slip of a room, but for the purposes of a temporary arrangement it might be helpful." Hugh said nothing. A silence elapsed and Lily immediately felt appalled by her misjudgement. He saw her offer for what it was, a ruse to lure him into a defined relationship that she had assumed they both desired. She flapped more vigorously at the persistent wasp.

"My sister will be relieved," Hugh said eventually, "but Helen, let's focus on my feelings." And he leant across the table and kissed her generously. "Quite frankly, I'm taken aback. By your generosity. You really do take care of the waifs and strays, don't you? First there's our lovely Stella in need of a home and now me. Are you absolutely sure? I mean there's your formidable aunt to consider. Would she not consider this an immoral gesture of yours, inviting a single man to move into her late brother's house?"

"It's my house now," Lily said swiftly. But at the same time, she realised that her intention had been entirely misconstrued. Her offer was for Hugh to stay merely at weekends, to confirm by her gesture that she would be happy for him to share her bed. She had not intended asking him to move in to Alfred Street and live with her full time.

But it seemed too late to retract. To define clinically the terms of their arrangement.

Already the matter seemed to have become a fait accompli. Hugh's mood was ebullient.

"I can't tell you what this means to me, dear Helen. And I promise not to get constantly under your feet. What with my various work engagements I certainly won't be sitting at home all day long. And naturally I'll contribute to household bills. Food and electricity and all that sort of thing. You must let me know whatever you think is appropriate." Firmly, he took both of her hands in his. "And the moment my own place is safe for human habitation once more, I'll be out of your hair within a day or so and that's a promise."

His gratitude was consoling. His need, after all, was greater than her qualms about the escalation of what she had intended. Besides, it was an affirmation of the depth of his affections for her.

"Of course, the house might be a bit chaotic with all the work going on," she said, "although the new kitchen should be finished soon and really there's nothing else urgent that needs doing. Stella seems to think a new bathroom would be a good idea, but I'm not sure that's entirely necessary." She paused. The pace of events over the past few minutes had been so rapid that she felt breathless. As if a divide had been inadvertently crossed with implications she had not even considered or intended. To convince herself as much as Hugh, she said, "It simply seems to make practical sense, you moving in to Alfred Street, doesn't it? With things as they are at present."

Hugh grasped her hands even more tightly. The signet ring he wore on his smallest finger crushed her flesh.

"It makes more than mere practical sense, Helen. At least for me. I so hope you are feeling exactly the same. About us, I mean. And our future. I suspect you are."

A couple hovered close to their table, staring at their empty glasses with intent. The wasp was still bothering her. Lily stood up.

"We should go," she said. "People need our table."

17

By mid-June, 8 Alfred Street no longer seemed a silent refuge at any moment of the day. Once the basement remodelling was complete, refitting took place. Lily had never thought about worktops. Had been unaware that people had begun to make social distinctions between materials and had relied on Stella's patient explanation that ceramic tiles or something called Corian had replaced Formica by choice. When it came to the flooring, Lily had been indebted to Frank, one of the plasterers, who had pointed out, during a tea break and another of his numerous cigarettes, that the original oak flooring, once sanded, would provide a perfectly serviceable, hard-wearing surface. Stella had been sceptical, but Lily for once had been adamant. She would, she said firmly, like to retain something of the natural fabric of the place. Something, she thought covertly, that her father would recognise.

One day she returned from school to see the carcasses of units being constructed and fitted along the walls and assumed that at some point in their lengthy discussions a choice had been made, although she was vague about the moment of resolution. Stella had introduced her to Rupert, whose services as a carpenter she said she had been fortunate in obtaining since he was evidently widely in demand in north London. *He owes me a favour*, Stella had said somewhat archly, perching against the new cooker that had been installed the previous day. Rupert, extraordinarily thin and pale as if he rarely ate or emerged from sunless basement kitchens, ignored the two of them, ignored the coffee and cake Lily proffered mid-evening and eventually left the house just before midnight, acknowledging Stella's promise to *settle up financially over the weekend* with a weary grunt.

The costs involved, the constant flow of cash, had initially shocked Lily. She had never thought of herself as parsimonious, but frugality was, perhaps, simply ingrained in her by upbringing. Stella carefully listed the break-down of outgoings, showed her the cashbook in which costs for materials and labour were being recorded and insisted that she had brokered good deals by using personal contacts. Lily had not objected. She was, after all, naïve about such matters. And she knew she could afford the work. Sums that sat passively in savings accounts appeared to be accruing interest at a surprising level, swelling the total so it was only appropriate to pass on some of her financial good fortune to those seeking sound employment. Anna and Simon seemed to be taking a particular interest in the renovations, standing outside the house one day to stare with blatant interest, commenting to Lily that the value of any property depended not only on the individual worth of a house, but on the collective quality of the road. Lily, indifferent to the point, had nevertheless accepted their subsequent invitation to a glass of wine and had sat at their enormous, scrubbed pine table, sensing her elevation in their view as a result of her radical expenditure.

And then Hugh.

He had swiftly moved in while she had been at work one day, resisting her offer to drive to Balham to help.

"There's still so much in Fulham, of course," he said as he carried two slender suitcases upstairs, "although much has gone into storage, naturally. Anyway, there's sufficient here to tide me over and I don't want to endanger my welcome by cluttering up your home, Helen."

"You won't," she said. But he was insistent.

"No. You are the most generous of people, but Stella and I need to remind ourselves constantly that we are your guests and must behave accordingly."

Initially, he occupied the single bed in the narrow room along with his possessions. Lily tried to feel grateful for his lack of presumption, the discretion of his attitude yet at the same time she felt marginally shunned by the continuing chaste nature of their relationship. As if, in spite of his endearments, his tactile gestures towards her, he thought of her as an unsuitable subject for a lover.

And perhaps, Lily thought, with private humiliation, she was just that.

For the first couple of weeks, he was frequently out, leaving early, returning late, a sudden flurry of tedious, uninspiring jobs, as he termed them, dismissing Lily's curiosity with a wave of the hand, saying he would be too embarrassed to explain the banality of the work. *It's hardly a summer season at Stratford, after all*, he said somewhat sourly as he left the house one morning around seven, a slice of toast and marmalade in on hand, a thermos flask of coffee in the other. She watched him walk briskly to the end of the road, wondered whether Anna and Simon and her other neighbours – the couple opposite with the new baby and an even newer red Porsche, the man next to them who was something in the City and went running every morning at an early hour – had noticed the addition to her household. Had noticed Hugh.

Lily hoped that they had.

And she began to be grateful for the muddle over her invitation, saw it as expedient rather than unfortunate. Why should Hugh not move in full time while his own house was uninhabitable? His presence would undoubtedly afford her visibility among her neighbours that her single, unremarkable self appeared to lack. These successful, striving inhabitants of Alfred Street, the Annas and the Simons, the bankers, the brokers, the fledgling politicians were like members of a tribe, with a shared sense of appropriate values. Stella understood this. She knew how to thrive amidst them, how to keep apace and emulate their material goals, acquire the trappings, the tropes and tokens of their prosperity. The zeitgeist, after all, was key and Stella breathed it, lived and transmitted it like one born for the purpose. Without Stella, without Hugh to complete their domestic triangle, Lily felt she would flounder, rudderless, ignorant, as the century shifted towards its final extravagant blazon.

★★★

"So rather a whimsical choice for the society's end of year extravaganza," Hugh said, sitting on a chair in the vast expanse of the new kitchen at the new table commissioned and custom-built by Rupert, Stella's carpenter acquaintance. "And American accents will be a challenge for a lot of the cast, I should imagine."

"I've always loved the play," Lily said, handing Hugh a copy of *Our Town*. "And it seems to be a popular choice with the other members. We can be lenient about accents, after all."

"So you want me to play the Stage Manager – the effective narrator of the piece?"

"We could divide the role into two if you prefer," Lily suggested. "I have seen it performed like that. Years ago."

She had seen the play with Toby Jessop. A drama school production, she remembered now, in a small theatre somewhere near the university. She had been anxious at the time that someone might see them, her unease spoiling the pleasure of the evening. Now she only chose to recall how moved she had been by the performance. Where Hugh might see whimsy, she found only pathos in the tenderness and truth of the story.

"That won't be necessary," Hugh said curtly. "I mean either I'm good enough to take on reading the entire role or I'm not. I don't think it's beyond my capabilities."

"I didn't mean that," Lily said, "of course not." She turned away, looked for the kettle and had to remind herself of the kitchen's new layout. There was silence between them for a moment, filled only by the enthusiastic gush of the new cold tap that was still a novelty after the sluggishness of the old one. Lily looked blankly at the cups.

"Sorry," Hugh said eventually. "I'm in an appalling mood after a day of role-play nonsense with a whole load of inane salesmen with the charisma of a bunch of toads. Hardly stuff to warm a thespian's heart."

"I can imagine," Lily said.

"But entirely unfair of me to bring my low spirits home to you, Helen. After all, you have your own frustrations with the school admin office, I'm sure."

"Not really," Lily said honestly. "Apart from elements of boredom."

"Anyway, I will be delighted to take on the whole of the Stage Manager as Thornton Wilder intended it. No need to see it as a burden for me, Helen. And I will make a reasonable stab at the accent, I'm sure. I played a bit of Tennessee Williams in rep days, some Miller too, of course. Those were the days when managements seemed capable of putting on decent drama and I was proud to call myself an actor."

Lily brought tea over to the table.

"I admire your resilience," she said, "your willingness to adapt."

He misunderstood her.

"Well, the former working men's club in King's Cross is hardly a glamorous venue, I'll give you that," he said. "And curiously enough, however seedy and run-down some of those old rep theatres were, there was a sort of raffish, louche allure to them."

"Not that, I meant the way you've embraced the changes to the profession. You haven't been tempted to give up and turned to – well, become a driving instructor. Or a bookkeeper or whatever disgruntled actors do." Hugh shrugged, but did not seem to be pacified. He drank his tea in silence, then picked up his copy of the play again, found a pencil in his pocket and began marking the text. Lily noticed that two buttons were missing from his light blue shirt and another was threatening to fall, lingering on a very loose thread. "I respect you for that," she went on, trying to shift his morose mood. "And your willingness to be involved in the Play Reading Society, of course. Some might see it as a busman's holiday without any pay."

He looked up and stared across the table at her as if only just noticing that she was there. Then his gaze shifted down the length of the room, to the French windows in the end wall that now opened onto the courtyard garden, encouraging light into the previously dark basement.

"I must say, Helen," he said, "Stella's done an admirable job. This place is a real joy now, isn't it? I'm sure you feel indebted to her."

"Of course," Lily said.

"She's someone with real vision. And imagination. Qualities not as common as you'd think. What does Lady Bracknell think of it all?"

"Who?"

"Aunt Dorothy, the dragon aunt. Something faintly Wildean about the woman, I'd say."

Lily hesitated. So far, she had been cautious with revealing too much about the level of change to her aunt. She intended being entirely silent on the cost.

"She likes Stella," she said evasively, "admires her enterprise and ingenuity. I think I've been a bit of a disappointment to her in that area."

Although even as she said the words, it occurred to Lily that it had been conformity and acceptance that had always been sought from her rather than initiative.

"Well, you know the saying, Helen?" Hugh said.

"Saying?"

"*They also serve who only stand and wait.* Or some such nonsense."

"Yes, perhaps," Lily said. "Although that could sound like an excuse for complacency."

Hugh, engrossed in his script again, looked up only briefly to ask if there was any more tea.

★★★

There was a full attendance. The last meeting of the season was always sociable, an extended interval for refreshments and the habit of prolonging the evening at a wine bar in Camden. Lily, with her commitment to drive Agnes home, had never been, but as she sat listening to the first half, to Hugh's dominating performance and to the play's tender depiction of life in Grover's Corners, Massachusetts, at the turn of the 20th century, she regretted her obligation. Previously indifferent to the idea of a crowded bar and drinking at a late hour, she was sure that Hugh would be eager to go and she did not want to disappoint him.

The evening was sultry after a day that had failed to provide a storm to break high humidity. Fire escape doors had been opened onto the narrow alleyway that ran behind the building so that the constant thrum of traffic, occasional sirens from ambulances, competed with the reading. In the interval, the hall emptied out into the confined space and paper cups were produced for the warm acidic white wine and cider that was circulating. Hugh, perched on a low brick wall, found space for Lily.

"My scepticism was misplaced, Helen. Clearly, everyone's loving the play. Although I have to say the American accent is something of a challenge for certain cast members." He lowered his voice, spoke close to Lily's face. "That woman playing Mrs Gibbs – not so much New Hampshire as New Orleans, I'd say. What's her name?"

Lily glanced across at the auburn-haired woman wearing a vivid yellow dress and high heeled sandals, wedged against the railings at one end of the alleyway. She was laughing loudly at something someone had said, spilling wine from the precarious paper cup onto bare toes.

"Amanda," she said, "Amanda Harris. She's one of our newer members. And I'm sure she's doing her best."

"Oh she's competent enough as an actress. Quite good, in fact, but accents are clearly not her thing."

"She has my sympathies," Lily said. "I would be far too self-conscious even to attempt one."

"Not even if I promised to coach you? Come on, Helen, you never know your strengths until you try."

"Too late now," Lily said with relief. She swallowed the remains of her cup, resisted Hugh's attempts to refill it. "And it's time to start the second half or the caretaker will be throwing us out before the final act."

"I think I'll just have a word," Hugh said, inclining his

head in the direction of Amanda Harris. "Suggest she relaxes a little and lets the words speak for themselves. Not sure if I can tolerate that inappropriate drawl for the rest of the evening."

"I wouldn't," Lily said firmly. But Hugh appeared not to hear, making his way towards her at the end of the alleyway, competing with the traffic of people heading back inside.

As expected, there was a move by a dozen or more to prolong the evening when the reading finished. It had been judged an enormous success, a highlight of the season, as the chairman termed it in his few concluding words, and Hugh's performance in particular was admired. Lily stood back, watching him receive the accolades from a few enthusiastic members who gathered around him, aware of the importance he would attach to such recognition. However much he would dismiss such a suggestion, even an audience of amateur enthusiasts was superior to no audience at all.

He was at her side within moments.

"The night is still young, I see," he said, as the hall began to empty. "We must join them. What could be better on a warm summer evening than to get mildly intoxicated? It's not even as if I have any work tomorrow, although that's nothing to brag about, of course."

"It's difficult for me," she said to him quietly, "I have to give Agnes a lift home. I always do."

Hugh looked irritated. "Surely she can make her own way for once. After all, it's midsummer and barely dark." Lily glanced across at Agnes, patiently waiting in anticipation, her pale paisley summer dress of indeterminate fashion suddenly seeming contrary to the vibrant mood of the evening. "But of course, if you feel obliged, more obliged to poor old Agnes than to me, I shall quite understand."

"Wait," Lily said swiftly. "I won't be a moment." She took a couple of pound notes from her purse, went over to Agnes and pressed them into her hand. "For a taxi," she said to her quietly. "They're so easy to pick up on the Euston Road. Would you mind just this once?" Agnes looked at the notes and passed them firmly back to Lily.

"That's entirely unnecessary," she said calmly. "The bus will do." She glanced over at the swelling number heading for Camden and the wine bar. "Enjoy the rest of your evening, Lily. And perhaps we can catch up over the summer if you have time?"

"Yes, of course," Lily said, gratified that Agnes was so conciliatory. "I'll be sure to ring you and we'll arrange something."

The wine bar was loud and dense with people and it was hard to see anyone they recognised. Lily lost sight of Hugh within moments as he went off in search of a table and she found herself stranded, trying to resist being stepped upon and buffeted by the persistent traffic. She felt self-conscious, unaccommodated by the surroundings. A distance of at least two decades appeared to lay between her and the crowd of drinkers and she wished she had made some effort to dissuade Hugh. The thought of the house in Alfred Street, of the routine of driving Agnes home, her quiet company, seemed curiously appealing and it was only the prospect of Hugh's confusion if she simply retreated that kept her rooted to the spot. Minutes passed. Ten, at least, and she began to feel ridiculous, an object that people had to circumnavigate with bottles and glasses held high to avoid her. Eventually, a gap cleared to allow her to see to the end of the room and some familiar faces sitting around a table in the corner, their heads close together as if trying to make themselves heard above the noise. There was the young man in the white T-shirt who had read the part of George, his girlfriend who had played Emily, and Amanda Harris in the vibrant yellow outfit with Thomas, the treasurer of the society. And Hugh.

Hugh, with an empty chair next to him, leaning forward and laughing at something one of the others had said.

"Helen!" He pushed a glass towards her, splashed the remains of a bottle into it. "We were wondering wherever you'd got to. We were just toasting the success of the evening, weren't we? Although there doesn't seem a lot left of this stuff. Anyone fancy making their way to the bar or attracting attention? There should be table service, although I doubt we'll have much luck with that tonight."

Thomas said something about trying his luck at the bar, but Amanda stopped him and stood up, waving the empty bottle wildly at a woman collecting glasses. Lily discreetly poured most of the contents of her glass into Hugh's. Her car was in the street and would need to be driven home. Conversation was near impossible, although that appeared not to trouble the others, who simply doubled their volume attempting to compete. Another bottle of wine arrived, which Hugh duly dispensed. He had just started to say something to Lily about others from the society abandoning the effort of finding space and moving on elsewhere when Amanda upset a glass and there was a confusion of hands, attempting to mop and stanch the pale liquid that dripped across the table onto laps and to the floor. Emily jumped up as the skirt of her pink dress behaved like blotting paper, at the same time upsetting another glass that redoubled the damage. Hugh retrieved broken stems and large shards of glass from the pool gathering on the floor and placed them like trophies on the table in front of them all. The situation was apparently viewed as hilarious. Lily watched with some detachment. Found tissues in her bag and passed them to the two women.

"How idiotic of me!" Amanda said, mopping her dress

extravagantly, "I am the clumsiest of people. I'm always doing things like this. So typical."

"Nonsense, anyone can see these tables are far too small," Hugh said. "As long as no-one's been cut by any splinters of glass, that's the main thing. They can be the devil."

"What a caring thing to say," Amanda placed her hand lightly on Hugh's. "Goodness, wish my ex-husband had been the considerate sort. But then of course, he wouldn't be my ex if he had been."

Again, laughter erupted. Hugh went in search of someone to clear the broken glass and conversation moved on to holiday plans. The young couple talked about camping in Cornwall, Thomas said something about Scotland and fly fishing. Amanda looked bleak and said that solicitors' fees over her divorce settlement had scuppered the notion of holidays for years to come in addition to being drained dry by two student sons. Then she turned to Thomas and started to talk about Scotland, a long tale about a trip to the Highlands that was barely audible. No-one, Lily noted, asked about her plans, for which she was relieved. Her obligatory week in Wales with her aunt was unlikely to be of any interest and she had not yet mentioned it to Hugh. He returned and suggested they move to another table, but it was near closing time, the place emptying around them.

"About time our old-fashioned licensing hours were revised," Hugh said as they all made their way to the door and out onto the narrow pavement. "Can you imagine bars in southern Europe closing so early? It's barely eleven, after all."

"So is that where you're heading for your summer hols, Hugh? Let me guess, southern Italy? The Greek islands?" Amanda grasped at Lily's arm as if in need of steadying herself. "How about popping me in your suitcase?"

"No firm plans yet," Hugh said, "and, of course, as a

jobbing actor I don't have the advantage of a paid break from work."

Amanda's curiosity seemed fleeting and she turned her attention to Thomas, suggested they share a taxi to Waterloo. As they all prepared to go in their separate directions, she suddenly called out, "Tell you what, how about a barbecue over the summer? At my place in Richmond, I mean. Yes, that's what we'll do. I mean, it seems such a long break without seeing each other and at least, Hugh, we can then all drink as late as we like in the garden with only the stuffy neighbours to complain." The idea was greeted warmly, although Lily imagined that Amanda would forget her suggestion by the next day once the effects of alcohol had worn off. "I'll be in touch with all of you about a suitable date, then! I must have your phone numbers somewhere," she called, waving as she headed down the road, clutching at Thomas's arm.

There was a new skip outside the house in Alfred Street.

Hugh said lightly, "More renovations, Lily? More disruption? You could at least give your house guests some warning."

"I don't understand," she said, manoeuvring the car with some difficulty into a space behind it. "I don't remember agreeing any further work with Stella. At least not at the moment." She felt overwhelmingly tired. As if the elation from the success of the evening, the subsequent hour or so spent in the fevered atmosphere of the crowded wine bar had drained her of all thought and energy. She wanted only to climb the stairs to her bedroom and lie down, incapable of confronting Stella, that mildly frenetic enthusiasm and decisive manner of hers when she was captured by an idea.

"I wouldn't worry too much," Hugh said. "She's a pretty capable project manager, isn't she? Leave it all in her hands if I were you. Anyway, it's far too late to worry about such things tonight. I'd suggest a conference around the kitchen table tomorrow evening."

Lily fumbled for door keys, let Hugh use his instead and followed him into the hallway. The house was dark, Stella either out or already asleep. She tried to remember when she had last seen her and realised it must have been before the weekend.

"Yes, good idea," she said, "and perhaps it's simply something I've forgotten about." She knew, however, that there had been no arrangement for any more immediate work, remembered saying she was relieved that her neighbours would not be disturbed by noise through open windows during the summer months. She turned towards the old kitchen in need of a glass of water and found herself standing in an empty room, the original geography of the house too ingrained for her to shift habit easily. Hugh had already gone downstairs and she heard the kettle being filled, mugs being lifted from hooks. She had no wish for tea at such an hour, but his gesture was thoughtful.

"Of course, there was that business about the bathroom," he said. "Not too strong? I always forget how weak you like it." He liberally splashed more milk into the mug.

"The bathroom?"

"The idea of an additional one. On the first floor. Stella was saying how you thought it would be a good idea."

"Did I? Well, at some point, perhaps."

"She said you weren't keen on the thought of all of us using the same one. I mean, after all, one has to respect boundaries."

"Boundaries?"

"Stella is a young woman, after all." Hugh spoke with deliberation. "I am an unrelated male and I wouldn't want there to be any embarrassing incidents."

Lily had no memory of such a comment to Stella. Perhaps the girl herself felt concerned.

"There's a lock," she said and tried the tea. It was tepid, drowned by milk. "On the bathroom door, I mean."

Hugh laughed.

"Of course there is, Helen! Really, forget the whole subject. One bathroom can serve the whole household perfectly well. A lot of people living in London would be grateful even for that."

"Exactly." Lily thought of the old, denuded kitchen, at the extravagance of the conversion when provision had, after all, already been adequate. But perhaps that was her trouble. She had lived an adequate, blandly satisfactory life for so long that she had not noticed the shift in attitude. Expectation, a certain sense of entitlement to material comforts which would have seemed the preserve of the excessively wealthy to her father, to her aunt, appeared to have become obligatory. At least to those who were fortunate enough to be living somewhere salubrious like Alfred Street. Lily was all too aware of the inequality of such privilege. Hugh was saying something about a call he had at the end of the week for extra work in a film to be shot in the west country. During August, he said resentfully, which would put paid to them having a decent holiday.

"I didn't know we were planning on one." Lily said. "We've not discussed it, after all." Hugh looked sheepish. "Well, as I said to Amanda this evening, when the work's around one just has to take it. That's the trouble with knowing an ageing actor who must grovel for every pathetic opportunity. Not ideal material for a partner, Helen."

"And are you?" Lily said impulsively. It was the lateness of the hour, that loose time past midnight that seemed to allow for uninhibited speech that could be forgotten if necessary by morning. "Are you my partner, Hugh? Are we in a relationship? Or do you see yourself simply as my lodger and likely to move out any time it suits you?"

He looked shocked as if Lily had insulted him. He reached out his hand across the table, took hers.

"My dear Helen, have I really been so remiss in letting you think such a thing?"

The front door banged, making them both jump and pull apart. There were rapid footsteps down the bare stairs and Stella appeared. She dropped her bag and headed to the sink, holding back her hair as she held her face under a running cold tap. She emerged, slumped down next to Hugh.

"So humid!" she said. "I swear I'm dehydrated. If this is going to be summer in London I need to be heading elsewhere."

"Curiously enough, we were just talking summer plans, weren't we, Helen? Or rather we were wondering about the skip outside. A bit of a surprise to come home to, I must say." He sounded gently censorious, the tone of a father whose indulgence was being tested.

"Oh that! Didn't I mention it to you both? I felt sure I'd checked it was all right. But skips can be hard to come by these days with everyone making demands for them so I just grabbed it when I saw it was available. Thought you'd be relieved."

"A little prior warning might have been helpful, but fortunately we are flexible individuals, wouldn't you say, Helen?"

"Possibly," Lily said. A headache was beginning to form, throbbing in her left temple.

"I know it means more upheaval," Stella swiftly admitted. "But minimal, actually, in comparison with all this." She waved her hand in the air meaningfully, a conductor of her own composition.

"We're talking about the additional bathroom?" Hugh clarified.

"Of course! Lily, you know it makes sense. I mean, this house of yours now has four floors!"

"I think you'll find it always had four, Stella," Hugh said somewhat proprietorially. "But we take your point. And where are you planning on siting this additional convenience? Just to keep us au fait with the changes?"

Stella looked surprised. As if the question was futile.

"Well, in that slip of a room where you've got your stuff," she said. "On the first floor, of course. It's the obvious place."

"And my stuff, as you call it, is to go – where, exactly?"

"My father's old study," Lily said firmly. "It's a far bigger room, after all."

"There you go!" Stella banged one hand on the table as if some sort of enormous resolution had been reached. "Which means, you two will have the current bathroom to yourselves and I won't be bothering you with my wet towels and long strands of hair clogging the plug hole. So disgusting, I know. And as for adding to the worth of the house, Lily, it's a win–win situation. The costs of putting a bathroom in are just negligible compared to the increase in value. I know you can see that. But sorry if things are going a bit fast for you both." She beamed at the two of them as if she saw her youth triumphing over the pointless caution of seniority. "But once a decision is made there's no point not acting on it, not while I've got the necessary tradesmen on board."

Lily wanted to say something about decisions over the house being solely her concern and of no relevance to Hugh, but she had no wish to sound confrontational. She stood up and placed her mug in the sink.

"All right," she said, "I can see that it makes sense to go ahead now if there are people available to do the work." She glanced at the time. Already it was well past one. She left the two of them talking about the difficulties of finding reliable labour and went to bed, expecting to fall asleep within moments. But instead she was restless, going over the practicalities of her spontaneous offer to Hugh. Although her father's study had been slimmed down, only a handful of his books now remaining, it was by no means entirely cleared. His desk, his chair and, of course, that casket was still sitting on the highest shelf.

His ashes, unscattered.

Before she went to work in the morning, she slipped into his study and removed the casket, feeling furtive as she placed it on the floor of the large wardrobe on the landing, partly hidden by the heavy hem of her late mother's fur coat. That evening, Hugh had moved the bed from the slip room up to the study, pushing the heavy desk against the wall and arranging his few possessions on the shelves, hanging a couple of jackets on the back of the door.

Her father, Lily noted, seemed finally and entirely absent from the house. Only his ashes remained.

It was another week before Hugh came to her bedroom. He had tried to return to their conversation, saying abruptly to her one evening when the two of them were finishing dinner that he had not wanted to presume. That the situation was delicate for him, living in Lily's house, but that perhaps he had been too cautious, too concerned with taking a wrong, premature step. Lily had said nothing. Her silence, however, seemed to serve as a sanction. And she surprised herself on that first occasion by her confidence in encouraging his embraces, by the spontaneity of her reactions as if this were a perfectly regular occurrence, a routine event in her life whereas in truth it had been years. Afterwards, Hugh had slept swiftly, easily. Whereas Lily had stayed awake. Relieved that what she and Hugh now shared gave them definition, a legitimacy, at least in the eyes of others who no doubt already assumed. As Stella had long assumed. She had glanced sideways at Hugh as he slept, his head turned away from her, his breathing even and deep, and had adjusted herself to the breach between expectation and truth.

There had been, after all, only Toby Jessop, that furtive time of intense, clandestine encounters, followed a couple of years later by a very brief and self-serving concern best forgotten. A solitary, strange man she had met in a queue for a play or performance of some sort, who had served her undefined purpose after she had learnt of Toby's marriage. She had loved Toby with blind ardour. For the near stranger, there had been utter indifference, even a faint repulsion and their few liaisons had, for her, been calculated, cold.

Nevertheless.

She had still been young.

At a stage in her life when any act of lovemaking was inevitably charged by the precipitous sense of possible conception. Of dicing with fate, with fortune, whatever the precautions. And however fearful Lily might have felt in the past about risk, with Toby, with the curious man on those random occasions in his dank room in Harlesden, there had been compensation in the heightened significance of the act, its enriched potency.

But no longer.

Lily blamed herself. Hugh had been, after all, perfectly attentive, considerate. Any sense of a perfunctory nature in the whole matter was no doubt her own failing. Her inevitable inadequacies as a woman over fifty foolishly anticipating the easy ecstasies found at thirty.

No matter. Hugh Murray was now undeniably her partner and his regard for her, a man with no motive other than his deep affections, was demonstrable. She was replete.

She wondered how much she would tell her aunt.

18

Dorothy looked disparagingly at the bowl of new potatoes and sliced tomatoes.

"It's too hot for a roast meal," Lily said defensively. She passed a plate with a substantial serving of cold chicken. "After all, it was nearly 30 degrees yesterday and it's forecast to get hotter next week. In London, anyway."

"Stella not here?" Dorothy said, salad server in hand as if her absence was mitigation for the meal.

"No, she's away," Lily said.

"Ah, well, of course. She's a sensible girl and no doubt got herself out of the city for the summer."

"Just the weekend, I think," Lily said. Although in truth she had no idea. Stella's movements were unpredictable, her absences random, but then she was under no obligation to explain herself. Hugh was always solicitous in such matters, excusing himself from Dorothy's visit that day as he had a call for a training film and had left early.

"I see we are no longer using the dining room," Dorothy said, dousing her potatoes liberally with butter. "It's all very modern, this kitchen eating, I suppose."

"I thought it would be cooler today." The French doors, wide open onto the courtyard garden, allowed some respite from the heat. Her aunt had been surprisingly reticent about the changes to the house. Even the news of the extra bathroom that was nearing completion had been met only by a mildly caustic comment that people nowadays were spoilt beyond measure. Lily had silently agreed. Yet at the same time admitted to Stella that she was looking forward to the practicality of the additional room. Dorothy was saying something about hoping for cooler temperatures in Wales. About the necessity to leave early in the morning to avoid gridlocks on the M4. Lily, who had spent the past month stalling in her mind the prospect of the week, agreed.

Hugh had been understanding when she had explained her holiday commitment to Dorothy. Her duty to her aunt was paramount, naturally, and anyway he was anticipating a busy working summer himself. But in future years, they must plan a proper holiday together and where else but Greece? He was counting on her to introduce him to the country, to share her knowledge and love of the place. The prospect was heartening to Lily.

Dorothy took more chicken. Another two potatoes.

"No doubt it will rain in Wales," she said. "It always does. A pity, really. They say the scenery is marvellous if you ever get to see it."

"We might be lucky. There seems no let-up in this heatwave." Lily gave up even making a pretence of eating, went to the fridge to replenish the water jug with ice cubes.

"This arrangement with these two friends of yours," Dorothy said, staring suspiciously at the carrot Lily had grated into neat mounds in the bowl of salad, "I presume it's all above board. Financially, I mean?" Lily pretended to be distracted by the splutter of ice against glass. "I wouldn't want to think that you were being exploited in any way."

"Of course not," she said evasively, swiftly adding to avoid further probing, "but it's more a case of my indebtedness to Stella. She's been wonderful, managing the renovations, finding the tradesmen. I couldn't have done any of it without her. And as for Hugh – well, he's a close friend. And, while his house is unfit to live in, it simply makes sense for him to stay here."

Dorothy said nothing, but her silence felt reproachful. Lily removed plates, placed a bowl of soft fruit, a jug of cream on the table. She was too aware of subjects unbroached to be comfortable with her aunt's curiosity. In spite of Hugh's initial insistence on contributing to household expenses, the conversation had never resumed and it now seemed awkward given their relationship. Besides, Lily reasoned with herself, it was summer, minimal gas and electricity bills, and his occupation in the house was only of a temporary nature. And he did contribute. In his way. He would bring home bottles of wine, ground coffee sought out from specialist shops, occasionally chocolates. And always the weekend newspapers that the two of them would sit over for hours, a habit that seemed to pertain to couples, Lily noted, and consequently embraced with pleasure.

And as for Stella.

Lily was sure that her gain was so much in excess of the extravagance of her household spending that it was not even worth defending. Fortunately, her aunt had moved on to more immediate concerns.

"Is there cheese, Lily? After all, it's been a very light meal. I always think that salad is unsatisfactory. Especially for Sunday lunch."

★★★

Hugh helped her with a meticulous route to Pembrokeshire. He brought home an ordnance survey map and spread it out on the kitchen table, pencilled in the village where her aunt's friend lived. Lily, who had not thought beyond the M4 and sufficient change for the toll on the suspension bridge, was grateful.

"Of course," he said, noting down B roads and ways of avoiding likely bottlenecks near popular coastal towns, "next year we'll be planning our Greek tour. Our odyssey, we could call it. In fact, Helen, we'll dedicate the dark months of winter to it. A way of relieving the oppression of the season by thinking of our Mediterranean destination."

The prospect of a week in her aunt's company immediately became more bearable for Lily.

"My father was so devoted to Athens. And Epidaurus and Delphi, of course," she said, "but it meant I didn't get to see other places very much. Crete, for example. I always wanted to go there. I tried to convince him, but with increasing age he just wanted to go back to the places he knew. As if he felt there wasn't time for more discovery and simply wanted to consolidate what was already familiar."

Or it was his obstinacy, Lily thought, a stubbornness that became more entrenched as he grew into old age, resisting change. Particularly any change that stemmed from a suggestion of hers as if it lacked validity and value.

Hugh folded the map with care, presented it to her with some formality.

"We will do it all, dear Helen, in our own good time. Mainland, sites of antiquity and myth. And the islands. Crete, of course, if you wish. Don't forget, you lead and I will follow. Now, how is that car of yours? Oil and water levels all checked? We don't want you and the aged aunt breaking down before you've even left the suburbs. And those Welsh hills will prove demanding."

Lily thought fleetingly of Hugh's late wife. No doubt he was excessively vigilant when it came to cars. To the possibility of tragic accidents.

"It's booked in for a service this week," she said, "and thank you for your concern. To my aunt, I'm merely the taxi driver."

"Nonsense. I'm sure she's looking forward to having you to herself for a few days. Or at least in conjunction with this friend of hers. She must feel very maternal towards you, given your circumstances."

"Possibly," Lily said uncertainly. For, although there had been scant demonstrable evidence from her aunt over the years, no doubt such love displayed itself in a myriad of ways.

"So, you and Stella are in charge," she went on. "Of the house, I mean. I'm leaving you responsible for restraining her in any more extravagant renovation projects!"

Hugh nodded with mock solemnity.

"You have my word, Helen. No gazebos or atriums or mezzanines to be constructed under my watch."

"And the cat, of course. It's such a relief not to have to go round begging neighbours to feed Hector."

"All in good hands. And you are to ring me when you arrive, remember. Just to reassure me. Am I being too appallingly protective?"

"Not at all," Lily said, "of course I'll ring."

His concern was heartening.

★★★

The house was not as remote as Dorothy had implied.

Within walking distance of a large village and a spectacular sandy bay, Lily was able to leave the two women after breakfast and head either to the shore or to browse in the collection of small shops until she felt obliged to return for lunch.

The heat continued.

Dorothy complained constantly that her bedroom was a furnace, sleep was impossible and that it would be unwise for her to venture out for any sight-seeing in view of the high temperatures. Her friend, Norah, was quietly hospitable but subdued and Lily could not help wondering whether she was regretting the invitation. She did her best to find shady spots in her attractive garden for them to sit and seemed anxious to placate Dorothy with regular meals and refreshments, but Lily sensed that her aunt's endless conversation was a strain on her natural reserve. The enormous stretch of bay was busy, cars parked at the rear of the sands to offload the paraphernalia of families eager to make the most of the sun, but Lily found it too cold for swimming, flinching when the chilled waters ran over her bare feet.

One morning, Dorothy appeared briefly at breakfast to say that, after a night with indifferent sleep, she had decided to return to bed for a few hours. Norah and Lily listened to her ponderous tread on the stairs, the door of her guest room firmly closing, and drank their tea in silence. The letter box flapped. A grey cat sneaked across the lawn pursuing a sparrow. The hall clock chimed nine.

"Could I join you this morning?" Norah said. "Wherever you were planning on going. I am feeling a little housebound, I must say. Although if I'd be a nuisance to you, you've only to say."

"Of course not," Lily said. "Although I don't have anywhere particular in mind."

"I'll be back by lunch time, for Dorothy," Norah added hastily as if Lily might be concerned her aunt was in danger of neglect.

They walked the short distance to the beach, then took the steps up to the headland that overlooked the bay with extensive views back over the village and out to sea.

"It's a beautiful place," Lily said, scanning the coastline. There was a soft breeze that relieved the heat of the day that was already building. "Although very quiet in the winter without the visitors, I suppose."

"Yes, some people would no doubt find it too deserted, isolated even. But there's a strong sense of community and I've never regretted moving here. And I enjoy my own company. I have my books. My hobbies. Of course, loneliness is inevitable at times, but that falls into every life. I can't blame the place for that. In fact, I have come to realise that a certain solitariness probably suits my nature. I have always found too much company rather overwhelming."

The friendship between her aunt and this gentle, tentative woman suddenly seemed improbable.

"I understand that you and my aunt used to be very close," Lily said. "The best of friends, according to Dorothy."

Norah said nothing at first. She headed them towards a bench that had just been vacated by hikers, heavy with rucksacks and walking boots and sat down with some relief.

"Do you mind? It's age telling on me, Lily. I find standing quite a strain these days." She paused again, found sunglasses in her pocket, a white handkerchief and wiped mild sweat from her forehead. Then went on. "To tell you the truth, I was very surprised when Dorothy got in touch and asked me if she could come and stay. Well, if both of you could come, actually."

"My aunt invited herself?"

"Yes. Naturally, I'm happy to see her. And you, of course, Lily. Please don't think I'm not grateful for your company too."

"You worked together, I understand, in the civil service?"

"A very long time ago, yes," Norah said. "It's how we met. But Dorothy was always very senior to me. If I'm honest with you I was always rather frightened of her. Intimidated."

"Yet you were friends, surely."

Norah placed a pale, very freckled hand on Lily's and smiled.

"I think I was always rather flattered that someone so accomplished and assured as Dorothy sought out my company," Norah said. "Not just in the office, but at weekends. Picnics and Green line bus trips out to beauty spots in the home counties. That sort of thing. We even had one or two holidays together. A walking tour of the Lakes, I remember. That would have been just before the war, '38, perhaps, or was it even '39? Just before everything changed, anyway."

"And then you married?"

"Oh goodness me, no. That came years later when I was on the point of retirement. The prospect terrified me, if I'm truthful, living a life alone without the structure of a job and, as I saw it, little else to occupy me. I felt I was too inadequate to cope with the possible expanse of years that lay ahead of me. I was wrong, of course. Entirely wrong. There is no reason to believe that diversion and fulfilment lie solely in the company of other people. Quite the contrary, in fact. But it took a long time for me to believe in my own resilience."

The strap on Lily's sandal was rubbing and she slipped it off, stared down at the red welt on her toe joint and wished she had brought more sensible shoes. Hugh was right about the hilliness of the terrain and she felt unprepared. She had rung him on their first evening, slipping out to a public phone box with the excuse of needing to stretch her legs since she had no wish to draw her aunt's curiosity to her call. It was consoling, to hear his voice, to imagine him standing in the hallway of the house in Alfred Street and to know of his concern. A batch of assertive seagulls squawked too low overhead. A dog, hotly pursued by its owner, brushed past them, barking.

"I don't think my aunt has ever felt inadequate," Lily said, "or admitted to it, at least." She smiled at Norah, but the woman seemed lost to her own thoughts, staring out at the distant white capped waves in the bay. Lily glanced at her watch. "Shall we go into the village?" she said. "To the café and find something to drink?"

"I would like that very much, Lily," she said. "As long as we are back in time to make a proper lunch for Dorothy. She is very fond of her food, isn't she? Rather like my late husband, in fact. He was never one to compromise with a swift sandwich, needed a knife and fork in his hand and the table properly laid for every meal. It was quite an adjustment, I have to say, after only concerning myself with my own needs for so many years."

The remaining days of their visit were similarly undemanding. Lily read, walked, talked more to Norah who seemed to enjoy her company. She wondered why her aunt had found it necessary to play with the truth in claiming that the invitation had been Norah's suggestion.

And she thought constantly of Hugh.

Of Stella, even, with a sentimental concern that her absence would be an inconvenience to them both. Hugh could even be missing her. She allowed herself to luxuriate in the prospect, in knowing of another's regard for her that was voluntary, unhitched to the duty of familial connection.

Then suddenly Dorothy wanted to go home.

"Let's go back tomorrow," she said abruptly as they ate dinner on Thursday evening. "It will be a better day for travel rather than leaving it to the weekend and, really, I can't imagine that Harrow can be any hotter than here."

Norah did not object and Lily, feeling the woman's patience had already been sufficiently tested, swiftly agreed. She thought of ringing Hugh to tell him of her early return, but it seemed unnecessary, as if she was implying he needed to make particular preparations.

The roads were again busy and traffic was painfully slowed by endless caravans. Around lunch time, they turned off the main route and found a village pub with a pleasant, shady garden and a menu that placated Dorothy. Lily began to anticipate the rest of her summer now that her commitment to her aunt was fulfilled. There was still, after all, the whole of August. Perhaps she and Hugh could at least get out of London for a couple of days, somewhere by the sea to take advantage of the continuing fine weather. Dorothy ate steak and kidney pie with appetite, ordered pudding. Lily finished a small salad, drank coffee.

"Well, I can't say I envy Norah living in such an isolated place. Very unwise especially at her age. That garden is already too much for her, I suspect," Dorothy said.

"She seems quite content." Lily watched a dance of two butterflies over a neatly tended flower bed. "I'm not sure your sympathy is needed."

"Always a mistake to marry late like she did," her aunt went on as if she had not spoken. "I do hope you won't make a foolish error like that."

Lily was taken aback. She had assumed that Dorothy viewed her friendship with Hugh as purely platonic. But perhaps her remark was random rather than significant.

"I certainly have no plans," she said truthfully.

The ice cream in Dorothy's Sundae was melting rapidly. She dunked a crisp wafer into the pool of pale pink liquid.

"I used to think you might," she said, "at one time."

"I might what?" Lily glanced at her watch. They were barely halfway home.

"Marry. Years ago, I thought there was a possibility if someone suitable came along. A vicar, perhaps, or a teacher at a minor prep school, that sort of thing might have suited you. Of course, it would have been terribly inconvenient."

"Inconvenient?"

"For your father. Although, naturally, you would have stayed. Yes, that was the plan. After all, the house was easily big enough for three adults. If you had, by any chance, ever found yourself a husband."

"You sound as if there were contingencies in place," Lily said starkly.

"One always needs contingencies," Dorothy said, "for life in general. But of course it made it easier that you stayed as you were."

"Easier? Who for?"

Her aunt looked at Lily as if she was being obtuse. She gave up on the liquidised ice cream sundae, opened her handbag to retrieve her purse.

"My treat, Lily. Have you finished that coffee yet?"

Lily drained her cup.

"Yes, we should get going. We still have a long drive ahead of us."

It was early evening by the time she had dropped Dorothy home in Harrow. She let down the windows of the car to lose the cloying scent of her aunt's eau de cologne and drove towards Islington feeling buoyant. Always she enjoyed returning to the city after any absence, reclaiming her sense of ownership, of belonging, but now there was the anticipation of welcome. No doubt Stella would be out or away for the weekend, but there would be Hugh. Hugh would already be thinking of her return the following day, possibly tidying the house, stocking the fridge, herself the centre and focus of his plans. Alfred Street was relatively empty of cars and she parked easily for once outside the house.

At first, Lily thought the sounds were coming from her neighbours' house, from Anna and Simon's, as there was the distinct cry of a child, a baby, followed by adults' laughing, glasses, plates, the general noise of a convivial gathering. But as she opened the front door and stepped into the hall, she realised that the noise was closer to home. Her home. Downstairs, the French windows were wide open, the kitchen busy with at least half a dozen people she failed to recognise and just as she was about to protest at the extraordinary intrusion, she saw Stella sitting outside in the garden, a young child on her lap. Then the front door banged, there were rapid footsteps on the stairs and Hugh appeared at her side.

"I saw your car," he said, his face vacant for a moment, absent of expression. Then he recovered, put down the bags of bottles and cans he held in each hand and embraced her warmly. "Well, this is a surprise, but welcome back, Helen. You should have let us know you were coming home early. You must come and meet everyone. Especially young Dylan."

"Dylan?"

"Yes. Dylan is Stella's son."

19

Within an hour, most people had left, leaving only a small group sitting in the garden.

Stella, Hugh, a young woman, and a man about the same age.

And the child. Stella's child.

Hugh had rapidly explained to Lily as she had stood in her kitchen surrounded by strangers that the gathering had been temporary, a mere staging post, as it were, for some of Stella's friends who were going on elsewhere for the evening. He had merely been aiding them with a quick visit to the off-licence to swell their stocks. Lily had been unconvinced, but her attention was too focused on Stella and her child to concern herself with his words.

"How old is he?" she found herself asking as if the question was paramount. The man, fair-haired with a stubble-like beard, unfolded long limbs from the ground and stood up to take the boy from Stella.

"Dylan's just over a year," he said in a quiet voice that Lily barely heard. The little boy burrowed his head into the man's shoulder, rubbed his eyes. "He's tired now. He missed his nap earlier what with all the – his routine's been broken, which is not ideal.'

"My poor baby," Stella said, "pushed into a routine from the very start. No wonder humans are creatures of dull habit."

"It works," the man said simply, staring at Stella. "We find it works."

The woman picked up a large bag by her feet and took keys from the deep pocket of her long skirt. Her skin was very pale, freckled, and long light auburn hair hung in a loose plait down her back.

"I think it's time to go," she said in a clear, firm voice. "We've quite a drive back to Kent and Dylan will sleep in the car." Then she turned to Lily and said, "You have a beautiful house. Stella has told us very little so we really had no idea."

"No idea about what?" Lily managed to say. It seemed absurd to her that someone she had never met had formed a view about her house. Hugh's explanation about the temporary invasion by Stella's friends seemed increasingly tenuous. She looked over at Stella, who had picked up a bottle of wine from the ground and was draining the dregs into her glass.

"Oh, are you all going now?" she said with some surprise at the general sense of departure around her. "It seems a pity when Lily's only just got back. And I've been absolutely appalling, haven't I? I haven't even introduced everyone properly. To Lily, I mean, my very good and incredibly long-suffering friend and landlady. We are good friends, aren't we, Lily? Or should I get into Hugh's endearing habit and start calling you Helen? Helen, the woman whose face launched all those ships. No, that was Cleopatra, wasn't it? I'm getting my classical women all mixed up."

Dylan began to whimper, small, gentle protests that the young man consoled by tenderly stroking his cheek. Hugh put a hand on Lily's shoulder.

"Ed is Dylan's father," he said to her. "And this is his partner, Jessie. That's right, isn't it? I'm dreadful with names, but I think I caught on to those correctly." He smiled at the couple and then at Lily as if wanting to suggest his understanding only just pre-empted her own. That he, too, shared her bemusement. Jessie held out her hand and Lily, mechanically, took it and watched as if from a considerable distance as Ed and Jessie headed back into the kitchen with Stella following, briefly planting a kiss on the top of Dylan's head, and saying something about visiting in a few weeks when her schedule was quieter. She had clearly been drinking steadily, her voice not so much slurred as unusually loud and emphatic. Ed and Jessie, Lily was relieved to note, both seemed entirely sober. She waited for some moments to hear the front door open, abruptly bang shut, then a hiatus followed by a car's engine starting and pulling away down the street. Then she turned back to Hugh who had not moved from his seat in the garden. He shrugged with a resigned gesture as if playing the part of a perplexed but fond parent.

"I didn't know," Lily said blankly. She sat down in the chair opposite him. "About the child, Dylan. Did you?"

Hugh shook his head. "Absolutely not. Although, of course, I hardly know Stella. About her private life, I mean. It's different for you, Helen."

"How?"

"Well, she's living in your house, for a start. One would expect a sharing of – shall we call them confidences? Woman to woman, or something like that."

"You are living in my house too," Lily said. "Can I be sure you have shared all confidences with me?"

Hugh laughed. "I think you know all there is to know about me, dear Helen. I'm terribly dull, positively plebeian, you could say. Certainly, no secret children to disclose or anything like that!" He leant forward, took her hand. "But when all's said and done, it doesn't really make any difference that Stella has a child, does it? I mean, it's neither here nor there to us."

"Neither here nor there?" The expression sounded absurd.

"Of course it must come as a bit of a surprise for you, Helen, I understand that," he added.

"It was a shock," Lily said bluntly, "finding all those people here. In my house. Let alone hearing that Stella has a child."

"But I've explained all that, surely," Hugh said with a slight hint of irritation. "They weren't actually here, so to speak."

"They seemed pretty much in evidence to me."

"Merely in transit, dear Helen. A stop-over, you could say. But, obviously, I can see that Stella's news has upset you."

"What I don't understand is why she didn't tell me."

Hugh picked up a bowl of crisps perched on the brick wall, ate several before replying. "Perhaps she didn't think it relevant for you to know. I mean, it's not as if she wants to move young Dylan in here. There appears to be a fixed and perfectly acceptable arrangement in place with his father, I understand. And that rather pleasant partner of his, Jessie. I assume they all live in perfect harmony somewhere down in rural Kent so nothing for you to worry about there, I'd say."

Lily tried to sound more phlegmatic than she felt.

"I'm suppose you're right. And it's really none of my business to know about her private life." Yet she could not help thinking that Stella had been evasive, elastic with the truth. After all, the birth of a child was hardly the sort of fact that was easily overlooked in conversation. Perhaps Stella had worried that Lily would be judgemental and hold an outmoded attitude to the cast-iron obligations of motherhood. To the idea of single mothers. In which case, perhaps she should reassure Stella to the contrary rather than reproach her for any duplicity.

"Helen, forgive me, I haven't even asked about your trip." Hugh looked crestfallen. He pulled his chair closer to hers. "How was Wales and the indomitable Dorothy? And the drive? Of course, I wasn't expecting you until tomorrow and I'd planned something of a special meal to welcome you home. But now – I'm afraid you'll find me and the kitchen very unprepared. You really should have let me know about your change in plans."

"It doesn't matter," Lily said, suddenly feeling very tired. The long drive from Pembrokeshire in the heat of the day coupled with her aunt's perpetual conversation had been taxing and she had little desire to do anything now than to be alone, prepare a simple meal and have an early night. But company was consoling, she reminded herself, and Hugh had already offered her appropriate perspective on the matter of Stella's son. And he was right, of course. There was absolutely no need for her to overreact. People behaved so very differently these days and Stella was a young woman unfettered by tradition, while Lily was of only fleeting importance in her life.

"Now dinner," Hugh said. "I'm sure Stella has plans for the evening – she seems to have disappeared, at any rate – and I need to look after you, dear Helen. Shall we go out somewhere? As I say, there's rather a Mother Hubbard situation here. Although, of course, being a Friday evening, anywhere decent is probably booked up and horribly busy."

They settled on fish and chips from the shop in Upper Street. Hugh headed down to buy it while Lily went upstairs to unpack her case. Since the additional bathroom had been fitted on the first floor, she had only used it once at Stella's insistence that she should be the first to try it out. Now she was tempted to shift the grime of the journey with a cool shower that the other bathroom lacked. Yet when she stood on the threshold it felt inappropriate, as if the room had been requisitioned. Stella, her untidy towels, creams, perfumes, discarded underwear, possessed the space and Lily withdrew, made do with splashing cold water on her face, changing into clean clothes. Hugh had arranged plates, cutlery and glasses on the kitchen table.

"Cod or haddock? I wasn't sure about your preference so I got one of each. I'm not sure if I can even taste the difference."

They ate while he talked of his week, the calls that had failed to materialise in jobs, but confirmation of the location work at the end of the summer. It would be dull fodder as usual, Hugh said, when Lily showed interest, crowd work on a classic remake for television, a lot of hanging around in period costume for scenes that would probably be edited out of the final version. His mood, however, seemed buoyant, she was relieved to see, aware of how morose he could grow at the prospect of such work. She went to bed early, the summer evening still holding on to the slightest light as she left Hugh downstairs, insisting that he wanted to clean the kitchen the way he had intended for her return. On the hall table were a few letters, regular bills, circulars, a postcard from Agnes on a day's coach trip to Canterbury.

And an apple core, the dregs of a mug of tea, a box of matches. Some loose cigarettes. She stared at the carelessly disregarded objects, insignificant in themselves, yet disquieting to her in some indefinable way. She picked up her post, went upstairs.

By the morning, they had gone.

She did not see Stella again until Sunday afternoon, when she came into the kitchen and placed several large punnets of strawberries on the table with an air of triumph.

"You'll never believe the bargain I wangled!" she said. "The market was about to close and I suggested I take the lot at half price to do the seller a good turn. He seemed to fall for it even though there was a queue behind me. I said it was getting late in the season for berries so he would be lucky to shift them." Lily found a large dish at the back of a cupboard, handed it to Stella. "Of course, there's far too many for us to eat so I'll make jam with the rest if that's all right with you," she went on. "Have you ever made jam, Lily? The homemade stuff is a revelation compared with shop bought, I can tell you. And it's great fun, we could do it together if you like. Only it would have to be today or tomorrow or they'll go mouldy. It's the water, you know: strawberries are full of the stuff."

There was a feverish air about Stella. She produced a pot of cream from her bag and called Hugh in from the garden and insisted they immediately sit down at the table together, placing a bowl in front of each of them. She talked incessantly as they ate. Something about a conversation with Anna and Simon, her opinion apparently sought over a colour scheme. And the couple from down the street had asked if she knew a reliable plumber. Ideally, an electrician too. Her masterminding of Lily's renovations, her reputation, she laughed, had spread. It was Hugh who eventually interrupted her.

"If I may speak for Helen," he said, "perhaps we owe her some explanation about Friday. I've been trying to enlighten her that it was all just random events that happened to coincide, filling her house with apparent strangers, and that there was no forethought to the whole thing. But I'm not sure I've done a very good job."

Stella bit her bottom lip as if suddenly aware of her transgression.

"Oh, Lily, how thoughtless of me. I didn't think you would be offended. You're always so welcoming to people in your house. Are you furious with us both? There's really no need."

"Of course not," Lily said, "Hugh has explained everything perfectly adequately. It was more a case of being surprised."

"Well, naturally! Coming home to a whole load of people after a peaceful holiday must have been such a surprise. We can't apologise enough, can we, Hugh?"

"I meant about your son," Lily said quietly. "About Dylan."

"Oh, that!" Stella said, pushing away her bowl and the strawberries that she had hardly touched. "Do you disapprove terribly, Lily? I mean I know we're different generations and I would hate you to think badly of me. Of my morals and my attitude to these things, I mean."

Hugh laughed. "Neither of us is exactly Victorian, Stella. I think you'll find we lived through the sexual revolution well before your time." Lily said nothing. For her, the so-called permissive age of the 1960s remained a decade of near celibacy after the implosion of her affair with Toby Jessop.

"Even so," Stella said and looked straight at Lily. "I can imagine you must look at motherhood so differently from most people, Lily. Because of never knowing your own mother. That sort of tragedy must have affected you and given you an overly sentimental view of the whole business. That's entirely understandable and fine with me."

"Yes, I can't imagine what that must feel like," Hugh said. "I can't say I ever had a close bond with my mother, but at least I knew her."

"Exactly!" Stella said. "I'm entirely estranged from mine now, but that's irrelevant. Lily's situation is just too sad."

"It was all a very long time ago," Lily said. She did not quite understand how the focus of the conversation had shifted and she had become its subject.

"Anyway," Hugh said, scooping another couple of strawberries and steeping each into castor sugar before eating them, "it seems to me you have an ideal arrangement for your son, Stella. Ed is clearly a very loving and attentive father."

"Oh yes, he is, I can't fault him there," Stella said. "A little dull as a personality, no drive or ambition to speak of, but kind in his way. Jessie's the same. They live in this very rural place in Kent, you know, chickens and stuff, a smallholding, they call it, and he makes furniture."

"Yet you had a child together," Lily said, "you and Ed." She felt a need to clarify.

Stella stood up, went to the tap, filled a tumbler and drank it swiftly. She leant against the sink, water dripping from her chin down her neck.

"I thought it would be interesting," she said eventually. "An experience."

"An experience," Lily said flatly. She thought of Dylan, rubbing his eyes in tiredness. Of his endearing vulnerability as he retreated into the safety of his father's arms.

"Yes," Stella said. "But it turns out it's not. At least not at the moment. Perhaps when he's older. Babies don't do a lot, you know."

No-one spoke. Through the open French windows, strands of children's voices drifted from a neighbouring garden, the splash of water followed by shrieks of pleasure.

"I wouldn't be surprised if there wasn't a ban on hoses soon, if this heatwave goes on through August," Hugh said abruptly. "Not that it can be a problem in such small city gardens, though."

"That reminds me," Stella said and came back to the table to sit down with purpose. "Have you asked her, Hugh? Asked Lily about our idea? Not that she's allowed to refuse, of course!"

Hugh smiled. Both looked at Lily with the knowledge of a smugly shared secret.

Then he explained.

It was her birthday the following week, he knew. And since the previous year she had been unable to celebrate as a result of her father's death, he and Stella had decided that it was time to mark such a significant landmark. After all, a celebration twelve months late was better than no celebration at all.

"It's the least we can do," Stella broke in. "After your extraordinary kindness to the two of us these past few months. I mean we have, after all, invaded your home."

"I don't think of it like that," Lily said quickly.

"Of course you don't, dear Helen. But that's why it's even more important that we return some of your generosity. We want to give you a party, don't we, Stella?"

"A party?" Instinctively, Lily recoiled from the idea. Yet she had no wish to seem ungrateful. To reject what was clearly a considered gesture. Birthday parties had never been a feature in her life even in her childhood. During the war, her aunt had instilled in her that any celebration would have been both inappropriate and impractical at a time of austerity and suffering. Thus, the habit had never taken root. Her father had always made some sort of gesture, a modest cheque, a card, and since her birthday fell in August they were so often away in Greece, which, as he would tell her, was present enough. She had been inclined to agree. But now, it seemed, Hugh and Stella had plans that they expected her to greet with alacrity.

"We've got things underway already, haven't we, Hugh?" Stella said. Her excited mood had returned and she started to tick off items on the fingers of both hands, prompted every now and again by Hugh. Eventually, she stopped and asked Lily for a list of the guests she would like to invite.

"This is your party, after all," Hugh said fondly. "You mustn't think we are taking over entirely! I'm assuming work colleagues and members of the Play Reading Society? I think Stella has already taken care of the neighbours."

Lily started to protest. But Stella interrupted.

"I've only mentioned it to them casually, of course. We were waiting for your go-ahead, Lily. But, when you think about it, it's only a gesture of neighbourliness after disrupting the street with the skips and building work over the past few months."

"I am not sure any of them are particularly interested in my birthday," Lily said, embarrassed even at the thought of such attention from people she scarcely knew. They might even feel compelled to bring gifts. The thought appalled.

"If you are unhappy with the idea, naturally we'll abandon it entirely, Helen," Hugh said. "And simply have a quiet dinner to mark your birthday. Perhaps just the two of us should go out for a meal? It's just that does sound awfully tame, doesn't it? More the sort of thing suited to octogenarian Dorothy rather than a belated 50th birthday celebration. But if it's what you want ..." He shrugged, sounding deflated.

Lily looked at the two of them across the table. It seemed simpler to comply than protest and, after all, it was what people did, on the whole. Her instinctive reservations about birthday parties made her the anomaly.

She agreed.

Immediately, Stella jumped up to find a notebook to begin compiling a guest list.

"Of course, a lot of people will be away," Lily said, with some relief at the thought. "There's really no point in me asking people from school." Her colleagues were congenial, but social events were rare beyond end of term lunches or leaving drinks. "And it will probably be the same with the Play Reading Society." She thought of Agnes's postcard, her day trip to Canterbury. She could not imagine Agnes feeling comfortable amongst her Alfred Street neighbours.

"Oh, I'm sure we'll find one or two still languishing the summer away in London," Hugh said. "Didn't Amanda say something about that?"

"Amanda?"

"Amanda Morris. The one with the ghastly American accent in *Our Town*. She talked about inviting us all over for a barbecue in her garden, after all."

"I'd forgotten that. But it's very short notice, isn't it?"

"Leave society members to me, Helen. I can have a quick ring round and see who's available."

"In fact, Lily, leave everything to us, guests and all!" Stella went out to the garden, calling back to the two of them, "We should have lights out here. It would make the courtyard look more like an outside room, an extension of the kitchen, rather than just a small walled space. I'll get onto the electrician and see if he can do me a favour before next weekend. And a cake – there will have to be a splendid cake!"

Hugh raised his eyebrows as if in amusement.

"Stella really is the most capable young woman, isn't she? You have to admire her."

"Yes," Lily said. She wanted to say something about her son, Dylan. About the perfection of his small features, his flawless skin, those wide eyes that turned to his father as his source of comfort and consolation. His mother's apparent indifference. But the right words eluded her. "Yes," she repeated, "she's extraordinary."

20

Dorothy had sent a card.
    She rarely gave presents. Even at Christmas her token tended to be in the form of chocolates or a box of festive biscuits that they inevitably shared. Her frugality had increased over the years, although Lily had never thought of her aunt as consciously miserly. It was more as if her habit stemmed from a suspicion of largesse, of ostentation, viewing it as vulgar and a sign of ignorance.
    But she had rung the day before.
    "An entire year since we lost Walter. I've not forgotten, of course. In many ways it seems longer."
    Lily agreed. Her father's death already seemed like an event hitched to another era.
    "A lot seems to have happened."
    "To some of us," Dorothy said. And paused so that Lily was uncertain how to answer. Her aunt's tone was unusually reflective, devoid of its normal stridency. She was aware of Stella downstairs, cooking in preparation for the following day, of Hugh cleaning the flagstones in the back courtyard and felt duplicitous in not telling her aunt about the party. It would be hard, however, for her to defend the event given her own resistance to it. "Of course, you are still young enough, Lily, to anticipate the future," Dorothy eventually went on, "to have another chapter in your life without your father in it. Whereas for me I have only memories."

"Memories are important," Lily said lamely.

"You wait until you are my age, then you'll understand what it's like living with everything in the past. Anyway, I must let you go, Lily. You don't want to be wasting your time on an old woman and her reminiscences. Enjoy your birthday tomorrow. I'm glad I managed to remember. What are you now – forty-seven or forty-eight?"

"Fifty-one," Lily said. "It was my fiftieth birthday last year."

"Good gracious," Dorothy said. "I'd lost track. Late middle age already. How swiftly life passes."

"These days people don't think quite like that. Fifty is considered relatively young."

"Nonsense, Lily. That lodger of yours, Stella, is young. That's what I call youth. Is she still with you, by the way? Useful extra income for you, I suppose. Not that you have the need for it."

"No." Lily said, "I'm very fortunate."

"Your father did his best for you, you know. Given the circumstances."

"Of course."

"Not easy for him. Sometimes I wonder whether I should have encouraged him to marry again. It would have been a sensible solution in many ways."

"He wouldn't have considered the idea, I'm sure. I think he was in love with my mother his whole life."

"That's the trouble with a premature, tragic death. Age shall not weary them, as the poem says. Walter was able to mythologise your mother for half a century."

Today of all days, his ashes should find a more appropriate final resting place than nestling under the canopy of her late mother's fur coat. Dorothy was reminding her firmly about the extortionate charges of day time phone calls, ending the conversation in her usual abrupt style. Hampstead Heath? A discreet corner of Bloomsbury near the university? Nothing seemed satisfactory and she pushed the prospect of a solution from her mind.

The house was full of flowers when she came downstairs on Saturday morning.

"Happy birthday, Lily!" Hugh said, presenting her with yet another cluster already arranged in a white vase she had forgotten she owned. "I had no idea what to get you, typical hopeless male that I am, but I thought I couldn't go wrong with flowers."

"Thank you, they're beautiful. But really – so many!" She bent over the arrangement of red roses sitting on the kitchen table, but found there was no scent to them.

"I thought they would help to show off the house for the party tonight. Nothing like flowers to make people feel they are at a real celebration."

"Do we have any idea of numbers?" she said. The prospect of the party had become no less daunting to her, but she tried to hide her disquiet. Hugh poured coffee. He had insisted on preparing breakfast and had been out early to buy fresh bread.

"Well, you know how it is – never easy to be sure how many will turn up. People can be so vague about parties, can't they?"

"I suppose so," she said vaguely, unable to recall much experience beyond the small gathering after her father's funeral service the previous summer.

"Anyway, we have the booze on a sale or return basis so no worries there, Helen. We will neither run out or be faced with endless amounts of alcohol to consume next week. And the glasses are on hire too so don't worry about all that. In fact, you are not to concern yourself about a thing!"

Lily began to feel very remote from the event, as if she was incidental to the occasion. Her birthday was supposed to be the catalyst for the evening yet the scale of these arrangements, the extravagance and noise of them seemed matched entirely to another self. She opened his card placed next to her mug of coffee, a Mediterranean impressionist beach scene that he had signed with his flamboyant signature and the words *this time next year, the two of us!* written underneath. She propped the card up next to his flowers, drank coffee, nibbled toast, feeling an increased sense of dread at the prospect of the party.

"I have to say that Stella and I have enjoyed ourselves enormously, preparing for this evening," Hugh went on. "And really, isn't it about time we started socialising a little more, you and me? We don't want to be considered pariahs of the neighbourhood. The odd couple of Alfred Street!"

"Of course not," she said automatically. But at the same time was aware of how few people she really knew in the street. Even Stella appeared to have befriended more. It was different in the past when generations of families had stayed for decades. Now there was a sense of perpetual change, not only with the residents, but the houses themselves. Only a few days before, she had noticed scaffolding being erected at the far end of the terrace and Stella had informed her that a builder had bought the neglected, subdivided tenanted property to restore it to a home for single ownership. Property development, she had added with apparent insight, was the future.

The phone went in the hall. Hugh leapt up.

"Leave that to me, Helen, it's probably one of the party guests checking times. You just relax. We have everything under control."

★★★

As the evening progressed, Lily realised that her main fears had been unfounded. No-one gave any indication that they knew it was her birthday. She was not at all its focus and, once she had opened the front door to the first arrivals, saw that the occasion was self-propelling, the assumption being that it was merely a summer party occasioned by the extended hot spell of weather. Neighbours talked animatedly to neighbours about parochial concerns, local schools, parking problems and policing of what they saw as the increasing vagrancy problem. She greeted several members from the Play Reading Society who had brought partners she had never met, the group drifting into the garden and gathering round a table as if reinstating the evening at the wine bar. There were faces Lily barely recognised until Stella prompted her with their names and a reminder that they had all worked on the house. The pale, lanky young man, Crispin, who had drunk endless mugs of tea in the old kitchen, the painter and decorator, someone called Sam and Alec, who had advised about showers and the wisdom of a new hot water tank. Lily had not expected them to be among the guests. Yet of course there was no reason for them not to be there to swell numbers. She had asked no-one, suspecting that her few close friends were too much of her own mind to welcome an invitation. She watched Hugh, attractive in a pale blue open-neck shirt, easily mingling with the guests, busily adept at keeping people's glasses filled as he moved from kitchen to the garden with a bottle in either hand. Stella had spread the table with endless amounts of food and Lily was amazed to see it all disappear so swiftly, having assumed it would also serve the three of them the following week. By the time she approached the table herself there was only a scraping of coleslaw salad left and a small slither of salmon, a fantail of cucumber clinging to the few flakes. The birthday cake that Stella had insisted upon to mark the occasion did not particularly distinguish itself amongst the flans and tarts and mousses. Someone swiftly cut into the pale pink sponge and shared slices so that any significance attached to the layers of butter cream and piped rosettes outlining her initials was soon lost.

It was a comfort, Lily told herself, to feel so irrelevant at the party when she had feared attention.

And yet at the same time the sense of dislocation, with no role at all to play at an occasion in her own home for which ostensibly she was the pretext, was disconcerting. At some point, she slipped upstairs to the top of the house and peered out from a back window onto the garden below. She saw Amanda Morris standing close to someone whose face she could not see, tossing back her head and laughing in an exaggerated way before turning to Hugh, her empty glass outstretched. He stayed, attaching himself for a while to the play reading group and becoming involved in their discussion. She envied the ease with which he infiltrated himself so that soon he appeared to be the pivot of their conversation. She went into her bedroom, found Hector curled up asleep on the bed in retreat from the invasion of strangers and felt tempted to stay upstairs until the evening began to wind down for it was unlikely that anyone would notice her absence. But the thought was cowardly. Hugh was right. She needed to be more sociable, to shrug off the habits of a lifetime of living somewhat reclusively. She must adapt to the way people lived now.

People like her neighbours.

Like Hugh.

And the Alfred Street guests did not stay late, leaving to relieve baby sitters by eleven or excusing themselves with concern over teenage children. At midnight Stella and Crispin and Sam and Alec moved on, grabbing remaining bottles and holding loud conversations on the pavement outside about the direction in which they should head. Suddenly, the house seemed deserted. Only Amanda Morris remained. She had failed to leave with the other society members when they had joined a general exodus as she had mislaid her bag. Lily found her searching amongst the debris of discarded glasses and plates in the kitchen.

"Wonderful party, Lily," she said. "Is this a regular thing? I do hope so. I mean as you know I'm a newbie to the society and, if I'm honest, I joined partially because I was after a decent social life with like-minded types."

"What colour is it?" Lily asked.

"Colour?"

"Your bag?"

"Oh that. It's... black. With beads on and a long strap."

Lily found a small leather turquoise clutch bag on top of the fridge, held it out to Amanda.

"Could this be it by any chance?"

Amanda peered at the bag as if about to deny ownership.

"Of course! Silly me, entirely forgot I swapped it at the last moment to match my dress. No wonder I couldn't find it. Clever Lily. Not only a first-rate party giver, but the finder of lost things!"

"I can take no credit for this evening," Lily said. She found the woman's exaggerated manner grating. "Hugh and Stella are entirely responsible. And the party is not connected with the society. It was meant to mark my birthday, actually." Since the fact had been overlooked all evening, now seemed a safe moment for Lily to claim it. Amanda, however, appeared not to hear.

"Stella is your daughter? That gorgeous young woman in the halter-neck purple dress?"

"No," Lily said. "My... a close friend."

At that moment Hugh came into the kitchen and seemed surprised to see Amanda still there.

"I assumed you'd gone with the others, safety in numbers and all that. It's very thoughtless of them to leave without you." He sounded irritated. Amanda waved her turquoise bag in the air. She was clearly more than a little drunk.

"All my fault," she said. "I'm a careless woman. But it's very gallant of you, Hugh, to be so concerned."

He looked at his watch.

"I tell you what, Amanda, how about I walk with you to Upper Street and we'll see if we can find you a cab?"

"A cab? I live in Richmond! I'll need to take out a second mortgage to pay the fare. No, a night bus to Waterloo or perhaps I could just sit on the District Line all night? One way or the other should get me home by dawn."

Hugh looked at Lily, raised his eyebrows marginally in exasperation.

"You can't possibly do that. I'd better drive you home, Amanda. That's if I'm allowed to use Lily's car?"

"But you've been drinking," Lily said more sharply than she intended.

"Oh everyone fusses so much about drinking and driving these days," Amanda said. "Put me behind a wheel with a bottle of wine inside me and I swear I'm a much better driver. More tactical."

"Actually," Hugh said, "I've drunk very little tonight. I've been too busy looking after everyone else."

"What an absolute treasure of a man!" Amanda said. "But, Hugh, I really can't impose on you like this. Have you any idea how far away Richmond is?"

"Nonsense," Hugh said. "It's no distance in the car. And we really can't have our guests subjecting themselves to public transport at this hour. Especially after such a wonderful evening." Amanda continued to protest mildly. "It's probably the only way to get rid of her," Hugh said quietly to Lily as she found the car keys in the hall. "Otherwise she'll be here for breakfast." Amanda appeared at their side, slipping into the sandals that dangled from one hand.

"And next time the party's at my place," she said, suddenly capitulating to the offer and following Hugh out of the door. "I'll be in touch before the end of the summer, Lily, just leave it with me to sort out a date."

It was only when she was back downstairs in the kitchen, locking the doors onto the garden and attempting to find a clean glass for a drink of water, that Lily remembered Hugh had never driven her car. She hoped he would manage its temperamental gearbox, its awkward clutch.

★★★

Stella, returning the following afternoon, was effusive about the success of the party.

"People were praising the food so much that it became almost embarrassing," she said, watching Lily as she put away the last of the washed crockery and cutlery. "In fact, if I'd wanted to start a catering business, I could have picked up my first clients from among your neighbours. On the other hand, I could also have signed myself up a couple of interior design jobs. They loved what we've done to your old basement."

"What did I tell you, Helen?" Hugh said, "You're really on the map now as far as the street is concerned."

"On the map?"

"People know you. Know us. We have a foothold on the life of Alfred Street, N1."

Lily stared at him in surprise.

"I've lived here for fifty-one years," she said. "My entire life. I think my foothold has always been secure."

Hugh attempted to envelop her in his arms, but she

sidestepped him, bending down to put away a heavy serving plate.

"Of course you have, darling Helen, everyone is aware of that, but you know what I mean."

"Not really," Lily said. She started to sort knives and forks, concentrating on the cutlery drawer so that she did not have to look at Hugh's face. All of a sudden, she longed to be alone, to avoid the conversation that seemed to be of her own making since it would have been so easy to agree with Hugh. Perhaps she was being combative. Stella, oblivious, started saying something about invoices for the food she had bought for the party, producing numerous receipts from her bag and placing them on the table.

"Cash would be great if you've got it, Lily. Oh, by the way, I might be off to the south of France at the end of the week. That couple at the end of the street with the twins?"

"She was an insufferable bore about her children," Hugh said. "If it's the same one I was talking to. Red hair and her husband's a lawyer?"

"She's something legal too. That's how they met, through the same chambers. And actually, those twins do sound like kind of prodigals. Musically speaking. They're already playing several instruments, evidently. Anyway, they wondered if I'd like to go and join them. On their holiday. Paid, of course, and I'd have to do some cooking and talk to the children in French so a bit of tutoring on the side. But it might be quite fun for a couple of weeks. They've taken a big house somewhere in Provence."

"Nice work if you can get it!" Hugh said. "You do fall on your feet, don't you, Stella?"

"But they hardly know you," Lily said, amazed. "Did they ask you last night?"

"Something like that," Stella said vaguely. "And this is

actually where you come in, Lily, and what I have to thank you for."

"Me?"

"They seem to think – Mark and Leonie, that is – that as I'm a friend of yours I must be trustworthy and of exemplary character. I mean those weren't their exact words, but I could read between the lines. If you allow me to live here and take responsibility for the house renovation, you clearly approve of me big time. You're like a full proof testimonial for me, Lily, as an upright and stalwart resident of the street!"

"Yet at the same time I am virtually unknown, an invisible entity," Lily said and immediately regretted it. She sounded churlish and irritable. Hugh, however, simply laughed.

"Oh dear, you're not going to let me forget my faux pas, are you, Helen? My heartfelt apologies and all that. You know I would never do anything to offend you. Quite the opposite." He carried two of the large vases of his flowers over to the sink and replenished them with water. "Important not to neglect the blooms, I'd say. The florist promised me at least a week's life if we keep them well-watered."

21

By the end of the week, Stella had left for the south of France, Hugh for a few days of extra work on location in Devon. He talked about the possibility of Lily joining him, to make something of a holiday while the weather remained hot, but he rang her on his first evening there to explain that the schedule was too tight to allow him any reasonable time off to spend with her. She was disappointed. She felt strangely restless in the house alone and rang Eileen, conscious that she had not been in touch for months, but Eileen, sounding somewhat distant, said she was about to go away. She tried Agnes, invited her to supper, ashamed that she was simply using her quiet friend to occupy a sudden vacancy in her time. Agnes suggested a walk in Regent's Park instead, to which she readily agreed.

And she thought about Stella. About the neighbours, Mark and Leonie, wondering whether they knew about her child, Dylan. Stella dealt so fluently with her life, shaping it with effortless economy, resilient, resourceful, even without the reassurance of parental support. Like a sculptor chiselling at a piece of clay to produce the required effect. Most people found themselves blundering through the years, content to court boredom to avoid disaster. And, even then, catastrophe called. Hugh's tragic loss of his wife, Louise, was evidence enough of that. Of course Stella was still very young. Even so, Lily could not imagine that the vagaries that visited most lives would at any point plague Stella.

Hugh rang two days before he was due home.

"There's respite in sight!" he said. "They're finishing with us a day early, soon after lunch tomorrow, so here I am, loath to waste these summer days back in sultry London. What about it, Helen? How about jumping in the car and joining me tomorrow evening?"

"Of course," Lily said, elated. "What a lovely surprise." Toby Jenner had once made a similarly spontaneous gesture, but the event had inevitably been couched in guilt and secrecy. And duplicity had been needed, a fake wedding ring and feigned surname in order for the two of them to gain a double room. A couple of decades later, no such subversion would be required.

"Although, thinking about it," Hugh went on, "there's absolutely no need for you to drive all the way to deepest Devon."

"I don't mind."

"No, I'm tired of this place now. Let's go somewhere different for a couple of days. Somewhere in… let's see, Hampshire? Dorset, perhaps."

He swiftly agreed to her suggestion of Lyme Regis.

"Now, where to stay? Do we just take pot luck when we arrive?"

"It's August," Lily cautioned. We might end up camping on the beach."

"And very romantic that sounds too, Helen. But I take your point. Trouble is, I've still got a day on set tomorrow so the chance of getting to a phone box and contacting the local tourist office or whatever one does these days to find accommodation is somewhat slight."

"Leave it to me," Lily said, thinking of the pleasure of looking at guide books in the reference library, phone calls on behalf of the two of them.

"What a practical woman you are, Helen, I forget that at times. It's so reassuring to be able to leave everything in your capable hands. We'll need an assignation, of course."

They arranged to meet at Axminster station. After an hour spent at the library compiling a long list of pubs and guest houses in the area, Lily spent another two making endless phone calls that produced nothing more than somewhat curt replies that there were no vacancies until October. Her final call was to the most expensive, a historic coaching inn called the Bear that she had only noted down as a very last resort. Yes, there was one double room available, she was told, but for a minimum of three nights. Out of desperation, Lily booked it, realising that Hugh had said nothing about the length of their stay. The price seemed extortionate, but her knowledge was limited to unpretentious, small hotels in Greece providing simple accommodation. No doubt Hugh would be far more accustomed to rates charged by decent English hotels and not flinch at the cost. There was the matter of Hector, but Anna happily agreed to call in and feed him.

"The babies will love it!" she said with her usual enthusiasm. "And once we start getting into pets, which I suppose we will at some stage, you can return the favour!"

The following day, Lily left far too early, telling herself that the traffic could be heavy, but in truth anxious to get away from the house for fear of a change in Hugh's schedule. She felt she could not bear the possibility of disappointment and being out of reach, however foolish the notion, seemed the best way of escaping it. She stopped in Winchester for coffee, went into the cathedral and sat in a pew in the cool interior for over half an hour before driving on towards Dorchester through undulating countryside parched by the long dry spell. She wasted time having a pot of tea in a village teashop and still arrived at Axminster an hour before Hugh was due.

And then he was late.

She watched a train arrive, then another, and began to feel conspicuous on the empty platform. It was close to seven o'clock and she began to wonder whether she should drive on to Lyme, to the Bear and the overpriced double room that now seemed to taunt her for her wild extravagance. Her linen skirt and shirt, pristine that morning, now felt grimed and creased and she went back to the car, rolled down the windows, combed her hair in an attempt to feel more presentable.

Finally Hugh arrived.

Not from the station, but from an approach road to the north of it, with a case in one hand, a jacket slung around his shoulders. He caught sight of her car, picked up his pace. He had missed his train, he said in explanation. They had finished filming later than planned then there had been a difficulty in getting a bus to the station. But fortunately, he had managed to beg a lift from one of the production team who was heading back to London and was willing to make a short diversion. Had she been waiting long? He couldn't quite remember what they'd arranged on the phone, the line had been unclear, but at least now he was here. They were both here. And he embraced her warmly.

The Bear, claiming 16th-century origins, heavily beamed with uneven floorboards and low ceilings, enchanted Hugh.

"I knew it was best to leave things to you, Helen. I am woefully out of practice with anything other than booking cheap theatrical digs. Congratulations on your exemplary taste!"

They ate in the dining room, an oak-timbered room, dark and cool in spite of the humidity of the night. Hugh was in a convivial mood, clearly relieved to be finished with the location work that he had found tediously dull and time-wasting.

"I suppose it's always like that, film work. At least that's what I imagine, a lot of hanging around waiting for the light to be right. Or the weather. Not that I know anything about these things," Lily said as Hugh studied the wine list.

"Chablis?" he said. "A prohibitive price, of course, in a place like this, but let's treat ourselves for once. In fact, it's my treat to you, Helen." He held her hand across the table. "It's the least I can do as you've taken care of the hotel expenses."

She had anticipated that all costs would be shared, the bill divided equally between them at the end of their stay. Yet now it felt inappropriate to suggest it since the decision over the booking had been hers.

They spent the following two days walking and exploring the area and spending time simply sitting and reading in the hotel garden. On their final evening, they found a small French restaurant in the town with an outside dining terrace and although the day had been hot, the night air was suddenly cooler with a dampness in the air that prompted Lily to think of autumn and the start of the new term.

"I know how lucky I am to be in safe employment," she said as they waited for their food to arrive. "But I do wonder if I should be a little more adventurous. I mean I could manage a more demanding job now that my responsibilities at home are lightened."

Hugh filled her glass.

"So what, my darling Helen, would you prefer to be doing? If you had your choice of destiny?"

Lily was silent for a moment then, feeling spineless, said,

"I've never given it a great deal of thought."

"Oh, come on Helen," Hugh said, sounding mildly irritated, "anyone with any imagination at all has dreams of an occupation even if they remain unrealised."

"The chance to travel, then," Lily said swiftly. "Yes, a job involving travel would be ideal. And to learn another language possibly. And now I have no ties," she went on with more conviction, "I suppose there's absolutely nothing to stop me."

"No ties?"

"After my father's death, I mean. Of course there's always Dorothy."

"Am I to consider myself of no importance in your life, then, Helen? I suppose I should be grateful that I'm not considered a tie in any negative way. Even so, a chap can't help but feel a little hurt."

Lily found his tone hard to judge. The waiter approached their table with food, relieving her of the need to answer straight away. When he had gone, she said,

"I was talking in an abstract way. You surprised me with the question."

Hugh laughed.

"Dear Helen, I'm not offended. One should always have pipe dreams, after all. But you might be interested to hear of a little project that's been put to me in the past few days. I wasn't going to say anything until details were clearer, but in fact, I'd value your opinion."

Hugh had been approached by a fellow actor, Robin James, who, like him, had become increasingly tired of the irregularity and tedium of the acting work on offer. He was starting a theatre school. Nothing grand or aspirational like RADA or the Central School, Hugh explained, but a training school, nevertheless. A hub where people could come and take classes, ad hoc, part time, in the evenings, at weekends, and learn the skills and craft of the profession. Robin had already taken a long lease on a premises in east London, a former drill hall that he was fitting out ready for an autumn opening and was now looking for professionals to run classes and workshops.

"It sounds ideal for you," Lily said. "It could be very rewarding work."

"Of course I wouldn't be abandoning acting entirely. That's the beauty of the thing, any classes could fit around other commitments. But you're right, Helen. I feel quite excited by the prospect of having another string to my bow, another source of income."

Hugh's enthusiasm was tangible, so different from the disillusion he so often expressed towards the mundane work that came his way. Although he never expressed the thought, Lily imagined he had dreaded the prospect of another ten or fifteen years of increasingly banal jobs as he coasted towards retirement.

"I think it's a marvellous opportunity," she said warmly. "And no doubt it's come just at the right time when you have so much you can offer students. I'm sure you'll be an inspiring teacher. You really do deserve it. After all, you've had such a difficult few years since losing your wife." She rarely mentioned Louise. It seemed insensitive to do so and left it to Hugh to talk of her which he very rarely did.

Hugh raised his wine glass towards hers.

"Ah, well, no-one promised life was all plain sailing. But we've managed to stumble across each other, Helen, so the gods of fortune sometimes have our best interests in mind, it would seem. Are there gods of fortune? You are my fount of all classical knowledge, remember!"

"There's Tyche," Lily said.

"Tyche?"

"But really she's more associated with the good fortunes of a city rather than individual good luck. And Plutus is all about personal prosperity."

"I could certainly benefit from his help, then," Hugh said ruefully. "Speaking of all things Greek, Lyme Regis has been wonderful, of course, but a little tame for our tastes, wouldn't you say, Helen? I'm putting myself entirely in your knowledgeable hands to arrange our Greek itinerary for next summer, remember." He reached over the table for her hand.

"I'll do my best," Lily said. It was only later as they walked back to the hotel, Hugh's arm holding firmly onto hers, that she realised the subject of her own dissatisfaction with her job appeared to have been forgotten. It seemed inappropriate now to mention it.

★★★

Back home in Alfred Street there was a postcard from Stella on the mat, her large bold scrawl protesting that she was *preparing endless meals* and that the company of the twins was *tiresome and exhausting* but the message was sufficiently sprinkled with exclamation marks to suggest she was enjoying herself.

"Do you think we'll ever be rid of her?" Hugh said light-heartedly as he studied the picture of a Provencal village. Lily pretended not to hear, busying herself with shopping they had picked up on the way home. She had begun to wonder herself if she should ask Stella about her plans. Yet each time the thought occurred she had pushed it away, uncertain what she wanted to hear in reply. Clearly, Stella could not live there indefinitely without paying some contribution to household expenses. Whilst she was project managing the renovations, it was excusable. But now the work was complete, the matter needed to be addressed again. Yet, at the same time, the prospect of Stella leaving followed by Hugh himself returning to his house in Fulham presented her with a reality she had shied from confronting. The renovated house, its expanse of space and spare rooms, no longer seemed fit solely for her occupation. She would be left with a folly on her hands, entirely of her own making. She watched Hugh pick his way through the rest of the mail, discarding flyers and handing her the rest.

"Things are going to be hectic over the next few weeks, Helen. What with catching up with Robin and sorting things there."

"Robin?"

"Robin James," he reminded her, "and the theatre school in Shoreditch. He's made a start, advertising the classes, finalising the venue, but he's ready for my input now."

"And your house? Surely the work must be drawing close to completion."

"Ah, that albatross," Hugh said darkly. "But you're right, I need to pop over to Fulham and arrange for a surveyor to check it's all up to scratch. And then… well, we can move on, can't we? The start of a new chapter. And you'll be relieved not to have me droning on about it all, constantly moaning about the crippling and escalating bills."

"Nonsense," Lily said. "You rarely mention it. I would be far more unrestrained in your position."

"Yet you've handled the upheaval of your precious home with dignity. Endured with such equanimity endless workmen smoking their cigarettes and drinking your tea while you've watched them pull the place apart. But of course it's been entirely worth it."

"I hope so," Lily said quietly.

"Think of it as a mission," Hugh went on. "8 Alfred Street has shrugged off its dusty past and can now sit proudly beside its smart neighbours. A success story without doubt, I'd call that, Helen!"

***

By the end of the month she was back at work in the admin office, preparing for the new term. Talk was of holidays and the long hot spell and there seemed interest in Lily's few days in Lyme Regis.

"I went to Wales as well." She tried to distract from the blatant curiosity. "For a week with my aunt. To Pembrokeshire. The beaches are extraordinary."

"We're more interested in your romantic walks along the Cobb with... Hugh, is it? Good for you, Lily!" Alison said loudly over the noise of the photocopier. Lily attempted to diffuse attention by asking one of the younger staff, Cara, about her recent engagement. But this seemed merely to fuel their focus.

"Perhaps there'll be another wedding to mark before the year is out!" said Angela who tended to turn anyone's life into a saga for entertainment given the slightest prompting.

Lily hoped her silence would deflate the topic of conversation. She found herself yearning for the privacy of her old office, for the status, even, of her former position as school secretary and wondered how she had grown to tolerate the noise and chatter of the admin office for the past year.

"But seriously, Lily," Alison said after cursing the temperamental photocopier for mangling several sheets of paper, "that's lovely. That you have someone to fill your life, I mean."

Lily, irritated, said, "I never thought of my life as empty."

"No, of course not," Alison said. "But you know what I mean. Inevitably there must have been a bit of – well, a gap, if you like, after losing your father."

Lily concentrated on counting copies of timetables and class lists intended for staff pigeon holes. Alison was a kindly woman and only stated what she knew others felt about her. What she had herself feared, after all. It was therefore contrary of her now to resent the suggestion. And yet she did. As if without a partner a woman's life was considered aimless and of little worth. She could not imagine Dorothy ever feeling like that.

★★★

Stella returned from France and set about pursuing leads she had apparently picked up at Lily's party in August.

"It seems all of your neighbours know someone who knows someone who is looking for a person like me."

Lily misunderstood. "To tutor their children in French and undertake some child care?"

Stella looked horrified.

"Absolutely not! I'm talking interior design. They saw the job I did here with your lovely house, Lily, and they've put me in touch with friends who have a project in mind. In fact, you could say that the renovations here have served me as a kind of walking advertisement."

"Well, you certainly come with a wealth of contacts," Lily said, thinking of the ease and speed with which Stella had manned the project.

"Exactly! In fact, me and Crispin are going to get some business cards made in order to launch ourselves."

"Crispin?"

"Your architect, Lily. Well, strictly speaking, not a fully fledged one, but he knows enough."

Lily felt it unwise to ask more. She had assumed that the elaborate plans for the basement had been entirely bona fide. "We'll need office space eventually, but for the time being we can base ourselves here, can't we?"

Lily, busy with sorting out the casting for the society's late-September meeting, said something non-committal. She was aware by now that so many of Stella's plans swiftly dissolved to be replaced by new notions. No doubt an alternative venture would soon present itself and gain her enthusiasm.

Hugh was constantly out. The theatre school in Shoreditch had started and although he conceded that calling it a school was somewhat inflated with only a few evening and weekend classes, the foundations were there. Lily was pleased. He seemed more settled and although he still searched through *The Stage* on Thursday mornings for potential calls and castings and went in pursuit of a few, he appeared resigned to the new work.

"It gives you more stability, surely," Lily said one evening as they sat over dinner. Swiftly, autumn was establishing itself with sudden gusts of winds and cool temperatures so that the long hot summer already felt remote.

"It's hardly a city broker's salary," Hugh said, adding caustically, "even when Robin actually starts paying me. But you're right as always, Helen. It's certainly a viable venture. Although ideally Robin wants a bit of an investment from me, some money upfront to help with start-up costs."

"I see," Lily said, "but I thought classes were already underway?" Hugh had spent most of Saturday teaching at the drill hall and had been in a positive mood on his return.

"Well, yes," he said, "but shall we say we're still negotiating the issue, me and Robin? He seems to hold somewhat inflated ideas about the spare cash I have to invest."

"Perhaps you could talk to the bank," Lily said. "I mean, isn't that what people do when they have a viable business proposition?"

Hugh laughed, pushed his plate away from him.

"In your world, no doubt, Helen. One has one's bank manager who offers avuncular advice and endless funds to serve one's needs. A jobbing actor does not have that advantage."

"No, I can see that," Lily said inadequately. She felt his

269

comment to be unfair, but later conceded that he had a point. After all, her needs had always been provided for thanks to the industry of hard-working generations past and no doubt a certain parsimony on their part, her father and aunt included.

Dorothy had cancelled her Sunday lunch visits in August, claiming the heat made the journey in the car too uncomfortable for her. But September saw a return to routine. On the final Sunday of the month, a wet and blustery day, Lily listened to her aunt's endless complaints about the poor cleaning services of the communal areas of the flats, the unreliability of the milkman and her irritation with her neighbour's nocturnal habits of piano playing. Hugh, who had come in late to lunch after a meeting with Robin, was diplomatic and patient with her and, when the time came to take her home, offered to drive her himself. Lily, in the welcome silence of the house after their departure, was grateful. When he arrived back around seven, he insisted that the two of them sit down with a drink in the new living room, a space that for Lily had not quite lost shades of the former kitchen. They sat for some time looking out at the darkening evening and the sodden leaves cluttering Alfred Street gutters. Then Hugh stood up, as if about to leave the room, before sitting down again, pulling his chair closer to hers.

"I've come to a decision, Helen. An important decision." He leant towards her. Took her empty glass and put it on the low table.

"Really?" Lily anticipated something to do with Robin and the theatre school. Of abandoning his waning acting career to focus entirely on teaching. "What have you decided?"

He drained his glass, placed it carefully next to hers on the table. Took both her hands in his.

"I'm selling my house," he said. "In fact, it's already on the market. I'm selling my house in Fulham."

22

Stella looked up from her magazine.

After the summer months when she had been absent so much, she had returned to spending most days in Alfred Street, at the kitchen table, in her room and frequently on the phone. Lily knew she needed to speak to her about the escalating phone bill.

"Crispin will be here in a moment or so," she said. "We need to finalise some plans for the project in Blackheath. And there's insufficient room at his flat share. Nowhere to spread ourselves."

"Blackheath?" Lily said.

"Well, Greenwich, really, according to the address. SE10."

Hugh put down the Saturday paper.

"And this is for Leonie's sister's house? It's a big renovation, isn't it?"

"Crispin and I are only involved in the kitchen planning. We're not quite up to a whole Georgian terraced house overhaul yet. Although, give us time…"

"There will be no stopping you, I imagine," Hugh said lightly.

"It's a good commission for us, potentially tapping into the south London market. Making waves there."

There was a knock at the front door and Stella slowly uncurled herself from her chair, dropped her magazine to the floor. "That will be Crispin, he's always horribly punctual.

Tell you what, we'll go into the old dining room, then we won't disturb the two of you. We'll probably be working all afternoon."

Lily waited until Stella had disappeared upstairs and she had heard the front door opening followed by voices and another door closing. She turned to look at Hugh, who had picked up his paper and returned to reading.

"I presume you know what this is all about," she said.

"What?"

"Stella and Crispin. I mean I know she said something about starting an interior design business, but I had no idea she was serious and going ahead with it."

"I must say I was surprised," Hugh said. "We both know that Stella's enthusiasms tend to be short-lived."

"Like the idea of motherhood," Lily said dryly.

Hugh looked up at her, surprised. "Helen, that's hardly relevant. Or fair. And it's not like you to be so judgemental."

"I'm allowed to have a view if that's what you mean. Is one considered judgemental simply by having an opinion?"

Hugh said nothing for a moment, turned back to his paper and then after a pause said, "Well, everything seems to have sorted itself out satisfactorily where the child is concerned. It's not as if little Dylan is being neglected. No-one has suffered."

"No," Lily said. "That's entirely true." Her disquiet over Stella's son still lingered. Yet she found it hard to understand the reason for her uneasiness since, as Hugh pointed out, the situation appeared happily resolved for all concerned.

"But as for this other business," Hugh went on, "I happened to be here the other day when you were out and the two of them – Stella and this Crispin fellow – were talking about their venture. They've even got a name for it and headed notepaper, would you believe! Fox and Hawkins, they're calling themselves. And it certainly seems to be taking off with a couple of clients already. One can't help but take an interest and encourage them."

"*In loco parentis?*"

"What? Well, I suppose so. Stella certainly lacks such guidance as we know. And I feel their enterprise should receive some backing if it's only our endorsement." He paused, looked across at her. "I thought you would be pleased. That Stella actually seems to be finding her feet at last. She is rather your protegee."

"My protegee? What a strange thing to say."

"Is it?"

"I merely offered her some stopgap accommodation when she was in need," Lily said. "No more than that." She knew she sounded defensive. And ingenuous. She had, after all, allowed Stella to become so very much more than a temporary, casual lodger.

"You've been kindness itself, Helen."

"And naturally I'm pleased that she seems to be settling down to something at last, but through no particular help from me. She's a very bright and talented young woman, after all. And beautiful too. Success usually comes easily to such people if they push themselves a bit."

"We are living in entrepreneurial times," Hugh said. "That's what counts. And there does seem to be an awful lot of money slopping around in certain circles that people are happy to bestow with wild extravagance. People like Stella's clients with their aspirations for the latest style that cash can buy. Good luck to Fox and Hawkins, Interior Designs, I'd say! I'm sure they'll be a huge success."

Lily agreed. Then added quietly, starting to clear the table of cups and plates from their late breakfast, avoiding Hugh's eye as she spoke,

"It's just that I seem to be the last person in this house to find out about things these days. I find that disconcerting."

But he appeared not to hear.

His explanation about his house in Fulham had sounded rational enough. He hadn't wanted to bother Lily with his concerns, but the rising costs of the subsidence problems and repairs had resulted in a final extortionate bill. He had seen himself in debt for years if he borrowed against the value of the house to settle it. Selling the house had been the obvious, sensible response. Besides, he had conceded to Lily, there were too many tangible hooks and attachments to the past, to his late wife lurking in the place so that he found he had no wish to return there now it was once more habitable. Life had moved on. He had moved on. Lily had sympathised. Understood. And Hugh had been anxious to reassure her that, once the house was sold and all bills settled, he would buy a flat with the remainder, somewhere small, but adequate that would be so much more appropriate for his needs. He was not, he insisted, planning on testing her patience indefinitely by overstaying her generous hospitality in Alfred Street. It was just a matter of time, finding a buyer, securing completion on the house and if the process really did drag on there was always the solution of him returning to his sister's home in Balham in the interim. Lily, grateful at least for his offer, had dismissed the necessity for it. Naturally he could stay as long as he needed. Yet she wished he had confided in her earlier, discussed his thoughts before acting on them. She disliked such secrecy with its suggestion of something underhand. Hugh had been suitably contrite. No more had been said about the sale of the Fulham house until a couple of weeks later when she had come home from work to find Hugh elated by the news that the estate agents had rung him with a reasonable offer that he had accepted on the spot. With any luck, he had said, and with a bit of plain sailing, he could be free of the place by Christmas and, for a week or so, he had shown some enthusiasm for inspecting flats in nearby areas, in Highgate and Camden and Kentish Town, but he had dismissed them all as too small and extortionately priced and Lily, inspecting a couple of properties with him, had agreed. She had suggested he widen his search. After all, she had pointed out, everywhere in London becomes fashionable eventually and perhaps he should consider Stoke Newington or Hoxton or even Shoreditch, where he would be close to the fledgling theatre school, places that no doubt would lose their undesirable labels within a few years and become aspirational. Hugh had been unimpressed. It was the sort of advice that only a home owner in Islington would voice, he said sourly, and Lily had felt duly reproached.

Stella and Crispin seemed absorbed in plans when Lily went up later to offer some tea. Stella beamed at her.

"Our life saver, Lily! We've not noticed the time, have we, Crispin? But we've got a lot done."

Crispin murmured a reply. His head of sandy hair did not lift from the pages of a large cash book. Lily recognised it from the one she had seen Stella use to record outgoings and payments during the renovation of the basement.

"Things seem to have got off to a very good start for your business," Lily said. "I'm so pleased."

Stella leant back in her chair.

"Well, it's just early days. We are at the teething stage, aren't we, Crispin? It's going to be quite a while before we're safely established."

Lily retreated, returned with a tray of tea and biscuits and put it down on the table, moving to one side a ream of headed notepaper, a box of business cards to make room for it.

Then she looked again.

Picked up a single sheet of the paper. It was headed in bold purple italic print with the name *Fox and Hawkins* followed by an address. Lily's address, *8 Alfred Street, London N1*. Stella caught her eye.

"It's just to start with," she said, floundering, and staring down at the notepaper, the business cards, as if surprised by what she saw. "We just needed something that gave us – gravitas? So that people would take us seriously. And your address has such an allure, Lily. An authority."

"You should have asked me," Lily said flatly.

"Of course, we should," Stella said. "I am so very sorry. It was quite an appalling omission. And please don't blame Crispin. This was all my own doing." She looked tearful. Fiddled with a strand of hair, nibbled at a fingernail.

"You had no right. And what about Crispin – doesn't he have an address to use?"

A sound in between a snort and a sarcastic laugh came from Crispin, who was drinking from his mug of tea.

"I've just been so thoughtless. We'll simply destroy it all." Stella grabbed a handful of the notepaper and began tearing sheets into pieces, tossing them to the floor until Lily stopped her.

"Really, there is no need for this."

"I just didn't think. I can see now how awful it looks, Lily. How it looks as if I was taking things for granted. Taking you for granted. Which I never would. Will you ever forgive me?" Her voice had become high-pitched and strained.

"Stella, this is all getting out of hand. I was just taken by surprise, that's all," Lily bent down to pick up the scattered paper, feeling suddenly weary and tired. The situation had become so inflated. "Yes, you should have asked me first. Out of courtesy. But it's done now. And I do understand your reasons."

"It's just until we have our own premises," Stella said.

"Which will be in no time at all. We're already looking at places, in fact, aren't we, Crispin?"

Crispin went on eating biscuits, brushing crumbs from the pages of the cash book onto the carpet. Lily turned to go, then suddenly felt this was the moment to bring up the subject of the phone bill.

"Just one more thing I've been meaning to mention."

Stella said, "I know what you're going to say. And yes, of course, once we're in profit we will pay you back a fair rate for rented office space. The going rate, in fact. Even just for the short time we are here, I mean. This old dining room really serves our purpose so well and it's not as if it's needed for anything else. In fact, you'll be gaining in the long run, Lily, getting paid for the use of a redundant room!"

Stella smiled broadly, as if she had just satisfactorily resolved a dilemma. Then she took a step towards Lily and gave her a gentle hug. She turned to Crispin.

"Didn't I tell you that Lily is just the best? Generous to a fault. Hugh is such a lucky man, you know. I must make a point of telling him more often!"

★★★

Hugh found Lily's copy of *The Country Wife* lying on the table.

"Restoration comedy this month? That's a bold choice for the society."

"Actually, I've had a lot of interest which is fortunate with quite a large cast to sort out. You'll read, won't you?"

He picked up Lily's list of characters with some rudimentary casting and pencilled his name next to a couple of names with a query. "I think I could do justice to one of those two, but of course it's entirely up to you, Helen, I'm in your capable hands. But have you thought about some dialect coaching? Just for the relevant characters, of course. It could make for a more consistent reading."

"I'm not sure that's strictly necessary," she said, wondering whether he was blurring the distinction between his work at the theatre school and the nature of the society. "But it's entirely up to you, of course." He was teaching more classes in Shoreditch, occasional evenings, most Saturdays, so that Lily found herself often alone the way she had been before they had met. But he was rarely late and always came home animated, energised, and talked at length about the students or a particularly successful class he had delivered. Lily listened, responded. But increasingly felt as if she was a fixed centre around which other lives were spinning. Flourishing.

Hers was beginning to feel static, inert in comparison.

Her neighbours opposite had recently let their house while they decamped to prestigious jobs in New York for two years and a couple had moved in with a distinguished-looking Bengal cat who proceeded to terrify Hector with ferocious howls and disparaging glares as if Hector's indifferent ginger status was beneath the Bengal's contempt. A house a few doors down had recently been bought as the result of a probate sale and was now occupied by a family, in residence only during the week, retreating from Friday to Monday morning to their cottage in in the Cotswolds.

And then Stella herself.

She seemed absorbed by Fox and Hawkins, putting in long hours that impressed Lily, used to her more erratic response to work. She no longer spent any time cooking or shopping for the three of them and Lily resumed the tasks, relieved that Stella and the taciturn Crispin seemed to be creating a viable business that would surely soon be occupying its own work space. The old dining room was resembling more and more a functional office and Lily had noticed that a filing cabinet and a couple of desk chairs had been moved in. She knew she should object to the increasing encroachment on the house, but she wanted to avoid such a confrontation, not wishing to subdue her eagerness. The sooner the business became a going concern, after all, the sooner Fox and Hawkins would be able to move out of Alfred Street. It still amazed her that the two of them appeared to be establishing themselves with conviction whilst lacking any relevant qualifications. Surely clients required authenticity. But Hugh said that her attitude was out of date. Of no relevance at all. The 1980s, he had pointed out, was a decade that welcomed style and assertion over substance. A restless era, he had said, where dissatisfaction with the status quo was driving ambition.

Lily questioned her own growing discontent with the admin office. Perhaps even her equanimity was being tested by the turbulence of the decade. She brought up the subject as they were walking in Regents Park one Sunday afternoon, the in-between Sunday as Hugh now called the weekend free of Dorothy's visit.

"I'm wondering if I should look for another job," she said impulsively. "Or at least do some voluntary work for a charity. Perhaps I'm too complacent. Lazy, even."

Hugh laughed, kicked his way through tranches of sodden, fallen leaves.

"Nonsense, Helen. You are the least lazy person I know."

"Lacking enterprise, then," she persisted. "Not sufficiently outward-looking."

"Whatever does that mean?"

"I'm not sure, really. But I feel I need to try something new. Or support a cause."

He stopped abruptly, looking horrified.

"You are not thinking of going off to join those ghastly women at Greenham Common, surely?"

Lily shook her head. "Nothing like that. Although one has to admire them. For acting on their convictions."

"Because, quite frankly, darling Helen, however much I love you, I don't think I could tolerate that. Absolutely not."

His words shocked her. They walked on, Lily aimlessly picking up some conkers, pocketing some, discarding others. Squirrels crossed their path. Hugh had never expressed love in any discernible way. He was affectionate, demonstrative, shared her bed and she assumed cared for her deeply.

But love.

The word seemed too potent for what she sensed in him.

And then there was the suggestion of possessiveness, of dominance even, in his language.

Or so it seemed to Lily. But perhaps she had been single too long to understand the intricacies and dynamics of a relationship.

"Maybe it's just the time of year," Lily conceded. "The shorter, colder days are making me too introspective. And, of course, you and Stella are making such strides. Perhaps," she added to lighten the tone, "I'm just jealous of your successes."

Hugh took her arm.

"No need for that, Helen. In fact, you are exactly right just as you are. And I know what a fortunate man I am to be at your side. After losing Louise – well, I didn't think even in my wildest dreams that I would ever love again."

His affirmation should have consoled her. Yet she felt alarmed by the intensity of such a declaration and could not understand why. After all, Hugh's companionship was surely now intrinsic to her happiness, providing the reassuring normality and routine that a woman such as her, placid, predictable, required. They walked on in silence, the soft autumn light of the afternoon gradually fading as it grew close to dusk. Lily shivered, her hands chilled. It was the turn of the year when scarves and gloves and boots were dug out of summer hiding places, found in the depths of drawers and at the back of wardrobes. Winter hovered spectrally.

"I'm looking forward to Tuesday's reading," she said as they picked up their pace and headed out of the park. "The society hasn't chosen any restoration comedy for years."

"I must say I've enjoyed getting to grips with it. Not the sort of thing that ever came my way even in the old days of weekly rep. It's been worth doing a bit of rehearsing to make sure we're finding out way around the text. The language is quite demanding for some of the cast."

"I thought it was just the dialect that was concerning you."

"That too," Hugh said swiftly.

"How is Felicity doing? She's just returned to the society after working abroad for a year, but she used to be one of our strongest members."

"Felicity?"

"She's reading Margery Pinchwife. So presumably you've been working with her?"

"Of course. Oh, you know how hopeless I am with names, Helen." He quickened his pace, glanced up at the sky. "I'd say there's rain threatening. Let's get a move on so we don't arrive home like drowned rats."

"Anyone else turn up?"

"What?"

"I wondered how many people came to your rehearsal call. It's not the way we normally do things, after all."

"Perhaps it's time for a change. Or at least a tweaking of procedure for the occasional play with particular demands. We certainly had sufficient cast there to make it worthwhile."

Lily stopped in her stride, bent down and fiddled with her shoe where a stone had wedged.

"Anyone in particular?" She was irritated by her own probing. She stood up, but the stone still rubbed.

"As I say, Helen, I'm useless on remembering names," Hugh said brusquely. "Just a handful of the principals popped in briefly. Will that do?"

They passed a couple with two dogs, King Charles' spaniels that leapt around their owners' legs, resistant to their leads. Hugh pulled her sharply away.

"How wise you are only to have a cat, Helen. Hector really is the perfect pet for a London household, wouldn't you say? Especially with such a distinguished name. Perfect taste on your part, Helen."

"My father named him."

"Of course. Highly appropriate."

He groped for her hand and she obliged. His fingers, as cold as hers, held on with a firm grasp. She waited to feel consoled.

But instead, was overwhelmed by grief, by a sudden longing for her late father that she had not felt for months.

For the peace and order, the understanding of her life, before his loss.

23

Agnes had been delighted. "I haven't seen the play for years," she said as Lily drove her home at the end of the evening. "Not easy, restoration comedy, but really, I thought it was a triumph. More of a performance than just a reading."

"Thank you, Agnes," Hugh said. "As you say, it's challenging, but it was my suggestion that we would bring it to life so much more if we interacted with each other. Obviously not staging it in any real sense, but at least adding a few moves and gestures rather than sitting stock still. Far more satisfying to perform that way."

"I am sure it must be."

"Hugh was quite a task master," Lily said, "insisting on a couple of rehearsals before tonight."

"How fortunate the society is to have gained a professional. And to have retained you. So often such people are with us only fleetingly, aren't they, Lily? It's good to see you still with us for another season. I hope you'll be reading next month."

"November could be difficult," Hugh said. "Work is piling up. And I really don't want to hog things. I know I'm still a relative newcomer compared with so many of the members."

"That really is of no importance. It's the quality of the readers that counts," Agnes said as they drew up outside her block of flats.

"That's kind," Hugh said. "But of course, one has to grab

work while it's there. There's a pilot for a new TV series – a hospital soap, in fact, being made in Bristol, which might take me away for a week or so. Possibly longer."

"I see," Agnes said. Her opinion of television was low, Lily knew, and Hugh's comment unlikely to have impressed her the way he expected. She gathered her bag, found her gloves in her careful methodical way. "Kind of Lily to give you a lift home too, Hugh. She's becoming quite the taxi driver!" He offered to accompany her to her front door, but she waved him away. "Quite unnecessary, thank you. No-one is going to intimidate me on my own doorstep."

Lily was pleased that Hugh had shared her discretion, preferring to keep an awareness of their temporary living arrangement from Agnes. Clearly, she saw Hugh as no more than an acquaintance from the society.

"So this TV pilot series is definitely going ahead?" she said as she drove them back to Alfred Street. Hugh often mentioned projects with some initial enthusiasm that then dissipated when he did not get a call. On this occasion, however, he was more positive.

"There's definitely some work available in a couple of weeks. Bit parts, one-liners, that sort of thing. Or possibly just extra work which will no doubt end up on the cutting room floor. But one never knows. Especially with a pilot series."

"And you can fit it in with the theatre school?"

"Robin's always happy to cover. Thinks we sound more authentic if one of us has to be away for professional work. He's probably right."

"I'd better not cast you for *The Doll's House*, then, if you might be away next month."

"Ibsen? Another challenging choice. Who do you have in mind for Norah?"

Lily turned off the engine. There were lights downstairs in

the kitchen and in the first-floor bedroom, Stella's bedroom, as well. Hector was sitting on the doorstep of Anna and Simon's house as if he had given up hope of his own letting him in.

"It's more democratic than that," Lily said. "As you know, people express preferences."

"Of course, but you don't want to end up with anyone weak in the main role simply because you're abiding by the so-called rules, do you?" He got out of the car and called to Hector who, after a defiant stare, came running to his side. Amanda Morris had already suggested herself for Norah, but Lily had been equivocal. She was, of course, too old for the role, but the society was usually indifferent to such considerations. It was the woman's assumption, her extravagant manner that Lily found irritating yet her personal feelings were clearly irrelevant when it came to casting. Stella was coming down the stairs as they went into the hall.

"Just off out. Oh, Hugh, a phone call for you. There's a message somewhere. You need to ring back sometime. Do you know, Lily, you really should think about getting an extension or two. No-one lives with just one phone these days. It's really quite antique, don't you think? Charming, but hopelessly impractical!"

"She's right, I suppose," Lily said as Stella went out.

"I'm afraid so," Hugh said, picking up a scrap of paper that had fallen under the hall table. "And one has to think of security with a house in London. You should have a phone in the bedroom, Helen, for any nighttime emergencies."

Lily, who remembered the house with no phone at all, then the excitement of its arrival in the halls where it had been regarded initially with some awe, found herself agreeing.

"I'll certainly think about it. What about your house in Fulham? How many do you have there?"

Hugh turned the scrap of paper over as if looking for more.

"Oh, we certainly had a second one put in at some stage." He looked up at Helen, smiled broadly. "Which reminds me, things are moving fast on the house. Exchange should be any day now. I heard from the solicitor this morning and it seems it's all systems go. So with any luck I can be out of your hair by the spring. If interest rates and property prices haven't gone through the roof by then, of course. I do hope I haven't been priced out of the market."

"Surely not," Lily said, ashamed of an inevitable ignorance on her part about house buying. "Won't there be some equity left after the sale?"

"Of course," Hugh said. "But remember those debts to the builders. And the money I've had to invest with Robin at the theatre school. I had to find that, of course."

"I thought that was only a nominal sum," Lily said.

"It all adds up," Hugh said bleakly. "But you're right, as always, Helen. I can't complain. Not after selling the house so swiftly. And this..." He held aloft the scrap of paper he had picked up from the floor and waved it. "It's about the Bristol job. The pilot for the hospital soap. The casting's definitely on so let's hope my fortunes are on the upturn."

★★★

Hugh went down to Bristol for a few days the following week. Back by the weekend, he entertained Dorothy with his stories of filming as they sat over Sunday lunch, although as Lily drove her home later she was more brutal in her observations.

"Not really the sort of thing a man of his age should be doing, surely," she said.

"What do you mean? He's an actor," Lily objected.

Dorothy raised her eyebrows.

"Exactly. Surely, he's better off with this teaching of his rather than spending time in some low-class television nonsense. How does the man make a decent living doing that? And remind me why he needs to be lodging with you at all, Lily?"

"It's temporary until he buys a new home," Lily said swiftly. "And he's just sold his house in Fulham."

"Really? He didn't mention that today. Selling his house, I mean. Whyever is he doing that?"

"He's keen to get something smaller. And to leave behind the hooks and memories of the past, I think. Which is entirely understandable."

Dorothy shrugged.

"One should never get sentimental about houses. A pointless thing to do. So, where's he off to now?"

"He's thinking about north London," Lily said. "A flat, probably."

"Well, I suppose that's sensible for a widower. I have to say that when you first told me that your friend Hugh was an actor, I was rather thinking of the West End. Subsidised theatre at a pinch. The National or the RSC. Not that it's any business of mine, of course."

"No," Lily said, "it's certainly not," and immediately regretted it. She had no idea why she was feeling petulant and defensive since the day had been pleasant enough. "Sorry," she said, "I didn't mean to snap at you. It's just what the profession is like these days."

Her aunt remained silent for the rest of the journey. Only as they reached Harrow did she say anything more.

"As long as you know what you are doing, Lily, and are being sensible about everything."

Lily smiled. "That's the sort of thing you said to me when I was a child."

"There's nothing childish about being sensible," her aunt said. "Something that a lot of adults fail to understand."

★★★

Hugh was away again in Bristol the following week and had another call for the weekend. It was turning out to be little more than extra work, he said, but at least it could be fairly regular if the series took off. Stella also left on Friday to stay with friends and was vague about her return. Lily firmly closed the door to what Stella had begun to refer to as her office, for the time being choosing not to confront her ongoing occupation of the dining room.

Saturday stretched before her with a freedom she had not felt for many months. Previously, the house had gnawed at her in free hours with the need to slim down its possessions, but the renovation had lifted that responsibility, with sleight of hand disposed into numerous skips the collections and dust of decades. She left Alfred Street mid-morning with no particular plan for the day, but to be out of the house and occupied. Already the hours of daylight were diminished. Lily felt unprepared for another winter as if the year was spinning too fast with the shops turning their minds prematurely to Christmas even before Remembrance Day. Her father had liked to attend the Sunday service at the Cenotaph, standing at some distance from the formalities of the ceremony, as if compelled to pay respect, but retain his own despair of conflict. The Falklands War, so shortly before his death, had saddened him profoundly and Lily had sensed that he would have been outraged by the victory parade that had followed months later through the city of London. She walked down Rosebery Avenue, on towards Holborn, cutting through Covent Garden for a coffee and a bun in a crowded, convivial café. Then, prompted by buying a poppy and with her father still in mind, she headed for Whitehall and paused for some moments by the Cenotaph, moving in its austerity. And thought with shame of his unscattered ashes, exasperated by her procrastination, her abnegation of a duty simply because there had been no instructions. And it occurred to her now how typical this was of her futility. She had spent over fifty years complacently obliging, but failing to initiate and now the habit was too ingrained to shift.

But such introspection was tiresome.

On a whim, she headed to Pimlico and the Tate Gallery, a memory, no doubt prompted by the poppy now pinned to her coat, of her aunt taking her there when it reopened after the war. London, beleaguered by bomb damage, limping through the early days of reconstruction and recovery, was bleak and inhospitable for a twelve-year-old girl. But some of the paintings had been a revelation. She had held a particular romantic attachment to Pre-Raphaelite art ever since, the opulence and intensity of colour and subject matter that had entranced her then, an escape from the drab realities of a war-weary city, never quite leaving her. The galleries were typically busy with Saturday visitors and she took her time, waiting for groups to dissolve in front of famous paintings before she could get close enough to Ophelia, to the Lady of Shallot, Beata Beatrix and Proserpine. She stood for several minutes in front of each one, noting detail she had forgotten or had eluded her on previous visits. After a while, she sensed that she was being watched. A man sitting on a bench in the middle of the room was staring at her, looking lost in thought as if trying to pin down a memory. A woman came in from a neighbouring room, sat down next to him and the way they spoke to each other, covertly, eyes darting towards her and away, was disconcerting. Lily made a move to leave, but they both stood up at that moment and their paths inevitably crossed. The man smiled.

"I think we've met. Briefly, at least. You're a friend of Hugh. Hugh Murray?"

For a moment, Lily's mind was blank. She could not ever remember meeting any friend of Hugh's unless it was someone he had invited to her party and she had failed to notice.

"My husband has a photographic memory for faces," the woman said, apologetically. "And expects everyone else to be the same."

"It was earlier in the year," he pursued. "On the South Bank. By the Festival Hall."

Lily remembered.

"Of course," she said. "I'm so sorry. We saw you after the concert. It must have been in May." She recalled also Hugh's disinclination to talk to the man, something about him being obnoxious or perhaps simply a bore.

"It's Ralph. Ralph and Fiona Fisher. And you are… sorry, your name's slipped my mind. Not as good at names as at faces and I'm sure Hugh introduced us."

"Lily Page," she said, "although Hugh always calls me Helen."

"Of course! Helen, that's right. We used to be neighbours, you see. Years ago, inevitably, but Hugh will have filled you in about all that business."

"Was that in Fulham?" Lily asked. The man seemed pleasant enough and she tried to forget Hugh's judgement of him.

"Yes, that's right. The good old Fulham days when we were all considerably younger. Well, they were good for a while, at least. Of course, it all went rather sour for Hugh. We were only talking about that the other week with Louise, as it happens."

"Louise?" Lily assumed that she had misheard. She waited to be corrected. But Ralph Fisher went on.

"Yes, Hugh's ex. We met her by complete chance at a wedding. Well, not really such chance as we all go way back a long way if you think about it. All friends of the bride's parents and our daughter's kept up with Sarah. The bride, that is."

The woman, Fiona Fisher, looked at her and Lily knew that she saw in her face what entirely eluded her voluble husband.

"Louise?" she repeated woodenly.

"Yes. Sorry, am I putting my foot in it? I don't suppose old Hugh talks much about her as it was all so bitter at the end. More or less having to evict him from the house when he refused to go."

"Ralph." His wife put her hand firmly on his arm. Lily noted a gold chain bracelet on her thin, freckled wrist. "I really think we should go. Time's getting on."

Lily ignored her.

"I thought she was dead," she said baldly. "Hugh told me Louise had died."

Now it was Ralph's turn to look awkward, to glance at his watch. At his wife, Fiona.

"Well, really, it's not for us to get involved. I'm so sorry if we've – best forgotten, probably. Ask Hugh for all the details if you must. And Fi's right, we should be getting along." They started to move away, but Lily stopped them.

"Please. Don't go. I want you to tell me. About Louise and Hugh. If I ask him, how will I know if he is simply lying to me?"

Neither of them said anything for a moment, then Ralph started to say something about it being Hugh's business what he told his friends when Fiona interrupted him.

"Don't be idiotic, Ralph. Helen is clearly not just any friend of Hugh's."

"He's been living with me for the past six months. Although it's a temporary arrangement while his house in Fulham is… he was living with his sister in Balham before that." Her voice faltered. Surely they were mistaken, Ralph and Fiona. Perhaps it was another Louise, a previous marriage, yet at the same time Lily knew that all she held to be true about Hugh was slowly eroding, all points of reference slippery and suspect. Helplessly, she looked from one to the other, from Ralph to Fiona, feeling as if she was the innocent in a bewilderingly corrupt adult world that had been hidden from her.

"Let's go and sit down somewhere," Fiona said firmly. Ralph began to protest, but she took Lily's arm and he followed.

He found them a table in the corner of the gallery café and then went in search of tea.

"You must think me a very foolish woman," Lily said.

Fiona shrugged.

"Hugh's a good storyteller," she said. "Quite the raconteur. We haven't been close for years, but he was always entertaining. Convincing even. But treacherous."

"Treacherous?"

"Oh, nothing criminal. At least as far as we know. But with women. With reality, you could say. No doubt Hugh half believes this story about a sister living in Balham who's kindly put him up for a while."

"He has no sister?"

Again, Fiona shrugged. She slipped off her jacket and her scarf fell to the floor. Lily picked it up and her head swam so that for a moment she thought she would faint.

"I have no idea. But he did move to Balham when Louise finally got rid of him and sold the house in Fulham. Last we knew, he was living in a rented bedsit in a shared house somewhere off the high street."

"And when was this?"

"Six years ago. It was around the time we were thinking of getting out. Out of London, that is. We moved to Dorset about the same time Louise sold and went off to Norfolk. I think she'd already started divorce proceedings by then."

Ralph returned with a tray of tea and scones.

"I wasn't sure what you would want," he said. "So I got a pot of each."

"Each?" Fiona lifted lids. Peered in.

"One of breakfast, one of Early Grey and one of – breakfast again, I think."

Fiona poured randomly into three cups, passed one to Lily.

"But I don't understand his pretence," Lily said. "What could he gain by it?"

Fiona and Ralph exchanged glances. They drank their tea.

"It's not for us to make moral judgements on his behaviour," Fiona said eventually.

"No," Ralph said sharply, "it's not."

"But you should know that there's a pattern," she went on. "Louise divorced him for adultery. There had been numerous affairs on his part, evidently. And she could have dragged various other factors into the equation, I'm sure."

"Other factors?"

"Oh, money matters generally. The house was hers, you see. She bought it before they met and – well, let's just say that Hugh was an expert in spending her money and not contributing to the household expenses."

Ralph took time buttering the scones as if distancing himself from the conversation and taking a merely practical role in the proceedings. He offered the plate to Lily. She shook her head.

"Has Louise remarried?" It was immaterial to her, but she felt she wanted to shore up her knowledge against the inevitable confrontation with Hugh.

"No," Fiona says, "although she has a very pleasant partner. A fellow lawyer. Did I mention that Louise is a lawyer? Specialises in family and matrimonial matters, ironically enough."

"And she now lives in Norfolk?"

"King's Lynn," Ralph added swiftly as if at last on safe ground. "Lovely house. Late Georgian, I'd say from the pictures. Of course, house prices are ridiculously low in that part of the world compared with London. Or Dorset, come to that."

"Ralph," Fiona said, "Helen is not interested in property values in East Anglia."

"No, of course not," he added hastily.

There seemed little more to say. The three of them went on drinking tea. Ralph ate two of the three scones.

"Of course, he might be a changed man," he said suddenly, brushing crumbs from the front of his sweater. "Where women are concerned. We wouldn't want to paint an utterly negative portrait of Hugh, would we, Fi?"

"He has lied to me. Endlessly," Lily said. "I think that tells me enough."

"He was often marvellous company," Ralph said as if Lily hadn't spoken. "Life and soul of any party every time. And not a bad actor either when he could get the work."

"And a fantasist. Always was. Felt the world owed him more than it was delivering. Still does, no doubt." Fiona looked across the table at Lily. "I'm so sorry if we have rather destroyed things for you. Will you be all right? You were bound to find out in the end."

"Yes," she said bleakly. "Yes, I was."

After they left, Lily sat on, trying to grasp the full extent and detail of Hugh's deception, at the same time feeling as if she had always doubted his story, as if Ralph and Fiona Fisher had merely confirmed suspicions she had cravenly chosen to repress. There had been, after all, certain inconsistencies. He had been guarded about his alleged sister in Balham, never suggested a visit to the Fulham house. And his claim to a sudden impulse to sell should have been questioned. Yet she had been complacent, blinkered in accepting his version of events. She had allowed him too much discretion in what he had willingly shared.

But his motivation bewildered her.

She simply could not understand why anyone would lie in order to pursue a relationship. But perhaps she was far too naïve about such matters. After all, Toby Jessop had made duplicitous claims in excusing his inability to marry.

It appeared that people lied glibly even to those they professed to love.

Her head began to throb and the clutter and crowds of Saturday visitors were suddenly overwhelming. Outside, the wind had picked up, the sunless day now heading towards an early dusk and she walked rapidly along the Embankment, clutching at the familiar surroundings for some sense of stability and reassurance. She felt both desperate to speak to Hugh, yet at the same time dreaded the confrontation. As if until the moment he admitted the fraudulence of his story it was still simply an abstract concept, a fanciful account from an imaginative mind intended to amuse rather than deceive.

Somehow, she had reached Victoria without being aware of her direction and she headed for the Army and Navy Stores as a distraction from her thoughts. It was airless, overheated, but Lily tried to concentrate on buying something she needed, desperate to catch hold of normality on a day that was proving so very other. In the hosiery department, she stared at the rows and rows of orderly arranged tights, plain and patterned, opaque and gossamer-thin, neutral and multi-coloured, then abandoned the task, defeated by choice.

Close to the station, there was a line of phone boxes and a small queue had formed partially blocking the pavement. Instinctively, Lily joined it. She needed to talk to someone.

A close friend, a sympathetic voice that would help her to reason and rationalise what she had heard. But no names came to mind. Of course she had friends. But none with whom she could share such confidences and consequently display her sense of humiliation. The queue was shortening until she was next in line. The young man in the box appeared to be making several short calls, scanning a scrap of paper as if working through a series of phone numbers, no doubt in search of accommodation with a large rucksack at his feet and the general appearance of a student travelling. Lily found herself growing concerned for him. There was something defenceless about him, as if he was struggling to understand the language or the system as he grappled for more coins, tried another number. It made her own sense of dislocation insignificant. She wished she could offer advice, help in some way with the problem that this obvious stranger to the city was experiencing. Then suddenly his calls were finished, his enormous rucksack heaved onto shoulders that seemed too frail for the task and she herself was standing in the box that smelt of stale, acrid smoke. A hint of urine. Her aunt answered within moments.

It was the only voice, Lily had realised, that she wanted to hear.

"Lily, is that you? Why ever are you ringing me from a public phone box? Is something wrong, the house on fire?"

"No, nothing like that," Lily said. "It's just that there's been a bit of trouble with my line." She improvised frantically. "And I didn't want you to worry if you couldn't get through. That's all."

"Well, I can't say I was intending to ring you today, child. I've nothing to say."

Dorothy's inflexible practicality was consoling.

"No, well, I just thought I would let you know. Just in

case. And no doubt it will be fixed by the time I'm home. The line, that is."

"I doubt it. I don't suppose engineers work at weekends. Anyway, was that all, Lily? I can't imagine how many coins you are having to push into one of those infernal machines to make this call."

"And we need to talk about Christmas, of course," Lily said wildly. The queue outside the phone box was forming again, faces fixed on her as if trying to predict the length of her call.

"Christmas? Whatever for?"

"When you come next Sunday, I mean. It's not that long away now, after all."

"Over a month, I believe. If we are sticking to tradition and the ways of the western world."

"Yes, I know. But time goes so quickly."

There was a pause. Lily wondered if they had been cut off. She had no more coins suitable to thrust into the slot.

"Lily, are you sure you are all right?"

Her aunt's concern was sufficient.

"Yes, absolutely fine. I'll ring from home as soon as the line is fixed. Just so that you know."

"Very well, Lily. Enjoy the rest of your weekend."

"And you. And see you next Sunday. Looking forward to it."

Her aunt, however, had gone.

24

Hugh was not home until Monday afternoon. Predictably, Lily had slept badly on Saturday night and had spent Sunday feeling both listless yet anxious to occupy the hours productively as if that would be a distraction. But the effort was futile. At times, she rationalised that she had only heard Ralph and Fiona Fisher's version of events and that Hugh might present the story differently.

Yet that was the entire point.

It was simply a story.

At first, there was no chance to speak to him alone. He was sitting with Stella over tea and a pile of toast in the kitchen when she arrived home from work and he pulled up a chair for her, offered to make a fresh pot. She found it impossible to look directly at him and the two of them, talking about his work in Bristol, laughing at the banal script, appeared not to notice that she said little. Conversation drifted onto a potential new client for Stella and Crispin who they were due to meet that evening. Eventually, she looked at her watch, said something about needing to make a phone call to confirm timings and disappeared upstairs.

"I ought to make a move too," Hugh said, "Sorry to rush off when I haven't seen you all weekend, Helen, but I'm teaching a class tonight for Robin. He's covered so much for me lately that I didn't like to turn him down. We'll catch up later."

He stood up, carried cups to the sink, rinsed them. Lily

took a piece of toast as a distraction. It was now cold, leathery, and butter had seeped into a greasy pool on the white plate.

"I met friends of yours on Saturday," she said.

"Friends of mine? Where was that, Helen?" He sounded indifferent.

"At the Tate Gallery."

"Haven't been there for years. We should go together next time. Lucky you, having a cultural weekend in London while I was earning my hard crust as a walk-on in TV trash."

"It was Ralph and Fiona Fisher," Lily said. "I believe you were neighbours when you lived in Fulham. With your wife, Louise."

In the brief silence there were sounds from upstairs, Stella's voice on the phone, animated, steps on the stairs. Lily watched Hugh as he walked to the French windows, pulling the curtains against the darkness of the evening.

"Years ago," he said dismissively and picked up his jacket from the back of a chair, slipped it on. "They moved to the country." Ignorant of the breadth of her knowledge, Lily could see that he was intent on salvaging the situation. Grappling for safe ground. "And we were never that close. Never really liked Ralph, in fact, and Fiona could be a bore."

"Yet they sounded as if they knew you well. Louise, too."

He patted his jacket as if checking for a wallet. Glanced up at the clock on the wall.

"So sorry, Helen, but I must go. It's later than I thought and I've got a class waiting for me."

"We can talk later, then," she said. "About everything I heard from them. From Ralph and Fiona. It was enlightening, I have to say." For the first time since Saturday, Lily felt controlled, resolute. She turned to face him fully. "Unless you'd simply rather leave this evening. Move out, I mean. That might be better. Take your things now."

Hugh's expression changed, complacency replaced by panic.

"What are you talking about, Helen? This is absolute nonsense. Whatever gossip you've heard from those two, well, it's all a misunderstanding, believe you me."

"They seemed very certain about the facts, these old friends of yours. Louise, for example. Apparently, she's not dead. They saw her the other week, alive and well."

Hugh's attitude altered. He moved slowly towards the table, sat down and tried to take her hand. She ignored the gesture, pushed the plate of limp toast away from her.

"My darling Helen, I've been such a fool," he said eventually. His voice was quiet, low. "You have to believe me when I say I never meant to hurt you. Or mislead you. Forgive me, please."

"What do you want me to forgive?" Lily said calmly. "I think you need to be precise. Is it your lies about your wife who divorced you? Or the fabrication of a sister? Or perhaps it's the sale of your so-called house in Fulham that never belonged to you? There's quite a list."

"I do have a sister," he said weakly.

"Living in Balham?"

"No. All right, no. She lives in Scotland."

Lily suddenly felt very tired. The last two nights of fractured sleep and the anticipation built up during the course of the working day had drained her. She ran a hand through her hair.

"You'd better go," she said. "If you have a class to teach."

He failed to move for a few moments, tried to engage Lily's face, but she avoided him for fear she might weaken or even cry.

"I can explain everything," he said firmly. "Absolutely everything. Just give me a chance, darling Helen. I know I've been an absolute fool, but we really mustn't throw away all we have. All we could have in the future."

Stella rushed down the stairs, took her briefcase that had been lying on the table and stood buttoning up a black winter coat, oblivious to the mood of the room.

"I'm out now. All evening until late probably. Crispin and I need to make a good impression tonight as this job could be the tip of the iceberg if we get it. These people we're seeing – well, if they like us and approve it could make all the difference." She beamed at the two of them and then disappeared up the stairs again. They waited for the front door to bang, Stella's footsteps down the street.

"I'll see you later," Hugh said eventually. "Darling Helen, don't brood about this all evening, will you? It really is so unnecessary."

"We'll talk when you come in," Lily said. And turned away when he tried to kiss her cheek, involuntarily flinching as if from an assault.

★★★

His proposal had startled her.

Lily had spent the evening anticipating Hugh's spirited defence of his behaviour and thus when he returned listened to it mostly in silence. Everything, he claimed, the pretence and the subterfuge had been grounded only in a desire to gain her affections. Her acceptance of him. He had been immediately attracted to her, he said, from that dark January night when he had inadvertently turned up for beginners' Italian class. Serendipitous, since his error had led him to her and the Play Reading Society. But he had felt ashamed of his past history, believed she would judge him negatively. A divorced man with no home of his own was hardly a subject likely to win even the temporary interest of a woman like Lily. Like Helen, he had amended. And what had begun as an innocent enough experiment simply to get to know her had become inflated, out of hand, as he realised the depth of his feelings for her. By the time he realised that what he wanted was not a transient friendship, but a permanent bond, it had been too late to retract his story. He knew he needed to confess his distortion of the truth – he had objected to her use of the word invention – but had been cowardly in his procrastination.

Ralph and Fiona Fisher's chance meeting with Lily had pre-empted the moment for it.

"In fact, I'm relieved," he had said eventually, leaning back in his chair with an air of capitulation. "At least now everything is out in the open. Although naturally I wish I had told you myself. Explained it all logically."

"Logically? Louise divorced you for adultery," Lily said.

Hugh shook his head resignedly.

"That was the detail. But our marriage was at an end, had been for some time. She hadn't been particularly faithful herself in those last few months if the truth be told."

Toby Jessop had been guilty of adultery and she, by implication, had been culpable. Thus it was not the fact, but the audacity of his narrative that troubled her. His ability to perpetuate such a lie, not only to her, but to her aunt, to Stella as well, was breath-taking. Although as far as Stella was concerned, she doubted whether she would take any interest in the falsity of Hugh's story. Her own personal account had, after all, been somewhat edited.

"I feel I know nothing about you now," Lily said simply.

"Nothing has changed."

"How can you say that? Everything is altered."

"Nothing in the present has changed. The past is irrelevant to us. To you and me, Helen. It's what is ahead that matters."

"You have humiliated me, made me look a fool. How do I know you won't do that again?"

He leant forward again, took her hand. She was too weary to resist and in some incalculable way it was of comfort.

"You are no fool, Helen. I am the clown who has risked losing everything in an effort to gain you. I am so very sorry. I don't know what else to say. But believe me, everything was done with only the best of intentions."

"You chose to mislead."

He hung his head. Said nothing. Lily knew her own reticence was also at fault. If she had asked more questions, insisted on clarifying his circumstances, the fabrication could not have flourished. She felt weary of the whole matter, wanted only to go upstairs to bed and slip into the oblivion of sleep. Wake in the morning to a day absent of conflict.

"Marry me, Helen."

Hugh's voice was low and Lily, assuming she must have misheard, ignored him. But he persisted, began to sound insistent. "I am asking you to marry me. Please. Or at least to think about it. I don't expect an answer straight away."

"Hugh, this is ridiculous," Lily said. She stood up and started to make her way to the door, but he stopped her, placed his hands on her shoulders.

"No, it's not. It's probably the sanest thought I have had in years. Why is it so hard for you to believe that I love you?"

"Because you lied to me," Lily said. "Over and over again. That does not sound like love to me."

She broke away from him and went up to her room, closing the door firmly behind her.

★★★

But her thoughts were far less disciplined than her words. Lily had never received a proposal of marriage. And the notion that in middle age she should suddenly find herself the focus of a man's desire, of his declared wish to marry, however devious his route, was hard to dismiss out of hand.

The alternative was the prospect of spending the years ahead alone.

She had, after all, no children, no assured company of any kind to soften and mollify the decades that, with luck and good fortune, stretched out in front of her. Hugh's deception towards her had been blatant. Yet, as the routine of the working week went on, the shock of it was diluted and she could even allow herself to believe in his words of mitigation. He continued to sleep in the spare room and Lily made no gesture to suggest he return to hers nor did he press the matter. He had picked up some extra classes at the theatre school and spent three more days working in Bristol so that she saw little of him and, when they were both home, Stella's presence was often a convenience. And a curiosity, for she appeared to have entirely changed her appearance as if the creation of Fox and Hawkins required a certain uniform and dress code. Gone were the trailing floral skirts and cheesecloth chemises, replaced by sharp suits in magenta and navy and black, jackets with padded shoulders that added breadth to Stella's narrow frame. On Saturday morning, Lily watched her as she pulled on a subdued camel coat she had not seen before.

"No fur this winter, then?" Lily said.

Stella smiled knowingly.

"Clothes indicate economic achievement," she said. "In this outfit I am a strong-minded, assertive woman of the 80s. The sort of woman our potential clients will believe in and trust with their money. You should try it sometime, Lily. Perhaps we should go shopping together and I'll help you choose outfits that are relevant to today."

"It's very kind of you to offer, Stella, but I don't think that's necessary for the admin office at school," Lily said.

"Ah, but that's the point," Stella said, "perhaps you'd get yourself out of the admin office and climb the professional ladder if you dressed differently." Lily, all too aware that a slide down the career path to demotion had already been her route, said nothing. "The thing about that fur is that I found it on a market stall selling second-hand stuff," Stella went on. "Somewhere in Haggerston. And it's not even decent fur, just rabbit, I think. The lining's all torn and the hem coming down so really, it's only fit for a cat to sleep on, if you think about it."

"I'm sure Hector would be delighted."

"But I'm not criticising the way you dress, Lily." Stella looked concerned. "Not at all. It's just that these things are important these days. Especially for women. Strength needs to be displayed on the outside as well as the inside."

"I'll bear that in mind," Lily said. It was a relief to have an innocuous conversation with Stella where she felt unguarded. "What about Crispin?"

"Oh, he's had to smarten up a bit, I can tell you. No good looking like a perpetual art student. Not if you want to get commissions worth thousands."

"I'm so glad it's all proving such a success. Fox and Hawkins, I mean. And in such a short space of time."

"Oh Lily, that's so sweet. And so like you." Stella took out gloves from the deep pockets of her coat. Leather, Lily noted, replacing the woollen mittens of the winter before. "But we're a long way from making a profit yet. You could call us a fledgling concern, but not yet flying. And we couldn't do any of it without you, of course. We really are totally dependent and ever grateful!"

Lily watched her go, listened as her high-heeled boots tapped down the steps and out into the street. The idea of

Stella's dependency seemed suddenly unwelcome, like a physical burden that Lily wanted to unload. At least her gratitude was of some consolation. She turned her mind to *The Doll's House*. The reading was only ten days away and she had just been let down by two members due to read major roles. After a few phone calls, she had managed to cast Christine, but Krogstad remained unfilled. It was the perennial problem of an inadequate number of men in the society and Hugh initially had been vague about his professional commitments for late November. Now she had no wish to pressurise him as if such a favour would be seen as a criteria for her forgiveness when the matter was too enormous for a facile resolution. But when he arrived back from Bristol an hour or so later he seemed eager to oblige.

"I thought you might be too busy," Lily said in a neutral tone.

"It's all gone quiet for a while. Apart from the theatre school, of course. Krogstad, you say? I wouldn't mind having a stab at him." He took a copy of the play from her, sat down by the window and started to read, looking up after a while to smile at Lily. "You know, I'm indebted to you and the society, Helen, for reminding me of real drama. It's like revisiting my younger days of provincial rep." He became absorbed again and Lily left him to read, relieved that she had promised to go to the school's Christmas Fair to assist on the tombola stall and thus, craven, avoid being in his sole company.

The day was bitterly cold with the first frost of winter overnight so the overheated assembly hall decked garishly with tinsel and paper chains, was cheering.

"Usual plans, Lily? For Christmas, I mean." Monica, the bursar's secretary, neatly lined up the bottles on the stall as if reluctant to see any of them won and their stock depleted.

"I suppose so," Lily said. "My aunt will certainly be coming."

And Hugh, she thought. Possibly Hugh. After all, where else would he go? Eviction was beginning to seem inconceivable, particularly at this time of year. Yet Dorothy would not have forgotten his claim to widowhood and she refused to perpetuate his lie. She gave the drum containing the tombola tickets a swift turn. "It's hard to think that it will be the second Christmas without my father. He always loved it."

"Oh, so do I!" Monica said. She was a large, kindly woman who had been at the school for over thirty years and rumours occasionally circulated that she was resolutely holding out against retirement. She had once confided to Lily that her fiancé had been killed in the Normandy landings towards the end of the war and she had remained single ever since. "I insist on embracing all the trimmings. Carol singing, Midnight Mass, stockings for my niece and nephew even though they are both highly successful young things and could buy me out of house and home if they wished. And a homemade plum pudding liberally laced and set on fire with brandy, of course."

"My father always insisted we buy ours each year from Harrods," Lily said. "It was his one indulgence so I feel obliged to keep up the habit."

"Of course!" Monica said. "Christmas is about family tradition. Even when the shape of that family has changed." She looked frankly at Lily. "Do you miss him terribly? It's allowed, you know, to go on mourning the departed endlessly. I know a little about that."

Lily served a parent who bought five tickets and waited until the numbers had been revealed and a bottle of Babycham handed over.

"This past year has been so different. Entirely unpredictable," she said eventually. "And, in fact, at times I've worried that I was losing sight of my father. Allowing him to be erased."

"Nonsense," Monica said firmly. "Life goes on and takes new directions, that's inevitable. But your father will always be there. In your heart and in your mind, Lily. Believe you me."

A huddle of girls crowded the stall, dithering over whether to buy a tombola ticket then moved off towards Lucky Dip instead. "The energy of the person lives on," Monica continued as if they had not been interrupted. "Call it soul or spirit if you like. I've always found that a comfort." She smiled, stared across the crowded hall. "It seems to give me a direction, anyway."

Later, back in Alfred Street, Lily found Hugh in a positive mood.

"All set for *The Doll's House!*" He greeted her warmly. "Such a powerful play, I'd forgotten. And really one that speaks to our age." He tried to slip an arm around her shoulder, but she moved out of reach, occupied herself with putting away draining mugs and plates. She was starkly aware of him watching her as she moved about the kitchen, eventually speaking with a sense of urgency. "Dear Helen, I know I promised to give you time. To make up your mind about marriage, that is. But I'm finding it so difficult not knowing your feelings. Would it be too much of an imposition if I could expect an answer by – well, let's say Christmas?"

"Christmas," Lily repeated, not so much in confirmation as in surprise at his insistence. They had not, after all, even resolved whether he was to stay living in the house. But Hugh seized on it.

"Thank you, Helen! I can live with that and I promise I won't say a word more about the subject until then. Won't nag you or make annoying hints. Now, how about a bit of lunch?" He moved swiftly to the fridge, taking out cheese, bread. Placed the fruit bowl on the table. "By the way, I was thinking of setting up a rehearsal for the principals in *The Doll's House* just as I did for *The Country Wife*. It seemed to make such a difference and really lifted the reading for our audience on the actual night. What do you think?"

"As long as people don't think it's a condition for reading," Lily said abstractedly, her mind more concerned with Hugh's ultimatum. "We're not an amateur dramatic society, after all."

"Of course. You're quite right," Hugh said. "Forget all about the idea. And tell you what, let's forget all about lunch here at home too and get ourselves out of the house right now!" He cleared the table as quickly as he had laid it. "I've been neglecting you lately, darling Helen, what with all this work in Bristol and the theatre school. Let me treat you this whole weekend for a change. Spoil you. We'll do whatever you like – just think of me as at your beck and call."

"It's Dorothy's Sunday visit tomorrow," Lily said firmly. Then regretted her tone. Perhaps she was simply too unversed in impulsive acts of kindness to recognise them. Too judgemental. After all, Hugh was clearly trying to make amends for his transgressions. He took her hand and this time she did not pull away.

"But there's today."

"Yes," she said eventually. "All right. Let's go out."

★★★

She was later than usual returning from work on Monday. She had offered to cover for one of the library assistants who was away ill and had spent a peaceful couple of hours returning books to shelves, supervising a few pupils who had remained behind in school to study.

A woman was standing on the pavement looking up at the house.

At first Lily thought she was a dog-walking neighbour

and prepared to smile and greet her as she got out of the car. But there was no dog and she failed to recognise her face. For one foolish moment Lily thought of Louise, Hugh's former wife, but instantly dismissed the idea. They were, after all, entirely out of each other's lives. She tried to move past, but the woman stopped her.

"Excuse me, I hope you don't mind me asking," she said hesitantly, "only I've tried ringing several times and no-one seems to be in."

There was a light in the basement kitchen, but Hugh was generally out at the theatre school on Monday evenings and Stella rarely remembered to turn lights off when she left the house. Lily waited for the woman to ask for money. A charity collection for the homeless at Christmas, donations for the annual party at the old people's home. Instead, the woman glanced up at the house again, then looked at Lily.

"I understand that Stella is living here. That's what I've been told."

"Stella?" Lily said, wary of confirming information to a stranger on the street.

"Yes," the woman said, "Stella Fox. I am Ellen Fox, Stella's mother."

25

Hugh showed little interest or surprise when he arrived home two hours later.

"It's really nothing to do with us, Helen. It's purely a family matter and just chance that you happened to meet this stranger at all."

"Stella's mother," Lily said.

"Yes, well, her mother."

"And Stella has given us such a very different idea about her parents."

"People have their reasons. Families can be very complex, you know. But really it's not your business, with absolutely no reason to get involved. In fact, my advice is to stay well clear of the whole subject."

"I suppose that would be best," she said. It was no doubt sound advice.

And she had passed on the letter left for Stella without comment, implying she had simply found it on the mat when she came home. Stella had responded with equal restraint.

But Lily found it impossible to despatch the visit from her mind.

She had been reluctant at first even to come into the house. Then at Lily's insistence agreed to wait briefly in the living room in case Stella came home. Ellen Fox was fair, her eyes pale, a face of small rather than striking features and a diffident manner that appeared to have no echo in her daughter. She sat quietly, looking up every now and again at the door as if half-expectant, half wary of seeing Stella suddenly standing there. She refused Lily's offer of tea or coffee.

"It's just that she hasn't been in touch for so long, you see," Ellen said, as if there was a need to justify herself. "I know I shouldn't have come, but we've been so worried. Well, at least I have."

"That's understandable," Lily said.

"Obviously, we hear from Ed and see Dylan as often as possible. Our grandson? But perhaps you didn't know about Stella's child. Why would you? I really shouldn't be bothering you about all this. After all, Stella is simply a tenant of yours, I suppose."

"Something like that," Lily said vaguely.

She apologised again for the intrusion.

"I just thought if I could see her, it would put my mind at rest. My husband thinks I'm fussing. And her brother too, of course. But once I had an address for her – Ed gave it to me – I hope you don't mind – well, I'm afraid I couldn't resist just coming to see where she was living."

"I didn't know Stella had a brother," Lily said. Already she was revising her understanding of indifferent, careless parents. The lack of a supportive family. "She's never mentioned him. But as you say," she added rapidly, "she's simply a tenant so no reason for me to know about her life."

Neither of them had spoken for some moments. A taxi had pulled up in the street and Lily had anticipated Stella's key in the door, but it had pulled away and there was silence again. Ellen Fox coughed, fidgeted with her wedding ring.

"She was always a very clever girl, very bright, you know," she said eventually. She picked up her bag from where it was sitting at her feet as if preparing to leave then put in down again, glanced around the room. "And very ambitious. I'm afraid she's always found us all very dull. Very ordinary. Me in particular." She attempted a half smile.

"I'm sure that's not true," Lily said.

"Oh, but it is." She had been adamant. "As if she thought we weren't quite good enough for her. And that's all right. Quite understandable, really, given what Stella is like. Of course, hearing about the baby was a shock at first. Not what we expected at all. But then it seemed like it might be a good thing, that it would change everything between us and bring her back to us. If I'm honest, I hoped she might find a need for me in particular. That I could be of some use to her. But then Stella made her own arrangements. It shocked us, to be truthful. That she could do that with her own child. But, of course, Ed is a very good father. And Jessie, too, is a natural so we couldn't wish for better for Dylan. In the circumstances. And we're always welcome when we can get to visit them."

"I believe Stella said something about you going to live in France," Lily said cautiously.

"Living in France?" Ellen Fox's face was blank. "Oh no, not us. You must be thinking of another tenant. Other parents."

"Ah yes," Lily said, "perhaps I am."

"We've always lived in Lincolnshire. Since before Stella was born."

She had been in London for the weekend seeing her son. Christopher, she said, had just started working in a primary school in Putney. She had stayed nearby with an old friend and had spent the day doing some shopping and seeing the Christmas lights. Oxford Street, Regent Street. The tree in Trafalgar Square.

She had handed Lily a letter.

"If you could make sure Stella gets this, I'd be ever so grateful," she said as if it was an enormous favour to ask. "Tell her, please, that I didn't want to risk it in the post, not knowing the sort of place she was living in. I mean it could have been a hostel or one of those squat places for all I knew and all very communal and no proper system. For the post, I mean."

Lily promised to hand it personally to Stella. The pale blue envelope clearly contained several sheets of paper and she wondered if Ellen Fox was partly relieved not to confront her daughter face to face, thinking rapprochement might be more calmly achieved this way. Just as she was about to leave, buttoning her navy coat, tying a woollen scarf around her neck, she turned to Lily and said,

"I just have to ask if she is up to date with her rent. I'd hate to think she was falling behind and owing you money. Her father would too and we'd insist on paying any shortfall."

Lily shook her head.

"That's very kind. But all is in order." She disliked misleading Ellen Fox. She was too open, too honest to deserve such deception. But the truth seemed to be slipping away from Lily, eroding rapidly so that she felt she no longer had any firm hold on facts. "And anyway, I believe Stella is moving out sometime soon. I think she has other plans."

"Really? That's a pity. I like to think of her somewhere as – well, as nice and homely as this." She glanced along the hall, to a coat over the banisters, a picture on the wall. "And you seem like a caring sort of person too. Silly, isn't it? But she's my child and however much Stella seems determined to keep us out of her life, to push us away, I can't help but worry and want only the safest and best for her."

"Of course," Lily said. "That's only natural. But as you say, she's a clever young woman. I am sure whatever she sets out to do in her life she will be successful."

She intended to reassure. Instead, Ellen Fox said, "I think that's always been our problem with her. She has always wanted so much. Expected it, really, since she was a young child. And as I said, we were never enough for her. Never interesting or exciting enough."

Lily spoke to Hugh only in general terms about the visit. Ellen Fox's comments about Stella seemed too personal to share as if she would be betraying confidences. And his dismissal of the subject seemed absolute.

"As you've already said yourself, Helen, she'll be moving out soon once this Fox and Hawkins business has truly taken off. I wouldn't be surprised, in fact, if we have the house to ourselves by Christmas or at least soon after." The proprietorial nature of his words disturbed her. But before she even had time to think of their implication, he went on. "Talking of Christmas, I assume 8 Alfred Street celebrates appropriately? All traditions observed? I imagine the street is awash with gatherings for mulled wine and mince pies. I have to say I'm rather looking forward to all that."

"If it is," Lily said, "I have never been invited."

The prospect of Christmas and the complications to be negotiated seemed daunting. Hugh had always been explained to her aunt as a temporary lodger, a friend in need of an act of kindness. But now there was no house in Fulham undergoing repairs. No property to sell and she could not imagine how she would reconstrue Hugh's situation to Dorothy when it still troubled her own comprehension.

Unless, of course, she accepted his proposal of marriage.

Somehow, however absurd the thought, that would seem to simplify matters.

Allow for a certain elision over details, even a mild mockery of the tale of his fabricated past. After all, his was not a story of criminal intent towards her, but simply a foolish, misguided error of judgement based on his affection for her and the consequent desire for her approval.

And he was probably right about the conviviality of Alfred Street at Christmas.

No doubt the place was a haven of festivities and with Hugh as her partner she would find herself duly invited. The single woman of a certain age, let alone a single woman with an aged parent, would always be anathema to any guest list. The previous Christmas had been sombre. Diminished. Dorothy had been unusually quiet and Lily had felt strained by the need to maintain conversation and attempt some degree of celebration. They had given in to watching television too early, eaten excessively, and, although it had always been the one night of the year that her aunt stayed, she had refused, insisting on being driven home before nine. Lily had returned along deserted streets to the empty house, rekindled the wood fire and drunk too much wine, regretting it the following morning. Boxing Day, at least, had been lightened by lack of expectation. Lily had taken a long walk and later Dorothy had rung and apologised for her morose mood the day before. She had not expected, she had said, with touching simplicity, to miss her brother from the day so very much.

And now December was looming again with what seemed like undue haste.

Perhaps it was as a result of living at a pedestrian pace for decades that the speed of change over the past months felt at times bewildering. As if Lily had unwittingly set out on a voyage without a compass, with little knowledge of the duration, destination, or even the route home. Yet she supposed she had been compliant. Or at least had failed to protest.

She could only imagine her father's quiet amazement at the inroads into the household. The possibility of her marrying. On the other hand, her aunt would no doubt be appalled.

But love was not commonplace.

Outside of familial bonds, love seemed to Lily to be such

a rare commodity that the thought of rejecting it out of hand seemed churlish. Preposterous, even. She was, after all, a very ordinary woman. The sort of woman to be overlooked even in a small gathering and as the years progressed such anonymity would only increase. Hugh, despite his flaws or even, perversely, because of them, drew interest. Attention. Surely she was extraordinarily fortunate to have gained his affections.

★★★

"Another excellent performance," Agnes said as Lily drove her home after *The Doll's House*. Hugh had headed straight to Shoreditch to the theatre school where there had been a break-in earlier in the day. The police wanted a statement about damage and theft, he told Lily, and there had been insufficient time for him to oblige earlier. "The society is most fortunate to have such strong members at the moment." Lily agreed. Hugh's insistence on a couple of rehearsals had clearly paid off again. "I suppose that's the last meeting until late January," Agnes went on.

"I'm afraid Christmas does rather overwhelm people now," Lily said, avoiding a cyclist who swerved precariously near to the car, tipping the wing mirror with his handlebars. "Although I believe there are plans for a social gathering of some sort. Amanda Morris mentioned something about Christmas drinks at her house just as we were leaving."

"Not for me," Agnes said firmly. "I am at least twenty years too old for that. But I suppose it's the sort of thing people want these days. Everyone has become so very sociable. One has to think of that."

"I suppose so," Lily said.

"She read very well. Amanda, I mean. It was good casting on your part, Lily. That final scene with Colin as Tesman was really quite moving. Of course, Colin was rather a natural for the part."

Lily pulled up outside Agnes's sprawling block of flats.

"Stolid and misogynistic, you mean?"

Agnes smiled. Her face, Lily thought, still had the delicacy and fine bone structure that in her youth would have been seen as features of great beauty. Fleetingly, she thought of her late mother who, if she had lived, would now have been about the same age as Agnes.

"That's unfair, Lily. But it's true that he always appears to be somewhat blinkered and obdurate. A loyal member of the society, nonetheless."

"Even if he only ever agrees to read after heavy persuasion on my part. It's an affectation of his that I've never quite understood. But you're right, it was a good performance this evening."

"We never used to talk in terms of performances, did we?" Agnes's hand hovered over the door handle. As usual, she seemed reluctant to leave the company and warmth of the car. "It's something Hugh Murray seems to have brought to the society. Ever since he joined and came up with these notions of rehearsals."

Lily sensed mild disapproval. She said nothing. Agnes was still unaware of the nature of her relationship with Hugh and for the time being there was no necessity for her to know more.

"Let's meet over the Christmas holiday," Lily said, trying to curtail the conversation. "Once the term finishes I'll be in touch."

Agnes gathered her gloves, her bag.

"I would like that very much, Lily. You always know where to find me."

★★★

Stella said, "The cake, then. I insist on making the cake. And the mincemeat for the pies. I have just the best recipe."

"That's very kind, Stella, but really, there's no need. Not when you are so busy with Fox and Hawkins. That must be your priority."

"Oh, but it is! We have new enquiries nearly every day. I tell you, Crispin and I can hardly keep up with demand. We'll be taking on more staff before long."

"And proper office space, no doubt," Lily said pointedly. But Stella was jotting something down in a notebook and seemed not to hear.

"But I do want to contribute to your Christmas preparations so please indulge me," she went on. "It's funny, but even though obviously I'm an atheist I just adore Christmas. But then everyone's like that these days, aren't they? There's no religious meaning left to it at all." Lily saw her write down brandy butter. She would cross it off later.

"I don't think the cathedrals and churches see it quite like that, Stella."

"I'm not talking about carol services. Even I might go to one of those. Everyone likes carols, don't they?"

"Midnight Mass?"

Stella pulled a face. "But I can imagine you going along to that, Lily. Just your sort of thing."

"You make it sound like an unfortunate aberration of mine."

"Not at all! I just meant you are so much nicer than me. A better sort of person, that's all. Really, Lily, you mustn't take offence when I'm simply complimenting you."

"I don't," Lily assured her. "But all these preparations seem rather excessive, Stella. We've never been the sort of household to overindulge and feed the fruit cake with port for weeks on end."

"Shame on you!" Stella said playfully. "Surely Dorothy expects a Dickensian sort of occasion."

"My aunt is not keen on what she would see as vulgar excess," Lily said. "As long as food is available in plentiful quantities she is usually satisfied. Although, of course," she added, in fairness, "she always admires your cooking, Stella."

"Would you mind terribly if I wasn't here for the actual Christmas Day itself, Lily? If I sneaked off a bit beforehand, in fact?" She doodled rosettes in her notebook like an adolescent seeking distraction from study. Lily was astounded she would even ask.

"I wasn't expecting you to be here. Surely you must have so many more appropriate places to spend the holiday." She thought of mentioning Stella's family, her young child, Dylan, but decided it was better to express indifference. "After all, this is all very temporary, you living and working here, isn't it? In a manner of speaking, you are just a tenant of mine." Stella looked up sharply, her face shocked, as if she had been unexpectedly insulted. Lily felt wrong-footed. "What I mean is that you naturally need to begin to think long term," she went on firmly. "A space of your own where you can live and work as you like. With people of your own age."

Stella said nothing for a moment. She fiddled with the dropped pearl of one earring then the other. Closed her notebook and placed it down on the table. Eventually, she said,

"I've never thought of our arrangement in quite that way, Lily. The word *tenant* is so… so cold. So functional. Whereas to me your home has always been a sanctuary. Yes, that has to be the word for it. And now that we've worked together as a sort of partnership to make it even more delectable, more desirable, I feel a connection with it that is not about bricks and mortar. Not about street value. It's so much deeper than that."

Lily stared at Stella. Ellen Fox was right. Her daughter was clever. She had never doubted that. But what Lily had failed to see was the brutality of that intelligence, how she could apply it ruthlessly to suit her own selfish whims, playing upon the vulnerabilities of others for her own advantage. Stella had exploited an obliging nature. And Lily had been too willing, too susceptible, to deter her. The young woman was a chameleon, changing colour to suit circumstance, dabbling at one role then another for the sheer novelty of the experience. Including a brief dalliance with motherhood.

Yet Lily felt relatively unscathed.

Stella had lived liberally in her home for the past nine months, but she could hardly blame the girl for what she had freely offered. Nor could she resent her persuasion to renovate the house for she had been complicit in the planning.

Or at least she had failed to resist Stella's momentum and had submissively agreed.

If at times Lily felt her grasp on events had become tenuous, decisions unwittingly delegated, debated without her knowledge, no doubt her passivity was to blame. Stella seemed to be waiting for an answer, her face expectant as if for an apology over Lily's turn of phrase. When Lily said nothing, went over to the sink instead and ran a tap over plates, she went on.

"Of course, you have made me feel part of a family, Lily. That's what has been special about living here. You've given me the roots I feel I've lacked for years."

"I've done nothing more than provide you with a room," Lily said disingenuously.

"Nonsense! You've given me the run of the kitchen to cook as much as I want for a start. Like all the Sundays when I've made endless roasts for Dorothy. Do you remember last Easter? And then your party in the summer. And of course simply getting to know your amazing aunt has enriched my life. All the long conversations I've had with her – really, I don't know who has enjoyed them the most!"

Lily set the plates to drain. Turned to a scorched saucepan and attempted to scour it. She had never known anyone before who dissembled with the ease and expertise of Stella. It was a performance of such consummate skill that she forgave herself for failing to penetrate the façade. Of course Hugh too was guilty of deception towards her. But, whilst Lily did not condone his lies, his ruse was surely of a different nature, with an aim that he had confessed with clarity.

Whereas Stella.

She continued to put away plates, pans, filling the hiatus between them with the noise.

She knew that she wanted her gone.

Out of the house swiftly so that Lily would be relieved of a confrontation about the strands of her life that she had sought to dissemble for no doubt her performance in self-defence would be exemplary. A tour de force that would be exhausting to witness. On an impulse, Lily turned towards Stella, still sitting at the table, her chin now propped on her two folded hands, and said,

"Of course, there will be some changes in the New Year. In the house, I mean."

Stella looked up as if agreeably surprised.

"More renovations, Lily? I have to say I was thinking that your next priority should be new stair carpet. It really has served its time." She beamed. "Do you have colours in mind?"

"No, that's not what I meant at all," Lily said. And, out of a need to fill the silence that grew between them, she found herself saying, "you see, Hugh will soon be moving in permanently. The fact is, Stella, that the two of us are going to be married."

26

Stella was elusive for the rest of that week.

Lily was relieved. Her announcement had been entirely rash and she had no wish to expand upon it or even share it with Hugh.

He had given her, after all, until Christmas.

And she was still far from resolute in her decision.

After all, she had simply used the claim of their marriage to serve as a way of giving Stella notice. She had looked shocked, surprised, but had said little, muttered a few words of congratulations then launched into a description of the latest commission she and Crispin were hoping to win. Lily had felt gratified that another sentimental, inflated speech had been avoided and had judged the matter settled.

And Hugh had been right about their neighbours in Alfred Street. Already Lily had received three invitations for December, holly-decked or mistletoe-embossed cards that she propped up on the mantelpiece in the way she assumed appropriate. She stood looking at them with caution.

"I can't imagine what we will all find to say to each other if the same people attend all three," she said. "And I suppose they will."

Hugh laughed.

"Helen, people don't say anything of worth at these parties. In fact, no-one really listens to what anyone else is saying."

"Really? So what's the point of them?"

"The point? Does there have to be a point in having a party?"

"I would have thought so. I can understand having one street event as a neighbourly celebration. But three? That seems excessive."

"There's always a certain amount of competition about these things, I imagine. Especially amongst the well-heeled of Islington."

Hugh picked up a log and pushed it onto the fire where it spluttered and caused a flume of smoke to billow into the room. The chimney needed sweeping, Lily thought mechanically, hoping it did not harbour any dead birds. It had been years since a fire had been lit in the old kitchen, but now it had transitioned into the sitting room it seemed appropriate to make use of it.

"Competition?"

"Oh, you know what these types are like. A chance to show off their elaborate decorations and resplendent trees, that sort of thing." He brushed soot from his hands, sat back in the armchair. "I must say, I'm looking forward to them all enormously, aren't you?"

"I suppose so. And anyway, we'll have to go. It would look so impolite not to."

Hugh laughed.

"Oh, darling Helen! How utterly typical of you! You have an inbred sense of duty. Do you know that? A little like royalty."

"I hardly think so," Lily said. Yet acceptance did seem obligatory which, perversely, suddenly made the prospect of the parties less alluring.

"Talking of trees, where do you suggest we put ours? Our first Christmas tree together, Helen, think of that!"

He held out his hand to her across the hearth, but she chose not to notice.

"My father always liked ours to be in the dining room,"

she said. "Although last year I didn't bother with a tree. There didn't seem much point somehow."

"Well, we will have to change all that. We need to establish some traditions of our own, don't you think? That's what couples do, after all." He glanced at his watch. Sighed extravagantly. Found his black sweater that had fallen next to the log basket where it had collected spikes of kindling.

"Time for your students?"

"Just the one class this evening. We're running workshops over this weekend, but after that there's nothing until the New Year. There's a couple of possible castings for voice-overs, but no doubt nothing will come from either of those. That market is so oversaturated these days."

"At least the theatre school is a success."

"Not exactly a financial gold mine, though," Hugh said morosely. "Our students are too poor to pay the going rate for tuition. And there's no point in pricing yourself out of your own market."

"No. That's sensible."

There was a knock at the door. Hugh raised an eyebrow.

"Expecting anyone?"

Lily shook her head. "Perhaps Stella has forgotten her key."

"Or it's carol singers singing flat and shaking a tin for charity in our direction."

It was neither. Hugh excused himself and slipped past the young man, vaguely familiar, standing on the top step. He appeared to look beyond Lily, into the hallway.

"I was looking for Stella Fox. She said to call sometime."

"Stella? I'm sorry, she's out at the moment."

"Will she be back soon?" There was an urgency in the man's voice that seemed misplaced if this was a casual call.

"I'm afraid I have no idea," Lily said. "Could I give her a message for when she does come in?"

"I've come to collect something, you see. Money she owes me. For work I've done for her?"

Lily suddenly remembered him. She assumed he was now part of Stella's team for projects with Fox and Hawkins.

"You worked on the new bathroom, didn't you? I am so sorry, I didn't recognise you at first. It's Jim, isn't it? Perhaps you'd like to come in." He seemed surprised to be asked, but followed Lily into the hall. "But I'm afraid I don't know anything about payment arrangements. Unless Stella has left something for you in an obvious place. A cheque, perhaps?" Lily looked at the hall table, half-expectant to see an envelope addressed to Jim. He went on standing there, looking confused.

"It's what you said," he said eventually. "Payment for the bathroom. For doing the plumbing. The tiling too."

"But surely that was settled ages ago," Lily said. She tried to recall the sum she had handed over to Stella for the work, the figures penciled on the invoice presented to her.

"No," he replied bluntly. "That's why I'm here. Stella has promised to meet me so many times to hand over the money. But she never turns up."

"There has to be some mistake. Just an oversight." But she knew her protest was hollow. If her doubts about Stella's integrity, the veracity of the young woman, had begun to grow of late, Jim's arrival at the house was final confirmation. A piece in a jigsaw that was slowly beginning to reveal a clear picture. Lily felt chilled at the possibility of a whole litany of debts, a persistent trickle of disaffected workmen trailing a path to her front door. The young man continued to stand in the narrow hallway, looking uncomfortable. "I tell you what, Jim," Lily went on, attempting to sound calm, "leave this with me and I promise I will talk to Stella. Do you have an address or a phone number where I can reach you?"

She took down the number he gave her. Wrote Jim Lowe in large letters and underlined it. When he had left, she went into the dining room and placed Jim's details in a prominent position on the table. Added *Jim called for his overdue payment*, and remembered Ellen Fox's concern about the possibility of unpaid rent. The adopted office of Fox and Hawkins now appeared to have lost all connection with its previous identity, with a couple of metal desk chairs, a filing cabinet and the surface of the mahogany dining table entirely covered in lever files. The faded beige shade of the standard lamp was tilted, the fabric scorched. Lily went over to straighten it, catching her ankle painfully on the edge of the cabinet.

Stella must go.

Along with Fox and Hawkins and its trespass on her home.

And sooner than she had implied.

Now.

After all, the room was required for Christmas. For a spectacular tree worthy of her father's memory, for the festive meal, a reinstatement of all that she and Dorothy had been unable to conjure together the previous year. And the addition of Hugh would inevitably confirm her own standing as if at last she had emerged into a life defined and worthy of regard.

The phone went.

It was Agnes, sounding hesitant, remote.

"I'm so sorry to ring you, Lily. Disturbing you like this in the evening. But I've done something very stupid." Agnes had fallen. She had tripped up in the street and fallen heavily while on her way home from shopping that afternoon and was at the Royal Free Hospital after badly fracturing her shoulder. "The thing is I had to give a name and phone number for next of kin. They require it, you see. I should have remembered from all my years as a hospital almoner. And I'm afraid I gave your name, Lily. I explained that my nephew lives in Australia and my cousin is in Hull so neither of them of much immediate practical use. I do hope you don't mind."

"Of course not," Lily said. In a perverse way she was relieved to have her mind shifted onto an immediate concern.

"Not that there's anything for you to do. It's just procedure."

"You must be in so much pain," Lily said. "Will you need an operation?"

"The pain is severe, I must admit," she said quietly. "But they're giving me pills to control it and everyone is being very kind. And, as for an operation, that's uncertain at the moment. Oh it was so foolish of me, all my own doing."

"An accident that could happen to anyone."

"They want to keep me in overnight, just to keep an eye on things. What with my age and living alone. But I'm sure I'll be discharged first thing in the morning."

There was just time for Lily to reassure her that she would ring the hospital in the morning to check on her before Agnes rang out of coins for the hospital call box.

The next day, she was put through to the ward and assured by the sister that Agnes had spent a reasonable night and was likely to be discharged that afternoon. Transport would be arranged for her. On her way home from work, she called at Agnes's flat, but it was in darkness and she resisted ringing the bell too many times in case she was sleeping. It was Thursday evening before she managed to speak to her again. There had been some concern about her blood pressure, Agnes explained, and the hospital had kept her in for another two nights before allowing her home. She insisted that she was coping alone.

"I'm resting," she said, "obeying instructions to help things heal. The bones need to knit themselves together again, but there's hope that I won't need an operation. That's if I behave myself and keep my arm still in this wretched sling. I have to say that the pain rather dictates that I do very little."

A neighbour had brought in some food, done some shopping for her, although she said she had little appetite. Lily offered to call in after work, but Agnes suggested she should delay visiting until the following week when she would be feeling stronger and appreciative of some company.

"I have my books," she added, "and the radio, of course. Even the television can be of use at times like this. In a week or so, I will be ready for some conversation."

"If you're sure."

"Lily, I am not a helpless old woman. It's my shoulder I have fractured, not my brain. In fact, my greatest fear in life has always been the loss of my eyesight. And my mind, of course. Whilst I have those two faculties in reasonable working order, I am not alone or in need of perpetual entertainment."

Lily felt duly reprimanded. She would visit, she said, in a week. As she put down the phone, the front door opened and Hugh came in with Stella, the two of them having met by chance in Upper Street. She had seen Stella only fleetingly since Jim had called the previous Sunday with no chance to mention either his visit or Fox and Hawkins's occupation of the dining room. Stella beamed at her as if reading her thoughts.

"You and I have hardly seen each other lately, Lily," she said. "But I'm cooking dinner tonight for the three of us so we can all have a good catch-up. I was just telling Hugh about a recipe I want to try out on you two, wasn't I, Hugh?"

"Something like that," he said, shrugging out of his overcoat and hanging it on the banister. "Although I have to say I got a bit lost in the culinary terms. But we're quite happy to sample the results, aren't we, Helen?"

He kissed her lightly on the cheek. Stella headed down to the kitchen, calling casually over her shoulder as she went, "By the way, Lily, that business about Jim – all just a mix-up on his side. He's a good workman, but hopeless at keeping track of things. Some people are just like that, aren't they?"

She was animated over dinner, relating a long and complicated story about some potential clients and Lily suspected that her self-absorption was such that she had entirely forgotten her rash comment about marrying Hugh. She was relieved. There were, after all, still three weeks until he expected an answer from her. Conversation turned to the neighbourhood parties and, in particular, the one at Anna and Simon's house that Saturday.

"She's calling it an Advent gathering," Hugh said, "no doubt simply trying to distinguish it from the others, determined to get in first, as it were."

"Typical Anna," Stella said. "The leader of the pack and all that."

"Simon's the same. They're a very driven pair, although quite charming, of course."

Lily was unaware that Hugh had spoken to the couple at any length to establish such an understanding of them. The familiarity was bewildering to her.

"Will you be able to come? To Saturday's party, I mean," she said. "I thought you were running workshops at the theatre school all this weekend."

"Oh no, there's now only one brief afternoon session," he said vaguely, dowsing his risotto in more grated parmesan. "I have to say this is delicious, Stella, most authentic, no doubt."

"Actually, it's far better to use champagne for the stock. But I compromised with a bottle of Chardonnay. Thought Lily might be taken aback by blowing the household budget on champers. And the trick is endless stirring, of course, to avoid turning the dish into plain stodge."

It seemed the right time to mention the dining room.

"I've been meaning to say something about the office,

about Fox and Hawkins and how much space you seem to need now, Stella."

"Ah yes! That room is evidently sacrosanct when it comes to the Christmas tree. Isn't that right, Helen? A Page family tradition going back centuries," Hugh said.

"Hardly that." Lily found his tone irritating.

Stella put down her fork. "Of course! I quite understand, Lily. Enough is enough. You'll need us to move out, won't you, me and Crispin? You can't be expected to enjoy your roast turkey and trimmings with cash books and ledgers encroaching on your space. That's totally fine."

It seemed to have been easily accomplished. Lily relaxed, accepted another portion of risotto. Clearly, Stella was at last beginning to take responsibility, relieve her of the need to provide. The thought of reclaiming not just the dining room, but the entire house for herself was heartening.

Of course, there was Hugh.

But that was different. If they were to marry her home would inevitably become his as well. Already, it appeared as if they were journeying towards that, events suggesting its inevitability. After his estrangement from her bedroom, the week or so spent in the spare room, he had returned wordlessly one night and she had not protested. Her point, after all, had been made and he could hardly do more to atone. She watched as if from some distance as he cleared the table, chivvied Stella to help, and turned her thoughts to the party the following evening, the prospect of two more to follow. Time was when one dress suited all such seasonal occasions and hung in the wardrobe ready to serve year in, year out. But no longer. Now, there appeared to be a compulsion to spend on outfits that drew attention to their relevance as if in confirmation of one's own significance. Lily, with an inbuilt sense of her own inconsequence, found the idea unsettling.

Hugh was late back on Saturday. The workshop, he said, had overrun, something about a late start after complications with the heating that Lily failed to follow. He insisted on changing his clothes, but eventually presented himself in the hall, where Lily was waiting for him.

"You look lovely, Helen," he said. "As ever. And appropriately festive."

"Is it too much do you think?"

She had bought a new dress.

Plain, deep claret in colour, on the hanger it had looked almost austere with long sleeves and a low, sweeping hemline. But she had been surprised, looking at her reflection in the mirror of the shop's small changing room. It had been many years since she had allowed herself an honest appraisal, too certain of dissatisfaction, but now, with youthful expectations long gone, she was not displeased by what she saw. As if at last she no longer viewed her appearance as a pale imitation of what it was supposed to be, but that of a mature woman with pleasant features that she inhabited with ease. Hugh's compliments were excessive. She had no need of his inflated flattery, but it sounded churlish to say so.

"On the contrary," he said. "Perhaps I should change into a matching shirt."

"Please don't," Lily said. "Anyway, we're already late enough."

"Parties never start on time, surely you know that. I should think we've judged things just right, in fact." He opened the front door. Other neighbours were crowding Anna and Simon's path, causing a slow trickle into their house. "See?" Hugh said, taking Lily's arm. "Trust an actor for perfect timing."

★★★

Stella said, "I've made the mincemeat. It just needs feeding with brandy every other day or so."

"I thought that was the Christmas cake," Lily said.

"That too. But you seem to have run out of brandy, Lily. Could you get some next time you're shopping? Or, better still, leave it to me."

"I'm not sure how we are going to eat all this food, Stella. After all, it's just the three of us." Lily had been surprised by Stella's sudden shift from the commitments of Fox and Hawkins to spending endless hours in the kitchen cooking. It was like the previous spring when she had first moved in and had seemed anxious to justify her stay.

"Surely you'll be inviting friends in now you and Hugh are such social animals."

"There are no plans," Lily said. Anna and Simon's party had been pleasant enough, but she was not looking forward to repeat events at other houses. She had felt detached from most conversations that had narrowly pivoted around subjects she had little knowledge or interest in and had found feigning fascination a strain. "But there's always Agnes. I suppose I could invite her." Agnes had already said that travelling to her cousin for Christmas was not going to be feasible with a broken shoulder in a sling. "She might even enjoy meeting my aunt," she added dubiously.

"There you are!" Stella said. "And much of it will keep so we'll be set up for weeks where food is concerned."

Lily wanted to repeat her expectation of Stella vacating the house before Christmas. Early January, she conceded to herself, at the latest. But it seemed easier to address the matter of the dining room and, immediately, Stella interrupted her.

"Oh of course, Lily, that's in hand. Besides, things have gone a bit quiet at the moment which is understandable. I mean who wants to be thinking kitchen renovations in December? Crispin and I have really put everything on hold for the time being. So it's no problem at all."

"I'm grateful," Lily said.

"You won't even know we've been there in a few days' time!" Stella went on. "Now, there's something else I've been meaning to ask you about. Presents?"

"Presents?"

"Yes, Lily, presents! What does everyone want? I mean, Dorothy, for example. And Hugh. Men are so hard to give to, aren't they? I've tons of ideas for you so you're not my problem."

"There's no need," Lily said swiftly. She wanted to say that presents were inappropriate, unwanted, in fact, when she was trying to cut the strings of Stella's hold. Stella picked up Hector from the floor and settled him on her lap, tickling the folds of his fur.

"Nonsense," she said, "I can't think of anyone more deserving than you, Lily. And as for Dorothy, well, obviously, she's part of the family so I couldn't possibly leave her out."

"What about your family?" Lily said. The opportunity had presented itself. "Won't you be seeing them over Christmas?"

Stella shrugged, affecting sadness. The young woman beguiled, Lily saw, with such exquisite mastery.

"No hope of that, sadly. Do you know, Lily, it's another connection between us, isn't it? Both of us motherless, if for different reasons."

Lily was outraged. Twinning her own genuine loss of her mother, of the late Helen Page, with Stella's chosen stance, was egregious. Hector suddenly jumped down from Stella's lap, wound himself instead around Lily's legs. She picked him up, stroked him.

"I wonder if your son, Dylan, will feel like that in the

future," Lily said measuredly. "Only time will tell, I suppose." And swiftly, to cover the potency of the silence in the room, carried Hector over to the back door to let him out.

27

Lily insisted on driving Agnes to her appointment at the fracture clinic.

"It's so good of you," she said, negotiating her way with evident pain and discomfort into the passenger seat.

"It's nothing," Lily said. "Term has finished now and I only have to go into the admin office for a couple of hours."

"Christmas seems to have crept up on me this year, but perhaps I say that every year. One of the habits of old age, I'm afraid, becoming a repository of cliches."

She dropped her at Outpatients and waited until she saw her safely inside the door. Agnes's gait was inevitably cautious and hesitant, reminding Lily of her father's vulnerability in his later years. Which reminded her in turn, with the familiar wrench of guilt and self-recrimination, of the casket of his ashes still residing in the cupboard on the top landing. And wondered whether such endless stalling was also the flaw in her handling of Stella, of Hugh, with her resistance to be resolute. She parked the car up the street and found a coffee shop to occupy the hour or two of Agnes's appointment, staring out of the window as if to better order her thoughts. To understand them. Compliance had been her perpetual watchword for so long that the will to exert her own desire had no doubt atrophied along with only a muddied idea of the nature of that desire. She drank one cup of coffee, ordered another, watched a sleek sports car park illegally across the road, the driver dashing into a florist to emerge moments later with an enormous festive wreath, bunches of mistletoe and red-berried holly. A busker set up a music stand, took a saxophone from its case and began to play a variation of "In the Bleak Mid-Winter". The notes drifted through the walls of the café, drowning out traffic noise, the hiss of the coffee machine, with the richness of its sound.

Agnes was relieved.

"No operation, the doctor said. As long as I am very careful and patient as things will take months to be normal again. And there'll be more X-rays and physiotherapy, of course, but that's all to be expected. I've been very lucky to escape relatively lightly. Especially at my age."

Lily drove her home, helped her move gingerly, painfully, into her flat and promised to visit again at the weekend. Saturday, she suggested, just a week before Christmas, and left with a handful of cards that Agnes had asked her to post. She spent the afternoon in the admin office at school, its corridors strangely silent with only a few office staff and cleaners in the place who were intent on removing the residue of end of term celebrations, drooping paper chains and cotton wool snow stuck to classroom window panes. The house was dark when she arrived back and she remembered that Hugh had mentioned something about a possible voice-over casting followed by a drink with Robin from the theatre school. She was relieved that Stella was also out. Since her barbed comments about Dylan, she had discreetly avoided being alone with her and was in no mood now for anything faintly combative.

Besides, there was that casket.

Resolved at least to move it from its place of obscurity for somewhere more prominent where she would be prompted to deal with it, she headed upstairs to the wardrobe on the top floor landing. The key, usually stubborn in the lock, turned surprisingly easily and the door swung back to expose it.

But it was an absence that drew Lily's attention.

Her late mother's fur coat was gone.

Foolishly, she moved the wooden hangers of the few items in there as if Helen Page's substantial coat was choosing to conceal itself. But there was nothing save an aged windcheater, two formal suits and the smell of very dry lavender and dust. Lily closed the doors, pointlessly pocketed the key and went straight downstairs to Stella's bedroom. The overhead light had been swathed in an orange paper lantern which gave off a strange glow, like the flicker and reflection of firelight, so that it was hard to discern detail.

But there was no coat on the chair.

Nothing in the cupboard or hanging from the hook on the back of the door and she felt ashamed of her suspicion. The room was untidy, on the floor a heap of papers, notebooks, ledgers that she recognised from the piles on the dining room table. At least Stella had kept to her promise to remove them from her adopted office. Mechanically, Lily bent down, started to stack them into some order, still resistant to see such muddle in her father's former bedroom. Out of casual curiosity she opened a cashbook that looked familiar and found details of the refurbishment of the basement. There was no surprise in the lists of work that she had agreed with Stella. Partition walls knocked through, plastering, rewiring, floors sanded, installation of new doors and units. Another page was devoted to the additional bathroom on the first floor, with plumbing and tiling and flooring all neatly itemised. But there appeared to be no costings, no record of the substantial amount Lily had paid out for the work. She flicked through the pages and towards the back found a section entitled *Finance*. Careful columns had been drawn and labelled *Materials and Wages* and duly itemised and completed.

But the totals were unfamiliar to Lily.

It was only when she turned to the final page that Stella's system became clear.

And there was a system.

A calculation of 35% had been added to all figures so that the amount Lily had unwittingly paid out represented not only costs of labour and materials, but an additional fee. A fee that Stella had labelled in the cashbook as *My Commission*.

The refurbishment of 8, Alfred Street had been at considerable financial advantage to Stella Fox. She had been covertly inflating the costs, presenting invoices to Lily that gave no indication of, effectively, her theft.

Her embezzlement of Lily's money.

Staring at the pages, Lily felt as if at last she was solving a cleverly crafted game, a perplexing enigma where she herself had been played as an expendable pawn.

Now she had to decide how to deal with Stella on her return.

If she acted on instinct, evicting her that night, she would be obliged to confess to Hugh what she had discovered and he would see Lily as ingenuous, a gullible woman who had been the easy prey for someone as mercurial and manipulative as Stella.

Which, she inevitably concluded, Stella's actions confirmed.

The knowledge was no solace.

Restless, she tried to distract herself by preparing a meal, but had no appetite. The fire she attempted to light went out twice before a blaze established itself. Around eight o'clock, carol singers called at the door. Lily heard them from down the street, no trio of inadequate voices, but a youth choir of twenty or so singing and collecting for a homeless charity. She found some change to give them then stood at her door, other neighbours at theirs, listening to "O Little Town of

Bethlehem". The purity of sound in the crisp winter evening, the ardent young voices were consoling and she could briefly shut her mind to the knowledge of Stella's duplicity, of her own foolish credulity.

Then Lily saw her.

She was walking rapidly from the end of the street, ignoring the carol-singing choir, the couple collecting for their cause, stopping for a moment under a street light to search for keys in her large bag.

Stella was wearing her late mother's fur coat.

The choir switched to "Silent Night".

She watched as Stella, her straight dark hair tipping over the collar of Helen Page's fox fur, approached the house.

"Lily!" She was surprised to see her standing there. For a moment there was slight doubt on her face, a young child unwittingly caught in the act. Lily stared. Waited. Then Stella flamboyantly turned a circle on the pavement and made a mock curtsey. "I can't imagine why you've been hiding this gorgeous creature away! I do hope you don't mind, Lily, but it makes me feel so glamorous. In fact, positively wanton! You know, like a kept woman or something!"

Lily said, "Take it off. Take it off immediately. You had no right." She had raised her voice and her neighbour opposite, listening to the final strains of the carol, glanced across the street. Stella swiftly came up the steps into the hall. Lily closed the front door, aware that she was shaking with an anger so profound that she could barely speak. But there was no need. Stella, brazen, said, "I do hope I haven't upset you, Lily. It's not like you to overreact. I mean it's just an old coat cluttering up wardrobe space, isn't it?" She had dropped the fur to her feet and stood looking down at it as at an animal felled. "Although obviously a good one in its time. Better than that old thing of mine, it has to be said. But no-one wants such things these days, do they? Hard even to give away, I expect."

Lily picked it up. Stella's scent, musky and cloying, clung to it.

"I want you to leave. Now," she said.

Stella laughed. Lily repeated herself. She laughed again, more hesitantly this time, and tried to push past, down the stairs to the kitchen.

"Tell you what, Lily, let's have something to eat. You look worn out. I bet you haven't eaten this evening. Me neither so I'll cook us something, shall I? Just something light. What do you fancy?"

"I don't want you in the house for one more night." Lily was relieved that her voice was strident. Controlled. "Take what you need now and you can come back at the weekend to collect the rest of your things."

Stella stared at her for a moment then leant against the wall, began to shrug off her boots.

"Come on, Lily, you're making a fool of yourself, you know. Is Hugh in? You obviously need someone to talk sense to you. All this fuss about an old coat."

"My late mother's coat that you had no right to be wearing," Lily said. "But it's not just about that. It's about your theft. Your lies. Your numerous deceptions, Stella. It's time for it all to end."

Stella was silent. She bit her bottom lip, drummed her fingers against the wall. Outside, neighbours' front doors banged as the last of the carol singers left the street. Then she moved suddenly, headed upstairs and disappeared for a few minutes, reappearing with a large bag and wearing a heavy coat. She stood buttoning it up, then smiled at Lily, who had not moved from her spot in the hall.

"I'll get out of your way for one night, shall I? Let you calm down about all this so that we can talk sensibly. Rationally. You're in no mood for that right now, I can tell." She spoke with the tolerant air of one who had witnessed a tantrum. Lily moved to the front door. Opened it wide.

"Good bye, Stella," she said.

It was only when Lily had watched her walk rapidly down the steps, pausing for a moment as if expecting to be called back, that she remembered Stella still had keys to the house.

★★★

She managed to say little to Hugh. Deception, she found, came to her aid.

She told him that Stella had found somewhere else suitable to live, a flat, and in order to secure it needed to move in immediately. He seemed surprised, but incurious. Even when she said she was changing the locks, he accepted her explanation that it was purely precautionary in case any of the workmen involved in the renovation had forgotten to return keys. Men, or at least men like Hugh Murray, Lily thought wryly, had little interest in a subject that did not place themselves at its centre. As the week went on, she expected Stella to return, with Crispin, no doubt, or another friend, to help her collect her possessions. Lily dreaded the event, but equally wanted it to be over, to dispense with her anger over Stella's exploitation and move on from her own sense of humiliation.

In the meantime, there was Christmas.

Hugh seemed to be embracing the season in particular good humour, his occasional morose moods entirely absent. Together, they decorated the large tree he had brought home, obliging her with setting it in the corner of the dining room. She looked at him candidly.

"I know you think it's the wrong place for it," she said. "It should be at the front of the house like all the others in the street so that the lights shine out."

He slipped his arm around her shoulder. "I know you like to preserve your father's preference, dear Helen. And that's fitting, I'm sure. But perhaps next year we can think of a change of habit."

"Next year?" For some reason his assumption startled her.

"But it's a small thing, Helen. A tree. As long as we are together celebrating Christmas, that's all that matters, isn't it?"

"Yes, of course," Lily said automatically. And supposed it was true. She was too bruised from events with Stella, she told herself, to feel anything close to pleasure at the prospect of sharing the season with Hugh. She had returned her late mother's fur coat to the wardrobe on the top floor, hoping fervently that any of her residual scent would soon be lost to the familiar dried lavender and cedarwood.

"I can't tell you what it means to me," he went on, "after so many indifferent years. Solitary Christmases in Balham were hardly celebratory occasions."

"You must have had invitations from friends, surely," she said. She thought of Hugh's natural sociability and gregariousness, a charm that managed to seek out convivial company as if it was somehow his birth right.

"I think I was always worried that people were simply feeling sorry for me," he said, "obligatory invitations rather than ones that came from the heart." He stood back, regarded the tree appraisingly. "Do we have an angel for the top branch?" Lily burrowed in the box of aged decorations, handed him a crushed object with only one wing intact. "She's a sorry sight, isn't she?" he said. "One for the dustbin, I think. I'll pick up something a little more resplendent tomorrow, shall I?"

She wanted to object, to explain that the battered, enduring tree ornament had become her father's joke, a family emblem of sorts, with a meaning lost over the years. But such a protest would sound sentimental.

"Thank you," Lily said firmly. "That would be a good idea."

★★★

Over a week had gone by and Stella's possessions remained. Her silence was unnerving with not even a brief phone call or a note to indicate when she would collect them. There was another Christmas gathering at the house of a neighbour down the road, one of the couples that Stella had befriended. Lily, comfortable to wear the new claret dress again since she doubted anyone would notice, had scanned the room, anxious in case she too had been invited and was overwhelmingly relieved to see she was not there. This time the guests were not limited to Alfred Street residents and Lily spent some time talking to a Greek woman who had been interested in her extensive travels with her father. She had found herself reminiscing at length, relishing the chance to talk with someone so alert and sympathetic to her affection for the country. The woman, Elena, was interested in whether she spoke Greek and when Lily admitted that she had yet to learn, she had been encouraging, offering suggestions of local tutors and classes.

They walked back the few yards to the house, Hugh, clearly a little drunk, holding on firmly to her arm.

"So tell me, Helen," he said, "how long are you going to keep me in suspense?"

"In suspense?" Lily was thinking of her conversation with Elena and failed to pick up on his inference.

"You're being very coy about it all. My proposal, I mean."

He squeezed her hand tightly. "I was hoping we would be able to make an announcement to your aunt over the festive meal. What do you say, Helen?"

"I'm not sure."

"Still not sure?" His voice was disbelieving.

"I mean as far as Dorothy is concerned. I think any such news would be better coming just from me."

She was intending to be evasive, to imply not her acceptance, but the manner of the delivery of any such news. But the lateness of the hour, the alcohol, had lowered her guard. Hugh tightened his hold on her.

"Whatever you think is best. I'm entirely in your hands, darling Helen, and will bow to your wisdom over this."

Lily pulled away from him, took out keys and opened the front door. Slowly, she took off her coat, shrugged her feet out of shoes that were beginning to pinch after standing for a couple of hours. Then she turned to him in the dim light of the hall, feeling an urgency to speak.

"I'm inordinately flattered, Hugh. Of course I am. But why marriage? Is it really necessary at our age? We could just go on with things as they are."

He looked taken aback, shocked even by her words.

"Just go on as we are, living together? But surely we want everything to be legal."

"Legal?"

"Yes," he said with a hint of irritation in his voice. "It must be – we need a legal bond between the two of us. With a certificate to prove it."

The description startled her.

"Why?"

"I mean," Hugh went on hastily, "when love is involved, you want it confirmed, don't you? And marriage is a statement of that love, isn't it? A declaration of sorts to the world!"

His mood seemed expansive. She started to reply, but then noticed a large white envelope on the mat, hand-delivered and addressed to her in Stella's precise handwriting. She bent down to retrieve it, imagining the tone of the content. Contrite, repentant even, with language that nevertheless portrayed Stella as an innocent and was consequently now cowed, wounded by Lily's actions. Hugh seemed to be waiting for a response. She said nothing, pushed past him down the stairs to the kitchen in search of a glass of water. Perhaps it was only the heartless that would reject love out of hand, turn away from one proffering it so eagerly, freely as Hugh. He followed her down the stairs, put his arms around her, pulled her close.

"Coming to bed?"

"In a moment," she said. "You go ahead." She broke away, filled a glass at the sink. He headed again for the stairs, then hesitated, turned back to her.

"So Stella's moved out for good, has she?"

"Yes," Lily said as neutrally as she could summon. "I told you, she's moved on elsewhere."

Hugh smiled. "I have to say I am relieved."

"Relieved?"

"Oh don't get me wrong, she's a delightful young woman. But I can't help feeling a little liberated, like a parent delighted to have the house to themselves again. No more *pas devant les enfants* and all that. Don't you feel the same?"

"Yes, it was time for her to go," Lily said although she was aware that Hugh's thoughts were purely carnal. Her own relief at Stella's absence was far more complex. She had extricated herself from a snare, the insignificant grub and easy prey for a magnificent yet amoral creature. She swallowed a tumbler of water.

"Don't be long, will you, Helen?" Hugh called back, his words slurring a little.

"I won't," Lily said although she knew that he would be asleep within moments. His amorous advances were so rarely matched by the actions of the ardent lover.

Stella's message was much as expected.

Her letter, tucked inside an extravagant Christmas card extending *Goodwill to all men at this blessed time* was a lesson in skilful manipulation. She was miserable with regret. Appalled by her own crass actions with regard to the fur coat. She had no idea that any sentimental attachment existed to what appeared to be a disregarded item of clothing consigned to forgotten storage. And as for the cashbook, the raw figures that Lily had come across misrepresented entirely the truth of the matter. The financial *intricacies* of the transactions between those employed for the *transformation* of Lily's beautiful house were a composite matter that Stella would be only too happy to explain, face to face. Around the kitchen table, over a pot of tea, a quiet meal, calmly, reasonably, so that Lily could have her understandable doubts removed and they could resume their very special friendship.

It was the prodigal expectant of the slowly tended and roasted fatted calf.

There was no address.

No possibility of returning Stella's remaining possessions, depositing them on a doorstep, and departing swiftly. Lily had no desire for an explanation. Nor even for the return of the considerable amount of money that Stella had, effectively, stolen or at least obtained by stealth. She saw the loss as penance for her inadequacies. She had been culpable of misjudging not only Stella's purpose and intent, but her own susceptibility. In her single, quiet, biddable life, she had simply grown too used to trusting people.

It was a grievous error.

She tore up the letter, the ostentatious card, placed the

tatters in the rubbish bin that was close to overflowing. Taking it outside to deposit the contents in the dustbin, she came face to face with one of the marauding urban foxes that were increasingly frequenting Alfred Street. She held his stare for several moments before the creature scampered away, bounded over the wall and disappeared into the night.

28

Hugh was gently disparaging.

"You'll excuse me if I absent myself from this shopping folly of yours," he said as Lily prepared to leave on Saturday morning.

"Of course, I wasn't expecting company. I'm sure it sounds foolish to you, but it's become a habit. A tradition."

Hugh inclined his head.

"I'm sure a plum pudding from Harrods will make all the difference to our celebratory meal. Add a touch of class, you might say, as well as remembering your esteemed father. And if you can tolerate the crowds of Knightsbridge just before Christmas, darling Helen, I am all admiration."

"That's why I'm going early," Lily said, "to try and avoid the worst of the crush. And I've promised to call in on Agnes afterwards."

But in the end, Hugh headed out before her. He was meeting Robin to make plans for the new term at the theatre school then had a bit of his own shopping to do, he said somewhat cryptically, and Lily suddenly felt stricken that she had not yet bought a present for him and added it to her tasks for the day.

And Stella's letter nagged.

It had been simple to dispense with its pages, but her message was not so easily removed. Swiftly, Lily went upstairs and packed up her remaining clothes, books, a collection of shoes, a silver necklace, a bracelet from the bedside table in an effort to eradicate evidence of her from the room. Stella's belongings had swelled since she had moved in months earlier with merely a couple of carrier bags. Now they required several boxes which, once filled, she carried downstairs to line the walls of the hall. At some stage, Stella would no doubt call unannounced and she wanted to be ready so that there would be no necessity to invite her in. For once, she would be a step ahead of the young woman.

For a moment or two, she thought of abandoning the idea of Harrods. She did not even particularly like Christmas pudding and was sure a supermarket version would serve. But the prospect of Dorothy suspecting a substitute was enough to propel her. Besides, there was a present for Hugh to find. She was unversed in buying gifts for men since her father's needs had always been so prescriptive and clearly defined. He had never invited innovation, whereas Hugh, she knew, would not welcome the socks and cotton handkerchiefs, the occasional pair of woollen gloves that had placated Walter Page. The Piccadilly Line resembled the worst of rush hour and she eventually reached the store just before one o'clock. The Food Hall offered little respite from the crowds, but Lily quickly found the required pudding then waited for another twenty minutes to pay for it, jostling with insistent customers. She was too warm, her coat heavy in the overheated atmosphere of the shop and she needed coffee before attempting to find a gift for Hugh. A book, possibly, from the department upstairs, or some cologne or a scarf. Surely ideas would present themselves. The queues at the store's cafes were endless, so instead she decided to head to a small snack bar in Basil Street that could be easily reached through the side doors into Hans Crescent. But the crowds milling around in the hallway at the bottom of the escalators slowed her and she stood wedged in a traffic-like jam, unable to make any progress towards the exit. She exchanged a sympathetic smile with a woman attempting to manoeuvre a pushchair and placate a protesting toddler, aiming for the same door. A soft toy dropped from the hand of the young child and Lily bent down amongst customers' feet to retrieve it.

Which was when the explosion happened.

The cacophonous blast of the bomb.

She had no idea if she was making any sound, but around her, pressing in on her, was a wall of screaming, crying, a mass of panic and confusion and she knew she had to stand up, to gain a firm foothold or be trampled underfoot. For a moment she caught a glimpse of the mother and her child and realised that she was still clutching his soft toy, but a second later it was brushed from her hand as crowds pushed and buffeted senselessly, struggling to move somewhere, anywhere, to escape whatever was next to threaten them.

Then someone suddenly appeared to be in charge.

Out of the clamour and chaos, a semblance of some order and calm seemed to be trying to impose itself. Instructions to leave, to evacuate the store as swiftly as possible filtered through the crowds and stilled the screaming. Lily followed, all slowly making progress towards an exit, obedient in their fear and grateful for a command that would release them from their immediate danger.

But the reprieve was brief.

Outside, black smoke billowed from cars on fire and jagged splinters of bloodstained glass carpeted the road. One car, in particular, was merely a framework of metal shards. An acrid, burning smell, in some remote way familiar to Lily, filled the air. And people, terribly injured, lay on the ground. Others sat or sprawled, holding limbs, heads, casualties of shrapnel or glass from the shattered shop windows. A police dog was dead in the gutter. Already there were attempts to help, assistance in staunching bleeding, binding wounds, offering some desperate words of support and comfort to the victims. Someone took off his coat and carefully, as if concerned not to injure further, placed it across the prostrate body of a man.

    Lily found herself propelled away by groups of evacuated customers. She walked hesitantly at first as if uncertain whether she herself was hurt, then with increasing speed in a need to get away. Sirens wailed. Traffic was at a standstill. Policemen were directing pedestrians and shoppers who had poured out of other stores, fearful curiosity and bewilderment on their faces with rumours about the cause of the explosion, the responsibility for the car bomb, swiftly spreading.

    Lily walked.

    Mindlessly, she headed in the direction of Hyde Park Corner, each time she passed a parked car flinching, her heart pounding, as if every vehicle now held the possibility of detonation. She wanted to get home. At the same time the prospect of reaching Islington seemed insurmountable. She had no wish to go underground to the Tube. Buses were caught up in stationary traffic as far as the eye could see and she felt inadequate to the long walk. It was only when she saw a café halfway along Piccadilly, went in and found a small table at the back well away from the window that she realised she was suffering from shock. Her entire body shook as if it refused to obey her mind's instructions to remain calm and she felt icily cold. She ordered coffee and worried she was drawing attention to herself when the cup clanked against the saucer when she attempted to lift it. But people's interest lay elsewhere. News of the incident was growing. One couple at a table near her told the waitress that there had been a bomb scare earlier in the day in Oxford Street, but it had amounted to nothing. An elderly man joined in the conversation, complaining that he had been heading for Harrods and seemingly more disturbed by a disruption to his afternoon plans than by the explosion. Lily wanted to tell him about the people she had seen lying severely injured in the road. She felt an exasperation with the man's blinkered selfishness, but the idea of confronting him was beyond her. She drank more coffee, tried to eat a buttered roll, recalling something about sustenance being sensible after a shock. Buses were still slow or stationary when she paid her bill and left. She skirted Piccadilly Circus, headed onto Trafalgar Square, down the Strand and into the relative silence of the weekend city streets where at last she slowed down and felt herself breathe more easily. It was only when she saw a phone box in Fleet Street that she thought of Hugh. If he had heard the news, he would be anxious, knowing where she had been heading that morning. Lily stood in the enclosed, dank-smelling space, imagining numerous similar calls being made from phone boxes across London, reassuring families and friends. But Hugh was not at home. No doubt his arrangement to meet Robin or his own shopping was taking up more of the day than he had expected.

But there was still Agnes, of course.

Agnes was expecting Lily and, however much she wanted to get home, to be secure within safe walls, she also felt a sudden need for company. And Hugh, probably unaware of the news, might not be back for hours.

It was already growing dark by the time she reached Agnes's flat a little after four. She ushered Lily in, settled her in an armchair in the living room, insisting on making tea for the two of them and brushing away the offer of help.

"I was so worried for you. I heard about it on the radio news, you see, and you'd mentioned going there today. To Harrods, that is. For something in particular, was it?"

For the first time since she had followed instructions to leave the store, to move away from the site of the car bomb, Lily thought of the Christmas pudding. She had no idea when she had dropped it and now imagined it lying amongst the rubble of plate glass and lifeless mannequins that had spilt out through the fractured plate glass windows onto the side streets of Knightsbridge.

"Was there much information?" Lily asked after they had sat for a few minutes in silence, drinking tea. The warmth from the gas fire was comforting, soporific in the small room. "About... about fatalities, I mean."

"No. Just that there were casualties. There will be far more on the evening news, I'm sure."

"It felt so strange," Lily went on, "walking away. Just leaving it all. It was what we were being told to do, of course, to get out of the way. But somehow it felt so heartless. Or irresponsible. Simply returning to ordinary life as if the incident was of no relevance."

Agnes nodded. "That appalling expression of *life goes on*. I've always despised it. There was a version during the war, of course, the Blitz spirit. As if it was one's patriotic duty to carry on mechanically without feeling."

"The smell," Lily said. "That's what it was. Where the memory came from."

"The smell?"

"In the street today. From the explosion. I remembered it from the war. Or at least I think I did. All those bomb sites and fires burning. But do you think I'm imagining that? It's hard to know what genuine memory is and what's fabricated. And I was only thirteen when the war ended, after all."

"Old enough to remember, I would have thought," Agnes said. Her hand and her left arm were now badly swollen and she shifted her position in the chair in an effort to find one more accommodating. Lily apologised for doing so little to help, but Agnes as always was forbearing.

"I am coping sufficiently well, Lily. This sling is a nuisance and sleeping is not easy, I have to admit. But my neighbour has been very thoughtful, popping in with a few treats and it could have been a lot worse if I'd broken a leg and rendered entirely dependent on others."

"But you won't be able to travel for Christmas. You often go to stay with your cousin, don't you?"

"In Yorkshire, yes. So no, that is disappointing, but not to worry. A visit in the spring instead once I'm more mobile will have to suffice. Easter, perhaps."

"You must come to me," Lily said impulsively. The events of the day seemed suddenly to make any reticence over the invitation absurd. "For Christmas Day, I mean."

"Oh no," Agnes said, "that is so kind of you, Lily, but I'm sure it's a family occasion just for you and your aunt and I wouldn't want to intrude."

"Nonsense," Lily said. "Anyway, it won't just be the two of us. Hugh will be there as well."

She prepared to explain, to enlighten Agnes about their relationship.

"Hugh Murray? From the reading society, you mean?"

"That's right."

"Oh well," Agnes said, smiling, "quite a party. Then I presume Amanda will be there too?"

"Amanda?"

"Amanda Harris."

"Why would I invite Amanda? I hardly know her."

Yet even as she spoke, Lily knew the implication of Agnes's question. She drained the dregs of cold tea in her cup.

"Of course, foolish of me to suggest it," Agnes went on. "It's just that if you're inviting Hugh – well, I believe there's some sort of entanglement between the two of them. As a couple, I mean. I don't know how one describes it these days – I'm so out of touch with such things."

"Obviously not as out of touch as I am," Lily said. She tried to force a smile, but failed. She looked down at her hands and studied the edge of a jagged fingernail.

"I assumed it was just idle chatter from other society members at first. People do like to gossip so, don't they?"

"I suppose they do."

"But then I happened to come across the two of them in the hallway near the cloakroom after the reading of *The Doll's House*. I don't think they saw me, fortunately, as they were rather absorbed in each other, if you understand me. But then why not? Amanda is divorced, I understand, and I suppose Hugh is a perfectly eligible bachelor. One doesn't know a great deal about the man. You probably know more as he lives close to you, doesn't he?"

Agnes smiled at her as if waiting for edification.

"No," Lily said.

"No? It's just that you've given him a lift home on the odd occasion. So I rather assumed."

"I mean, no, he's not coming on Christmas Day. I got that wrong. I don't know why I said that."

Lily was afraid she was going to cry. She suspected that if she tried to say anything more, her voice would break and betray her. She turned to look at a tall book case in the corner of the room, trying to concentrate on the titles arranged alphabetically on solidly packed shelves as if committing them to memory: Austen, Bronte, Dickens. Hardy, James. Lawrence and Woolf. Lower down, Greene, Orwell, Lessing, Spark. Agnes followed her gaze.

"Too many books," she said. "Or rather too little space for them. There are piles on the floor in my bedroom."

"It was the same with my father. I had to get rid of so many yet now I regret it. I mean I regret being quite so ruthless. I wish I had held on to more."

And suddenly tears became inevitable. Obligatory, even, and she wept silently so that there was no need for either woman to acknowledge her distress. But, after a minute or so, Agnes stood up, went into another room and returned with a pressed white linen handkerchief with a flower motif. She handed it to Lily apologetically.

"Terribly old-fashioned of me, I know," she said. "But somehow more comforting than tissues. And it is new."

"I'm so sorry," Lily said.

"Nonsense. You have been through an appalling event. Such a reaction is normal."

"I think it must be the shock."

"Yes," Agnes answered, "of course." Then after a brief pause added, "And I do hope I haven't said something to make that worse."

Lily shook her head. The handkerchief smelt faintly of lavender that reminded her of the wardrobe on the top floor, her mother's fur coat. Those ashes of her father. Agnes drew the curtains against the drear December day, insisted on making more tea and encouraging her to a slice of the dense fruit cake her neighbour had made. Lily felt resistant to leave as if the small room offered a protective cocoon from the reality of the news. Of the implosion of her own sense of truth.

"You will come to me on Christmas Day, won't you, Agnes?" It seemed suddenly urgent to insist. To put in place a plan within her control. "My aunt will enjoy your company and so will I."

"If you are sure, Lily, I would be absolutely delighted. It really is most kind of you."

Agnes's gratitude touched her. The gesture, after all,

was self-serving. She had no wish to replicate the previous Christmas alone with her aunt, which would, after all, only serve to underline Hugh's treachery.

At six o'clock, they listened to the news on the radio before Lily left. There were already five fatalities with many more taken to hospital with critical injuries. Policemen as well as members of the public who happened simply by chance to have been in Knightsbridge were among the victims. Lily wondered where Hugh had been all day. With Amanda Morris in Richmond, perhaps, and imagined them walking by the Thames, slipping into one of the riverside pubs, Hugh brazen and unabashed in his betrayal. As she walked back to Islington, wary of sudden noise, a dustbin lid rolling in the road, the sudden cry of a child, she allowed the full knowledge of his actions to engulf her. And was aware of feeling not so much profound shock as inevitable acceptance. As if his unfaithfulness was woefully predictable and she had only been waiting for confirmation to clarify her understanding. Hugh's protestations of love, his flattery and demonstrative affections, the repertoire of the practised deceiver, the classic cad, had muddied her judgement for too long. The marriage proposal, she now saw, had been his ultimate card, a step in his calculated path towards his mercenary goal. Stella Fox had been patently duplicitous. But Hugh's crimes towards her were far more heinous.

She wondered how much Amanda Morris knew.

And how many other deceptions there had been over the past year, remembering now the numerous times when his plans had changed. Or he had been absent, late, delayed and she had blithely believed in his explanations.

Wanted, no doubt, to convince herself of the plausibility of his stories.

The house was dark. Relieved, she went swiftly upstairs

with a sudden need to shower, to wash her hair and remove any suggestion of the smell of smoke from the explosion. The detritus of the whole day. In the kitchen she found a note from Hugh. *Not back until around 8 – wait dinner for me? Hope shopping was successful!* Two scrawled, elaborate kisses, his initial. There were crumbs on the table, a cup with the dregs of coffee. His black sweater discarded over the back of a chair. For a moment Lily felt her resolve wane. It would, after all, be possible to go on as they were. Some couples chose to survive on compromised fidelity, only seeing what suited in order to maintain a semblance of a relationship.

There was, in fact, a choice.

She poured herself a glass of wine and carried it to the sitting room, where she lit the fire and then sat in the large armchair, relying only on the flames for light. It was after half past eight when she heard Hugh's key in the door.

"There you are!" he said, snapping on the overhead light. "Sitting in the dark, Helen. Sorry I'm so late, but you know what things are like at this time of year."

"Not really. Tell me," Lily said.

She watched as he threw off his jacket, unwound a scarf and muttered on about crowds and traffic and endless queues for the bus. Every phrase now seemed loaded with significance, with dissimulation. How exhausting it must be, Lily thought, to maintain a shadow life. And how humiliating to be perpetually wary, on guard for signs of such deviance.

"You haven't eaten, have you?" he said. "I'm starving." He knelt down and adjusted a log that was threatening to fall into the hearth.

"Did you hear about the car bomb? At Harrods?"

"Oh that, yes, of course, dreadful business."

"Weren't you concerned?" Lily said.

"Concerned?"

"You knew I was going there today."

"Goodness, Helen, so were thousands of other people, I imagine. The chance of you being affected by it were – well, just so low. And clearly you weren't."

He turned to her and smiled, as if despatching the matter.

"So you weren't worried at all?"

"Let's just say I trusted your judgement not to be in the wrong place at the wrong time."

"As if it was that easy," she said.

"I mean I know one can't be complacent about these things," he added as if to appease her. "But when all's said and done, the statistics show that—"

"It's something that happens to other people," she said caustically. He looked at her with surprise, unused to her being at all combative. It seemed a good moment to go on. "Did you see Amanda Morris today?"

"Who?" He turned away, glanced back towards the fire. Held his hands out to the flames. Lily said nothing. A log sparked and he pulled away from the hearth, sat down in the chair opposite her. "Oh, that woman from the reading society, you mean? Why ever would I see her? It's not as if there are any plans yet for the January meeting. And even I'm not such a task master that I'd insist on rehearsals a week before Christmas!" He attempted to laugh, but it was shallow, thin.

"You are having an affair with her," Lily said. He looked across at her as if she was absurd, started to protest, but she cut in. "There's no point in pretending otherwise, Hugh. In fact, it's so obvious that I should have realised months ago. No doubt it started the night of my party when you drove her home to Richmond."

Again, he attempted a reply, but then sunk into silence, his face expressionless, rudderless, defeated. He was not a man, Lily saw, familiar with being lost for words. After a few moments, he got out of his chair and abruptly left the room, returning with a glass and bottle of wine.

"It's not what you think," he said quietly, sitting down opposite her. She pulled a bemused face.

"I think I understand the nature of an affair, Hugh. The terms of it, as it were."

"But it means nothing."

"It is not nothing to me. In fact, it's a very great deal."

"Of course, I didn't mean that. Oh darling Helen, I've been such a fool."

She was anticipating this move. And was grateful that her experience with Stella had prepared her for such craven games.

"You are no fool, Hugh."

"It's all over, anyway. It was just – she's a neurotic woman, you know. I was an idiot to allow myself to be pulled into the whole wretched business in the first place."

He sank back in the chair with an air of being the victim rather than the perpetrator of the event.

"So it was entirely against your will?" Lily said. "You are far too old to play the seduced younger man, Hugh."

And suddenly, as he sat there floundering to regain ground that was slipping irretrievably away from him, Lily saw the inadequacy of the man. And saw him in the decades ahead, those lean good looks of middle age, that easy charm dwindling until he became no more than a sad spectacle, a figure to pity and avoid rather than indulge.

"Of course there was error on my part. I entirely misjudged things, I admit that. But you have my word, darling Helen, that nothing like this will ever happen again."

"And nothing you say will make any difference now, Hugh."

"I know I have to win back your trust and I quite understand that might take some time." He appeared not to be listening to her. "I just can't believe what an idiot I've been."

"So you've said. More than once." He looked at her, a weak smile on his face as if beginning to see a path through to safety. To redemption. He refilled his glass. "But that's not true, is it? In fact, you've been extraordinarily clever and scheming from the start. From the very first moment you met me."

"I don't know what you're talking about," Hugh said. His expression had lost its complacency.

"If there has been any foolishness it has been entirely on my side," Lily said calmly.

"Darling Helen, you're talking in riddles. The day has clearly taken its toll on you. All this awful news about – the car bomb business." He held out a hand towards her as if expectant of her capitulation. "Shall we eat? It's getting late, you know, and I'm sure you could do with some food. Let me look after you after your appalling day." He stood up, reached the door then paused when she did not follow. "We can sort everything out, you know. All this… this confusion of yours."

He smiled at her. Lily felt in danger of hitting him. For the first time in her life, she wanted to strike out, to cause physical pain and disturb his self-satisfaction. Instead, she began to talk, surprising herself with her fluency, her clean and categorical account of his mercenary pursuit. He had seen from the start his opportunity. Acquisitive, mendacious men evidently lived beyond the pages of sentimental Victorian literature, preying on single middle-aged women living without dependents in substantial homes whose worth had been inflated prodigiously by the soaring London housing market. Add in Lily's excess of good will, her sense of obligation and an emotional vacuum following bereavement and Hugh's challenge was set. After all, what was he sacrificing in setting about gaining her affections? Swapping a rented bedsit in a shared house in south London for a home in Islington was worth suppressing any feelings of repugnancy for a very ordinary fifty-year-old woman. In fact, he no doubt salved any slither of a conscience he might possess by seeing his actions as compassionate, selfless, providing her with relief from her prescriptive life. The touch of claiming widowhood was possibly an excessive gesture, but no doubt he viewed it as useful bait to snare her sympathies. Hugh did not protest. He sat staring initially into the flames of the fire then down at the floor.

"I asked you to marry me," he said eventually. His tone had lost all pretence of warmth. "I was willing to do that much for you."

"For me? It was all for your own gain. Material gain. You wanted a financially assured future. No doubt even Dorothy came into your calculations when you realised I would eventually inherit from her. Love was never at the forefront of your mind."

"Oh, love!" He stood up abruptly, knocking over his glass, which shattered on the floor. "You're so naïve, Helen. No idea of the real world. Just a closeted, spoilt child who is out of touch with the way people live their lives. The games they need to play to survive."

"I know the way I choose to live my life. And it is not with subterfuge and pretence."

"Can you hear yourself? God, how pathetic you are." He had raised his voice. She looked down at the broken shards of glass, the spilt red wine soaking into the floorboards.

"I would like you to leave, please," she said. "Now. Within fifteen minutes. Get out of my house."

"Don't be ridiculous," Hugh said. "You can't insist on that."

"I think you'll find that I can," Lily said.

"But it's late. It's Saturday night and it's …this is all so idiotic." His resistance was at its last gasp.

"Call a taxi if you wish. Or call Amanda Morris. I'm sure she'll manage to put you up for the night if not for considerably longer."

"I can't." He sounded beaten, a man surprised to find himself finally run dry of luck. "Not at the moment. Her kids are coming back for Christmas tonight."

"How inconvenient of them. But I'm sure you have other friends."

"You are behaving in the most ridiculous manner, do you know that? You're going to regret this when you calm down and come to your senses. I should have known, of course."

"Known? Known what?"

He stepped closer to her chair. Involuntarily, she flinched.

"Do you know what happens to women like you who've had nothing meaningful ever happen to them? They become petty and petulant. You're just eaten up with bitterness and now you're throwing away your only chance."

Lily welcomed his words. If the slightest doubt had lingered over the wisdom of her decision, it was now entirely eroded. She stood up, went into the hall and opened the front door wide. He followed then hovered for some moments as if still expectant of a reprieve. Even held a hand out towards her. She stepped out of its reach.

"Goodbye, Hugh."

"Helen, I …"

"It's Lily, remember?" she said firmly. "It's always been Lily."

29

Dorothy had been delighted with Agnes's company on Christmas Day.

"I can't think why you haven't invited her before," she said when Agnes had finally left late in the evening. "Even when your father was alive she would have been welcome. Walter liked strong, independent women like Agnes."

Lily had been relieved by the success of the day. The two women had talked endlessly and had been comfortable and at ease with each other, so that the burden of the day that she had dreaded was entirely lifted.

Hugh's absence had seemed an irrelevance.

In the week after he had left Lily had been bewildered by her shifting moods. Raw anger and rage at his betrayal, at his ruthless exploitation of her, had alternated with painful regret for the loss of an anticipated future that was no longer hers. She was, after all, a single woman once more. Yet, after the events in Knightsbridge, the random chance that had delayed her in the shop rather than thrusting her into the heart of the atrocity, this was a mere sidenote to consider. And gradually, as the days passed, she became aware of a sense of relief. She had never, in truth, wanted to marry Hugh Murray, or even entirely believed in the carapace of the character he had presented to her. Yet no-one, she allowed herself, was entirely immune to flattery and adulation and can resist its lure. Least of all fifty-one-year-old Lily Page, who had known little of such attention. Then on Christmas Eve, she had gone to the midnight service at St Mary's in Upper Street, greeted entire strangers and vaguely familiar faces with seasonal wishes and returned home aware of feeling content with salvaging her own autonomy. As if her life that had always been tethered by circumstance had been granted freedom, an emancipation, and her only obligation was not to squander it.

She had still heard nothing from Stella.

Her remaining bags cluttering the hallway had felt offensive so Lily had carried them out to the back garden, deposited them in a heap where they had soon become sodden from night frosts. She had parcelled up Hugh's clothes and stowed them in the cupboard under the stairs and it had only been inertia that had prevented her from delivering them straight to the Salvation Army, where she would certainly consign them if they remained into the New Year.

Dorothy had been easily persuaded to stay overnight.

"Just as I used to when Walter was alive. Although I have to say it's strange to have his bedroom."

"It's appropriate," Lily said. She had swiftly neutralised the apricot drag effect that Stella had imposed, rendered the walls plain again and removed the vibrant rug. "No point in having a room go to waste."

"Quite right," Dorothy said. Then added, "You seem to be rid of those two friends of yours, Lily. That young woman who appeared to have attached herself and… Hugh, wasn't it?"

"Yes," Lily said dismissively and was grateful when her aunt asked no more. She had always thought of Dorothy as a woman with little curiosity into others' lives. Now she wondered if it was tactful diplomacy that curbed further interest and saw that her aunt and Agnes belonged to a generation where it was considered prurient to enquire too much into personal circumstance.

They took a short walk on Boxing Day morning, down to the canal, where they negotiated a path through a plethora of young children attempting to ride new bikes and scooters along the tow path.

"You could stay longer if you like," Lily said. "There's no need for you to go home this afternoon."

Dorothy seemed fascinated by a father's patient encouragement of his son to conquer his fears of the two-wheeler.

"Well, I suppose one more night would do no harm," Dorothy said eventually as if bestowing a gift. "I have to say, Lily, the changes you have made to the house have been successful. That enormous kitchen of yours still seems somewhat extravagant, but I suppose the additional bathroom is practical. And I don't suppose it cost you a great deal, did it? Just knocking down walls and so forth?"

Lily thought of the enormity of the sums. Of Stella's abuse and exploitation of her trust, not just for her own gain, but for that of her so-called contacts whose wages had no doubt been speciously inflated.

"No," she said, "and it's not as if I can't afford it."

"Yes," Dorothy agreed. "And it's your asset, after all, Lily, as I'm forever telling you. Goodness, when one thinks about it, you'd be quite a catch for an ageing man without his own property. You want to watch out for that – beware any fortune-hunting widowers or divorcees!" Her aunt laughed and took Lily's arm in a gesture that felt unusually companionable. "But I know you're far too sensible to fall for any trickster like that."

"I hope so," Lily said. And felt tears sting her eyes, managing to blame them on the sharp wind that had begun to pick up.

"Of course you've no doubt increased its value. If you decide to sell, that is."

"Sell?"

"Well, why not? It's a big place for one person. I dread to think of your heating bills."

"But the house has been in the family for generations!"

"Exactly. Time for change, perhaps."

"Wouldn't you mind? After all, you must have so many memories attached to it."

Her aunt looked at Lily as if she found her sentimentality amusing.

"It's a pile of bricks and mortar, child. Not a repository of feelings. And it's yours, to dispose of as you will. You'll find no objection from me whatever you decide to do with the place."

Dorothy stayed one more night, but was anxious to leave early the following morning. They drove back to Harrow on quiet roads and Lily carried her aunt's bags up to her flat, stowed the remains of the turkey, trifle and ham in her fridge. In the living room she picked up a photograph taken decades before of her father and her aunt, Walter in a formal suit, broad lapels, his sister at his side in a floral summer dress, white gloves.

Their youth was startling.

Dorothy came into the room.

"One of my favourites," she said, taking it from Lily. "Taken a year or two after the war at a remote cousin's wedding. Your father always photographed well, although he despised having any taken."

"I remember," Lily said. "It's why I have so few of him. You both look so young."

"One forgets," her aunt said. "It's only the face seen in the mirror each morning that's familiar. Of course I would only have been about the age you are now, Lily. Or thereabouts. Still with decades ahead to live. Just like you." She replaced the photo on the side table, adjusted its angle. "Tea? Coffee? Would you like a cup before you drive back?"

Alfred Street was unusually empty. The hiatus between Christmas and New Year had seen an exodus of households as if there was a compulsion to leave the city until the restoration of order and routine in the New Year. The unlit trees in drawing room windows suddenly looked tawdry rather than festive as if the season had overstayed its welcome. For the first time since Hugh's departure ten days before, Lily had time on her hands to fill. She felt restless and the sight of her aunt's bedlinen, stripped, folded and piled with precision, the mattress bare, underlined the sense of an ending. She headed out of the house, walking briskly up to Highgate Fields, then changing direction towards Clissold Park. She had no thought in mind about a destination, but simply kept on walking, indifferent to the fine rain that had started to fall.

The photograph lingered.

Dorothy in her print dress, those gloves, a small hat perched on the back of her head, her familiar slim figure and a face still young enough not to be considered old. About Lily's age, her aunt had said. And she tried to recall her then. Her father, too, yet stubbornly it was always their faces in later years, as if their more youthful selves had been eroded by memory. It was getting dark by the time she was back in Alfred Street. Soaked through, her woollen gloves sodden, hair matted flat against her head, she was thinking only of a hot bath, dry clothes when she realised there was someone sitting by the front door of the house.

Stella Fox.

She stood up as Lily drew close, holding out her arms, a gesture of surrender.

"Lily! Oh, Lily! Thank goodness you're here. I was so worried that you might be away."

Lily said nothing. She found her keys and waited for Stella to move aside so she could reach the door. But she failed to move. Lily recognised her attitude, as she stood stubbornly on the top step, expectant of dispensation.

"I'll fetch your things. Please move away from the door and wait on the path. It will only take me a moment," Lily said curtly.

It was not the reaction Stella had prepared for.

"Lily, we need to talk. I realise I have just been so foolish the way I forgot to explain everything to you. All that business about the money. I mean, money! We might live in a materialistic age, but no-one should ever fall out about it, should they? Least of all someone as kind and giving as you."

"They might be a bit damp, the bits and pieces you left. They've been outside, you see." And with a swift movement she slipped past Stella and into the house. In the back garden, she shook off surplus rain from the saturated paper carrier bags, carried them through the kitchen and out to the basement stairwell and up the steps. "Here you are. Rather wet, but no doubt they'll dry off." She deposited them at Stella's feet and swiftly retreated, locking the door behind her. For a moment she heard nothing and imagined that either the bags had been abandoned or that Stella had resentfully slunk off with the bedraggled contents.

Then the knocking began.

First repeatedly at the front door, then at the stairwell entrance where it was louder, more insistent, as if the door was being struck with undue force. When it became clear that Lily was not going to answer, Stella substituted screaming and ranting, attaching numerous expletives to Lily's name and kicking the terrace railings with her heavy boots. Then, after a brief silence, she began to spill the contents of the sodden bags, spreading them over the front step and path with wild gestures that made her look either deranged or very drunk. Watching unseen from an upstairs window, Lily was surprised to find herself amused rather than alarmed by the spectacle. She noticed a light going on in the porch of a house opposite, someone twitching aside curtains as if drawn by the disruption to the quiet street. Eventually, Stella stopped. She stood for a few more moments staring up at the house as if trying to conjure a final trick to reinstate herself. To gain, once more, the upper hand. Then, hefting her bag onto her shoulder, kicking her way through her discarded possessions, she turned and walked rapidly away and down the street.

★★★

On New Year's Eve, her next-door neighbour, Anna, called in.

"No big celebration tonight," she said. "Quite frankly we're still exhausted from Christmas! But do pop in for a drink early evening. Just to toast the New Year and all that. Hugh, too, of course."

"Hugh is not here," Lily said simply. "We are no longer together. And Stella has moved out. But yes, I'd like that, thank you."

Anna seemed indifferent to Lily's news.

"Lovely. See you about seven, then? By the way, I heard you were at Harrods that Saturday when the bomb went off. How terrifying to be that close."

"Yes," Lily said. "But I was one of the lucky ones, still inside the building."

"There's been another fatality from it, I believe. A policeman. Dreadful business."

Lily thought of the injured she had seen lying in the road outside the store. She shuddered involuntarily.

"All in all," she said, "I'll be pleased to see the back of 1983 and welcome in the New Year."

"Well, you win some, you lose some," Anna said brightly.

"And, let's face it, every year is a bit of a voyage, isn't it? We steer our way through the high seas as best we can. See you around seven?"

★★★

Hugh's letter was hand-delivered. Lily found it early the next morning and the idea that he had been at the house without her knowledge disturbed her. She read it, hoping at least for his deep, unqualified regret.

She should have known better.

31st December 1983

My dear Helen,

I do hope you will forgive me this clumsy approach of writing. We are so very much more to each other than a formal letter would suggest, but the last time we met, you made it very clear that you did not want to see me again.

And I entirely understand your reasons for saying such a thing. I was crass. Indiscreet. Vulgar, even. Possibly a touch arrogant.

Displayed, in fact, traits of personality that I have always despised in others and have strenuously guarded against developing.

Until that appalling Saturday. And you, my dear Helen, are the last person deserving of such treatment.

But then passion and profound emotion know few bounds. And I am, after all, merely an inadequate, weak man, overcome and in thrall to my feelings. I do not even begin to apologise for that or to pretend that I can ever be otherwise where you are concerned.

So here I am grovelling. The repentant sinner, so to speak. And asking, in my awkward, stumbling way, for some sort of pardon. An absolution, perhaps.

Can we start again? Or at least remove that last unfortunate scene from our memories? You were not yourself, I know, and I was insensitive. Neither of us were at our best, were we? Let's blame it on the time of year. These dark winter days when the light is gone in the wink of an eye are so dispiriting. No wonder we both snapped. And I can quite understand your reaction even though, I have to say, you got things entirely wrong. Or at least woefully out of perspective.

But let's put recriminations behind us and move on. The future is what matters, not some sordid disagreements from the past.

And we have a future, my dear Helen. And I know that in your heart of hearts you believe that just as much as me. Don't let this small setback spoil the possibility of quite magnificent days ahead with adventures we have yet to imagine and realise. Let 1984 be the start of that future. Together.

Ever yours,
Hugh

There was an address in Neasden. A phone number that had been underlined several times. Like Stella, he would be expecting a submissive response. Biddable, acquiescent Lily Page, only too grateful for his attentions, willing to turn a blind eye to any dalliances and affairs of his. A prerogative for men like Hugh Murray, he would no doubt consider. She folded his letter back into its envelope, stared at the flamboyant style of his writing, the *H* with elongated lines, an enormous *P* dominating her surname. She would use it to start the fire in the sitting room later in the day, enjoy seeing the paper catch, ignite and burn.

★★★

The decision was impulsive.

"When do you want to go?" the woman in the travel agents in the Clerkenwell Road asked.

"When?"

"Yes, when exactly?"

"Now. I mean tomorrow, perhaps. Or tonight even? There are always night flights, surely?"

Lily had given the matter little clear consideration, but the desire to leave, the possibility of it had refused to leave her mind. The woman reached for a file of dog-eared timetables, turning pages swiftly between thumb and forefinger.

"From Heathrow?" Lily nodded. "For how long? I presume you want a return ticket?"

"A return flight, yes. For a week, perhaps?" Then added, with a sudden compulsion to despatch the hooks and restraints of a lifetime, "I suppose it's always possible to change the return date? If my plans alter?"

The woman looked up at her wearily as if her request was tiresome.

"Then you want an open return. But that would be more expensive."

"An open return," Lily said firmly. "That would be best."

There was more thumbing of pages, a red varnished finger nail running swiftly down columns.

"There's a flight leaving tonight at ten o'clock. I can try and get you on that one if you like. Or would you prefer midday tomorrow?"

"Tonight," Lily said. "That would be ideal." She did not want to risk the impetus leaving her. She watched as a phone call was made, a flight requested, fares and figures jotted down on a pad that was thrust across the desk towards her. She nodded, beginning to feel a sense of distance from the event as if it belonged in the life of a woman that she did not entirely recognise.

"Accommodation? Your flight will arrive very early in the morning, you know." The woman's tone suggested that Lily was a hapless traveller.

"Thank you, but I'll make my own arrangements," she said brusquely. And wrote out a cheque, waited to be handed her airline ticket. Two luggage labels in a slim folder.

And that, it appeared, was all that was required.

A decision, a simple exchange and transaction had served. Lily felt light-headed at the speed and audacity of it.

Back in Alfred Street she made plans. A call to the small city hotel she knew. To Agnes, explaining her absence. Anna happily agreed to feed Hector, who had already grown into the habit of living between the two houses as if it was a cat's prerogative to have such choice.

Finally, she phoned her aunt.

Explained.

"I see," Dorothy said after a long pause.

"It's a sudden decision," Lily said in mitigation. "Going away, I mean."

"You don't have to justify yourself, child. You are free to do as you like now. Value that, Lily."

"Yes," she said. "I will."

"Is it legal? What you are proposing to do?"

"I've no idea. But I don't suppose anyone will notice."

"No. Or even object if you needed to explain."

"Exactly."

"But won't your term soon be starting again at that school of yours?"

"Actually, I'm thinking of resigning." The thought had flitted through Lily's mind daily since Hugh's departure, but, once spoken out loud to her aunt, the idea seemed binding.

"Splendid, Lily!" Dorothy said with enthusiasm. "You don't want to spend the next decade or more in the same institution. And, with your skills and experience, you'll easily be able to pick up work. I've always thought you were wasted, simply labouring over the photocopier."

"Thank you," Lily said, surprised by the compliment and enormously gratified. Already, she was drafting a letter of resignation in her mind.

"A postcard, please. And I'll look forward to hearing about your adventures when you return. Quite an odyssey for you, in fact!"

★★★

It was barely dawn when the airport bus arrived in Syntagma Square. The unpretentious family hotel had not changed and the owner greeted her warmly, insisting on serving her with an early breakfast. From the window of her room on the second floor she looked over the narrow streets and roofs of Plaka towards the Parthenon and, although she was tired after the overnight flight, she washed quickly at the small corner basin, changed her clothes and headed out to the Acropolis. Even at that hour on an early January morning, she was not alone. But the crowds she had always known in the summer months were missing and once she reached the Parthenon it was possible to ignore the handful of tourists and simply stand in awe under a brittle winter sun and opalescent sky. The events of the past year slipped away amongst the magnificence of the ancient stones as if Stella and Hugh's treacheries were mere transitory irritations too banal to consider.

But Athens was only her temporary destination.

After two days in the city, relishing her solitary status, Lily boarded the overnight ferry from Piraeus. Just before docking at Souda Bay on the island of Crete, she went up from her cramped cabin onto the deck, deserted in the chill of the winter dawn, and scattered her father's ashes into the swell of the Mediterranean Sea. In the dim light of the early morning, she watched them skim the surface of the water, then disappear, as if Poseidon himself was claiming them for eternity.

At last, Walter Page was despatched.

And he would have approved of his final destination.

The White Mountains were snow-heavy, their peaks like pink quartz in the rays of the rising sun. Lily stepped from the ferry onto the bustling harbour, disorientated for a moment after a night of little sleep. She watched as passengers were greeted or dispersed to taxis, cars, coaches, a moment of mild uncertainty as she stood alone, suitcase at her side. Someone nudged her shoulder with a large rucksack, apologised. Then stood a little distance from her, similarly hesitant. Eventually, he turned and asked tentatively,

"Do you know if there are buses into the city, into Chania? It's my first time on the island."

Lily smiled, nodded. "Mine too. But I've always wanted to come. And I'm sure there must be buses. Shall we go and find out?"

She picked up her suitcase and, with the fellow traveller in tow, headed towards the street to enquire.

Postscript

Hugh Murray stands staring at the front door of 8 Alfred Street.

The *For Sale* sign astonishes him.

Spring is making a valiant attempt to show itself in the diffident crocuses and bulb hyacinths in the window boxes of the street, but he is too distraught to notice them.

He has not expected this. Not at all.

The onslaught of loss that wakes him each morning, hovering at the parameter of his days, astounds him.

It had all been a matter of pragmatism, after all. A suitable arrangement, a marriage of convenience to serve his needs. To allow him to go on endlessly living his careless, casual life.

He had not planned on falling in love.

And only in the absence of the woman has come to understand it.

He is amazed, infuriated even, to find himself truly ardent, besotted, and the prospect of losing her is like viewing a grief that he has no wish to bear.

Anna appears at her front door.

"Hugh? It is Hugh, isn't it? Are you looking for Lily?"

"Yes," he says.

"She's away."

"I see. And the house is…" he points at the sale board.

"On the market."

"Right."

Anna stands there in the weak sunshine of the March morning, a gatekeeper, Hugh suspects, of more than she is willing to share. He shifts from one foot to another. The thin soles of his cheap shoes are inadequate for the cold pavement slabs.

"Well, when you hear from her, perhaps you'll say I called." He is grovelling, desperate for acknowledgement. Anna says nothing. Hector sneaks between her legs and she picks him up, holds the purring cat close. He starts to walk away, making an attempt at a cheerful wave. Half way down the street he stops, looks back at the house. A car draws up outside, a couple get out and stand on the pavement, expectant. Within a minute or two they are joined by a young man, keys in his hand, who leads them up the path and in through the front door of 8 Alfred Street.

Helen, Hugh Murray mutters under his breath as he walks away and heads for the bus stop in Upper Street. *My darling Helen.*

This book is printed on paper from sustainable sources managed under the Forest Stewardship Council (FSC) scheme.

It has been printed in the UK to reduce transportation miles and their impact upon the environment.

For every new title that Troubador publishes, we plant a tree to offset CO_2, partnering with the More Trees scheme.

MORE TREES
LET'S PLANT A BILLION TREES

For more about how Troubador offsets its environmental impact, see www.troubador.co.uk/about/